Awaken

To Mike,
Welcome to Sophia's
World. I'm proud
to share the Indie book
world with you. xxx

Awaken

G.R. Thomas

Copyright © 2015 G.R.Thomas

First Published by CreateSpace, 2015

Cover illustration: katartillustrations.com
Editing: Betareaders.com.au
www.grthomasbooks.com
Interior designed and formatted by:

emtippettsbookdesigns.com
Printed by Clark & Mackay, Brisbane

To Rochelle Maya Callen,
But for you, I would not have put pen to paper.
Thank you.

"Be not afraid of greatness. Some are born great, some achieve greatness, and others have greatness thrust upon them."

William Shakespeare,
Twelfth Night

Prologue

As charcoal clouds mustered on the horizon, the sun still shone bright and warm from behind the billowing mass. With sleek, muscled arms, Nik'ael gripped at an overhanging branch leaning out from the shade, plucked a hard, green olive, and inspected it. *Perfect!* Beads of sweat glistened at his temples; the heat of summer was at its peak. A white linen chiton kept him cool as it flapped in the breeze against his thighs. He let go of the branch and unclasped his water pouch from the woven belt strung loosely around his hips. He drew a long, refreshing gulp. The rolling clouds mirrored across his sparkling blue eyes as he caught sight of his reflection in the silver clasp, reminding him all too well of what he was. He smiled as his alabaster hair blew around his square jaw as an emerging breeze rustled the leaves above his head.

A storm was brewing; he would have to cut short his walk today. He enjoyed his long walks where he surveyed his crops and rested his mind amongst the peaceful quiet of the orchard. He smiled broadly to himself, deepening the dimples on his golden cheeks. The harvest was plentiful-they would all eat heartily this year. A rumble of thunder in the distance set him on his way down the grassy hill towards home. He rolled the unripened olive between his finger and thumb as he went.

Nik'ael surveyed expansive plains as he descended from the rise of the hilltop. *This is a paradise on Earth,* he thought. He contemplated the small village that was his home—a collective of family and friends who lived and worked in harmony. It was an eclectic mix of people who laughed and loved, regardless of who or what they were. Illness was rare, lives were long, and the land upon which he stood sustained them well. Nik'ael looked skyward and wondered why, even now, he and his kindred were still unable to visit their true homeland, despite all their good works for the human population.

Many years had come to pass since life was breathed into the first soul in this world. Distant thunder rumbled as he took in the parched surrounds, and he thought about his ancestors who had been sent to watch over this new mortal species called humans, both a blessing and a curse. For, once on Earth, these Watchers of the Kingdom of A'vean succumbed to the impulses of the human condition, breaking the law of the Kingdom. They discovered urges of the flesh that they had hitherto never known, and fell in love and lusted after these weak but beautiful beings, creating offspring such as he, Nik'ael, son of Toth'iel.

These offending Watchers were sent to Earth to oversee and protect humans, nothing more. Breeding with them was considered heinous by the Throne, a great betrayal of the innocence of humankind. The Watchers were banished without recourse to live amongst humankind, forever unable to return home. New afflictions beset the Watchers, no doubt punishment for their weakness. Bitterness and anger brewed within them, a new scourge which they suffered in the human form, and which divided them into factions. Nik'ael was one of the Eudaimonia—the Flourishing Ones—hybrids who had merged through necessity into a peaceful life on Earth among the humans. They continued to teach and care for man whilst learning from their ancestors' painful experience to no longer mix their progenitors' bloodline with mortals.

Realising the damage they had caused, many of the offending Watchers had largely removed themselves from contact with humans, preferring to retreat within the shadows into a hidden life. A select few stayed to guide their Eudaimonian offspring in the ways of the ancestors in the Secret Places hidden throughout the world. They protected the descendants from themselves and their enemies.

As strong as Nik'ael was, even he feared the others, those in exile who became The Daimon—vengeful Watchers who had vowed to rise against A'vean. Reviled by their predicament, they disappeared, not heard from for centuries, but remained ever-present, ominous and unseen.

As Nik'ael travelled home, leaving behind him the olive trees he loved so much, something touched him lightly upon his shoulder. He turned, and his eyes widened in surprise for a moment. In his three hundred years, he had never seen such a being. Uriel, an Archangel from the High Council of A'vean towered over him.

Nik'ael bowed deeply, eyes cast down.

"Stand, young Nik'ael, I wish you no harm. I wish only to speak with you."

"Kindred, you have my ear and my heart, but I cannot stand in your presence," he quietly responded as he laid his arm upon his bent knee.

"Many years have passed since we could consider ourselves kindred, Nik'ael, yet I bring you a warning at the peril of my divine soul. You are descended of my brother Toth'iel who sinned along with the others. I have watched with regret his fate and that of his lineage. Entrenched in the mortal realm eternally is truly horrendous." He shook his head in despair. "You, Nik'ael, have lived with dignity amongst humankind and have not followed in your father's way."

Nik'ael cringed inwardly at the insult. His father had been a great warrior who had made one simple mistake. He was too scared to share these feelings. He did not know the temperament of an Archangel first-hand to dare to contradict one.

Uriel continued. "I have heard your confessions of remorse for the sins of your forebears. Your undertakings to be of service to the Throne in protecting man and woman from further degradation have not gone unnoticed."

Nik'ael attempted to speak, but Uriel struck him silent with the wave of his hand.

"For this reason, I grant you a small mercy. I am here on the orders of the Throne, directly from the great I'el, to warn our humble servant Noah of a great flood. It shall deluge the Earth catastrophically, so as to purge all of the evil from this once beautiful creation. Take refuge Nik'ael. Warn your worthy kindred, for I pity your poor souls."

Nik'ael was silent for a moment, his mouth hung slightly open in shock. He looked upwards, barely daring to meet the eyes of Uriel. *Surely this could not be? His Creators were not vengeful. Were they not benevolent, especially to those who shared the spirit and power of A'vean running through their veins?* His mind raced for answers.

Uriel rose into the sky as glaring white light and heat emanated from behind him. His eyes swirled like supernovas, a mishmash of coloured, sparkling light. In a booming voice he called out, "You have been warned. Dismiss me at your peril."

He was gone in a blinding flash that left Nik'ael reeling from the aftershock, thrust back onto the ground with the breath knocked from his lungs. As he recovered from the encounter, he drew himself up and fled.

Despite a superhuman speed, he worried that his mortal legs would not get him home fast enough to warn his village. Against all his instincts, he forced himself to stop, close his eyes and relax his mind. Connecting with the elements, he drew in the energy surging on the breeze, and rose up into the sky just as Uriel had. Nik'ael felt the ripples of energy surging from within-an instinct he had suppressed more often than not. Doubt plagued him as his back burned and his muscles flexed. He could never match the power of an Archangel yet he knew he possessed an immense strength which was unusual for a hybrid. He comforted his confidence with this thought as he let himself relax. Nik'ael flew upon the cooling breeze, through the ever-darkening sky. The ground flew by below, but not nearly fast enough in this moment of desperation. He quietly cursed himself for not practicing his higher abilities more often. He never really needed to. By the time he reached the valley where he lived, an ominous and heavy rain was drenching the landscape.

Nik'ael called out frantically to his family as a feeling of doom suddenly overwhelmed him. Neither human, Eudaimonian, nor Watcher responded. The bang of a door against a nearby house set him on edge as the breeze screeched wildly through the village, like the howls of a Daimon in the pits of Hell. Distressed chickens clucked and squawked as they dashed for cover. A cow had pulled itself free from its tether and seemed disorientated, nosing through barrels of grain, the whites of its eyes bulging.

Searching every home and field, he found nothing but signs of hasty retreat. The rain pelted his body. In the distance, through the hideous sounds of the angry storm, he thought he heard a scream. He felt fear and pain, but not his own. Drawing as much energy as he could, he crested the rocky hill that protected his village from the ocean winds, only to be confronted by a scene of utter horror.

There, upon the beach and bathed in a blinding light, were his family and friends being slaughtered by High Angels. Humans were being thrown like sacks, smashing their brittle bodies into barely recognisable remnants. The odour of blood made his stomach lurch with nausea. The unnatural redness running into the sea foam was hard to watch, yet he could not look away. Watchers and Eudaimonians had their spines ripped out rendering them unable to commune with the elements. Fresh muscle and bone littered the sand, leaving them vulnerable and paralysed, unable to save themselves through flight or transference. The dark blood of the Watchers and the crimson of the humans, congealed into pools of horror before it was lapped up by the incoming tide. Nik'ael hid behind a large rock, watching the bloody murder with disbelieving eyes. He was frozen in place. He could not have moved from his hiding spot even if he'd wanted to.

As though time stood still, this scene seemed to last forever—like it was occurring in the slow motion of a nightmare. The paralysis of shock numbed him, and his body was immovable from the ground.

When all of the humans were dead and the Earthbound Watchers were rendered completely defenceless and unconscious, the avenging Angels ascended up to the clouds and disappeared, their mission complete.

Torrential rain fell with a deafening roar. NIk'ael's hair was plastered to his face. His tears and the hammering droplets of rain were indistinguishable now. Shock had heightened his senses—every hair on his body stood frozen, every cell intimately aware of the suffering below. Pain shot through him as though he himself was under attack. His stomach heaved at the metallic odour of the inconceivable torrents of thick, glistening blood as it drained from the sand into the ever-encroaching tide. What was once pristine white, was now stained a dark, sickening red.

Nik'ael slowly rose out of his hiding place, shamed by his cowardice. *Uriel warned me too late,* he thought to himself. They had no chance at all. *Was that his intention? Was he being fooled by design? Was he to be punished by bearing witness to such carnage?*

Still in shock, he made his way unsteadily by foot down to the beach. Stepping through the masses of bloodied bodies, he kneeled by a human companion, a young man so broken from within that he was now a mere sack of skin. Lifeless eyes looked up at him. *Poor Evane—such a kind soul.* He scanned the beach, short of breath from the sorrow as he found himself surrounded by hundreds of lifeless and dying corpses, most of whom he knew. The wind blew hard into him, whipping at him from all directions. The sea spray burned his eyes and the sand bit hard at his skin as he searched on. He was unable to heal the mortal wounds of his kindred by himself—there were too many—and the poor humans had no hope at all.

Furthest away from the menacing tide, high up on the beach, he came upon a figure whose familiarity brought him to his knees instantly. Lying atop a small rise of craggy shoreline rock, a female lay prone. Her back was flayed wide open, her beautiful earthly body completely ruined. Nik'ael crawled to her on hand and knee—such was the effect that the sight had upon him. He reached out to her still warm but ghastly pale flesh and rolled her over into his lap. He knew who she was even before he saw her beautiful face. He could tell by the curve of her body, the impossibly long plaited white locks, now bloodstained and cascading down her lithe physique. Across his lap, mortally wounded and limp as a rag, was his wife, Neren'iel. Her soul was no longer with him. As a half-breed, she was unable to withstand the immense power of an avenging Angel, and these wounds could not be healed. He gently picked up her hands and kissed her fingers, already tinged blue by the touch of death. He wanted to die right then and there with her. Pulling her up higher into his lap, he cried out, his head thrown back in anguish. Hot tears cascaded down his face, mirroring the rain pounding upon his back. The physical droplets of his grief diluted the blood that encrusted her angelic face. He could not feel her energy any longer. He could not feel anything at all.

After a time, Nik'ael was forced to carefully lay her back upon the ground. A soft and lingering kiss was placed upon her lips, a whisper of eternal love promised into her unhearing ears. He ran his hand one last time down the length of her hair, caressing her soft, pale skin under his trembling hand, embedding her visage and feel into his memory. He rose into the sky, weakened by what he had seen on the ground. The ocean was rising and raging at an incredible speed. Tsunami-like waves crashed further and down deeper onto the peninsula, engulfing everything in sight. *Were any of his kind able to survive this?* He turned his back, no longer able to look. In the distance, he saw her—she was fleeing over the farmland. *Had she sat there like him and done nothing, too?* He closed his eyes. He was utterly alone, deserted, betrayed.

Nik'ael flew for what felt like an eternity, his own tears adding to the steadily filling oceans. The sky overhead was smudged crystalline by the icy comet that had exploded above the earth, now raining its remnants down. He found small ports of rest on the peaks of the highest hills and mountains not yet engulfed by A'vean's wrath. Nothing made sense. I'el was peace, A'vean the ultimate place of oneness, or so he had been taught as a child. His confusion slowly turned to the beginnings of anger.

Finally, he spotted out at sea a vessel of such magnitude that he thought for a moment that he was hallucinating. His body was weak and ravaged. Following the ship's path for a time through the roiling waters, he finally flew down and rapped on its doors.

An oaken porthole opened on the side and an aged fellow thrust his head out, looking about for the disturbance. The wind and sea spray blew savagely into his greying hair and beard.

He glared in surprise at Nik'ael, who cried out to him, "Noah, beloved of The Most High of A'vean, please will you offer me sanctuary? I was warned too late by the Archangel Uriel, of this horrific tragedy. I've witnessed my family slaughtered. I am lost." The human weakness deep within him surfaced as he begged for help.

Noah looked at him momentarily then wordlessly shut the window.

Shock, abandonment, utter misery, and loneliness assaulted Nik'ael's senses.

He clenched his eyes and fists, his mouth thin with building rage. All the muscles of his body rippled beneath his golden skin. Tossed around in the sky by the cyclonic winds, he threw back his head and let out a scream so primal, so loud and reverberating, that it penetrated every corner of the

Earth. His veins strained against his skin through this outpouring of passion. The swirling mark upon his face lit up like a beacon, blazing across the waters below. Something snapped within him. When his energy was finally depleted, he quieted. Nik'ael opened his eyes wide and clear. He looked back up to the furthest reaches of the sky and spoke with an unnerving calm.

"I will have my revenge against you. A worthy servant was I to you and of all those seated by your table. You reward me, a victim of circumstance, with such betrayal? I curse all that follow the Throne of A'vean, and I vow to cause chaos and harm for the rest of my days."

Nik'ael drifted silently through the air, his head low in defeat. Through bloodshot eyes, he glared at his reflection in the glassy water below. Angry tears worked their way slowly over his flaring nostrils, then languidly dripped from the edge of his locked jawline. His shadow and reflection suddenly disappeared as the dull sunlight was blotted out behind him. He spun around, still dominated by fear, and his hands flung back in defence. There before him hovered five malevolent figures. Instinctively he knew them.

Yeqon, Ged'erel, Asbel, Pineme, and Kasadya. *The Five Satans, forever present but always unseen.*

Yeqon moved forward and spoke. "Brother, we heard your grief from every realm. We are one and the same. Take my hand. Join us. Together, our power combined, we shall avenge all that have wronged us."

Without hesitation, and in a moment of pure weakness, Nik'ael reached out and grabbed Yeqon's hand.

A powerful, dark energy shot through Nik'ael, piercing every cell in a nanosecond of pure agony. His eyes turned from blue opals to black, and his heart went from feeling, to stone cold.

Nik'ael was now the sixth Satan.

I always knew I was different. Not weird or quirky, just different. I look just like everyone else my age, mostly. But on a deeper level, I knew that what made me human was more ethereal than I was comfortable admitting, even to myself. Snippets of my abilities had been shining through all my life. What I thought I was and the truth of its meaning were about to bring me crashing down into a level of chaos that I did not know could ever exist.

Chapter
One

Cockatoos screeched like washerwomen shouting orders for the day as I emerged from the fog of sleep. A blaring alarm, getting louder by each ignored minute, was nearly imploding the iPhone by the bedside, until my hand finally touched the *dismiss* button. Then I flung the whole device across the room.

"Ugh, God no, tell me it's not morning!" Refusing to open my eyes, I slithered from my bed. In a well-practiced routine, I made my way to the bathroom by feel alone. Flipping the light switch on, I shoved my face towards the mirror, opening each sleepy eye by just a slit with two fingers. "Ugh." *Who invented mornings? Were they thinking straight?*

Turning the worn brass faucets on, I waited for the shower to heat up. The gentle spray of water on the curtain and rising steam beckoned me in. I stepped in to the steaming luxury, leaned against the wall and relaxed.

Shift work. I hated the concept, the early starts and night shifts, but it's what I did, because I loved my job. Nursing rewarded that selfish part of me that liked the indulgence of making a difference, of saving a life, and knowing that it was my actions that did it. I would have preferred it though if people could choose their moments of sickness to occur in more socially acceptable hours.

Healing came naturally to me from my earliest memories. Anyone I saw in pain—be it a person or a poor creature that I found on the side of the road—I had to care for them, to will them back to health. A legacy from my family. Generations of healers, seers, mystics, you name it. Everyone, according to Nan, would experience something different as his or her gift. We could all open up a sideshow at a carnival, except that our powers were more than a money-gouging stunt. They were organic and real, but hidden. On the wards, I could gently and discreetly unfurl small amounts of my closely held secret gift as it developed. The unfortunate hours allowed me the freedom to be me—Sophia Woodville—without standing out too much. I liked ordinary life—it was comforting and safe. It shadowed me from the more confrontational things that life could throw at me, or so I liked to believe.

After a few minutes I felt slightly more human and stepped out. Lavender moisturiser melted into my still-warm skin. I swiped the steam from across the mirror and slid in my contacts. Warm brown eyes reflected back at me. I slathered on some foundation, a sweep of mascara, and plain aloe lip balm. A touch of makeup was necessary whenever I left the house, just enough to cover the large birth mark on my face. I'd never been ashamed of it, but the veil of light beige saved strangers from staring at me, or voicing the odd awkward question. It wasn't particularly bad. In fact, Nan always instilled in me that it was beautiful, with its swirling tendrils of mocha that enveloped my right eye and cheek. It was a part of me.

My ordinary, covered up reflection stared at me as I grabbed my brush. I did save a little rebellion for my hair—I wasn't a complete bore. Rainbow-tinted tresses slid through the bristles as I wound hues of pale blue, pink, and green up into a small, messy bun atop a backdrop of indigo. I smiled as it reminded me of my rotation in paediatrics. A nurse who looked like a fairy broke down all the scary barriers that kids hid behind. It was an icebreaker and a crowd pleaser, especially if you were five years old. I thought Nan's proper old world ways would object, but she was surprisingly modern by suggesting that it looked enchanting.

Back in my sunlit room, I threw on aqua scrubs, a worn pair of Sketchers, and a spritz of lavender perfume. I placed my lanyard over my head and chuckled to myself as I looked at the white-out smeared under my photo with the name Sophia scrawled in my own messy writing. For some reason HR had deemed that I was called Soon Yi. I didn't really look like a Soon Yi, so I amended the ID badge myself.

As I was still smiling to myself it suddenly occurred to me that I hadn't received my regular, silence-shattering 5:45am wakeup call from my bestie, Jasmine. Then I remembered why when I caught sight of the smashed phone in the corner, resting on the ever-growing pile of crumbled clothes.

Crap, another one. Annoyed, I grabbed it off a red top. That's the third time I'd assaulted an innocent phone to death this year. I could deal with this by offsetting it against the fact I didn't do it to living things. It was becoming a costly character fault though. I rummaged around on my bedside table, looking for the landline under a pile of books, when my door creaked open. Within seconds, I was flung to the ground by a mass of black and white fur.

"Shadow, you smelly old thing, no morning breath kisses!" I was plastered to the floor under my beautiful Alaskan malamute and constant shadow, hence the name. I wriggled out from under his sloppy, love-struck licking and pointed to the bed. "Go on now, back to bed." All seventy kilograms of dog heaved up onto the bed begrudgingly. He grabbed the quilt in his mouth and pulled it up over himself. He then rested his head ceremoniously upon the pillow. I giggled, thinking I should have YouTubed that.

Dusting off the white fluff from my outfit, I picked up the landline and dialled Jasmine's number.

"Hey you, what's up with voicemail?" she demanded. "Don't tell me you're not coming in today. It's our first day in the ER, and I'm sweating bullets here. I need you as my wingman, or person—or whatever!"

I could hear *Ride of the Valkyries* blaring in the background of her phone. Jaz liked to present herself to the world as a hard-core emo, gothic chick. Her true self was closely guarded, even from me at times. Never a dull or unsurprising moment was had in her company, such were the contradictions of her personality.

"'Morning to you too, Sunshine. Stress not, I just murdered another phone!" I confessed. "I'm going to have to pad my walls to protect the next poor device that succumbs to my morning wrath."

"You're going to be working just to fund new phones," she chastised me. "We've got to work on your morning mood," she warmly laughed, vastly improving my attitude in an instant.

"If you're lucky, I'll pick you up in twenty." Then mumbled though my parting goodbye, "Isn't it about time you got a licence?"

I snuck downstairs, avoiding the third last step with the betraying creak and peeked in on Nan. All quiet. The purr of the cat was whirring away on the end of her bed. As usual, every morning I would put out a teapot of English breakfast leaves and a blue willow teacup and saucer, covered with a lace doily. I filled the kettle, so that when she woke up she just had to press a button, wait 60 seconds, pour, and enjoy. The latest teapot cosy looked like a ladybug. Nan knitted anything, and I mean *anything*. Our modest cottage home was forever covered with knitted animals, cushions, blankets, slippers—just about anything kitsch and slightly ugly. I grabbed my keys and handbag, a knitted one of course, a slice of sourdough bread, and headed out the door.

I crunched along the gravel path to my Mini Cooper. It started with a welcoming rumble. Plugging in my iPod, I reversed out of the steep driveway of my forested home in the Dandenong Ranges. This beautiful Eden was green and alive with nature all year round. Even in summer, the unfurling fronds of tree ferns bulked up the landscape in an enchanting green hue. The mountainous shire was dotted with cute little villages crammed with teahouses and antique shops. It was a close-knit community who fought to keep the towns free of big corporations. That's what drew in the tourists—the lack of sameness here, and the individuality of each and every nook. This place was one of a kind.

As I waited for the flurry of early cars to pass, I wound the window down and took a deep breath of the crisp morning air. The unearthly magic surrounding the Mountain Ash forest was never lost on me. The many and varied creatures hidden in the shadows, and even the sound of the breeze caressing its way through the trees made it simply breathtaking. When I was young, I was so very positive that I could hear the fairies whispering in the trees around me.

Turning onto the tourist road, I noticed the familiar flashes bursting through the pulled drapes of Brennan's house. He was the paraplegic photographer across the road, a really nice guy who worked all hours on his art. He'd given me a few beautiful nature shots as gifts for running some errands for him. He was quite young and completely stunning to look at, which was always a bonus and made helping him out all the sweeter. Apart from his amazing good looks, he was truly a kind soul. For this reason, it often struck me as strange that he was always alone. I regularly drove off at dawn with reflections of his snapping camera flash in my rear view mirror.

A few kilometres along, I tooted the horn a couple of times outside Jaz's place as I drove right up to the front door. The songs of bellbirds kept my mind from nodding off as I waited. The birds trilled with more enthusiasm than usual this morning. Like my own home, the sounds, sights, and smells around this place were as comforting as a hot cocoa on a cold winter's evening.

I recalled the day we met whilst I was waiting for her, as it always gave me a laugh. We first found each other when we were twelve. We both started a new school the same day. I'd been home-schooled until then, so hadn't a clue about how to navigate the formidable social terrain of junior high school. She, on the other hand, had been to seven different schools, had three expulsions under her belt, and knew how to establish herself as the top dog in three minutes flat. She was a nightmare, unkempt and foul-mouthed. We actually had a fistfight on our first meeting at lunchtime. She did the punching, and me—the running around a tree. That's how we became best friends.

The front door finally opened. I expected Jaz to come bounding out, but it was her brother, Ben, ducking under the doorframe. He looked up at me as he turned to head to the garage. He paused a second as he wiped his hands down his work pants.

"Hey."

"Hey," I replied.

"Big day today?" he leaned on my door and smiled. I immediately felt a little warmer.

"Yeah, bit nervous but it should be fun. What about you?"

"Just more of the same. Picked up a nice old Fat Boy to do up."

"A fat what?"

"A Harley, Soph! Picked it up for a song but it needs a heap of new parts though. We'll have to scale back on the partying!"

"Yeah, hard core ravers aren't we? We'll have to cut back on those crazy popcorn-filled movie nights!"

"Maybe just crawling after Jaz. Costs me a fortune ferrying her around."

"She'll exhaust herself out eventually. At least you've got me. A hot tea and a DVD and I'm sweet."

He smiled warmly at that then pushed back from the car. He looked at me just long enough to make me squirm a little, wondering if I'd said too much.

"I love those nights," he said as he stepped further back. The space left between us was an unwelcome void. I smiled back as he tucked his shoulder length black hair behind his ears and turned away.

"Catch ya later, Soph." He waved and disappeared into his man cave to work on this latest motorbike. My cheeks burned as he walked away in his calm and measured way. *Oh God! Keep it together Soph.*

Eventually, Tinkerbelle's emo cousin emerged from the house. Jaz sprayed deodorant on the run as she grumbled her way out to the car. I smiled as she rammed herself into the front seat, cursing to herself about pigs, brothers, and missing clothes.

"Just shows you that genes do count for something. He's such a slob. My scrubs were under his gag worthy work socks. I'm sure I originate from a more sophisticated heritage somewhere! His parents clearly came from Slumland!"

"He's not so bad. He's just a regular guy, none of them care about clean socks!" I laughed as I took the peppermint Mentos she offered me every day for 'un-kissable breath.' She was still in a state of half dress, pulling impatiently at her shoelaces and combing through her hair with her fingers.

"Just floor it. Oh my God, you too? Is that last week's noodle box, Soph? You are such a slob just like my brother! I'm surrounded by heathens!"

"Again—licence, car, get one. My car, my space." This was standard character bashing for us, but it was our routine, and made me laugh.

We had a smooth run down the tree-lined, winding roads, listening to Imagine Dragons. Making good time, we detoured for a coffee at my favourite haunt, *Miss Marple's*. It was the cutest little teahouse on the mountain, with amazing coffee, and scones the size of your head. I'd worked there from age fifteen as a waitress for the loveliest couple, Harriet and Alfie. Alfie was running the place, since poor Harriet fractured her hip. Being a back of the house handyman, he never looked too comfortable as a barista, but surprisingly made a mean short black. He was a kind of pseudo-Dad to me, a wiry man with a strong Scottish brogue, despite being a forty-year expat. Every kid around here grew up knowing that he was Santa, ringing the bell through the streets of the shire every December. He was brash and loveable and one of a kind.

Jaz grumbled about how Ben had spoiled another 'opportunity' last night, following her around a nightclub. She didn't get it that he was just watching out for her. Bad guys were always her poison. She went inside the café ahead of me, swearing to herself about him as I grabbed my bag and locked the car. A surprising chill prickled up and down my spine as I did so, and my head throbbed with an intrusive, sharp pain. The unnerving tingle was like that feeling you get when someone sneaks up quietly behind you, so I instinctively turned to look behind me. The café was on the main road, but was surrounded by dense gardens and an old lane. I could swear I saw someone disappear into the back of a mass of wisteria that grew down from an overhanging tree. The swinging vines were in conflict with the still morning air. I looked hard through the dawn light, but saw nothing with my crappy vision. I jogged to catch up to Jaz and kept the strange incident to myself, hiding my trembling hands in my folded arms.

Around the back of the building, we pushed through glass-panelled doors. The perks of being a former favourite employee meant that I could pop in before opening time to grab a coffee whilst the fresh morning scones were baking.

"Morning, Sisters of mercy. Come to cure my ailments?" called a booming voice. He used the same line every time we walked in.

"Morning, Alfie. And no, no one could cure your ails—there are too many! Can we please have the usual?" I asked sweetly.

Jaz whispered sideways in my ear through her teeth, "If his ails didn't live in a bottle of Glenfiddich, he'd be just fine!"

I elbowed her in the ribs. "Shut up and play nice. He's harmless."

For a girl you would cross the road to avoid walking past, Jaz had some pretty ironic social standards. She had never divulged more than a few snippets of her early childhood to me, and from those I'd made an educated guess that her parents fell far from grace in her eyes. I never pressed her for more, but she knew I was always here if she needed to talk.

I watched the old man with the sparse grey hair fumble around at the counter. As ever, he proudly wore a piece of clothing baring the Fraser family colours. These days, he drew the line at a kilt. He said it got 'too nippy for his nether regions.' I always responded with, 'T.M.I., Alfie!' Today it was a tattered, old green and red vest, proudly ironed, with polished silver buttons.

"How's Harriet today Alfie?" I asked.

"Oh, she's never better since your dear old Nan come see 'er. She's an angel that woman."

"That she is," I responded as he turned to busy himself, re-filling the coffee grinder.

We waited on the window bench seat out front whilst the intoxicating smell of Arabica filled the room. Miss Marple looked down upon us from every direction. A hundred framed photos covered the papered walls. This place was an homage to the great British mystery sleuth.

"So," Jaz began, "we need a night out in the city. There's a great band playing at a new club on Flinders Lane. I've so got to make up for last night. Bloody Ben!"

"Just the two of us?" I asked. "In the city? You know I'm not really into that scene anymore. I like it just fine up here. And you know Nan, she's so overprotective."

Yes, yes, I was a young woman in the prime of life, and I did enjoy the odd clubbing experience. I'd just lost interest in the nightlife scene as a weekly—*or even monthly*—thing, since my last experience. My idea of fun was being outdoors, experiencing nature. I know that sounds like a tick off the bucket list of a retiree, but so be it. It killed Jaz. I was quite sure I was her social *faux pas*.

"Listen, Ben will be there—unfortunately, for me. Even though we know he's a pussycat, no one messes with him. You've seen trouble back away from his mass of muscles! You'll be in good hands. Hopefully, I'll be in hot ones!"

I smacked her leg reflexively. "Be a lady!"

"Oh, shut up."

She always ignores me.

"Anyway, you could tell Nan that you're just spending the night at my place. You've got to let your hair down—literally. By the way, have I ever pointed out to you that you never actually wear it down? If you let that rainbow mane down with me by your side, we'll look like Helena Bonham Carter and Barbie on a date! That's sure to guarantee us a hot night!" she laughed wildly at her own joke.

"Jaz, I know you think I'm a geriatric in a twenty-year old's body but…"

"Ka-ching! That goes without saying, sister!"

"Hmm, anyway, I love hanging with you, but you know the downtown scene isn't my thing anymore. All those sweaty bodies squeezed into dark spaces—I can't breathe. It makes me claustrophobic just thinking about it. And I'm not going to lie to Nan. I can't believe you even suggested that!" I eyed her disapprovingly. *I was a geriatric.* It was too embarrassingly true.

She rubbed her temples in exasperation. "Sophia, I love your Nan, and I know she means well—hell, she was right about that last dipstick I dated. But you have to actually live a little outside your comfort zone *and* her shadow. What do you want to do? Go to work, come home, make tea with Nan, and knit your own line of handbags for the rest of your life?"

I hugged my handbag to my side in mock shock.

"You can't go to the same two pubs up here for eternity! That's a very small X-Y gene pool to dip into! You're young, gorgeous, and never had a boyfriend. You seriously don't realise what you're missing out on!" She grabbed my hands as I felt my cheeks burn from the unintended insult.

"You owe yourself a bit of room to take a risk and enjoy yourself. Not everyone's out to get young girls! There *are* some nice guys out there. I know what happened in June gave you a fright, but that's not representative of every nightlife experience." Her eyes were sympathetic, though her words were trying to galvanize me into action.

"Ah, that's what it is! You still want to hunt me down a boyfriend!" This was a never-ending issue with us. "I'm not interested. Unless you can deliver Theo James to my front door, forget it." I threw my hand across my heart and sighed. She needed to have a boyfriend constantly, but I was happy to wait for the right guy. I never felt the need to throw myself at guys like she did. *Well, I'd certainly reconsider that stance for Theo, though.*

Annoyingly, she'd reminded me of my last experience in central Melbourne. We'd caught a train downtown to the new Docklands development. A boutique club had opened there, and she'd managed to procure a few opening night tickets from some poor sap who was after her. Unfortunately for me, Ben was under strict instructions to stay out of her face that night. If he hadn't, my night may have turned out differently.

It was a nice place, actually. It had a modern medieval-chic feeling to it. It was Jaz's taste, down to the finest detail. The crowd looked loaded, and not just with money. Glassy-eyed distant stares surrounded us as bodies moved hypnotically to the reverberating beat under minimalist lighting. It wasn't quite the crowd we were expecting—*that* kind of partying was totally not our scene. However, we stayed, out of politeness for her friend who bought the tickets for us. We stuck by the bar for a while until, as expected, the ticket guy turned up and got the guts to ask Jaz for a dance. She loved the seductive power she had over the opposite sex.

"You all right for a while?" she'd asked.

"I'm fine. I'll just be here, admiring the stoners. Try and show some class tonight, Jaz." I implored her with a mocking, motherly raised eyebrow.

"Always." She blew me a provocative kiss as she batted her eyelash extensions and disappeared onto the dance floor.

After a while, a guy in a black hoodie sat next to me and started the usual small talk. Oddly, he stared straight ahead at the mirror behind the bar, not glancing in my direction at all. His face was shielded by the hood. He seemed slightly underdressed for the place. He picked at a coaster through black gloves.

"You here with anyone?" his voice was strained. He coughed to clear his throat.

The hairs on my neck reacted like internal alarm bells. I edged away slightly.

"Yes, actually. My boyfriend is just in the bathroom," my voice wavered with the quick lie.

"Thought you walked in with that chick over there?" He shoved his head in Jaz's general direction.

"My boyfriend is her brother, he brought us in, okay? Look, he'll be back in a minute, I'm not interested, sorry," I looked around for Jaz but she was nowhere to be seen.

He stopped talking at that, got up, and walked away with a limp.

Nervous sweat had sprung down my back. *This creep has been watching me.* The value of having a boyfriend right then seemed to suddenly skyrocket.

My head started to ache, and I felt a little nauseous. I needed some fresh air.

I made my way down a dimly lit hall to find the ladies room, catching my heel on a ripple in the rug as I went. As I bent down to reposition my shoe, a large, gloved hand yanked me down from behind and dragged me out through a door, into an external corridor.

"Don't even think of making so much as a squeak!" the words rumbled cold and wet into my ear.

Immediately, I was sure it was the guy from the bar—his voice sounded the same. His arms were covered in a black polar fleece, but I couldn't see him. I couldn't scream if I'd tried, because his hand was pressing onto my mouth so hard. My lips were pushed painfully into my teeth, and I could taste my own blood. I struggled so hard, thinking that this was it—*I'm going to be tomorrow night's six o'clock news.* He roughly pushed me, face down onto the concrete floor, and felt me up all over my back. My skin crawled with revulsion at his touch. He then brazenly turned me over.

"Move and your throat will open like an oyster shell!" Images of all the worst possible things that could happen to a girl in this situation flashed through my mind. My pulse pounded frantically in my ears.

What actually happened though was completely different, but just as terrifying and bizarre. He leaned forward, his face still hidden in his hoodie by a shadow cast from the overhead lights. His breaths were ragged, laboured like someone struggling to breathe. He moved with urgency, his head swung around frequently to check that we were alone. He seemed to sniff at the air, like a dog trying to pick up a scent. My limbs froze as he reached for my eyes. I could barely draw a breath, his weight was so heavy on my chest. I squeezed my eyes closed as my lips trembled wildly. He forced my eyelids wide open, inspecting inside—for what, I didn't know. He grumbled, seemingly annoyed. His breath was hot and rancid in my face. Next came a flash of silver. I screamed and struggled for my life then, regardless of his threat. He growled like an animal as I reached up, pushing and grasping at the silver weapon with every ounce of my strength. I punched his face, shoving it into a glimmer of light, immediately wishing that I hadn't. His hoodie fell back slightly. I could see half of a bald, sallow-skinned face with dark, unforgiving eyes. He looked like a corpse. His lips were pale and bloodless. As I frantically lashed out at him, my fingers registered the coldness of his skin.

His strength overpowered me as he slashed at my arm, making sharp and painfully deep contact. He immediately stood up after slicing me and gazed at the small, scalpel-shaped blade. I shuffled away, taking quick advantage of his weight being off me. I frantically looked around for an escape route. I glanced back at his position, just in time to see him slowly lick my blood off the knife. I retched, got up, tripped over myself, but then managed to explode into a run, expecting another grab at me to finish me off. A bright flash from behind me bounced off of the metal wall art by the door that I was yanking open. I looked back momentarily to see that the dreadful man was lying spread-eagle on the floor, a large gash opening up on his head. Dark fluid seeped slowly from the open wound. Repulsed, I turned and ran. All I heard as I disappeared through the door was a malicious laugh and the words, "Now, now, I know who you are. I'll be seeing you real soon, sweet angel. *Mmmmm.* Yum, yum." He drawled this out slowly, emphasising the evil of his intent. The night was a blur after that. I'd run back into the club, dragged Jaz out by her hair, and screamed practically the entire way home. It took me two days to tell her what actually happened.

"Soph! Soph? Oh don't go thinking about that, please? He was just a pervert, high on some kind of dust and trying to scare you. He's probably dead or someone's girlfriend in prison by now." Jaz's voice pulled me back from the vile memory. "Will you at least come out somewhere, off the mountain at a minimum, just to get away from here?" She held up her arms wide in an exaggerated gesture, indicating the general vicinity around us.

"How about a compromise?" I offered as I pushed the memory far away. "We'll go down to *The Mill* in The Gully after work tonight to celebrate our first day in the ER. They have great bands, and I'm sure the crowd there aren't the Neanderthals you think exist up here."

She brightened slightly at my concession.

"But, you have to come for a hike in Sherbrook forest with me on our next day off together."

"Oh, come on. That's not a fair deal—nature and bugs and *ugh*," she grumbled. Outdoorsy was not her thing, just like clubs weren't mine. I often wondered how we were even friends.

Thankfully, Alfie interrupted with our steaming cups. "You girls goin' out on the town tonight?" he asked.

"Yes, Alfie. And yes, I'll mind my manners." I gave him a gentle squeeze on the arm.

"It's those boys who need to mind their manners nowadays. You be sure 'n take that Ben with you, he'll keep their grubby hands off of you. You hear me?" His eyes sparkled with a little moisture. He was a gentle old soul.

"Don't worry yourself, old man. She's a big girl now. We can look after each other. C'mon, Soph. We're going to be late."

Jaz shuffled me out of the front door, the bell tinkering as it opened and closed. "If you go listening to old McDougall there and his nonsense, you'll end up a spinster, living in a house full of cats!"

"Nice, Jaz! Anyway, I like cats," I said as I pushed her away.

I looked back to wave at Alfie, catching him swigging a morning pick-me-up from a silver flask hidden under the till.

Chapter Two

The drive down the mountain was warm and clear. The horizon of warm weather loomed in early December. Soon the dry heat of another Australian summer would arrive. I loved the natural warmth of the sun on my skin. It was comforting and familiar, and I didn't rock winter clothes.

At 6:50am we arrived in the staff room of the ER at St. Xavier's Public Hospital. Judy McPhail, the mentor for graduate nurses, was waiting by the door with our allocations for our first shift. Jaz and I were both nervous—*anything* could come through those doors, and that kind of unpredictability was daunting. I may have had a natural gift, but that didn't mean the horrors of what could happen to the human body freaked me out less than anyone else.

"Okay, Jasmine Armitage. Good morning." Her face exuded warmth, and with a broad smile she handed Jaz a welcome pack. "You are going to work alongside me today in the Short Stay wing. We should get a few sprains and fractures, and there's usually a lot of suturing to do down at that end. Have you put in stitches before?"

"No, but that sounds sensational." Jasmine was determined to work in the high stress and pace of the ER. She was an adrenaline junkie. The more action the better for her. She only had one speed, and that was full throttle.

"Sophia Woodville," she flipped her notepad over, scanning the staff roster. "You will be partnered with Cindy Beal. She's in the Resuscitation bays today, so that's going to be a real eye-opener for you. Take in as much as you can. There's always a handful of heart attacks, so keep your eyes and ears open. You should learn a lot today."

I was sure my life force had left me then and there. That's big time scary stuff, dealing with people on the edge of life and death. I glanced at Jaz, my eyes wide with unadulterated fear.

"Whoa, you're like Super Nurse already. Just don't zap yourself with the defibrillator!"

"Thanks, friend!" I squeaked as I headed out the door to what would become the day that started it all.

What I thought was going to be the most terrifying experience of my life actually turned out to be great. Cindy was a patient and kind educator. Twenty years of experience and not at all jaded yet.

By lunch I'd done numerous electrocardiograms, taken enough blood to satiate a vampire, and roused more than a few overindulged ravers. I'd actually confused a few of them as they happily thought they'd arrived in Fairyland when they woke up with me in their faces. *Thank you rainbow locks*, I mused to myself.

The mayhem of the place was overwhelming, though. People of all persuasions came and went nonstop. Groaning, crying, screaming and arguing, with countless eruptions of unpleasantness spilling on the floor seemed par for the course here. Lunch with Jaz was a welcome break for me and an expletive-filled venting session for her.

"That was so not what I was expecting! I've been showering stinking old homeless men all morning. I was yelled and spat at by a woman complaining that aliens stole her methadone and she needed more before they came back to abduct her!" She blew the fringe out of her eyes with a look of disgust as she pinched her nose, attempting to rid her memory of all offensive odours.

"That wasn't the worst of it. I was sent into the kids' wing to relieve the staff for morning tea. All the little ankle-biters cried and hid from me. Couldn't even get a temperature taken!" she complained as she popped the top of her Gatorade off.

"Have you looked in the mirror lately?" I giggled. "Smudged black eye liner, blood red lips, emo hair do? Not exactly a fairy party for the kids, Jaz! You'd do better where I've been today. You'd frighten the OD's into not risking death anymore if they woke up to your pretty face!" I scoffed playfully. She pursed her lips, with one eyebrow kinked up in annoyance. Clearly, my attempt at humour was unimpressive.

"You literally stop my heart with hilarity. I am choosing to ignore all of those insults. So, what about you? Any hot Docs to drool over while stabbing in adrenaline?" Her ovaries had obviously just switched on.

"Oh, for God's sake, turn off your hormones. I'm trying to eat here!"

"That crud is not food. That's not nutrition in my book. Here, you can have my apple." She rolled it across to me.

Whilst she bit into a pastrami and cheese toasty, I tucked into my quinoa and vegetable salad. "Do I ever look like I'm lacking energy, J?"

"No, but you'd be more fun on pizza night!"

"There is such thing as a vegetarian pizza you now!"

"Yuck, why bother? Anyway," she drawled, "remember that cute new intern we worked with on Southward? You know the one, all muscle and no brain? Well, there must be *some* brain since he's an intern, but I tell you, one bat of my lashes and he's just a hormone with legs!" She had her sultry, *come hither* face on. I didn't like her like this. She was worth so much more than a one-night stand.

"You're disgusting. Leave the poor guys here alone. They don't understand that you are the lioness and they're the gazelle."

"Shut up! Anyway, I've got a date with him—*tonight*. Do you hate me? Do you mind if he comes with? He's actually offered to drive. I hope his car is cleaner than yours, though."

"Just do whatever makes you happy. I'll stay in. I wouldn't want to crowd you." I was kind of relieved. I was feeling more exhausted than usual. I stirred slowly at my coffee, taking a bitter sip, forgetting I hadn't actually sugared it yet. Jaz groaned as I ripped open a small stick of sugar.

"God, you're such an old bag! No way, sister, you're not getting out of it. You better be there, too!" she stood up preparing to leave, pointing her Gatorade at me. "Be there, woman!"

"Okay, okay," I said. "But I'll just hang for a little while. Satisfied?"

"Excellent. Oh crap, I need to wax!" Jaz winked provocatively at me.

"Ugh, how much is he going to see on the first date? Actually, don't answer that!" I huffed, flashing her my palm.

Soon the clock ticked on the half hour, cutting short her reverie about which lippy and black dress she should wear—she only had black dresses. I pushed out from the table, gulping my drink down. "See you tonight, J. I hope you find some hot homeless man to wash this afternoon to rev you up for tonight," I giggled and ran from the swipe of her hand, just vaguely hearing a string of insults as I whipped out the door.

Back in Resuscitation, it was quiet for all of thirty seconds. Cael, the RN in charge today, called out to me with an Irish-tinted voice to prep a patient bay for a 'screamer.' It seemed like Jaz might have handballed one of her 'fun' patients to me. As I was double-checking the bedside equipment, I could hear the growing howl of what sounded like a cornered wild animal.

Heading up the ambulance gurney as it wheeled through the door was Cael, his eyes wide with amused alarm.

"Sophia, ready for some fun?" A devious grin dressed his face. He was going to enjoy my inexperience.

"Um, what do you—?" I didn't need to finish my sentence as I caught a glimpse of our patient from behind him. I had to look a couple of times before I could work out if it was a male or female. Pulling up into the patient bay was a thrashing mess of arms, legs, and blood spatter attached to a body that had seemingly ripped out its own hair. Fistfuls of long auburn locks entangled the fingers of what I now realised were female hands.

She was screaming, howling the name, "Annie! Annie! Annie!" Heavy panting followed a rumbling growl. Bloodshot eyes looked desperately left and right for an escape route. Lashing out everywhere, even scratching herself with blood-caked acrylic nails, she was a fearsome sight. Anything she could grab hold of was fair game. The attending Registrar reached in to give her a shot of Valium in the arm to calm her down. *Bad move.* Lightning quick, she grabbed at his wrist, twisting it with a sickening *crack*. The syringe flew across the room as the doctor fell to the floor, grasping his flaccid hand. I pressed the emergency call button, as we clearly needed some decent manpower with this woman. The black harness securing her to the ambulance trolley was keeping her body down, but she fought so fiercely that the entire gurney shimmied across the floor as she thrashed.

"Get me out, get me out! Get me a corpse!" she screamed. The paramedics looked more than pleased to be depositing her with us.

"Do you think we need a psych consult, Cael?" I shouted rhetorically over the incessant howl. He had meanwhile called a code grey, indicating the presence of an aggressive patient. This received an immediate response as more medical personnel entered the room, backed up by some burly security guards.

"Considering she was found trying to scratch some poor sod to death at Ferntree Gully Station, that'd be a yes," he called back over the noise. "That ain't just *her* blood under her nails. I paged for the consult when we got the heads up from the ambos while they were in transit. I'm hoping he'll be here sooner rather than later. Having fun?" he asked cheekily as he leaned in to hold the patient's arms down, hopefully preventing more fractured staff. His smile was calm while my heart pounded with the thrill and fear.

As Cael tried to calm her down there was a wet *pfft* sound as she spat in his face.

"Oh, come on woman, that's just not nice!" he growled back at her. I grabbed a cloth and antibacterial lotion and wiped his cheek, glad that I wasn't the one in the line of fire. The woman writhed around, panting like a dog. Saliva and blood trickled down her chin. A few more spit bombs were dodged by all but the contorted face of the poor Registrar, who was still in agony on the floor as another nurse put an ice pack and splint on his arm.

"I didn't sign up for this shit," he said through clenched teeth and barely repressed tears of agony.

The woman mumbled and growled to herself, straining vigorously at the chest restraints. Her neck arched back almost unnaturally. Her muscles flexed so hard that I could see the pulse pounding rapidly under her skin. She seemed to be struggling desperately as sweat poured like rain down her face. Cael eased up off her for just a moment, watching her intently. My heart heaved for her—she was suffering immeasurably. I sensed a great negativity about her, like her life force was all wrong.

She had no ID, but as I looked through the fearsome façade, I could see evidence of a previously well-kept woman. There were remnants of neatly applied makeup on her face, and one rather glamorous gold earring still dangled from an ear. Her clothes looked expensive, like she probably worked somewhere corporate, apart from all the bloodied rips.

She eyed me up and down for a moment, grinding her teeth and chewing at her lips.

"Don't be scared, we're all here to help you. Try to calm down." I attempted to reassure her but was met with the gnashing of those perfectly white, straight teeth.

"You, remember me? Hmmm?" she smiled broadly, her expression maniacal. "*Mmmm*, you tasted so delicious." She sung this melodically in the creepiest tone. Her smile was crooked and just plain scary. I involuntarily took a step back from the bed.

What the hell? It can't be, I thought, rubbing at the silvery scar peeking out from beneath my sleeve. Without warning, and her with eyes fixated on me, she yanked her arm back towards her face. To my utter disbelief, she began biting deep chunks out of her own flesh.

"You are not worth this torture, though. *Argh*! Get me out of this *thiiiing*!"

she screeched through a mouthful of muscle, her eyes still glued to me. Arterial blood splatter hit the roof and walls. I copped a spray across my chest and cheek.

"Oh my God, stop! Stop!" I screamed at her. I tried grabbing at her wrist to stop the self-mutilation, but she just spat blood and tissue at me.

"You burn, you bitch! Get your filthy hands off me. *Argh!*" She wrenched her wrist from my grip, as large blisters pillowed out from where I'd held her.

"Holy hell!" yelled one of the paramedics.

Cael moved with lightning speed, grabbing both her arms, holding them firmly down across her chest again.

Throughout this horrific episode, she screamed in agony as well. Attacking herself and begging for mercy, all at once. For a split second, her eyes cleared of their glazed and fanatical stare. She looked pleadingly at Cael.

"Help me! Please?" A milder voice begged, choking on the bloody mess in her mouth. It was as though there were two people battling each other within one body.

"Settle down Ma'am, settle down. You're safe here. Relax, listen only to me and I'll help you," he soothed in his liquid voice. "I see you, I know the pain you are suffering. Let me help you."

In the next moment, her eyes reverted to a berserk, bulging glare. The menacing voice returned, along with continued attempts to chew any part of herself that she could reach.

I grabbed at some fresh bandages nearby to cover her wounds if at all possible, never letting my eyes leave the scene in front of me.

She glared long and hard at Cael whose expression was now deadly serious. "No one can help me, I am dead!" she screamed. "You're burning me, bastard—bastard, let go of me!" Her thrashing escalated exponentially. Between us all, we held each limb down with immense effort. She was tiny, her strength seemed disproportionate to her size.

As if perfectly timed, the Psychiatrist arrived, eyes glued to an iPad. He addressed us briefly with a curt nod of his head, barely making eye contact with anyone, least of all the patient. Cael, still leaning heavily on the now physically subdued woman, gave him the limited information he knew.

"Send her to H ward. We will assess her in the morning when she has calmed down and her wounds have been attended to." His voice was monotone, his face even more lacking in personality. Ward H was not where you wanted to be allocated. It was locally known as Hell Ward, because that's what it was like to work there. It was the locked down section of the hospital, where prisoners and psychiatric patients were securely kept whilst treated.

"Keep her restrained, and we'll sedate her for assessment up there. She's in no condition at the moment to be interviewed by those police officers I saw hanging around outside the door," he said authoritatively.

The Psychiatrist looked my way for the briefest moment as I was trying to put a pressure bandage over the pulsing wounds across her arm. The edge of his mouth quirked up, not in a smile but in a way that gave me the creeps. Wordlessly, he looked back to the patient. Exhaustion seemed to have settled into her as she was merely panting through her teeth now, her crimson lips were peeled back with the strain.

"Can you tell me who you are? What is your name?" he calmly inquired of her.

She considered him for a moment, grinned, and then spoke in a foreign language. It sounded like Greek. The dialogue was getting her worked up again as she spoke in a careful and calculated tone. Her voice was husky and way too deep for a woman.

"Sounds like Greek. Anyone speak Greek around here?" I asked.

Cael's expression read deadly serious. "I speak a little," he answered. His eyes were glued to the patient.

"That isn't any Greek I've heard, and I'm Mikonos born," interjected a pot-bellied security guard.

"It's a dialect. Perhaps you missed it growing up," Cael answered quietly.

"I'm telling you it's not—"

"Quiet. If you can't help, just be quiet while I concentrate." Cael snapped at the guard.

"No need for translation," said the Psychiatrist, clearly impatient. "She is highly distressed and needs to be calmed down before we try to make sense of her. Call the orderlies for an immediate transfer."

He moved to leave the room, but stopped at the door, looking back as the woman began muttering randomly again.

"Annie, Annie, Annie!" she panted, pointing at the Psychiatrist with a restrained finger. She spoke briefly to him in the strange language, her tone was terrifying. She then reverted to English. "Her blood is on all of our hands. Get it, get it now! You will answer to him if you do not do his bidding!"

My hair would have stood on end had it not been in a bun.

Something seemed to wash across the Psychiatrist's face. *Was it understanding, or perhaps fear?*

He left without another word. The orderlies arrived and were given their instructions by Cael. They gingerly manoeuvred themselves around the patient to avoid the renewed onslaught of spitting and wheeled her out. Her screaming echoed down the corridor until it was cut off by the closing of the elevator doors.

I took a deep breath, the back of my gloved hand pressed firmly against my forehead as I leaned against the wall, exhausted.

Cael was running his hands though his pale hair, his face to the corner. The pot-bellied guard was ghostly pale.

I asked him if he was okay.

His lips moved silently open and shut a moment, making his double chin wobble. "Ah, she was as Cael suggested, speaking some dialect of Greek that I've not heard before, but I could pick up enough." His voice was shaky, haunted. He hitched up his pants. "She was saying, 'You know me,' then something else I couldn't understand. Then she said, 'I am Deumos, loyal servant. Get me out, trapped, pull me, wretched thing.' And also, 'Peel this flesh from me.' It sounds crazy. The last thing she said was, 'I bring you the Earth-born.' There were some other words I couldn't make out. Then, 'Bring the blood, or pay with yours.' She repeated these same phrases over and over. Freaky shit—oh sorry miss, um—freaky *stuff*, ya know?" He made a quick exit after that, leaving just Cael and I in the room.

"Peel this flesh from me! What the hell? That poor woman was terrified and clearly very disturbed. Did you hear all that, Cael? Do you think it's some new street drug?" I asked as I rubbed my arms that had pricked with goose bumps from the creepiness I'd just witnessed.

Cael responded in a kind of bland way. "Not sure, Sophia, but I wouldn't want to be the one trying to draw a blood sample from her at the moment for a tox screen. Seems like she's the one doing the bloodletting!" he laughed, but not with his intense blue eyes.

My gaze fell to the floor for a moment. Ruby smears glistened back. I could see the path of the patient's trolley as thin red wheel lines tracked out through the door. Cael called my named softly, pulling my eyes up from the foul sight.

"Hey, look at that!" he pointed to the wall clock, a little more animatedly.

"It's only fifteen minutes until we knock off. What do you say we grab some friends and meet at *The Mill* for drinks tonight? I could use a debrief after this day in the shape of a shot glass!"

"Actually, Jaz and I were meeting up there tonight anyway. She's got herself a hot date, so I'm meeting her there."

"Well then, how about I pick you up, so you don't have to drive alone? Is 5:45 ok? Text me your address."

"Oh, that'd be great." I'd rather arrive with someone than walk into a packed club alone, so this was a handy turn of events. I'd already been trying to think of excuses to give to Jaz for a no show. "Here," I passed him a paper hand towel with my address written on it. "My phone needs repairing," I said with a smile.

I arrived home after dropping off Jaz and took a quick shower. I threw my scrubs and shoes in the garbage can. I wasn't going to bother washing those. That woman's face was imprinted on the inside of my eyes, and I needed all physical evidence of that experience out of my possession.

My wardrobe was a disaster. I surveyed the crammed mass of fabric and accessories. Having little care for fashion, I settled quickly on a pair of black skinny jeans with a simple white shirt. My Nine West flats with a bit of bling on the toe were my only 'good' shoes, so on they went. To make my bestie happy, I straightened my hair and left it down. The multi-coloured layers nicely pepped up the muted tones of my outfit. I noticed the indigo on the top was due for a touch up, as the pale blonde was peeking through. I took a mental note to visit my hairstylist ASAP.

Nan was out on one of her charity days, and as she didn't 'do' mobile phones, I left her a note on the kettle, since it's the first place she went when she arrived home. *Tea is the essence of the gods* has always been her motto and life philosophy.

It was right at 5:45pm when I heard a rev in the front garden, heavy footsteps crunching toward the house, and finally a knock at the door.

I opened the door just as he was taking off a motorcycle helmet. Cael's pale blonde hair cascaded down to right below his ears, the afternoon sun glinting off it. Distressed denims, a white t-shirt with a black stallion on it, and a retro aviator jacket had him looking like a Calvin Klein commercial on my front porch. From hospital scrubs to—this. *Wow!* I was momentarily left speechless.

"Are you going to let me in, Sophia, or do I need an invite like a vampire to step over your threshold?" he said with a bemused smile.

"Oh, God. Sorry, I'm just flustered. I was, um, rushing to get ready. Sorry."

He stepped in, practically ducking through the doorway. *Clearly no jockeys in his family tree*, I guessed.

"Nice house."

"Thanks, I'll just grab my bag and we're good to go."

I ran back upstairs, rummaged through the clutter I'd left on my bed, and found it. As I walked back down, I saw Shadow preening all around him, tail wagging and flat out on his back with Cael scratching madly at his tummy.

"Wow, look at you. He generally goes all attack dog with anyone other than Nan or I. Even Jaz and Ben get a good dose of '*don't mess with me*' from him." I was impressed, Shadow was my *nice-o-meter*.

"Animals know who the good guys are," he said, giving me a wink.

He stood up, heading out the door. "Come on then, let's go and unwind a bit, shall we?"

I followed him out and looked dubiously at a red motorbike.

Seeing my face, he explained, "2012 Ducati. This is *my* pet. Here, put this on and jump on the back."

I grabbed the silver helmet and wrestled it onto my head. I sat on the pillion behind him, sheepishly holding onto his waist.

"If you don't want to go flying off around the bends, I suggest you hold on a little tighter. I don't bite," he mused at me.

I reached around his impressively taught abs wishing it could be someone else.

We roared off at an alarming speed, so much so that I deduced speed limits and Cael were foreign to one another. After realising he actually did have control of the bike, I started to really enjoy the ride. The wind whipped loose strands of my hair everywhere, and I hugged tighter into Cael, hoping to not to fly off the back. About half way down I felt an intense onset of dizziness. The closer I held onto Cael, the more pronounced it became. It wasn't female hormones causing me to girl crush on him, it was different. If I pulled slightly back, the feeling dissipated, when I hugged closer around the bends, my head began to thump. *Weird.*

We pulled up to *The Mill* in grand prix record time. Cael was red cheeked and pumped from the ride. Plenty of cars were there already, so it looked like it would be a busy night. It was a cute place—a two-storey bluestone building with a pub downstairs and a concert venue upstairs. A blue neon light was already blinking, indicating the way to the entrance. It had a country atmosphere, but served killer tapas and booked some great bands. Tonight was a Pink tribute band called Moore Pink.

Pushing through the double doors, I saw that there were a few familiar faces here already from St. Xavier's. We veered over to a table near the entrance to the beer garden and joined them. I greeted Gus, Jane and Olivia, all from the ER, whom I'd only met today. Cael rescued me from an awkward silence after the brief hellos, ordering a round of drinks and some tapas to share.

After some general chit chat, Gus asked us about the woman who had come in.

"I hear it took two hours to get her sedated enough to assess. They needed to use an anaesthetic to get her under control," he said with raised brows.

Jane nodded, adding, "The cops have already sent in Forensics to scrape her nails, and intend to charge her with the attack at the train station. Apparently, her victim was a seventeen-year old girl. My mate Pierre has been nursing her and told me that the poor kid copped a hundred stitches down her back and another fifty around her eyes. What kind of animal does that?" She shook her head in disgust.

The squeal of my name suddenly flew across from the doors as Jaz entered with a googly-eyed young boy. I say *boy* because this intern looked like he'd just stepped out of high school.

"Soph, you came! I so thought you'd wimp out!" I received a big, over-exaggerated hug. She had her cutie-pie façade on in full effect—the one she dazzles all of her fresh catches with before she goes in for the kill. I noted that she'd toned down her look tonight. She'd gone for a less vampy lipstick, and covered her tattoo with a long-sleeved dress, black of course. A little less intimidating for the poor guy, probably. He was cute, but way out of his depth with Jaz, and I think he knew it.

"I didn't see your car out there," she said. "That's why I'm so surprised to see you."

"I got a lift with Cael, actually," I informed her.

"You minx, I knew there was a tiger in there somewhere. Word is, he's very, *very* single." She punched me playfully in the shoulder.

"Shut up, you. It was just a lift," I sighed as I brought her to our table.

After a delicious meal and some tear-inducing laughs, we could hear the band doing a sound check upstairs.

Jaz was the first to get up. "Who's going to join us?" She pulled her pet to his feet and they sauntered over to the staircase, with her grabbing at his backside.

"I'm on first thing in the morning," said Cael, "but I'll stay for a little while. Do you need to get home, Soph?"

Despite feeling exhausted, I was having a nice time.

"I'm good for a while, let's go on up."

As we climbed the stairs, Cael grabbed my hand and we walked up together. My skin was instantly on fire. My head swam again, and I had to grab the bannister to remain upright. He stopped a minute, regarding me as though he knew how I felt. "I'm fine, let's go," I volunteered, pushing him onwards.

The first set had just begun. The lead singer was probably not the best Pink lookalike, but her voice was spot on. Jaz was already dancing, amongst other things, with Mr Googly Eyes. We all stood as a group, but Cael still grasped tightly to my hand. He seemed to make nothing more of it, so as it wasn't an unpleasant experience, I didn't pull away.

After a while, we drifted into the flow of the crowd and started dancing. The distraction helped me let go and forget the day's worries. Despite a persistent headache and the fact that Cael was strangely keeping very close to me, I was having a great time. In the middle of 'So What', I spun around catching a fleeting glimpse of a face in the crowd staring at me. I looked behind me to see if there was another person he was looking at, but all the others had their backs to him. The intrusive stare became heavier as I turned back to see he was a step closer. Dark eyes. Pale skin. He was jostled back by the crowd, becoming a silhouette behind a support post. Then he disappeared behind a group of girls as I tried to see who it was. I kept spinning around slowly and caught a glimpse of the face again. My heart rate sped up as fear instinctively crept up my spine. Visions of the other club came to mind, causing anxiety to set in. I continued dancing, trying to appear normal despite feeling completely creeped out. I attempted to get a better view with every move I made. He darted away again. I felt a shiver all over despite the heat of the crowd. I craned my head left and right, standing on my toes to see where he went. The flashing of the disco lights left the room looking like a flickering, black and white motion movie. In it, I saw this face weaving in and out of the crowd, peering back and forth at me. It was close, then far, then close again. I was just about to tell Cael when there was a loud crack as a light overhead exploded, raining down over the crowd who scattered to get away. The lights all suddenly went out. People began to shuffle and panic as the band called out to *hold on* until the power fired back up. I was jostled around. I felt someone rush past me, cool and way to close. A hand grabbed at me as an emergency spotlight turned on revealing the surging crowd, looking for the way out. I looked for Cael, I couldn't see anyone I knew as I was pushed around some more. Another grab at my arm. I was freaked out now. I spun around looking desperately through the mass of bodies for whoever it was. The lights blared back on. I spun around again, trying to find my bearings, looking wide eyed for this freak who was watching me. I turned and ran almost face first into Ben. I'd ended up by the doorway to the stairwell, and he was glaring my way, arms crossed. He often looked broody, but I could see that his expression was especially dark. He looked angry or hurt—I couldn't work out which.

"Ben, I'm so glad to see you. I was just—"

"Soph, I think it's time to go," Cael's voice called as I felt a gentle pull on my shoulder from behind. I turned around, smacking straight into Cael's expansive chest.

"Hang on, I'll just be a sec." I turned immediately back to continue speaking to Ben, but he was gone. In the space of a fraction of a second he'd disappeared into the thickening crowd. Something was up, what it was I hadn't a clue. Ben frequently came out with us, but he always hung with the group. I'd never seen him skulking alone in the background. It was always his perfect smile that greeted me. Not this time though, leaving me with a nagging worry. *Perhaps he was annoyed at another social snub from Jaz. It couldn't be that I was with Cael, could it?*

"Are you stalking me?" I queried Cael, eyebrows raised. I forced out normalcy to hide my still shaking body and voice.

"Just checking that no one is hassling you," he replied, grabbing my hands and pulling me back to the group. An electric shot ripped up my arm, causing my breath to catch in my throat. *What the hell?*

"No one's hassling me, I just thought I saw my friend." I had to squeeze the words out, breathing through them like a woman in labour. The irony of what Cael said was not lost on me. I could have told him about the weirdo in the crowd, but I chose to keep it to myself for now. Cael didn't seem to notice my shakiness. I found Jaz as I blinked my eyes, recovering from that awful, strange sensation. Unsurprisingly, I couldn't see her face at all, as it was so deeply glued to Googly Eyes' mouth. Seeing her overt public display of inappropriate affection with strange boys would be enough for her overprotective brother to lose it with her. Perhaps that's why Ben had a thundercloud expression.

Still slightly dizzy, I wondered if my electrolytes were off. *Perhaps I was dehydrated?* I rubbed at my still-stinging arm in confusion.

"I'd like to go home actually, Cael. I'll go call a cab," I said as I checked my pockets for my IPhone, forgetting I'd killed it.

"No way. I'll drop you off, I insist. I'm on early tomorrow, too. Plus I've got a couple of things I need to catch up on before I call it a night, anyway," he said.

We said our goodbyes quickly. I didn't bother with Jaz—she was mauling Googly Eyes in a booth in the farthest, darkened corner.

The ride home seemed to clear my head. The air was sweet and fresh, and the evening had cooled considerably. The steep mountain road at night was pitch black, with only the small light of the motorbike hinting at the forest that surrounded either side of us.

Pulling up to my house, Cael got off his bike and, ever the gentleman, walked me to the door. "Thanks for coming, Sophia. It was a great night. Good to see you smile."

Then he leaned in towards me.

Oh God! I thought my heart was going to pop out of my chest. I could smell his cologne, fresh and light, like the ocean. I shivered as he whispered with warm breath, close to my ear.

"Don't move." I tensed automatically. He cautiously reached his arm behind my head, then swiped and kicked something out into the bushes.

"What was that?" I asked, rather alarmed.

"I thought if you turned around and saw that massive, eight-legged hairy fiend by the door knob it would spoil your night. I hate those things," he said with an exaggerated, creeped-out look.

"Well, thanks. You've saved a damsel in potential distress," I said, bemused.

He kissed me on top of my head in a brotherly kind of way, then waved goodbye.

Through the revving he called out, "Keep your doors locked after you go in, Soph." He gave me a thumbs up, then disappeared at alarming speed, leaving nothing but moonlit dust in the air.

I watched him ride off. There was something about him. Something I couldn't quite put my finger on. I didn't want him to leave.

Cael suddenly felt very familiar and I didn't know why.

Chapter Three

The soft beeping of a heart monitor broke the midnight silence. The room was dark, other than the small stream of light peeking up from low hung wall lights. Nurses chatted quietly in the distance as they busied themselves with the night shift routine.

A large figure, silhouetted by the night, slipped quietly and unseen into the Intensive Care room. It made its way over to the patient lying deeply sedated in the bed. Her arms were shackled to the bedsides, covered with thick bandages. Dried blood sullied the white crepe. Her legs were secured to the foot of the bed. A blood transfusion was still in progress through a large IV in her neck, replacing the immense volume of blood she'd left on the floor of the ER that morning. Oxygen tubing lay slightly askew under her nose.

The figure reached down and straightened up the tubing, so that the gas was flowing correctly into her nostrils. With this gesture, the monitor showed static interference, and began to alarm. A palm waved across the screen. With a brief flash of white light, the monitor silenced itself.

Beep, beep, beep. Back to normal.

The individual placed a hot hand across the woman's chest. Her body jerked up, as if shocked with electricity. Then her eyes flew open. Black matte orbs glared back. They were venomous, but her body was so heavily drugged, only her eyes could react with hatred and intent.

Wordlessly, the figure placed a large hand across her whole face, gripping gently and slightly inward with the edges of glowing fingertips. The woman's head arched backwards, not of her own will, but from the energy being infused forcefully into her brain. Her mouth gaped open with silent screams, to be heard by no one. Her eyes bulged, begging for mercy. The blackness within them slowly receded, revealing a hint of jade as a hazy, coal-coloured substance oozed out from her nose, mouth, and ears. It amassed upon the pillow around her head.

The smoky entity began to rise up, attempting to take form. Before it had a chance to, the large figure by the bedside thrust two hands within its depths and let a maelstrom of electrical energy attack it. The room lit up briefly with the intensity of the force. Then a miniature thunderstorm raged silently above the woman's head. The blackness swirled and writhed in defiance. Only the individual inflicting the attack could hear its screams as it collapsed within itself, on its way to oblivion.

Once satisfied that the job was done, hands were once more placed upon the woman. One over her heart, the other upon her head.

With these immense hands glowing brightly and warmly upon her skin, in the distance of her consciousness, she heard a message. *You are free.*

The room was now quiet and empty, apart from Annie. She lay still in the bed, serene, peaceful, and healed.

Chapter Four

Another early morning wakeup went as well as yesterday, except that this time, I had to mind my manners. Nan was my alarm clock today, so I couldn't very well throw anything at her. My regular call from Jaz was a bit more surprising, though.

"I don't need a lift today, Soph. I, ah, already have one."

"Did you go home last night?' I asked.

Silence.

"Good luck explaining that when you see Ben. By the way, he was there last night. Did you see him? He was just hanging out by himself, looking pretty peeved, but he left when he saw me. You have to stop sneaking out on him."

"Sorry, I didn't see much, other than Adrian's face, among other things. Ben will live—he's a big boy. He needs to get himself a girlfriend. He needs to stop panting over what he can't have." Her tone was unsympathetic, the last part irked me.

"Again, you're disgusting and mean, so I'll see you at work." I hung up. She actually was pretty awful to him sometimes, yet he never complained. I got the feeling this part of their dynamic dated back to her childhood. His was a complete mystery. All I knew was that they ended up as foster kids together and had looked after themselves since their foster parents died. They'd done it pretty tough, but always had each other's backs. Well, except when Jaz was prowling for male company.

It was a matter of life and death that I had to have a large mug of coffee when I arrived at work. The staff room was empty, save for the cleaning lady who politely waved hello. I was ridiculously tired—lately, I seemed to get more exhausted every day. Yet it still took me ages to get to sleep at night. My mind seemed to be constantly racing with empty thoughts. I'd only had two drinks last night, but I had a killer headache now. I didn't have time for *Miss Marple's* this morning, so I had to put up with the crappy, generic instant hospital-issue coffee. With enough sugar in it though, the hot liquid was bearable to get down.

As I left the staff room, I'd barely made it out of the door when I was knocked to the ground by a gurney as it sped through the ambulance doors. I hit my head on the doorjamb as I went down. A brief sensation of blackness and stars peppered my sight as I was quickly hoisted up by a staff nurse who I didn't know.

"You ok? Sorry, sweetie," said a soft female voice.

I rubbed at the back of my head and leaned against the wall. "I think so. I—what happened? Do you normally drag-race patients through the doors?"

"Ha, humour, you must be fine. In that case, follow me. We need all hands on deck, we've got family here. I'm Kea, by the way. Come on." She yanked on my arm as she guided me down the corridor.

I followed her to the Resuscitation bay, watching the pendulum-swing of her long, black braid as I rubbed at my head. *What did she mean we've got family here?* When I entered the room it was mayhem, a far cry from the usual, methodical calm. The patient area was surrounded by a huge medical team. I could smell the sickly metallic odour of blood—*lots of blood*. More blood than with Annie yesterday, and somehow richer and more disturbing to my senses. It made my stomach lurch, not the best weakness to have as a nurse. As I stood by and watched, I caught snippets of conversation.

"Where was he found?"

"The Police said he was draped over the top of a two-metre high statue inside the Rickett's Sanctuary. The caretaker found him when he opened up this morning. Had to call in the fire brigade to haul him down."

"Apparently, the place was a mess—trees were ripped up, and one of the statues was smashed to rubble. Like a tornado had been through the place, so they say. The strange thing is that his bike was crashed further down the tourist road, just back from the shopping strip."

"That's got to be a couple of kilometres away. How did he get to where he was found?"

"I've never seen an injury like this. This is no motorbike accident."

My ears pricked at this. *Motorbike accident?* I knew two people with motorbikes, Ben and Cael. I pushed forward in a panic, trying to see who it was.

"What the hell?" someone exclaimed.

"Looks like it's just been ripped out!" said another shocked voice.

"Crank up the oxygen, this blood is too dark. He's oxygen-starved. Get a blood sample."

Then a doctor in navy scrubs called me over. "Hey you, we need an extra set of hands. Get some gloves on, and stand here. I need some pressure over these wounds."

I froze for a moment.

"Well come on girl, get over here!" he grumbled.

Shaking myself out of a fugue, I snapped on some blue gloves. My head ached severely up the right side of my face the closer I got to the bedside. That bang to my head could well have been developing into a concussion, I'd worried.

As I caught a glimpse of the patient, I felt every nerve light up in my body, and my head pounded like a drum. My vision blurred at the edges, and a wave of nausea rolled through me. I had to grasp the bedside for a moment to regain control of my balance. *Blip, blip, blip.* The cardiac monitor sang harmoniously next to me, but it seemed a thousand decibels too loud. The sight in front of me was a naked male, face down, with blood literally everywhere. Barely any skin was visible under the tide of red liquid. He had a gaping gash on either side of his spine, so hideous it would surely impress the likes of Stephen King. My head throbbed harder. I squeezed my eyes shut just for a second. Rough hands grabbed my gloved ones and pressed them down firmly over one of the spinal wounds.

"Press here, and don't move until I say so. Got it?"

I nodded affirmatively to the doctor, trying to mask my efforts to slow down my irrational and panicked breathing. I could see exposed vertebrae all up the left side of the body. I assumed that's what the wound under my hands also looked like. I was both mesmerised and horrified all at once. The thick blood oozing out was dark, very dark. Yet the small snippet of skin I could see was a healthy golden tone, where I'd expect it to look pale and sickly. As the blood pulsed, I was sure—but quite possibly concussed—that it actually sparkled in the light.

The skin was torn and ragged, as though hacked at with a saw. Exposed muscle was flailing with every breath the patient took. The muscly mess glistened as it protruded so wrongly outside of his torso.

The doctor was cleaning out the other wound whilst inspecting it. I could hear the distraught shouts of staff as they frantically busied themselves with various jobs around the patient.

"I'd swear to Jesus himself that this guy has had his spinal bone ripped out! Look! There's exposed spinal nerves that look exactly like cord tissue, yet the central column is intact! I want a Neuro consult!" This was the senior ER registrar, Doctor Davis. I'd met him earlier. He seemed nice enough, but his face was in such a contortion of confusion right now that I was sure he was feeling like he'd landed in Oz with no yellow brick road to follow.

He packed the wound heavily with gauze to stem the bleeding, calling out, "Nancy, call the OR! He needs exploration and patching up. Book a CT on the way, I need to see what's going on in there. Draw some blood for standard trauma pathology, and get some O-neg blood down here ASAP!"

Nancy nodded wordlessly and moved with a well-practised precision.

Davis looked at me and said, "You're new. What's your take on this?"

"I, ah, well—ah, it's horrific, it's—oh um, it's bloody, very bloody." *Why was I so dumbstruck?* I burned with humiliation. I was an honours grad, for crying out loud! *Where were my neurons hiding?* My body was numb, yet pulsating all at once.

"Don't bust a brain cell! Take your hands off there, I'm ready to clean that side out now," he barked the order at me as he moved around to my side of the bed.

Kea quietly appeared and placed her hand on my shoulder. She whispered sympathetically in my ear, "Hon, don't mind him. He tends to lash out when he's frustrated. Why you don't stand up at the top end and note the poor boy's vitals every five minutes. That'd be a great help, and I'll take over here."

I removed my bloodied gloves, quickly washed my hands, and grabbed a pen and his chart.

The victim's vitals were all normal, other than an elevated temperature, which was perplexing, given the exposure he'd had in the elements and considering the amount of blood he was still rapidly losing.

Davis snapped again, "Neuro status? His pupils, have you checked them? Has anyone checked this guy's pupils?" he was clearly stressed.

"I checked them on the way in," said Kea. "They were fine then. Sophia, could you check them again now?" she prompted.

I pulled out my penlight and knelt down so I could get to his face.

I gasped out loud, "Oh no—no, no, no! It's Cael. Oh my God!" I welled up.

"We all know who it is!" Davis barked, "So get on with making sure our teammate here has the best chance of recovery."

His face was serene, his breathing steady, but he was ripped to shreds. *From last night to this, how could it be?* Just hours ago, we were laughing and dancing.

I nervously reached toward him, removing a twig stuck in his muddy, matted hair.

"What happened to you?" I whispered to no one but myself. I reached my bare hand to his eyelid. I very gently opened it, my fingers shaking and tingling. I shone the torch's beam in, and then felt a blow as though a bomb went off at point blank range in front of me. Blinding light shrouded me as pain seared up my back and through to my face. Indecipherable images flashed through my mind. Crashing waves, black eyes, women and children, intense white light. Arms reached out to me dripping with blood, grabbing at me. I felt such immense terror, I could not move or speak.

Then it all went quiet.

Chapter Five

A loud knock on the door drew Diane's attention, only because it was frantic and clearly they'd forgotten to press the intercom buzzer to request entry.

Being morning teatime, she was alone in the Pathology lab, and as gross as it sounded, she'd happily snack by herself amid the sight of the various specimen containers.

Annoyed, she pushed out from her desk and opened the door. A clearly inexperienced intern was standing there with a pathology bag full of tubes.

"Is this where I drop off urgent blood samples?"

He was quite a looker, but clearly not at the top of his class, because right in front of his face on the door a bold sign read, *Deposit samples through chute. Please press intercom for urgent samples. Thanks, Pathology.*

"Yes, thanks. I'll take that. How quick do you need it?" she asked.

"Straight away. It's for Cael from the ER. He's been badly wounded in an accident, and Doctor Davis needs some results immediately," he blurted breathlessly. He'd obviously taken the stairs down here, not the elevator.

"Oh no! Poor Cael. I'll get onto this immediately—let them know I'll bring up the results myself."

Diane had known Cael for a number of years. He was one of those really decent guys, the kind who looked after his staff as well as his patients. For someone so young, he was of a class of gentleman long forgotten.

"Thanks," the intern puffed as she shut the door in his face, threw her sandwich in the bin, and headed straight to the work benches.

Despite feeling distressed about Cael, Diane immediately prepped the slides and tubes with careful precision. The first analysis immediately showed that his blood-oxygen level was at 100%, which was very strange. The blood appeared to be completely oxygen deprived. It was dark blue in colour, when it should be a bright shade of red. She was slightly excited by the possibility of a mystery on her hands, but then immediately felt embarrassed and guilty because of whom the sample belonged to. The routine in the lab could get a bit dull, so something challenging was like pathologist porn. *Sad, but true.*

All of the other elements of this blood sample were at the highest end of normal as well, so she just needed to work out why the oxygen was not lighting up like a neon red sign on his haemoglobin.

Popping her hair back in a headband and a new set of gloves on, she got comfy in her chair. More slides at the ready, she carefully slid them into her microscope. After a few adjustments to the scope, she leaned in to get a good look at this mysterious blood.

As her eyes adjusted, she sat back up and furrowed her brow in slight confusion. *Was there something swirling and sparkling back up at her?* Diane made another adjustment to deepen the image and sharpen the focus. She leaned back in to look, and then she screamed. A bloodcurdling, horrific cry of shock and pain.

The chair rolled away from under her as she fell to the ground.

"Help! Help me! Help—please, oh God, help!"

She pushed her hands hard into her eyes. Blood dripped down the side of her face as she knelt. She panicked, knowing all too well the aroma of that metallic tang. She bent forward onto the floor, gripping her head fiercely in agonising pain.

Colleagues came running from the tea room.

"What's going on?"

"Is that you Dee?"

"Oh, Dee!" Jamie, her supervisor, placed a gentle hand on her back. The emergency fluid spill kit sat by his side. She barely acknowledged him. He leaned in closer.

"Diane, it's me, I'm here. What happened?"

"My eyes! Oh, my eyes!" she whimpered.

"Did you get a blood spatter?" he asked.

"No! No, nothing. I just looked at it and, oh God it hurts. I just looked!" she gasped.

With that, Diane collapsed to the floor, unconscious.

"Call a Code Blue, Amy. We need some help here!" Jamie ordered. He checked her pulse and breathing, which were all fine, then repositioned her carefully onto her left side. He removed her hands from her eyes, noting with shock that blood was trickling from the corner of each tightly shut lid.

"*What the hell*?" he mumbled.

"Oh my God! What's happened?" exclaimed his Intern, Sarah.

Sarah placed two squares of moistened gauze over each eye as Jamie put an oxygen mask onto Diane's face and checked her pulse.

The code team burst through the door with an experienced calm. Senior ER nurse Kea was running the team today.

"What's the story?" she asked.

"We don't know. Diane was just examining some blood slides during her tea break, and suddenly she was screaming on the floor! She's unconscious now, with blood pouring from her eyes," Jamie answered, shock hitched his voice.

Kea leaned in while other colleagues hooked Diane up to a cardiac monitor. Gloves now on, she removed the gauze and pried open one of her eyes. Kea immediately recoiled back at what she saw. Then she opened the other eye and saw the same thing.

She sat back, very concerned. Kea turned to Jamie. "Jamie, what chemicals have you got down here? Could anything you use do this?"

Jamie was wrenching his hands through his hair. Diane was more than just a co-worker. This was his wife on the floor. He panicked.

"Oh my God! Shit, shit, shit—what the hell is going on? There's nothing in her workspace that could do that to her! Help her, please!" Jamie choked out the words.

He turned to Sarah and spat out, "Go see what samples she was looking at and cover that microscope. Do not let anyone use it."

Sarah called out, "There are some tubes here with Cael's name on them."

Kea looked up sharply at that, then back down to Diane. "Definitely do not let anyone else use that scope, or examine those samples. Quarantine it until we know what's going on."

Jamie looked back down at his wife. Her open eyes were pure white. No iris, no pupil, just white.

Chapter Six

Flashes of light and dark flickered before my eyes. A groan and a sickening thump sounded to one side of me. Trees rustled in a breeze I could not feel. *Thump, thump, thump—crack.*

"Argh!" an agonising scream roared from behind. Groaning, mumbled curses that I could not make out followed. I turned and saw two silhouettes clashing, floating in the air and throwing themselves at one another mercilessly. Blinding flashes of light exploded each time they came into direct contact. Both figures panted, as though this had been going on for some time. Each time there was a burst of light, I caught a glimpse of ancient, knowing faces—male, female, children. Soiled rock faces, covered with moss.

The brighter figure flung its arm forward, and a great explosion of lightning emanated from its palm, slamming the dark creature to the ground so hard, he seemed to be half buried. But that did not end the fight. The dark one, the more terrifying of the two, clawed back out of the dirt and grass and rose back up into the air. Huge trees were silhouetted in the distance by the moonlight. The dark figure raised its arm, repeating the same gesture. Fire, hot and stinking of sulphur, burst from its palm, hitting the lighter being square in the chest. The contact spun him around, rendering him prone on the ground. Advantage gained, the dark figure quickly descended and knelt by his victim. He grabbed the head of the overwhelmed being, wrenching it backwards. A pale, glowing trident stabbed down around his neck, pinning him helplessly to the ground. A *third figure emerged from the darkness, leaned over the defeated one, and said in a cruel tone,*

"She is mine."

The creature atop him then ran its hand slowly down the wretched form's body. It rammed its hand into the other's back and ripped upwards and out with immense force. The tearing of sinew and crunching of bone, tinged with the smell of blood, filled the air.

I screamed.

"Stop! Please stop, whoever you are, just stop!"

The helpless creature groaned with such misery as its light was fading. It turned its face and stared straight into my eyes. It extended a hand out toward me, palm up. An image of concentric circles glowed white back at me. It was him—it was Cael!

The creature that I now knew to be pure evil stepped up from Cael's limp body and disappeared into the blackness beyond. The other dark being focused its attention onto me as it stepped over Cael's body. I wanted to run, but my limbs wouldn't budge. This new evil presence advanced upon me quickly and grabbed hold of my arms with a great and merciless strength. It was barely restraining itself from breaking my bone. It leaned forward, holding me close to its muscular body. Black eyes pierced into mine, its form frighteningly familiar. It caressed my hair in a strangely loving gesture. It breathed slowly, controlled, as though in contemplation, and then said,

"You are mine, Sophia."

I willed myself back to consciousness.

I heard the distant call of my name.

Help me, I thought, as words refused to come.

"I think she's coming round," said a familiar voice.

"Sophia! Sophia, it's me, open your eyes," I heard.

"Call a doctor," another voice instructed.

My eyes wouldn't open, and I thought I was still in the grip of the evil thing—a dark silhouette, masculine in shape, indistinct other than those black eyes, still held me tight.

"Sophia!" a shout close in my ear jolted me awake. Throwing my arms and legs about, I tried desperately to be free of this dark terror. "Soph, it's me, Jaz. Nan's here, and Ben, too. It's okay now, you're all right."

The odour of disinfectant assaulted my senses.

"Sophia, I'm here now, dear. You are safe," spoke a smooth, proper, and familiar British voice.

Nan's with me, I thought. *Ok, I'm ok.*

Slowly, my eyes cracked open to the glare of bright lights and many faces peering down at me.

I tried to sit up, my vision blurred as it adjusted to the brightness.

I briefly panicked. "My contacts, where are they? I can't see," I mumbled.

"They're still in, dear," soothed Nan. "You've been unconscious for an hour or so. Relax and let them adjust. You're here with us now."

Nan rested a warm hand across my head, which was instantly soothing. I felt her energy willing calmness me into. There was a spark that I felt pass between us, though I wasn't sure if it was going from her to me, or the reverse.

Fully alert now, I removed a blood pressure cuff from my left arm just as it began to automatically inflate again. *Thank God.* I was just dreaming about that thing pumping up on my arm. Just a stupid nightmare—nothing had hold of me after all. I barely convinced myself of it, remembering the image of Cael's face as he lay on the ground, ripped to pieces.

"Well, thank Christ for that. I thought I was going to have to buy a new black dress. Geez Soph, are you trying to give me a frigging heart attack? You don't have to go and pull this kind of crap to get attention!" This was Jaz's version of sympathy.

"Just trying to save those poor interns from you!" I mused at her. My mouth was stale and dry as I spoke.

"Ugh. So funny!" she grumped back at me.

Her smudged eye makeup betrayed dried tears. Never one to let her prickly exterior show too much weakness, I must have given her a decent fright. She gave my hand a reassuring squeeze. Another shock zapped between our hands, and she quickly yanked hers away. My face and right arm were left burning hot.

"*Ow*, Soph, did you feel that?"

"No, what?" I lied, panicking.

"You okay Soph? Ben asked from the end of the bed. He looked pained.

"Yeah, I think so," I wasn't quite sure it was true, but all limbs seemed intact and working so I figured I must have been alright. He stepped forward as though to say something else but the moment was interrupted when a female nurse with a severe crew cut entered the room. She checked me over, put the blood pressure cuff back on, and noted my vitals down on the bedside computer.

"Hi there, sleepyhead. You're awake!" She stuck a thermometer in my ear. "Oh, your temperature is quite elevated—39 degrees. How are you feeling?" Her bedside manner was far softer than her appearance.

"I feel fine I think—a little dazed, perhaps. I've got a bit of a head and back ache, but otherwise, I think I'm okay." My voice sounded distant and sleep drunk.

"Well, in light of this very high fever, I'll be back shortly to take some blood so we can see what's going on. It could well explain your fainting episode. I'll alert your doctor, fetch the equipment I need, and be back shortly. You just lay back and rest, honey." She gave me a motherly caress across my forehead as I snuggled back into the pillow. I'd never had blood taken before, as I'd never had an ill day in my life.

After the nurse left, in a most calm and proper manner, Nan announced, "Well, that won't be necessary at all. We like to keep our fluids in our own vessels in this family. Come on, Sophia, we are going home. I'll have dear old Aunt Esme come tend to you."

"Uh, Nan?" Jaz piped in, "Something really weird happened to her. You don't just fling three feet across a room into a wall, lay unconscious for an hour, and then go home for afternoon tea!" Her eyes were incredulous.

Jaz had guts, talking to Nan like this. I'll give her that.

Jaz continued. "What if she got an electric shock or something?" Jaz looked back at me, rubbing at her hand. "Shouldn't you let the experts check her out properly first? Is that 'fluid in the vessel' thing some religious guilt you peeps have never told me about? I've never pegged you guys as the religious type!"

"Experts? Lord preserve me, Jasmine." Nan smoothed down her platinum hair, her effort at composure. "Have I taught you nothing, young lady? Although Sophia and you choose to work in these mechanised, disease-ridden institutions of drug intoxication, I have no time for them. You know perfectly well that we are more than capable of providing our own health care." Exasperation with a plum tone was Nan's specialty.

"Yeah, yeah, natural healing mumbo jumbo, I hear ya." Jaz ducked as Nan's glare was about as tangible as a clip around the ears.

"Leave it Jaz, I'm fine," I said, giving her an encouraging smile.

Not wanting to cause a fuss though, I did as Nan said. I'd never gone wrong with her healthcare to date, so there was no valid reason in my mind why I should stop taking her advice now. As I was easing up out of bed with Nan and Ben on either side of me, a different nurse entered the room with an equipment-laden trolley. The fluorescent lights suddenly intensified my headache, and the room spun for a moment as she parked the trolley next to me.

"You shouldn't be up out of bed yet. I need you lying down whilst I draw the blood in case you become lightheaded," she snapped. She didn't have the comforting bedside manner of the previous one. She scratched incessantly at her arms and her neck was inflamed with some form of lumpy rash. She looked like she needed the bloodletting, not me.

"Where's the nice nurse?" asked Jaz, matching the new nurse's bitter tone.

Her curt response was accented with a killer glare. "She had to attend to another patient!"

Her smooth intake of a calming breath prefaced Nan's next sharp, yet polite interjection. "With the greatest of respect, we will not be requiring anything further care from yourself or this—" she looked around, waving a limp hand through the air, "ponderous place. I will be discharging her in a moment's notice, thank you."

Taken aback, the nurse sought out a response, scratched some more, mumbled weirdly to herself, and finally said, "I *must* take her blood." She had a strangely determined expression on her heavily wrinkled face.

"Yes, I understand. But we have the right to decline treatment, and are exercising it today, thank you." Ever so polite my dear Nan was. Watching this exchange was as amusing as it was unnerving.

"I'm going to get the doctor to discuss this with you. I need your blood." She left quickly, wringing her hands as though nervous. So hasty was her exit that she banged into the trolley as she went, sending blood collection tubes all over the floor.

"'*I need your blood!*'", mimicked Jaz. "That was a little ghoulish. Clearly, she got her nursing degree at the '*Up end of Backside*'!" she exclaimed.

"What's the problem, Nan? It's fine. I take blood from people all the time. It's no big deal—I can lose a few drops and still survive." I said, hoping to ease Nan of the worry.

Now Nan was patting down her lilac morning suit. *Oh dear.* Whilst Nan, with her soft appearance, elegantly tall stature, and knitting proficiency might lead others to believe her to be mild and meek, I knew otherwise.

"Sophia, you are indeed an adult, but believe me—there are lessons you have yet to learn, and perhaps at this very moment you are now realising that?" She stared at me intently before turning away and gathering her handbag.

Was she referring to the energy that passed between us? The unsettling zap I gave Jaz? How could she possibly know?

Nan continued as she picked through her bag for something, "You are best off heeding my advice on this matter. Now, unless you wish me to have a conniption in front of your friends, get off of that bed this very moment!"

"Fine. Can you help me again, Ben? I actually do feel a little lightheaded still."

He moved immediately to my side, quietly supporting me. "I've got you," he said. His muscles trembled with the effort of holding me ever so carefully as I went to stand. He smelled so nice, so familiar so—I don't know.

"See!" exclaimed Jaz, her hands raised in vindication, "She's dizzy. She needs to be monitored a bit longer. It's not like I'm a nurse or anything—I do have a brain, you know," she grumbled.

"Jaz, just stop," snapped Ben. It was rare for him to share a real opinion on anything, he always just went with the flow.

"Since when are you the qualified nurse, Benny boy?"

"Don't be a smart mouth, Jaz. I'm not qualified in much, but I think she looks okay. She's just a little weak, that's all. Nan's right, she'd be better looked after at home."

Ben gripped my hand a little tighter as I planted my feet on the floor. My stomach lurched as he did so, and I had to sit straight back down against the edge of the bed. He looked at me, and after a brief stare, he stood back, let my hand go and mumbled, "Jaz, perhaps you can help? You're better at this nurse stuff." She huffed at him in vindication as he backed off to the far wall of the room. He rubbed his hand over and over as he looked back at me with an odd expression. No electric jolt this time, but he certainly felt something. *What was it?* This day was getting stranger and more surreal by the minute.

The door banged open, revealing a familiar face.

"I understand you are refusing essential medical care, Ms Woodville," spoke the Psychiatrist who took that poor woman away yesterday. I never caught his name. Squinting my eyes, I noticed there was no actual picture or name on his ID badge. *Very odd.*

"And you are?" Nan questioned him authoritatively.

"I'm Doctor Hyde, head of Psychiatry, and I'm here to assess Ms Woodville's state of mind to see if she is fit to make her own medical decisions. She has suffered a concussion, has a high fever, and is likely not in a fit state to refuse important diagnostic care."

"Doctor Hyde, oh my God!" Jaz sneered into my ear. "It'll be Doctor Jekyll next!"

A smile tickled the edges of my mouth.

"Excuse me, sir, but I am her grandmother, and I have made the decision to discharge her from your care."

The dark haired doctor closed his eyes and rolled his head side to side as though trying to release a tense muscle. He looked back at us, completely emotionless.

"As she is an adult, you have no legal say in the matter, I'm afraid. If you are going to be difficult about this, I'll have security escort you out."

He looked at me with a cold stare. "You must understand it is in your best interest that we ascertain that you are fit and well. Don't you, Sophia?"

The way he spoke my name tugged at a memory that had my flight response fully armed. Ben's head snapped up, eyes sharp, as he stood to his full height moving quickly in front of Jaz and I. Nan placed her handbag back down and faced the doctor square and centre, unmoving. She simply glared at him for a moment. From my vantage point, I could see her hands clenching behind her back, fingers twining in and out of each other. She was *reading* him. I'd seen her do this many times before. It was her sixth sense to know a good energy from a bad one.

She turned to me and mouthed something, but I couldn't quite get it. Her eyes were wide with alarm, which was unnerving since she was the most composed person I knew.

"Soph, what's going on?" whispered Jaz casually, seemingly oblivious to the bizarre unfolding situation. I ignored her, as I was unable to take my eyes from the doctor.

Ben moved closer behind Nan and spoke calmly to the doctor.

"You need to leave, you're not needed here now. We're taking her home."

The doctor inclined his head, a look of confusion on his face.

"It's all right Ben, I have this under control. Go and fetch the car, dear." She handed him the keys.

He shoved past the stonily silent doctor, firmly shouldering him as he went. As he made contact, the doctor's image stuttered, like static on the TV. His face became nondescript as his features just seemed to swirl in the oval of his face. Nan gasped. Ben yelled, "What the hell?" as he pushed Nan out of the way and stood in front of me protectively. I felt like I'd gone back into a dream-like state.

The doctor's guise evaporated, revealing a resplendent man with glistening olive skin and black eyes. Looking at him was like seeing something through tunnel vision—blurred around the edges, with no definitive lines to his shape. He was there, but not there. He was bare-chested, wearing what looked like black leather pants, the kind you'd expect to see in the middle ages.

Ethereal, stunning, and frightening. Horns pierced through a thick mass of dark, ashen-tipped hair. I was clearly seeing things—the bump to my head must have been worse than I thought. Thick at the base, two dark horns swirled up and backwards to a point from just behind both temples. This was a mythical creature, something out of a scary fairy-tale from my childhood.

What followed next happened in seconds.

"I *knew* it was you," Nan spoke calmly. "I've sensed you for days."

"No time for reunions," he coldly responded.

At that moment, with one hand, he grabbed viciously at Ben's throat, lifting him high into the air and thrashing him to the ground, limp. "I'll deal with you later, you weren't meant to be here boy!" he snarled as he looked down at Ben's limp body.

Jaz and I screamed in unison as she ran at the creature, black polished nails bared at it. I was frozen to the floor in shock.

This creature eyeballed Jaz and spoke one simple word, "Unsee."

Jaz screamed again, falling to her knees this time in agony as she rammed balled fists into her eyes. Fresh droplets of blood cascaded freely around the edges of her temples. In that instant, I knew what Nan had whispered to me earlier. I threw myself over Jaz' body, both of us falling heavily to the ground. I don't know whether I was blinded by the headache that was a permanent resident now or something else, but either way, I couldn't see anything for a few moments.

With Jaz struggling in pain and frustration underneath me, I could hear a scuffle behind me. Voices argued in that strange language again and there was a sudden rise in the room's temperature. The lights flickered, I detected a *snap*, and then a loud *crack*.

A male groaned.

"Leave him be!" yelled Nan.

"You betray me over and over," said a deadly smooth voice.

"You betray yourself," Nan replied.

"What the hell is going on?" screamed Jaz.

"*Quiet, shhh*," I whispered to her.

An emergency evacuation alarm sounded. The pounding of what seemed like thousands of feet pressed in from every direction, as the hospital converged to respond.

The pain in my head had thankfully dulled, but still ebbed in the background. I just somehow knew this meant that the vile creature had gone, but where, and for how long? I turned to check on Nan as I pulled Jaz up from the floor, my arm around her shoulder for support.

"What the hell just happened? Crap, Soph! Are we in the psych ward by mistake? He flung a frigging weapon or something at me!" Jaz whimpered, swiping at her bloodstained eyes.

"Come now, we must leave immediately. This place is not safe." Nan spoke with an unnatural calm, as though nothing supremely paranormal had just happened. She straightened her skirt and hair then beckoned us out the door.

I yanked on Jaz's arm and we followed her without question. Now I was Jaz's support, as she could barely see. There was no other logical option but to listen to the only person who seemed to know what to do in such a whacked-out situation. Noise was blaring from every direction. This was not any ordinary fire drill. I heard panic in the voices pushing past us. Then I caught a hint of smoke in the air. Through the chaos of hospital staff running to and fro, wheeling patients on beds and wheelchairs to emergency evacuation points, we didn't immediately realise that we'd left Ben behind.

"We've forgotten Ben!" I screamed out.

"We can't stop, Sophia. You don't understand the danger we are in. I'm sorry, but you must leave him!" yelled Nan over the noise as she ran.

"What? Ben, we've lost Ben?" With that, Jaz pulled away. She ran back towards the room that we had just fled.

I ran after her despite Nan screaming for me not to. I ignored Nan, calling for Jaz to wait for me. I didn't want to be separated from her. After twisting and turning through a few corridors pushing through the fleeing masses, I found her back where we started. She was still as a statue and unflinching. An evolving emotion of utter confusion and horror marred her pale face. I followed her gaze. There on the floor, where Ben had fallen, was a human-shaped black scorch mark burnt into the linoleum floor.

"This is the reason you must follow my every word, Sophia," Nan said in a quiet tone behind me.

Chapter Seven

Running at full speed, through the labyrinth of corridors, I was in a state of shock every bit as real as the look on Jaz's face. Wondering where Ben was, I found myself maintaining Nan's impressive pace while dragging my friend's resistant form along the way. My mind ached and raced for answers, achieving no port of call.

I didn't speak, as I didn't know what to ask—although, there was something stirring in my gut, like a cord about to snap. Incapacitating talons of fear snared out through my insides. The feeling invaded every screaming cell of my body, and it was a struggle to keep my burning eyes focused and clear enough to follow Nan. I tripped over myself in the thickening smoke, pulling Jaz down alongside me.

"You trying to bloody kill us, Soph? Let me go!"

"No, we've got to get out! Come on!" I yanked her back up, coughing on the black cloud wafting at head height. I saw Nan just ahead, looking back for us through the rush of escaping patients and staff. She looked panicked, for what I thought was the first time in her life. Instead of heading out an emergency exit, she pushed through the heavy door of an internal stairwell.

"Come, Sophia! You must hurry. We are running out of time—we need to get out of this place!" she yelled back as she raced down with an alarming speed.

Running out of time?

For what? Why?

Jaz was fighting me the whole way, screaming at me. "Let me go! I'm… going to…find…my brother!" she screamed at me through gritted teeth.

Then she swung at me. I dodged and pulled at her harder. "I don't know what the hell is going on Jaz, but we've got to get out of here now. Stop fighting me, God damn it!"

Her screams were manic and guttural. I pulled at her with a renewed strength, half-tumbling down the worn stairs. My sweaty hands made it impossible to grip the handrail for support, so I just hoped I wouldn't fall in my haste.

The lights began to flicker on and off, and the buzzing of the incandescent tubing became menacing.

What were we running from?

This was madness. There I was, careening down a staircase with my white hospital gown flapping behind me, like a mad woman escaping an asylum. At the final landing on the ground floor, everything went dark as I ran into the back of someone. I screamed.

"It's me, Sophia. Hush, be still and be quiet," Nan whispered. Her voice echoed inside my mind.

The lights burst on, and there stood that same creepy doctor. Again he was blurred around the edges, blocking our exit. He spoke in that same Greek-sounding language that Annie had screamed at us yesterday. It was a language foreign to me then, but surprisingly now I understood it as though it were English.

"Enl'iel, put your ancient soul at ease now. Finally, after eons, we have found The One. Stand down and give me the one we seek, and all will be well. We shall have peace between us and be once more among the exalted and our kindred." His voice was soft and enticing. It dripped like sweet honey laced with poison.

Nan surprised me as she replied in the same language.

"I know your true intent with this child. Your course is misguided. You are clouded by an eternity of hate. You know not the correct path to our salvation. I choose the path of light. I am a seeker of repentance, and I am the keeper of the Earth-born child. Stand aside, rest your vengeful and wearied soul. Let us pass!" Nan spoke with a surprising tone of authority.

She ordered him away with a commanding defiance, "Leave this place, and get out of our way!"

"Nan, what's' going on?" I screamed along with Jaz, who was incoherent by my side as she continued to struggle against me.

The figure shimmered. His features morphed in and out of focus. A great heat and light emanated from behind him. Blinding whiteness pulsed outwards, shaping into a familiar form, like wings but made of light.

These wings of light rippled and pulsated as he elevated himself into the air. At this point, Jaz had fainted, either from exertion, shock or both—I really wasn't sure. I felt like I could repeat the gesture as I laid her down softly behind me. I stood in front of her like a mother bear protecting her cub. I checked her pulse with trembling fingers, she seemed fine for now.

"Get away from us!" I screamed till my throat hurt. "Nan run! Run!"

A gusty wind blew up inside the stairwell. Howling like a storm, the high-pitched screeching was deafening. Lights continued to flicker, and some were now exploding, causing micro shards of glass to spray down over us. I knelt over Jaz's body to protect her.

The figure faced off with Nan and spoke again. "You possess the key to our salvation. I will have it now, or the wrath you will face from my brothers will make the curse we have all endured seem but a mere joke. You know not the danger you are in. We are unseen, yet ever-present around you."

How could something so beautiful be so very ugly?

As my fear for Nan heightened, my entire body began to shake, feverishly heating up from head to toe. I'd never felt such fear, confusion, or dread. As I watched the scene play out, my mouth became desert dry. I couldn't swallow to wet my mouth, and was too afraid to let out the million screams of terror building from within me.

Nan stood her ground and reached out her right hand. "You will leave this place!" she bellowed.

Her hand glowed brightly, and without so much as a flinch, a shot of crackling lightning exploded from her palm, straight at him. It was like a bolt from the sky, hitting this creature in the region where a heart should have been. He reeled, stepping back a pace or two and looking down briefly at the scorch mark upon his heaving chest, though he was shaken little. His black eyes glowed crimson with rage, and he too reached out a glowing hand, threatening the same gesture to Nan.

"Don't test me, Enl'iel! A half-breed can never defeat me!" he yelled in a voice thick with rage. With a quick swipe of his huge hand, Nan was flung across the small landing, smashing her skull with a crack on the wall. Nan slumped over, silent.

Before I could react, think, or move, he came for me. My body felt like it was on fire now, but my arms and legs were jelly. I could barely stand to defend myself. *How am I going to fight this thing?* Gasping and breathless, my backbone screamed to peel itself from within my body the closer he came to me.

He reached out to grab me, but I dodged him. I circled back around and pulled Jaz out of the way, laying her closer to the bottom stair.

"Come, child, don't fear your destiny. It will be in your best interest to come willingly." He reached out an enticing hand to me. I could barely breathe. I felt like I was having a heart attack. I grabbed my chest as pain shot through it from front to back.

Then I fell to my knees.

"Please—don't. Please—leave me—alone." I could barely string the words together coherently. He laughed as I glimpsed at Nan in a heap on the floor behind me.

"Oh child, there is no chance of that now. It is what is written, and so it must be done." He lurched forward with one flap of the immense wings.

An explosive, lava-like heat ripped up my spine, and I was suddenly pulled vertically into the air. I thought the figure had me for a moment, but when I glanced up, his face was a picture of shock. I looked down at my dangling legs in disbelief. My arms were flailing as they sought support that I quickly realised I didn't need. I could see the glimmer of a white light on both sides of myself that lit up the darkened corners of the landing. Impossible heat coursed up my right arm to my face and back down again. Without conscious thought, my arm shot out as Nan's had, and burning, crackling energy exploded from it toward the shocked creature. The right side of my face throbbed painfully as the pulse in my head thundered in my ears. Another nuclear bright crack of light shot from within me a moment later. My own free will was not present as all of this happened to me. All I could do was look across at the creature as he faced off with my rebelling body. This man—or *thing*—in front of me screamed with rage and pain. He backed away, then advanced once more, and my body intuitively reacted in exactly the same way a second time.

He roared and advanced again. This time, he made it close enough to grab at my neck, cutting off my air supply. I gaped and gasped like a fish out of water. Panic overrode my ability to think. My vision blackened around the edges as his immense grasp became hotter and tighter by the second. I was still elevated off of the ground in his massive grip when he spun me around as though to slam me face down onto the cement floor. A quick glimpse my unconscious best friend drew a renewed strength and anger from deep within me. My body burned agonisingly again and shot lightning bolts in every direction. I felt like I might actually combust. The monster dropped me as his hand singed to blackness from the heat of my neck, and for a moment, he receded into the shadows.

I collapsed to the ground, exhausted. The wind still howled, blowing anything loose into a vertical stream. I felt as though I'd been kicked in the gut by a horse. In fact, it was more like I'd been under a whole stampede of them. I was in agony. My hair, glued to my face with sweat, hindered my vision as I crawled over to Nan. She lay still and unconscious. I placed my shaking hands on her smooth face. She was warm, her life force strong. I glanced back at Jaz who was stirring behind me. With horror, I saw him standing above her, hundreds of swirling black puffs of smoke danced around his body.

He smiled a beautiful, deadly smile.

"I, Belial, servant of The Six, am in awe of your power. I underestimated your emerging strength, Earth-born. Enl'iel has protected you well. I will not risk myself against your untrained power on this occasion, but I shall give you incentive to offer yourself to us willingly."

"Pick up the weakling," he spoke to the black swirls, which immediately congealed into an opaque, featureless human form, like a person made of smoke. They descended on Jaz, enveloping her. They swirled and pulsated, until I couldn't see any part of her at all. *Was I screaming out loud, or in my head?* I couldn't tell. The chaos I was witnessing was so surreal that the line between reality and delusion was too blurred to know what I was doing. I half ran, half crawled to her, not thinking of the danger. In a few paces, I was within reaching distance and grabbed through this swirling mass of foul-smelling smoke. My hands just ran through it like water—there was nothing to grasp within its roiling mass. The blackness began to rise back into an erect human-like shape and there, within it, arms flung aside as if in crucifixion, was Jaz. It was truly horrifying. She appeared engulfed and contained within its mass. The wind in the stairwell was blowing harder now, debris flying everywhere. Yet Jaz was still, her eyes closed and her physical form serene. I was forced back onto my knees by the ferocity of the wind and the stinging, airborne glass shards. I struggled hopelessly against the onslaught, unable to help my friend. Then with one last blinding flash, the smoke monstrosity was gone, and all that was left on the painted red floor at the bottom of the stairs was a burn mark, Nan, and me.

I sat in utter stillness for some time. Comprehension and shock merged into an emotion that was indecipherable. I crawled numbly back to Nan and laid my hands upon her heart and forehead. Through stinging tears, I weakly drew from within and around me the elemental power of the Earth's magnetic fields. I willed all that was positive into her, and my hands warmed and glowed as though a light was being shone from behind them. It was nothing like what had just happened to me. That—well, I didn't know what that was. Nan roused, as a thick trickle of dark blood running down her neck rapidly dried up and shimmered into nothingness. She wordlessly took my hand and pressed it against her cheek. She spoke with her eyes. She knew what this was.

As she gathered herself up in silence, I went back over to the blackened patch of ground where Jaz had been. I ran my fingers slowly, disbelievingly, over the charcoal stain on the floor. The rough blackness pricked sharply. I placed my hands flat on the floor, shaking uncontrollably. I could feel what was left of Jaz's energy in the cold concrete. I pressed hard until my knuckles whitened and my hands ached, willing her back. I cried silently, my shoulders heaving with sobs.

"Nan, what's going on?" I asked quietly.

As the words left my quivering lips, more footsteps were coming down the stairs, echoing off of the walls above. I got up and backed away fearfully and protectively towards Nan in the bare light that was left in the stairwell.

"Let's get out of here," I whispered. She grabbed me protectively.

As we turned for the door, it suddenly opened with a loud bang. Kea, the ER nurse, was standing in the doorway, dangling keys in her hand. "Hurry, follow me!"

As she spoke, the footsteps behind us arrived. I glanced back with fear, only to see that it was Ben. He was dishevelled and pale-faced, with dark circles under his eyes, but alive.

I threw myself at him, exhausted. He returned the gesture with a fierceness that shocked me.

"Are you okay?" He held me back and looked me over carefully.

"I don't know!" I sobbed as he drew me back into his familiar embrace.

"Where's my sister?" he asked softly.

I looked over to the scorch mark on the floor, then back at him with eyes lacking any form of explanation.

His grip tightened as he scanned the room.

Before he could speak further, Kea interjected. "Enl'iel, I'm your only safe ticket out of this hell hole today. Come with me, please?"

"I don't know you," said Nan. Curiosity, not fear, laced her voice. "Who are you?"

Kea shook ever so slightly and shimmered. As she came back into focus, she straightened into a tall and regal posture. Smiling sympathetically, her dark hair faded into the purest white locks.

I reeled. Ben stiffened, and Nan breathed a sigh of relief.

Kea had eyes that swirled like supernovas, the colour of blue-specked opals.

Chapter Eight

I don't remember how I got into the car—everything was a blur of pain and confusion. All I remember was that Ben held me tightly to him. His familiarity was the only common sense as I looked up at his face. The moon was high in the sky as it highlighted the silvery scar along his chin. It must have been close to midnight.

Ben's hand hadn't left mine even for a moment. He looked and felt rigid. A sheen of sweat beaded across his face. I hadn't the energy to ask him if he was in pain, I didn't need to anyway. I could feel it oozing from him. All I could do was hug tighter into him. As I nestled my head into his shoulder, that strange lurch in my stomach returned. As though he felt it too, he gently pushed me up. "Nearly home," came his throaty whisper. He seemed suddenly remote, like a stranger as he physically distanced himself. It was so confusing, along with all of the other frightening events I had just endured. I was overwhelmed, to the point of complete physical and mental exhaustion. Although I fought it, my battered body betrayed my will to remain alert. I fell asleep against the window to the quiet murmurs of Nan and Kea in the front, and the sound of Ben breathing softly, ever so controlled, next to me.

I roused as the car eased to a stop. Doors opened and closed. Footsteps followed. Then more murmuring outside, and I could hear a new voice in the mix of the familiar ones.

"I'll carry her up." Ben's deep cadence pulled me further into wakefulness.

The cool night air was eclipsed by the strong arms that slid around me. Warm breath whispered into my ear.

"It's just me, Soph. I've got you, relax."

And I did. I found that I did not have the strength to do to anything but relax. I felt as though I had the flu—I was burning up, my head spun and ached, and I felt sick to my stomach. My nerves were screaming for the likes of morphine to get some relief. It was like nothing I'd ever experienced—I didn't *do* ill. I let myself melt into Ben's comforting warmth. He was so safe and familiar. He carried me carefully, with gentle, measured steps into our house and up to my room.

I could hear the kettle boiling and cups tinkering as he pushed the door open with a shove of his hip. Laying me on my bed, he hesitated ever so briefly, watching me with a pained expression as he pulled a blanket up over me. He opened his mouth as though about to speak, then checked himself and turned to leave.

"Ben, stay. Please?" I beckoned in a tiny voice.

He looked back, this time his eyes anywhere but on mine.

I reached out for his hand. He sat on the very edge of my quilt and gently took it. His hand was shaking. That long silver scar that ran the length of his jaw seemed more prominent as his cheeks burned with an emotion I was unable to decipher.

I needed to talk. "Jaz...I...she...I don't know what happened to her. I saw something, but I can't even bring myself to put it into words. I tried to save her, I was reaching for her, but I just couldn't grab her. There was this weird blackness everywhere, I couldn't see where she was, and then she was just gone!" I was babbling as I sobbed my heart out to him. His hand tightened on mine, he leaned forward, and to my utter surprise, he kissed me ever so softly on my forehead. The gentle touch sent shockwaves through my whole body. He jerked back quickly enough that told me he'd felt something too. His red-rimmed eyes glistened, which he swiftly wiped at with his black sleeve.

"You need to rest, Soph." Those emerald eyes found mine again. "Esme is here, and she'll be checking on you soon."

"What happened out there? Did you see what I saw? I can't be losing it, I can't. You were there, and then you weren't. Jaz was there, and then she was gone. I was—God, I can't even say what I was doing. It's just plain madness."

"You look exhausted. I didn't see anything until I found you at the bottom of the stairs. I'll find Jaz—she probably ran off in fright from the alarms. She nearly died in a house fire as a kid, she was probably just freaked out. She's disappeared before—you know that. She puts on this bravado, but she's just a lost kid on the inside. Whatever you both saw has probably triggered some memories she'd rather forget. I'm not doubting what you said Soph, but you whacked your head pretty hard today. It was dark and chaotic during evacuation. The black smoke—well, apparently there was a small fire at the hospital. You're not mad, Soph. You've just had a really crappy day. Don't worry about Jaz. She'll turn up tomorrow, I'm sure of it."

"But, that doctor—he was so not normal. And Kea, she did that thing with her hair and eyes!" I was too exhausted to argue with him, and also slightly offended that he'd politely accused me of imagining what I'd seen. Then again, if I were him, I would probably not believe me either. "Ugh, you're probably right." I threw up my hands, resigned to my sudden madness. I gave in to what was sensible as I rubbed my eyes. "Thanks for looking after me. Let me know when you hear from her, okay? I'm so worried."

"No problem, you know I always look out for you guys. You're my only family. Rest up. I'll come check on you tomorrow." With that he got up and left, leaving the lingering scent of sweet ashes and spice, like the smouldering embers of incense.

I gathered up my quilt and pulled it tightly as I rolled to my side to have a self-indulgent sob.

I'm lying in my bed, like any other night. The sound of cicadas murmur and click outside the window. Streams of moonlight beam in through the slits in the shutters, casting highlights across me. I feel as though I'm going to get up, but when I try, not a muscle will move. Only my eyes can open and close. The cicadas are suddenly silent. Everything is silent. No sounds of anyone awake downstairs or rustling of wind through the trees. I see a shadow glide past my window, breaking the pattern of moonbeams on the bed. At this, heat rises inside me. My heart thunders at full pelt behind my ribcage, but my arms and legs are leaden.

The door that leads to my balcony creaks slowly open, even though it is always locked. I watch it helplessly from my paralysed state. A shadow enters, moving unnaturally. Not walking, not gliding, but jittering back and forth, as though stuck between this world and another. If there is a higher level of fear than abject horror, I am now in that place. I don't want to look, but like a car wreck, I can't take my eyes from the sight. It stutters its way silently towards me, a recognisable figure emerging from the blackness. A female vision in an ethereal, flowing black gown. Head cast down, it hovers at the end of my bed. Silent. Menacing. There is a sense of sadness emanating from it. I can feel lonely energy, fear, and regret. She is somehow communicating with me through emotion. Then she raises her head. I scream, but not out loud, as every part of me other than my eyes is utterly frozen.

Jasmine stares at me. Her short black hair is in a perfect state, but her heavily made up black eyes looked at me with such sorrow, I hardly recognize her. She is weeping. Blackened tears run down her face and over her ruby lips, pooling onto the floor. Drip, drip, drip. She leans her head from side to side while she looks down upon me, as though she is contemplating something. I will her to hear my thoughts, to understand that I will find her. I would do anything to find her.

In a voice that is not hers, a faint yet deep scratchy whisper, she says, "I am lost."

I squeeze my eyes shut for a second, and when I open them, her face is inches from mine. Her eyes bore into mine, black as night. A growl emanates from deep within her. She screams a single word, right into me.

"Awaken!"

Chapter Nine

The immense heat of volcanic energy emanating from the depths below the plain made the mountains in the distance shimmer like a mirage.

Great expanses of red and black were crumbling with desolation. An ochre, cloudless sky blazed overhead, undisturbed but for the ashen gases spewing from the mountainous peaks engulfing the horizon in the distance. Pungent, sulphuric odours permeated every corner, every rock, and grain of sand. Long dead tree carcasses stood as silent sentries lining the length of an avenue leading to a massive platform of pumice. Upon this altar, an incongruity to what was natural to any known world, stood The Six.

Six tall figures, powerfully built, stood proud and brooding. They were bare chested males, each gripping a weapon in his left hand. One, a blackened sword, as long as he was tall. The second, a trident spear that glowed red like molten metal. The third, an orb of pulsating light, balanced upon his palm. The fourth a cross bow that held six bolts of static, lightning arrows. The fifth, an axe head made of the clearest crystal, and the sixth, nothing at all. His weapon was hidden and decidedly more destructive—the power of manipulation.

With an unnatural stillness around them, silence reigned as they contemplated the situation that had driven their every move, every thought, and decision for millennia. An endless battle, created by their own actions, plagued their sanity.

"It is becoming increasingly evident that finally, we have found the Earth-born," said the sharpened tongue of the first.

"We must strike now, while she is in our sight," added another.

"She is well protected. Her power is unbalanced, and lacking control. She nearly killed Belial without knowing what she was doing. I say we wait until she awakens. We should draw her out, see her power for ourselves, then find a weakness. We already have the leverage we need. There is no need to rush in like fools," added a third.

"Why the concern, my brother? Belial is but a servant, a pawn in our war. He barely deserved the title of Watcher even in the beginning. His loss for her gain would have been well worth it. You have a weakness in you, brother. Worry not for others when it concerns our mission," the first retorted sharply.

"This is the best time to strike. She cannot overcome us, she has no control of her power. I say we take her and force her awakening. Then she will become ours, available to use at our leisure. If we bring her here, no one else can stop us." Frustration dripped from this new voice.

"I am tiring of this. My time has been long away from home. We have wasted too much energy foolishly chasing false leads. Are we sure she is the One? Do we really understand how to harness her power?" The words rumbled from the deepest and most aged of voices. A mumbling of acknowledgment to these questions resounded with the nodding of five horned heads.

The third voice spoke again. "She shows all the signs and has been protected since birth by the most powerful of Watchers and Eudaimonia. There are unprecedented energy signatures spiking around the world. My spy informs me regularly that there are increased gatherings in the sacred places, and all discussing her. We have never seen such activity. But I know we are missing something. We have one part of the solution, which is her in the flesh, but I am certain there is something else that we are missing. In all of these years, we have always been a step behind, blinded by our own rage. This is the time to think clearly and shield our wisdom from our vengeance so as to bring this war to an end. There is more to this prophecy than we first thought. We must wait and watch. We have misinterpreted something, I'm certain of it now. We should not draw her out before the entirety of the advantage is on our side." Before he continued, he glanced to his left at the figure suspended in a sphere of swirling black mist. A girl, young and serene, who—in this world or that—was now a player in a game far beyond her comprehension.

"Brothers, you are wrong about Belial, he was wise to protect himself. He is an immensely powerful ally. He is entrenched with the closest of ties to her protectors. This keeps us within an arm's reach. He is invaluable to us." He bowed reverently to the others as he said this.

The first contemplated this for a time. He turned to survey the Hell he called home with an unabashed disgust. It made even Tartarus look luxurious. He inhaled deeply, his expansive chest widening as taut, powerful musculature strained under smooth, golden skin. He turned back, ashen hair billowed out down his back. His face was chiselled with Angelic exquisiteness.

Beauty had never been so skin deep as with he.

"As you have gained so much insight with your many years of reconnaissance, and an equal amount of opinion, it is to you that I charge the task of unravelling that which we do not know. Immerse yourself to the fullest in that wretched place, and find the answers that elude us. Take the Rogues, send them far and wide. Use whatever resources you can find. I will have no more mistakes. My patience has been wrung through. I am sick to the core of my dealings with this forsaken human world. It once amused me to meddle in their evolution, but now they just cause me to wretch. The mere thought of another day spent looking down at them wearies me. What a waste they were. A'vean has done so much better on the other worlds and none of those has brought such reckoning upon us for our dalliances. Why these humans hold such standing will for eternity be a mystery to me. The Throne is entrenched with fools!" He struck his trident hard into the soil, causing a rumble deep within. Screams reverberated from somewhere far off.

With that, the first, his voice echoing off the mountainous ranges, raised his arms to the sky and called, "Belial, come forth!"

Rumbling thunder like that of a storm on the horizon filled the air. The sky darkened dramatically over the heads of The Six. Wind raged around them as they stood, unmoving. A distortion in the air about them developed into a spinning vortex. Red and white swirls of electrically charged energy clashed against each other. Static buzzed in the air. An opening in the sky emerged, revealing the blackness of space on the other side.

"My Masters, I am your humble servant." Belial appeared, stepping casually but reverently through the fresh opening between time and space. Ferocity dripped from him like beads of sweat.

"Get rid of that!" The first pointed a finger at the girl. "You know what to do with it."

Belial glanced at the foul mouthed girl, who he had only just transferred here, a tactical move he hoped would be pleasing to his Masters.

"Yes, Master, as you wish." As he moved to go, he thrust his glowing white trident into the dusty earth beneath him. A crack appeared just wide enough for him to squeeze his hand into. He reached down and fished around, immersed up to his elbow. Screams emerged, growing louder as he slowly withdrew his arm. In his grasp was a writhing mass of black smoke, flashes of light popping out from within it. Stretching in and out of the undulating form, tortured faces appeared and disappeared. They were pushed out and sucked back into the smoke haze, like a snapping rubber band. Gruesome mouths gaped wide, a look of horror in their eyes. Agonised screams resonated from within the billowing blackness.

"You will all do nicely." Belial responded to pleas of mercy. He pulled a piece of smoke out of the mass and threw it towards the girl. "You know what to do, if you know what's good for you," he laughed to himself.

He turned to the Six, bowed deeply, only grimacing with malice towards them all when he was low enough in submission that they could not see his face. He stood back up proudly before them, reaching a hand toward the levitating girl and beckoned, "Come."

The swirling smoke surrounding the girl sparked with life. It moved, dragging her with it, and followed Belial back through the portal.

Chapter Ten

As I awoke, I realised the gut-wrenching screams were coming from me as the horrendous images of my nightmare dissipated all too slowly. I shimmied up to the head of my bed, pulling my knees up tight and hugging them in self-comfort.

My bedroom door opened with such suddenness, I imagined that they had been camping outside my door. Nan and Esme entered wearing equally concerned expressions. Esme sat on the bed close to me, while Nan was wringing a fresh washcloth into the basin beside my bed before patting it across my head.

"Child, Esme's here. You're safe now. What troubles your sleep, my sweet?"

Esme was one of the most beautiful souls I've ever met, and someone I'd known my entire life. She was descended from the Wurundjeri people. She'd called me her spirit child for as long as I could remember.

Her beautifully soft, ebony hand caressed my face. "Baby girl, you tell Esme what ya seen. I see fear in them eyes," her voice was smooth and sweet. "Oh Lord, you're burning up, sweet pea. Nan, go boil the kettle, she needs some 'o my special tea. And my bag, would ya please bring it up? I've got some lovely things for soothin' in my bag o' tricks. I musta known strange things were gonna be going on here tonight." She mused to herself with a smile that was fraught with something other than hilarity.

"Of course, Esme. I'll be back shortly, Sophia." Nan kissed me lightly on my hair. Her necklace fell forward, and the large white gem she always wore grazed my cheek. It vibrated softly on my skin. For the briefest moment, my headache eased, but just until she stood back up. *What was that about?* Nan let me play with this gem as a child when I was frightened or unwell, to distract myself from my worries. I'd always cherished it. But I'd never known it to do that. I thought I was truly going mad.

Esme leaned over me. "Esme will have you feelin' better real soon, honey pot. You tell me what's got those eyes like saucers when you're good and ready. But first, let's get you up and out of that God-awful hospital rag and into somethin' nice. What ya think about that, eh?"

"Ok," was all I could manage.

"A shower is a fine start, I think. I'll get one running for ya. When you're done, you'll have some nice Kakadu plum tea. Then I'll tuck ya up, snug as a bug."

"Esme, I think I'd like to sleep downstairs for the rest of the night."

"No girl, you'll stay right here with me. I'll sit by you all night. I'll keep those restless spirits away," she soothed as she smoothed my hair back.

"How do you know that's what's upset me?" I asked.

"Sophia, I told you many a time that I've a deep connection with my land. These ranges is where the spirits roam. I feel 'em, and I 'specially feel that one's been here tonight, but it's a strange one. Somethin' not right about it. Not one bit." Her head was slowly shaking, whilst she mulled over this thought with an expression of deep concern.

"Yes, something is so very not right about today. Tonight. Everything!" I added, exasperated.

Nan arrived back from the kitchen with a brewing teapot on a tray and a weathered brown bag slung across her shoulder. "Do as Esme says, dear. Take her remedies, get some rest, and we will have a long overdue discussion in the morning."

Nan sat by me for a moment and rested her hands across mine. I could feel an infusion of her energy. It was warm and tingling, so familiar. It gave me just enough fuel to heave my aching mass out of bed. Nan swiftly left the room again before I could say anything more.

As I stood up, I caught sight of a photo of Jaz and me when we were sixteen. Me, all girly in pink, and Jaz, already in the Goth phase, with her newly tattooed right arm pulled tightly around my neck. She was planting a kiss on my cheek. You couldn't see her face in the picture, though—it was obstructed by her mane of dyed blue and black hair. I picked up the homemade mosaic frame and rubbed my fingers across it. A tear slipped down my face and dropped onto the glass, blurring the picture.

"*What happened to you?*" I whispered to myself.

By the time I pulled myself together enough to walk to the en suite, Esme was busy humming an enchanting indigenous lullaby to herself while she tested the water temperature for me.

"I miss hearing that song. It brings back nice memories," my words caught each time I tried to speak. "It's still comforting."

"O' course it is—that's Esme's purpose, sweet pea—to soothe all of my children. There now, you hop on in. I'll wait outside the door, just right here if you need me."

Esme closed the door behind her, and I stepped into the shower. The sting of the water woke me right up, though I'd have rather remained asleep, locked in that nightmare. At least that way I wouldn't have to face what had happened to me. *To Jasmine.* However, the heat and moisture eventually soothed my aching frame. I used an abundance of soap, trying desperately to wash away the day. It stung all the way down my back. My poor back, by God, it felt like it was trying to explode. I concluded that I'd bruised my spine during my myriad of falls in that one twenty-four-hour period. *Or, let's be honest, whatever the hell happened in that stairwell.* The floating thing, that lightning shooting out of me—that couldn't be good on the body. Just thinking about those events made me feel like a complete nutter on the verge of insanity.

Perhaps I was still dreaming? Could I be that lucky?

I reluctantly stepped out. As I towel-dried my hair, I stared into the mirror. It hadn't steamed up too much, so I could see myself clearly enough. The reflection was—*surprise, surprise*—alarming. I barely recognised myself. My hair had faded. The rainbow of colours were a pastel palette, the boldness of the colours just a memory. Sunburn-like red glowed angrily along the inside of my right arm. I hesitantly touched it—it was insanely sensitive. Most shocking though was the birthmark on my face. The mocha swirls were now maroon welts, raised and ugly. They too were terribly painful to touch. It was like my life had become a horror movie, with me as the star. My lips trembled as tears welled. Before I could indulge in a fresh cry, my entire back began to itch. *What now?* It felt like ants were crawling under my skin. I grabbed frantically for my back scrubber, reached it round, and gave my back a good hard scratch. *Wrong move.* It hurt like hell. Pouring vinegar on an open wound would have been more pleasurable. I had to lie down. This was all too much. I took out my contacts, and with blurred vision, tiptoed over the cool floor and back into my room, wrapped only in my towel.

"Don't look at me, Esme, I'm a freak show!"

"Oh sweet pea, there ain't nothin' could happen to ya that would ever worry 'ol Esme."

She was waiting for me with a clean set of pyjamas and didn't flinch at the sight of me. It was as though I'd always looked like this to her. She smiled warmly as I shimmied into the bottoms. I turned my back on her to discreetly put the top on. It was then that I heard a sharp intake of breath.

"What is it?" I asked, immediately fearful.

"You feelin' a little itch on ya back there, honey?" she asked.

"Oh, yes! It started in the shower. I tried to scratch it, but it hurt like hell! I'm red and sore all over. Can you see a rash there, or some bruising? Anything?"

"Don't you be scratchin' that itch. Esme will get you something for it, just a touch o' this and that."

"What is it, Esme? What can you see? You're freaking me out!"

"Don't ya worry now Sweet Pea, just relax while I get a couple extra things from downstairs. I need some fresh boiled water, petal. I've got a little sage and lavender burning for you by the door and window. It'll keep them spirits away. Your big 'ol fluff ball is sleepin' outside your door, too. He's stinkin' up to high heaven. That smell would keep the devil 'imself away!" Esme laughed heartily. "You best be givin' him a bath tomorra'. *Pee-ew!*" She waved her hand in front of her nose as though swatting Shadow's stench away. "I'll be right back to see to that back 'o yours, and then we'll settle you in for the night, all nice and cosy, eh?"

Although I was terrified to be left alone, I also didn't want to seem childish, so I simply nodded and she bustled quickly out of my room.

For the first time in my life, I felt like I was seriously ill. I actually needed healing myself for a change. I was about to snuggle back into bed when I heard Nan and Esme in what sounded like not so much a disagreement, but certainly a fervent discussion of differing opinions.

I couldn't help myself. If they knew something I didn't—which I was fairly positive was the affirmative at this stage—I was going to find out.

I tiptoed over to my door, stepping lightly so that the floorboards didn't give my movements away.

I kneeled and placed my ear gently to the wood. I listened.

"I really insist we wait until morning. I need time to prepare, and I would like Brennan's support." Nan's tone was firm and unyielding.

"Enl'iel, she's entering the Change, and I see it's a Quickening. I seen it on 'er back just now. She's gonna need to know before too long. I can soothe 'er somewhat, but that girl's gonna get some big fright if she awakens suddenly and don't know what's goin' on! Poor child."

That word again. *Awaken.* What the hell does that mean? I am awake!

"It's all too early. She hasn't reached her comin' of age, and her body ain't ready yet! It hasn't had the right kind 'o preparation," Esme added, sounding distraught.

"Yes, you are correct of course, Esme. It *is* too early, but I have my suspicions as to why. I too believe she is experiencing a Quickening, and I believe Cael has sparked this. She is the one we have been waiting for, Esme. We have known this for twenty years. Unfortunately, she has grown up very human, and it will take care and training in the right way by the correct individuals to prepare her properly."

"Yes, yes, I see ya point. My heart cries for what that poor girl might go through. She's like my own birthed baby, Enl'iel. I'm frightened for her."

"I never would have been able to protect her so well without you, my dear friend. I know you love her every bit as much as her own mother, myself included. You and I are on the same side, but there are encroaching forces that are working ever more fervently in opposition. Please, tend to her wounds and let me make the appropriate arrangements? I need to work out what to do with Ben and Jasmine as well. They were never meant to be a part of this. Stay nearby my Sophia, Esme. We must dull this Quickening as best we can until she is in a safe place to awaken. Here is most definitely not safe."

"All right then, I must trust ya judgement. I just don't wanna lie to my baby."

With that, I heard Esme's heavy footsteps plodding back up the stairs.

I nearly fell over myself trying to run back to my bed quickly, tripping over my floor rug as I went. I'd barely made it into bed with the covers up when there was a knock at my door.

"Sweet pea, it's just Esme. You ready for me to come on in and tend to that troublesome back?" she asked sweetly.

"Yes, come in," I answered, trying to mask my breathless voice. I lay in such a way as to give the impression that I'd already dozed.

I was feeling frightened, angry, and betrayed all at once. *Is there a name for that emotion? What did they mean I'd grown up 'human?' Who was Enl'iel? What was that talk about Ben and Jaz?* Being frustratingly non-confrontational in nature, I just bit my lip before I blurted out something I'd regret. I needed Esme to be in and out as quickly as I could push her, so I could attempt to process what I'd just heard. I needed to make some sense out of this strange, evolving madness.

Softly closing the door behind her, she entered carrying a tray covered with fresh eucalypt leaves, some white cloths, and a steaming pot of water.

"Here now, my sweet baby, a nice cup o' plum tea for your aches." She poured this from the pot that had been brewing by the bed. "Drink up." I wordlessly took a cup from her as she dropped her bag onto my bed. The tea was hot, sweet and fruity. It was delicious as it burned its way down my throat. Esme was a well-known natural healer around the Ranges. She imported indigenous ingredients from all around the country and conjured up her own well-loved natural teas, lotions, aromas, and compresses. I watched her silently as she readied whatever was coming my way. She hummed to herself, and I detected an undertone of nervousness in the melody.

"Esme?"

"Yes, dear?"

"What are you making there?"

"Oh just a bit 'o this an' that. A nice eucalypt compress to calm that fever, and a soothing tea tree lotion for your back, dear," she answered as she pounded away at a mortar bowl, not meeting my eyes.

"What's wrong with my back? Is it bad?" I inquired, carefully watching her every move.

"Oh no, honey, no! Just a bit of a rash. I expect it's from all ya stressin'. You're always lookin' after everyone but your own self."

I was busting to see my back. I needed to know what she'd seen, but I needed to do so without raising her suspicion.

"I've just got to go to the bathroom while you're finishing that, okay?"

"Yes, dear," she replied, seemingly lost in her own thoughts.

I did one of those walk-run things that you do when you're trying not to appear to be in a rush. I closed the bathroom door and nearly hit the roof as I was met with a pair of glowing green eyes.

I flipped on the light, and for a change, it was something normal, rather than another heart-stopping apparition. Our cat, Pumpkin, sat perched on my vanity, undoubtedly he'd been licking drips from the tap. Pumpkin was fluffy, orange, and overfed, hence the name.

"Hey puss, I've had enough scares today." I picked him up, giving him a brief snuggle before putting him down on the floor to purr away with satisfaction.

I ruffled at the toilet paper roll to convince Esme that I was doing what she expected as I grabbed a hand mirror from the second drawer. I took off my top, and my skin instantly pricked up with a chill, despite my feverish state. I manoeuvred around so that my back faced the large vanity mirror and I could dangle the handheld one in a way that helped me get a good view of the damage.

After a bit of adjusting, I caught sight of my back. I drew in a none too silent breath of surprise and dropped the mirror onto the floor, where it immediately cracked.

"You okay in there, Sophia?" called Esme.

"Ah, yeah, I'm fine. I just knocked something over. All good," I lied.

I bent down and picked up the mirror with a quivering hand.

I took a slow, deep breath in and repositioned myself again.

In the cracked reflection of my hand mirror I gazed hypnotically at the vision within it.

Down either side of my spine was a ruby redness, beginning from halfway down my back and spreading out in an organised, fernlike pattern up either side of my backbone. It reached outwards, curling around and enveloping the edges of my shoulder blades. It was uniform and symmetrical, as though etched by an artist. The tattoo of inflamed foliage-like skin was punctuated with small nibs of what looked like spinal bone beneath the skin. It was like looking at something or someone else, not me.

I must have stood there too long, mesmerised by the sight, because the door suddenly opened, and there was Esme.

"Oh, sweet pea," was all she could say, her voice dripping with sadness. She pulled me out of there with a swift gentleness.

"Nan, you better come on up here!" she called out calmly.

I was awake, but felt like I was moving in a dreamlike state. *How much can a body take in one day? How much can my sanity take?* I had questions— so many questions—but they just could not form upon my lips. I wasn't sure I knew how to compose the right words to ask for answers to things I didn't comprehend at all.

Next thing I knew I was in bed, face down, and feeling a distinct wetness on my back. I tried to get up, but a gentle hand pushed me down with a comforting, *"Shhhh."*

"Just lay while I finish the compress to ya back. It's burnin' up and needs settlin' down," Esme soothed. "Be still. I know there's a lot goin' on in that pretty head o' yours right now, but it's near on five o'clock in the mornin' and ya need to rest."

In a drunken kind of voice I slurred, "W-where's Naaan?"

"I'm here, dear," replied a hollow voice to my left. I turned to look at her. An expression of sorrow was on her face, the likes of which you only see when there's been a death. *Was it Jaz? Was it my own?*

"I don't want to know, Nan. I just don't want to know."

"I know, sweet girl, I know. We will talk after you have rested. The time has arrived to tell you the truth about your family. It has, however, come sooner than I anticipated. You have a future that you could not possibly imagine, Sophia."

I didn't want a new future. I just wanted to go back to yesterday, back to when everything made sense. Back when I had a crazy best friend trying to pimp me out to potential boyfriends, and a career that brought me such happiness. Back to hanging with Ben, helping him put his bikes back together. I wanted to un-see the things I had seen and un-feel the rebellion going on inside my body. I wanted sleep now, to forget it all. I looked past Nan, out into the darkness of my window. I stared into the nothingness of it and willed it all away as I drifted off to the sensation of Esme rubbing my back. In the furthest reaches of consciousness, where you know you can't turn back from sleep, I heard Pumpkin hiss and Shadow growl.

Chapter Eleven

The large, shadowed figure hung in the predawn air, looking down upon the three women in the room below. He'd been there every night for twenty years, observing his charge. The two older ones he could just wrench to pieces right now. The other one though, he would just bide his time as he done for so long already. Her death was coming—it was imminent. Unstoppable. Necessary. She was merely a player in a larger game, yet she was the queen, the most powerful piece on the board and she did not even know it. What happened today or tomorrow mattered not.

The two older figures hovered annoyingly in his line of sight. They fussed over her endlessly. She was never alone long enough for him to get as close as he wanted to. Out here, he was less detectable. That Enl'iel was painfully strong for a half-breed, and cloaking himself from her had become a true art form, though it drained his energy greatly. And that witch-woman burning her God-awful smells made him wretch. He might dispatch with her sooner rather than later.

"Why were you at the hospital, Belial? Did Yeqon send you?"

"Yes, he grows impatient," answered the other male voice from behind the overhanging jasmine bush. "The Rogues are sloppy when left to themselves, making mistakes the humans will pick up on. One of them infected a live human. They will have us exposed before too long. Brainless filth. He sent me in to right the mess. It was a coincidence she was there at the same time.

Almost poetic, don't you think, brother?"

"The time is not right. I told them that."

"Indeed. She is too human, yet her power great. She is dangerous."

"Perhaps we should bring her in, Belial? We could observe her until her awakening. She couldn't hurt anyone in the pits. I question whether she would be any use at present though."

"That is what Master Yeqon wants. He was displeased I did not return with her. I have been given orders."

"I understand. Carry them through as you must. I have a plan of my own."

"As you wish, Nik'ael."

"Did you return the human girl?"

"Yes."

"Good."

"You enjoyed roughing up that boy in the hospital today. No? Miss the old days of war and torture?"

Belial simply laughed in response.

"Get out of here!"

Belial obliged by blinking away instantly.

Nik'ael dared to venture a little closer to the upstairs window. As she rested serenely upon the bed, half naked and face down, he watched. A muscle flinched across the bare expanse of his chest. He would follow his own plan. He sighed in frustration as the old hag covered her back with lotions and healing leaves. The young woman's beautiful form was slowly hidden from his sight. He was mesmerised by her. She had grown into such a beauty inside and out. He'd become impossibly enchanted by her. Nik'ael fiddled with the wooden bracelet around his wrist as he wrestled with these unwelcome thoughts. Strong fingers pinched forcefully at the little brown beads. It was tempting to let her live a little longer, to savour her. But that was not his call. He was just one—the whole made all of the decisions together; well most of them.

She must be entering the Change. He could see the redness glowing from under her skin—her energy tracts were emerging. From what Belial had reported, her powers were beginning to pulse, so her body must be in complete agony. He remembered that feeling all too well. A hint of sympathy tugged at his heart for the briefest of moments.

Nik'ael watched and listened to them console her. She had no idea what she was. They thought she was being protected by keeping her in the dark, but it actually made her exquisitely more vulnerable. It would take her too long to harness her power, as her humanness had left her body and mind weakened. She did not and would not know her own strength before he took her. This made his mission seem all the easier to complete, and time now seemed less of the essence.

She turned her head to face the window, and he instinctively drew back to guard himself from being seen. Her eyes gazed out as though she were looking directly at him, into him. Without realising it, he had moved forward again to look deeper into those eyes. She would not see well without her human-made enhancements, not yet. But soon—soon, she would see into the furthest depths of the universe with those beautiful eyes. He imagined that they were actually looking into his own. The Mark of A'vean burned deeply on his face. His hands were clenched knuckle-white by his sides. The desire to reach out and touch her crept up on him again, to run his hand along the smooth curve of her body. Her soft skin, warm under his touch. His fists trembled. He held his breath as his dark heart quickened, rebelling against him. He shook his head to clear his thoughts and glided backward again, accidently brushing against a tree branch, rustling its dewy leaves.

A growl from below and a hiss from the sudden appearance of a cat's face in the windowpane surprised him. He was getting sloppy. Thousands of years of no results and chasing false hope across the earth could do that. It could make you just a shell of what you once were and leave you a mere ghost of your old self. Desperation was something he never used to feel, but it was an affliction that the passing eons had now brought out in him exponentially.

Nik'ael was tired.

He moved off to leave, taking one last look over his shoulder at her. He touched his right hand to his head, and vanished in a flash of light.

Chapter Twelve

I opened my eyes and, for a beautiful moment, forgot what had happened yesterday. Then all too quickly it crashed back down on me like a tidal wave pounding at the shores of my memory. Poor Cael and Jasmine. *What the hell was going on?* My heart thundered in an immediate panic.

Every square centimetre of skin reminded me of the whole mess when I rolled over onto my back and reacquainted myself with that dreadful, searing pain in my spine. I sat up on the bedside with my head in my hands as it too, pulsed mercilessly up the side of my face. I looked around the room. Thoughts of escape washed through me as I felt something wet on my feet.

Shadow was already dutifully kissing my toes. "Hey boy." I gave him an unenthusiastic scratch behind the ear, which was still met with a thumping hind leg and a groan of pleasure. Dried eucalyptus leaves and towels lay neatly folded on my side table, a tangible reminder of last night's events.

I seemed to be alone. I stood up gingerly and made my way back to the bathroom. Groggily, I threw some cool water over my face and put my contacts back in. Reaching down slowly like an old lady, thanks to the nerve war in my spine, I picked up a glass shard from my broken hand mirror off the floor. I didn't recognise the face staring back at me. I turned and took a quick glance at my back in the vanity mirror. Yep, the ugliness was still there. *Not a dream, God damn it.* My heart thundered harder. That red design of capillaries was there in the centre, even brighter and thicker, if anything. It looked raised now, like hives from an allergic reaction. At least the itching had subsided.

I leaned heavily on the wash basin and examined my reflection. I considered running right there and then. I looked deeply into the eyes staring back at me. They were fearful and brimming with tears. Despite myself, my lips trembled and I let my head hang loosely. Finally, I released a sob. *What was going on with me?* I watched the blurry tears slip slowly down the porcelain basin, towards the drain. They glistened like liquid diamonds as they trailed away. For a moment I gave into the fear. I ran in a panic back into my room, taking a quick look out the window. Could I trust Nan? I didn't know in this moment of irrationality. I just had to get out of there. No one was out the back. I unlocked the square pane of glass, ready to jump out that way. The damn balcony door would creak too loudly if I used that.

I squeezed under the bed to grab any old bag I could find. Shadow thought it was play time and yanked at it. "No Shadow, not now! Let go!" He backed off but stayed annoyingly in between my feet as I threw open the wardrobe and crammed an assortment of clothes into the bag. As I headed to the window, arms and legs like jelly, I caught sight of the picture of Jaz and me, still smeared with last night's tears. Shadow followed and pulled at my bag again. "Stop it!" But he pulled it clean out of my hands with a loud rip as the contents went flying everywhere. "Look what you've done! Bad dog!" I growled at him as I knelt down to pick up everything. I stopped just as quick. I sat there on the cool floorboards staring at the small peels of paint curling off the wall. *What was the point? Where was I going to go?* I grabbed the picture of Jaz. It was so simple then, two friends just messing about, having fun. It suddenly dawned on me that I was helpless and vulnerable. Just like Jaz, just like Ben. I wasn't so sure about the rest of them. If I ran, who knew what was out there waiting for me? Where was I going to go anyway? Did I run in ignorance and leave everyone behind? No! That wasn't me. I wasn't so much a fighter as I was loyal. I couldn't just tail-it out of there like a coward and leave those that I loved, no matter what hand they may have had in all of this deceit about whatever was going on in my life. "Ugh! Damn it!"

I balled my fists in frustration, slammed the floor and tossed the remnants of the bag back under the bed.

"You win Shadow," I gave him another scratch behind the ears as his tail wagged furiously. I puffed out a couple of quick breaths to compose myself.

"All right, Soph. If it doesn't kill you, it makes you stronger." I worried about the potential killing part. I wiped my eyes clear. The clock ticked over to 11:45am as I threw my pyjamas onto the bed. *Death!* The thought had me recounting what I'd witnessed at work. Had the place burnt down in the insanity that had occurred? Had anyone else been injured? Was that creature going to come back? I decided in that moment that running was definitely not the right choice. I had to know what was going on, to protect myself at the minimum. I needed to find out if Cael was okay, and even though I didn't know where to begin, I was determined to find Jaz. Besides Ben and I, there wasn't a soul on Earth that would notice her absence. She needed us. I hadn't even told Nan what happened to her. She knew Jaz was missing, but she was out cold when that thing abducted my best friend. How I was going to ask about a smoke monster-abductor was something I'd have to think long and hard about. I wasn't even sure I could discuss it with Ben after what he said last night. I felt vastly alone.

My room was toasting up from the warm midday sun. The day shining through the open window was beautiful, perfect almost, mocking my inner Hell. I rummaged through my cupboard again and found a light, floral sundress to throw on. Without bothering about my hair, I took a slow, calming deep breath and left the room, not in any way ready for whatever was about to come. At the bottom of the stairs, I forgot about step number three, and it creaked predictably. The noise had Nan out of the kitchen in a flash.

"Good morning, dear," she spoke softly. "Would you like breakfast?" She smiled sweetly, but I could see her wringing her hands nervously through her apron.

"Just some tea please." I was short with her and she noticed it. I was actually ravenous, but I didn't feel like hanging around her for too long. I'd eat later. There was too much clouding my mind for idle chatter over pancakes.

I followed her into our small kitchen and sat at the table for two. The silence was awkward as she brewed the tea. Normally, we would be gossiping like parrots, but today the silence flowed like molasses, slow and painful.

"Where is everyone?" I asked. "From last night, I mean."

She paused a moment, then said, "Esme went home, and Ben is back at his place, with Kea keeping him company. He has had quite a night. They both want to be there when Jaz finds her way home."

"I'm not so sure she will." My voice trailed off as I tried to blink the smoke monster away. Then I decided to just dive right in. "I didn't know you knew any of the staff at the hospital. How do you know Kea? You seemed to recognise her when she did that changing…thing. Actually no—don't answer that. I can't handle any more surprises right now." I looked away to avoid her expression. I'd asked questions that I didn't quite know I wanted answers to.

Nan maintained the uncomfortable silence before she put a steaming teacup in front of me. She felt my forehead simultaneously.

"You are still burning up. How does your back feel?" she asked, almost sheepishly. Her tone annoyed me.

"How do I feel?" I snapped. "I feel as though my life has just taken a tumble into Crazyville, and my body is rebelling by trying to both combust and rip itself apart simultaneously. That's how I feel! And to top it off, my best friend has seemingly disappeared into oblivion, abducted by some possessed cloud-thing and a goat man!" I yelled at her, I think, for the first time ever. She tried to speak, but I held up my hand to stop her. I stood up from the table, spilling my tea everywhere in the process. I inwardly cringed at the echoes of teenage frustration in my voice. "Whatever it is, I don't want to hear it, not now. I can feel it's something that I will never be able to un-hear, so please just give me today, just today to pretend I have a normal life." Tears welled again in the corners of my eyes, but I sniffed them back. I felt a sudden unfamiliar anger surging. I needed to get away.

"One day, Nan. Just one day, and then I'll listen to you." My voice ached to scream again, but I pulled my anger back to a controlled, cool simmer.

I walked out of the kitchen without looking back, fairly sure her face was the picture of disbelief. I slammed out of the back door to the veranda, grabbing a dried corncob from the half-barrel by the back steps and a peppermint from the sweet jar I always left there. I marched barefoot towards the back of our property. I followed the lavender-hedged path, running a hand over the tops of the purple buds, upsetting the bees dining on them. They buzzed with annoyance, but settled back down as I moved along. The crunching of dried gum leaves mixed with the velvety grass felt divine under my feet. It occurred to me that my feet were the only pain-free body parts I had, so I stomped harder than necessary down the stone steps towards the back paddock, like a toddler having a tantrum. But man, it felt damn good.

We lived on ten acres of bushland, which provided me with a childhood alien to many twenty-first century kids. I lived and breathed the outdoors. Too much time inside, away from the sights, sounds, and smells of nature, drove me stir-crazy. Already, the serenity of my surrounds had my nerves calming slightly.

I stomped angrily past the shed, a run-down old wooden cube. It sat proudly upon the edge of a large pond brimming with huge goldfish. Another year of neglect and it may well join them on the silty bottom. The building leaned like an aging monolith. The two windows at the front were whited out with grime, and the peeling green door rotting at the base left it a sorry sight. It was a creepy kingdom for the only creatures that I really struggled to love— *spiders*. I tried, but no, I could not shake that goose bump inducing, get-the-hell-outta-there feeling I got when I saw one of those hairy puppies crawl by. And that shed was huntsman central. I never ever went inside it. Ever. A wide berth was always necessary, just in case one was out sunning itself.

About fifty meters further down, I saw him, and my anger instantly melted away.

"Hey boy!" A magnificent grey head with a show-stopping flowing mane swung up to the sound of my voice. He trotted over with a friendly whinny, knowing that a treat was surely coming. "Good morning, Grey."

Grey was beautiful. Seventeen hands of gentle storm-coloured equine. He enthusiastically crunched on his corncob as I stroked his neck lovingly. When he'd finished his treat, I asked him, "May I?"

He gave me a warm snort and shuffled his hooves a little, indicating he was ready for a run. I grabbed his mane and swiftly flung myself up onto his bare back with a long practised ease. The familiar warmth of his body beneath me was comforting beyond description. I leaned forward, rubbing his neck and whispered to him, *"Off you go, handsome."*

Riding Grey was like an extension of myself. I did nothing, just moved along with him. If he walked or galloped, it was up to him. Today he took off through the wooded acres as though he felt a need to run off the nervous energy that was coursing through me. I held fistfuls of his soft mane tightly as warm air rushed over my face and through my hair. His energy thrummed underneath me while his powerful muscles sped us all over the beautiful landscape.

Under towering Mountain Ash goliaths, the sun filtered through the canopy, casting momentary bursts of heat across me. The pounding of Grey's hooves was melodic and calming. For a moment, time stood still. The chirping of the birds slowed, the sounds all around me dulled as I let go for just a moment. I let my head fall back and lifted my face to the sky as I slipped briefly out of reality. His pace felt like slow motion as I experienced what I knew were the last remnants of my old life crumbling away. Somewhere deep inside of me, I always knew that with my upbringing, life was never going to be ordinary, no matter how much I wished for it. In modern society, bucking most of the trends of conventional living was always going to set me apart. Always wondering the fate of my parents and living with Nan who gave little away, left many unanswered questions. My life was set apart in so many ways from others and what happened yesterday was a sucker punch, jolting awake the part of myself that had been happily hibernating.

Grey slowed down to a trot, then a gentle walk at the rear perimeter of our property, where a small stream crossed the back corner. I jumped down, giving him a *thank you* nuzzle and a peppermint to crunch on as he lumbered off to slurp in the clear water.

I found a spot where the sun was highlighting a cosy piece of ground and laid down. A ray of sunlight light warmed my chest. I closed my eyes and listened to the sounds around me. The trickle of water was accompanied by a family of lorikeets screeching in the distance. The sun was strangely soothing on my already hot flesh. I snuggled deeper into the ground and curled up on my side, wishing it would swallow me up, at least for a time. From my earthen bed, I could hear the tiny rustling of the miniature world that lived in the leaf litter. The musty smells of another realm, of life invisible to the naked eye, but comforting to me.

The warmth pushed me into a lazy and comfortable nap.

The sounds of nature entwine with the forest emerging in my dream. I am running, arms open wide. My fingers graze along lavender bushes, chasing butterflies as they try to land for lunch on the surrounding flowerbeds. I am young now, maybe six. My pale hair flies wildly as I giggle that joyful, carefree laugh that the innocence of childhood keeps only to itself. The fairies swirl around me, tickling at my ears. They wanted to play hide and seek. I run from them and hide down behind the retaining wall by the pond. I struggle not to laugh, trying to keep impossibly quiet. They always find me—that was the fun of it. I poke my head around to look up the steps, and a bright, floating white light pops out at me and whizzes through my hair, creating more of a mess than before. I run, laughing and squealing, as a whole cluster of my fairy friends chase and tickle me until I reach the back steps of the house. My dress is now a mess of mud and leaves. I turn to wave at them as I move to walk inside. They cluster into the shape of a heart before darting off with immense speed, disappearing into the forest. I hear the whinny of a horse and put my hand over my eyes to shield them from the bright sunlight. Then I look off into the distance. Someone is out there, but I can't make out who it is. I call, but no sound escapes my mouth.

Another loud whinny forced my eyes open, bringing me out of the dream and into the blinding glare of the sun that was now burning hot through a gap in the overhead wattle tree. I woke with my mouth halfway open, as though I was still calling to the mysterious person in my dream. I hadn't seen my fairies in a long while. I missed them. I was always sure they'd been real, despite the mocking I'd received from Jaz and Ben when I shared my secret with them.

Grey whinnied again and I sat up, shielding my eyes as I had in the dream. I screamed in surprise as someone loomed over me. My eyes didn't adjust quickly enough in the glare of the sun before the person leaned down over me.

"Hey you, it's just me."

"Ben?" I said, shifting so that I could see him better.

"Sorry, yeah, I didn't mean to scare you."

He knelt down next to me, his dark hair covering his eyes as he studied the ground. Then I bombarded him.

"What are you doing here? Nan said you went home. Are you okay? Have you found Jaz?"

"Slow down, Soph. One question at a time." He half-smiled and ran his hand through his hair. For some reason, the action caught my attention and made my heart flutter just a little quicker.

He studied me intently for a moment, then reached towards my face and gently lifted some stray locks away. Suddenly aware of what he was seeing, I roughly shoved his hand away and pulled my hair back down, pressing it firmly to the side of my face. It suddenly mattered to me how I looked in front of him. I turned away to watch where Grey was grazing on some ferns. I was at a loss for words, not sure what he'd seen, not sure what to say, not sure why I cared.

"I've just gotten up, don't look at me. I might scare you half to death!" I tried to use self-deprecating humour to divert him away from what he may or may not have just seen.

"You don't need to worry, Soph. You're beautiful," he responded, looking back at the ground.

I peered up, confused as my hair fell away from my face again.

"I only see a tired girl in need of cheering up," he reached for my hand.

I wasn't sure if he was lying to save my dignity, or if he really hadn't actually noticed the glaringly obvious scarring. I took his hand and we stood up. Again, there was the stomach flip and bizarre hum as our skin touched.

It was like with Cael, but different. With Cael I was left with a strange feeling of familiarity but with Ben, I just wanted to reach back to him, be closer and run away all at once and it scared the hell out of me. This was just all too much.

"Come on Soph, let me cheer you up," Ben's liquid voice yanked me out of my thoughts. He held onto me like he was scared I might disappear if he let go. I felt like I wanted to disappear.

"How could you possibly cheer me up?" I asked, still shielding my sensitive eyes from the sun's glare.

"Just follow me."

We walked slowly back to the house, as it was the only speed my body would allow me to travel. We remained silent for a time. The gentle padding of hooves kept us company as Grey followed behind like a puppy. I snuck glances at Ben as I wondered on everything.

Since he wasn't divulging anything about yesterday, I couldn't contain my silence anymore. "What happened to you yesterday, Ben? You just disappeared."

"I don't know. I remember the drive home, but not who was in the car, other than you. I vaguely remember putting you to bed. Other than that I remember waking up down the hall from the room you'd been in with a killer headache!"

"You can't remember anything at all?"

"Yeah, bits and pieces from St Xavier's, but nothing that makes too much sense. I heard screams. At first, I thought it was all the people running to get out, but then I ran past a door, and I was pretty sure I heard Jaz's foul mouth, so I followed the sounds down the stairwell. That's where I found you. Then it's a whole lot of blanks. Glad you're okay Soph." He squeezed my hand softly.

"That depends on your definition of okay."

"What do you mean?" he stopped and looked me over. I panicked and changed the focus. I couldn't let him be dragged into this any more than he already was.

"No, no, I'm just exhausted. You're okay though? Let me see where you hit your head."

"I'm fine. Nan checked it last night. All good. Let's put a smile on that face. Come on, I think Nan has made you some weird, vegan dessert thing." He smiled. I liked his smile.

He pulled me into a run, making my body scream quietly in defiance. Everything was incredibly sensitive. The breeze teased each nerve ending on my skin like pinpricks. The smell of lavender, crepe myrtle, and eucalyptus rushed through my senses as the entire landscape seemed to come alive in a way that I'd never noticed before. Something in me felt like it was unfurling. All the while, my palm sweated and tingled inside Ben's warm, dry grasp.

When we arrived back into the kitchen, he didn't let go. He guided me into the lounge, where I screamed with surprise. A mass of black hair and a dragon-tattooed arm lay casually over the edge of our sofa.

"Jaz!" I was all over her in an instant.

There she was, lying tucked under a knitted blanket, a strong coffee in hand and Nan fussing by her side. A plate of untouched avocado chocolate mousse lay crusted over on the tea table. How Nan thought she'd eat that, I'd never know.

I hugged her so tight, she squealed. "Easy, sister. I've got a concussion. I don't need a fracture as well!" Jaz's attitude seemed intact, so that was a good sign. Her hair had the lingering smell of smoke. *Was it from the hospital fire, or those black entities that I knew I saw engulf her?*

I hugged her again, and she pulled away quickly. "You look like crap, Soph!"

Awaken

"Where have you been? What happened to you? Did you, um—do you remember yesterday at all?" I asked, visually checking her over for cuts, abrasions, anything serious. Despite the rain of glass that had poured over us, her skin appeared perfectly smooth. The only evidence of anything untoward was in her eyes. They were bloodshot and puffy, with a hint of dried blood caked into her long, mascara-smeared lashes.

"More than I care to discuss right now. Let's just say that what I saw makes *Twilight* seem like *Sesame Street*!" She looked straight into my eyes, giving me a meaningful glare that read, *please don't make me remember it.*

"Please, Jaz. I know it's hard, but I need you to tell me the last thing you remember?" I begged, desperate for her not to have seen what I had seen.

"Again, not feeling like an Oprah-style spill-my-guts sesh just now, but the last thing I saw, unfortunately, was Alfie's face at least a mile too close to mine! Ugh, and it wasn't coffee breath I was smelling, either!"

"What's she talking about?" I looked at Ben and Nan who were standing behind the couch.

"Alfie found her, unconscious, in the back of the café this morning when he was getting supplies from his storeroom. He said she was huddled up by the back entrance, sleeping. He used plenty of descriptive words that'd even impress Jaz! Something about too much partying and not enough working! Guess he wasn't too impressed." Ben answered with a smirk in Jaz's direction.

"Huh, he's one to talk! Mister, one shot coffee, two shots whiskey! He's no friend of mine!" snapped Jaz.

"Jasmine, there's no need for that. Alfred simply misunderstood what he saw, though I might like a word with him about his foul tongue at some point. That redheaded temper of his gets the better of him much too often." Nan continued, "Apart from you, dear Ben, whose amnesic episode, thank the heavens, has protected you, we have all witnessed some rather frightening events over the past twenty-four hours. It has been shocking and confusing, I understand. I myself have been overwhelmed, as I know Sophia and Jasmine in particular must be. The reality is, though, you are all in danger because of it. I need you girls, and you too, Ben, to trust in me that I will explain what I know where and when I can. Trust in me that I *will* protect you."

"What's going on?" asked Ben as he walked around to our side of the couch. He hadn't really questioned anything since all of the strangeness began. "I don't understand what you're talking about. What's going on? I don't understand anything, aside from wanting to smack my irresponsible sis for running off—again!" I covered Jaz's mouth, as she was about to interject. "What are you talking about, Nan?" His eyes were wide, and his mouth was a thin seam of frustration as he balled his fists.

"Ben, your ignorance keeps you safe at this stage, be grateful for that. The girls were unharmed. I am expecting a couple of acquaintances any moment now to help me sort out this ungodly mess. I just need you to do as I ask for now. Please?" Nan had politely fobbed off his questions.

Ben raked his hand through his hair in an act of frustration. "You know something. Tell me! What's going on with Soph?" He was agitated as he probed for information. I shrugged. I didn't have a thing to add.

"The less you know, the better. You just have to trust me on this. I will keep you all safe, Ben. However, I do need some help. Please, I beg you to trust in me. Faith is difficult when you feel in the dark, and can't find anything tangible to hold onto. But you *must* have faith in me," she tried to console him. He just turned his back in frustration, pounding his fists together.

"Holy hell, this is all starting to sound like a B-grade movie plot, guys!" said Jaz as she moved to get up from the couch. "I'm outta here. I'm sure there's a party somewhere that I'm meant to be at. Tell that to Alfie, will you? You guys can go—"

Ben turned and pulled her back down. "Sit down, sis! Shut up and stop being difficult. You insisted on coming straight here instead of seeing a doctor, so be nice, huh? I need you somewhere that you can be looked after. Just behave!"

"I'm sorry that the middle of my sentence interrupted the beginning of yours, Ben! I was speaking. Now get your hands off of me, bro. I'll go wherever the hell I want. Who appointed you my parent? I'm old enough to know what's good for me!"

I grabbed her free hand and let a small wisp of healing pass through to her. It actually hurt, pain sang down my arm as the energy flowed slowly, catching my breath. I tried to send her some calming energy, which given my present state, was nearly impossible.

"What *are* you doing, Soph? Will everyone please stop touching me? Leave me the hell alone! It feels like needles, and it's creepy. Plus, you stink, too. What kind of perfume have you got on, *eau de puke*?" She spat the words like venom at me. This level of nastiness was out of the ball park, even by her standards. Something was so not right with her.

"I'm sorry, I was just trying to help. We're all trying to help." I maintained the calmest edge to my voice that I could. "We've both been through something horrible. We should stick together, yeah? Like always?" I asked softly. "We've got to make some sense out of this." I glared back at Nan. Clearly, my last day of oblivion was not meant to be. I needed to know what was going on in this little world of ours, and now.

"Yeah, well, keep your hippie healing crap to yourself!" Jaz' expression was vicious. I sat back, trying not to feel hurt. Ben's hands were in his pockets as he just glared at us both. The angry and fearful tension in the room was suffocating.

A knock at the door cut the mood in the room momentarily. Nan discreetly placed her hand on the door to feel the energy on the other side. We so didn't need a peephole. As I watched her, I noticed that she was actually still in her nightwear, something I'd never seen her do before. She was also completely not herself.

"About time," she sighed. In walked Esme, followed by Kea, who was pushing a wheelchair with Brennan in it.

What in the world was the neighbour doing here?

They came in quietly, almost reverently, like it was a Sunday service. I was put right back on edge by their behaviour. Nan came over and scooted me closer to Jaz's end of the couch so that she could sit by my side. Jaz scowled like a toddler as I tried not to bump into her.

"Ben, dear, would you mind heading to the *Whole Foods Market* and grabbing a few things for Jasmine? Here's a list." He grabbed it, scanning it from top to bottom

"I'm not eating your—"

Nan cut her short. "Hush, dear. You've been through an ordeal. Just relax and let me care for you as your mother would."

"Mother? I've never had a mother! Don't talk to me about mothering. I've always taken care of myself just fine, thanks Nan!"

"Jaz! She's just trying to help! Please, try to calm down." I exclaimed.

She just turned her head away and looked at the floor.

"Don't worry about it, dear. This is fear talking, not your friend. It takes more than a snappy mouth to upset my constitution." Nan turned back to Ben. "You and I shall have a chat when you get back, Ben. Kea will keep you company, just in case you still feel a little under the weather from yesterday. Now be a dear and grab those things for me, won't you?"

"Sure, no worries, and I feel just fine for the record." he said, grabbing for his keys and looking totally peeved.

Kea picked up her keys, too. "Nuh-uh, you're co-pilot today, buddy."

"I'm not your *buddy*," he snapped as he followed her out the door. He glanced back at me, worry and hurt shadowing his eyes.

Jaz piped up again to say something as the door slammed shut, but Nan, clearly frazzled now, laid her hand across Jaz's forehead and commanded, "*Sleep.*" And out she went.

Chapter Thirteen

With Kea and Ben now gone, it was just Brennan, Esme, Nan, a lightly snoring Jasmine, and I left in our tiny living room.

"How long have you put her out for, Nan?" She used to do this to me when I had nightmares as a child if I couldn't get back to sleep on my own. I often thought she bordered on the cusp of magician, rather than healer.

"Long enough, dear." I tucked the blanket around Jaz's neck, she looked peaceful.

Brennan, of all those present, was the first to break the uncomfortable tension in the room. "Hey, Soph. She'll be fine, don't worry."

I looked at him, suspiciously, wondering what the hell he was doing here.

"I'm guessing you're not here to ask me to run out and grab you some milk," I said dryly.

"I am short on supplies but no, I don't need milk. I suppose you're wondering why I'm here, of all people," he smiled weakly.

"That would be a yes, but frankly, I don't know why *anyone* is here."

"Well, Nan needs a hand. There's a little something about your past you don't know and it's time for you to know. It's something she's been dreading and looking forward to since the day you were born. I'm here to support her and you. I know that must sound completely ridiculous."

"Okay," I drawled out in that way you do when you think either yourself or the person who's talking to you is completely cray-cray.

"You're not losing the plot. Don't worry about that. I'd be the first to tell you, if you were! We are all perfectly sane, I assure you. Well, I can't vouch for Kea, but—"

"Brennan, please!" snapped Nan. She looked unashamedly nervous.

"Sorry. Anyway, you are perfectly safe and normal. Well, kind of."

"Brennan!" Nan exclaimed again.

"Fine, it's been a while, okay! Soph, there's something we need to tell you."

There it was. I stood up, leaving Jaz to her slumber. I couldn't sit to hear bad news, I began to pace. I moved between the bookcase and sofa, wringing my hands. Esme moved in and took over, comforting the indifferent, snoring Jaz.

I looked to Nan who seemed to be taking a back seat as her eyes remained fixed on Brennan, urging him on. Her face was pained.

"Soph, you have an immensely important heritage that you have never known about. We've allowed you to grow up in the human world, oblivious to it all, in order to give you the best start to your life. You, little princess, have a future and abilities that you could never even imagine. The forced ignorance has been for your protection, not to simply keep you in the dark," Brennan explained. He wheeled himself over to me and placed his hand on mine. I felt that buzz of energy from him, too. I pulled my hand back fearfully. *Stop! Just Stop!*

"What did you mean by, 'the human world?'" It was a just plain crazy question.

Azure eyes regarded me with such a warmth that I couldn't look away from them. "Don't be scared. I'm as much family to you as anyone, kind of like a big brother."

Hearing this, I looked back at Nan. She nodded her head, indicating all was fine. *Fine?* Alarm bells were firing in my head to run for the hills. Not for fear of danger, but rather fear of a truth that I didn't want to know.

"Listen to Brennan, Sophia, please?" she said softly.

"Esme, would you mind?" Brennan inclined his head towards the front door, and Esme ambled over to retrieve a set of crutches that I hadn't noticed leaning against the wall. She passed them to Brennan, who put the brakes on his chair and began trying to stand up. Despite myself and my own worries, the nurse in me fired up, and I immediately went to assist him.

"It's okay, I can manage," he said with a smile and a wink.

"I didn't know you could walk at all, Brennan." I remarked, astonished and relieved for him, too.

"I've been in an extended and intensive rehab program, so to speak. I'm just about done with these things." He eyed the crutches and winked again. "Follow me."

He hobbled slowly but steadily over to the book cabinet and leaned himself against the empty fireplace mantle. Only now that he was standing could I appreciate how tall he was—he must have been close to seven feet. His shoulders were wide and muscular, and as he steadied himself, his t-shirt sleeve slipped back to reveal an impressive set of white scars circling his bicep. He opened the glass doors and shuffled around some books. Then he said to Nan without looking back, "It's time. Enl'iel, why don't you slip into something more comfortable?" I bristled at this unexpected innuendo. Brennan must have seen my expression that felt to me like, *go get a room and Ugh,* all at once.

"Hey, it's not what you think, get that sweet mind out of the gutter princess." I blushed and looked anywhere but in his direction for moment.

That was when Nan took her cue and launched into an excitable frenzy as she headed towards her room.

"Oh, thank the heavens," she exclaimed, "just let me change first. Oh, my Lord! I'm still in my nightwear!" she gaped down at her linen nightie.

With Esme stroking Jaz's brow, Nan in her underwear, and a semi-stranger helping himself through our belongings, I was just lost for words.

I simply watched the trio; whatever they were up to was going to play out right there. I felt Esme's eyes fall heavily upon me, watching for reaction to the unfolding events. The ticking of the wall clock and Jasmine's slumbering breaths seemed as loud as a freight train in the confined space. I even felt the air weighing me down. The slam of Nan's bedroom door brought my focus back to Brennan.

"What are you looking for in there?"

"Just a second princess, have to remember which books—ah, yep, that's the spot."

As he spoke, he pulled out two vintage *Encyclopaedia Britannica's* that I don't think had been opened in my lifetime. The amount of dust that flew off as he threw them onto the floor confirmed this assumption. He seemed very at home here, considering I'd never known him to visit.

He reached in again and a light seemed to shine back out, then a clicking sound drew me closer to see what he was doing. I wasn't short at all, but his impressive stature eclipsed my view. His arm then fully extended into the wall cavity. Now we had Indiana Jones-type hidey-holes in the house, it was just getting more surreal.

Brennan pulled back his arm, and in his palm was a key of sorts. It was large, about the length of a ruler, with a rounded handle. The end was very unusual, a kind of three dimensional swirling orb of metal. Sort of like a coil. It was quite beautiful.

"Here, hold this, will you?" he passed it to me.

Immediately, it glowed white, then red-hot. I dropped it in surprise.

"Hey, that's an antique. Careful there!" he said jokingly.

He picked it back up and passed it to me again.

"I don't want it. You hold it!" I was afraid of the strange object.

"It won't hurt you, but it will lead you to some answers," he replied.

"Sophia, take it, dear." Nan was back. She was dressed in khaki camouflage pants, a very tight white t-shirt—revealing assets I didn't know she had—and some army-style boots. I dropped the key again.

"Nan!" I gaped.

"Hang on, I'm not quite done." With that, she placed her palms flat against her face. They began to glow as mine did when I used them to heal. She slowly stroked them back over her face towards her hair, shaking her whole body slightly as she did so. A visible change in the air around her caused the edges of her body to blur, like that freak at the hospital.

"Oh my God!" That's about all my brain could manage.

Nan had changed her appearance. I mean, seriously freaking changed what she looked like. She went from Helen Mirren to Cate Blanchet in under ten seconds flat. With my eyes bulging out of my head, I edged cautiously over to her and reached a hand out hesitantly to her face. Her skin was smooth and youthful, and very, very real. She wordlessly placed her hand upon mine and kissed my palm.

"What are you?" I asked tentatively.

"I am a mere shadow of what you are."

The hand holding mine had not a crease, nor an age spot. Her short hair now flowed long and white down the length of her back. And her eyes. I was sure they'd been brown, but were now a shade more akin to Brennan's. I backed off slightly, though fear wasn't pushing me away, I just needed to back off and stare.

"Enl'iel," Brennan said in a husky voice, his breath catching before he could say another word. She gently pushed past me and rushed over to him. They embraced—very lovingly. He bent his head and kissed her lips in a way that told me that they were more than just neighbours. My cheeks burned with embarrassment. I tried to avert my eyes from this intimate scene, but curiosity was fuelling my every move.

"I've missed you so much," said Nan in a voice that was soft and alien to me. She cupped his face in her hands, their eyes melded to one another.

"It's been a long time," he kissed her again, slow and lingering. His pale, shoulder length hair fell down over their faces like a natural veil of privacy.

"Oooooo, I love a good 'ol romance, he, he!" Esme was clapping behind me as though this was all perfectly normal. Her commentary broke the moment, and they stepped out of their embrace.

I finally found my voice again. "How did you—and I—ah, your name, what did he call you?" Again my brain and vocabulary were not in sync. "This is, just whoa!" My palms were pressed either side of my nose, half covering my eyes, as though seeing less of the situation would make it easier to process. "Um, Nan I don't know what is going on here!" My eyes refocused on her, transfixed by her youthful beauty. I was gaping at something that my brain couldn't quite accept.

"Don't be afraid, Sophia, it's still me. I'm the same as I ever was, perhaps just a little different on the outside. Enl'iel is my real name, Lily was just a nickname. This will all make sense to you soon. It's too much to explain over a matter of minutes. First, we need you to follow us—there is something you must see that will help. Esme dear, will you please make sure Kea follows on after she has secured Ben?" She was still hugged to Brennan's side as she said this, their elbows clung tightly together.

"Don't you worry. I'll sit here by this young one and wait for 'em," Esme answered as she patted Jaz's arm.

"What do you mean, 'secure' Ben?'" I questioned.

"Sophia, Ben is not like us. He may have seen some things that he should not have, despite what he has indicated. Kea, well she *is* like us, and she is just going to make sure both he and Jasmine are safe from their memories, which in turn will ensure their future safety. Knowledge of what you don't understand can be very dangerous."

Like us? She seemed to be defining us as something different from others. *But in what way?* Clearly, I knew I had a sixth sense for healing, like her, but how did that qualify me to be part of an *us-and-them* scenario? Then again, after what I'd witnessed recently, there was definitely another kind of something out there. What I knew as normal and real was now a train wreck smouldering in front of me.

"Will he be okay? Are you sure he and Jaz will be safe?" I asked.

Nan came over and took my hands firmly, rubbing her hands across mine. She contemplated me with furrowed brows. As Nan spoke, I listened, but her voice seemed far away, like I was in bed dozing, listening to someone read a bedtime story to me.

"My job for a very long time has been to protect you. When Ben and Jasmine came along, I brought them into that safety net as well. I will always do whatever I can to protect them, Sophia. Right now though, *your* safety is more important than anything else in this world—theirs, mine, anyone, and that is not said lightly." She then gestured that we should head out the back door.

"Come, follow me. It's time for you to know." She took my hand and led me away.

Our hands glowed in each other's, her newly youthful hands nearly identical to my own. I found myself stealing glances at her frequently, convincing my brain that what I was seeing was actually real. Right there and then, everything was like a smack in the face to me. My senses were on high alert, taking in every detail around me. The energy in the air was intense, like the static of a thundering sky. My pulse raced with Nan's, which I could feel through her palm. Her breathing was loud, too loud. Her pants rubbed like sandpaper as she walked, the annoying sound grated in my ears. Even the smell of tea and eucalyptus in the air were like punches to my senses. My own body temperature became hot and unbearable. The growl of a desperate hunger called from within. Each little clue was evidence of something new and surreal. My subconscious was desperately trying to grasp at something, making every cell in my body hypersensitive. Confusion and curiosity had fused into a pull that was overpowering my fear, so I didn't resist it. Something in my gut was pushing me forward.

As we stepped into the warm sunshine out back, I could hear the swing of Brennan's body between the gentle thuds of his crutches as they crunched into the leaves on the path. Shadow appeared and followed us, keeping a protective watch over me. His soft fur rubbed against my legs as we made our way down the garden path.

We made a bee-line down the back cobbled stairs, straight to the wooden shed.

"We're not going in there, are we?" I asked, quite alarmed.

"Of course, dear. Much of what you need to know lays within those walls." She gestured straight to the horrid grey cube.

"No, it's spiders that lay within!" I said. It was kind of a ridiculous thing to worry about at the moment, considering everything else that was going on.

"They will leave momentarily." She giggled to herself. "I am sorry, my darling, but I deliberately left them there specifically to keep you out. I knew you would never voluntarily go in there that way."

Nice! I thought. Twenty years of feeling the creeps walking past that thing was all her doing.

Nan placed her hands upon the weathered grey structure. Again, her hands lit up, and she voiced the words, "Thank you." Every hair on my body stood on end as I heard the scurrying of thousands of hairy little legs move en-mass, like an army marching off to battle. I swear they had tap shoes on, as the intensity of the sound made my ears want to curl in on themselves. I stepped back and bumped into Brennan in my haste to get out of the way.

He put a reassuring arm around me. "Not a fan myself, but don't share that. I've got a reputation to maintain." He gifted me with another warm smile. He felt strangely and suddenly very familiar to me, like Cael.

From where I stood in his protective embrace, I saw from every corner thousands upon thousands of hairy, eight-legged fiends emerge and swarm their way off into the surrounding forest.

Nan pushed open the shed door. "There we are, nothing but rusty tools and dust in here now. Come on, dear," she said brightly, as though it were a flock of fairies that had just flown by.

I was ushered through the door unwillingly, ducking my head and checking for any stragglers in every corner in the dim light.

The small space was thick with an earthy, mouldy odour. Nan pushed aside an old workbench with a physical strength I never knew she had and grabbed a heavy broom. She began brushing firmly until a wooden door, of all things, was revealed in the dirt floor. It seemed as large as a regular door, but was clearly very, very old. The original colour of the wood had faded to grey, and there were divots and chips gouged all over it. A large keyhole of sorts was centred into the edge closest to my feet, but there was no apparent handle with which to pull it open. As my curiosity pulled me in to look closer, I could see a faded carving in the middle. It looked like a word. I kneeled down and brushed off some remaining dirt, revealing the word, *Biblionia*. The script was old, but I could see an elegant hand to it, telling me it was once brilliantly and ornately decorated. I ran my fingers lightly across the letters on the rough wood. The word meant something to me—I could feel it intrinsically. My face burned once more.

"It's a dialect of an ancient language akin to Greek, dear. It means 'library.' It's a safe place for us. Well now," she tut-tutted as she swept away one last layer of dirt, "it hasn't been used in such a long while. Sophia, I need you to take that key and unlock this door. I know you well, and you will only come to understand who you are by cold, hard evidence. I know you can feel a power growing within you—use it to open the door." Her smile was warm and sympathetic as she urged me to take the key.

She was right, of course. I was transparent to her. She knew that I could only accept whatever this was with facts, not faith alone. The only real faith I'd ever had was in her. It was Nan who had shown me my healing abilities, by demonstrating her own. I'd never have believed it possible otherwise. I needed to see, hear, and feel cold, hard evidence. Blind faith was not natural to me.

The door at my feet would open a new world, away from the illusion of life I had been living. I was being railroaded into new territory, which was terrifying. What I realised immediately though as I looked at the key Brennan was holding out to me, was that getting upset or defensive was not going to put a stop to what was going on. It was happening to me and around me, so I decided that I just needed to go forward and find out whatever the truth really was. I knew Nan would never allow me to be hurt, so despite my innate desire to run, I put my trust back in her hands.

"Come on, Soph, you can do it. This will lead you to answers to the questions you never even knew to ask," Brennan said.

I took the key for a third time, and again it glowed white, then red hot the second it touched my skin. Surprisingly, it did not burn. I turned it over a couple of times then held it for a moment with my eyes closed. *Deep breath in, slow breath out, repeat.* It had a vibrating energy flowing through it, as though it were a living thing. My hands trembled, yet my curiosity was piqued. There was absolutely no way to not go with the flow.

"What is this made of?"

"An ancient and rare metal," Brennan replied.

The key was probably a good kilo in weight and getting heavy very quickly, so I knelt down and slotted it into the deep keyhole in the base of the door. It sank in easily with a *click*, and I turned it clockwise. As I tried to work out how I was going to pull it open, the whole door shook. I reflexively pulled my hands back as it shimmered. Its wooden beams lolled, like waves in an ocean.

"Do you see this?" I wondered aloud. It was an amazing sight.

"Yes, dear. It's perfectly normal. Just watch and wait."

"*Normal*? I hardly think anything is normal right now!" I mumbled, more to myself as I watched the door become hazy and almost transparent.

There was a dull and deep rumble underfoot, like an earthquake's aftershock. The whole room lit up with two rapid, blinding flashes, white then red. When the brightness subsided and my vision cleared, I saw that there was no door left at all. A black, rectangular hole gaped in the floor. I inched away from the side as a wave of vertigo hit me.

"Well done, dear, well done. Seeing is believing. Look what you have done!" She was positively beaming, like a proud mother hen.

"Now, you just need to reach your hand inside, Sophia. Use your energy, as if you were healing someone. Move some positive light into the darkness," she instructed, as though it was a logical next step.

I was never one to believe that it was smart to put one's hand into an unknown hole. "Can't you do that?" my voice was a whisper as I gazed into the blackness below.

"Sophia, you need to exercise your power. This is just the beginning. Don't be afraid," she purred like a mother cat, gently caressing my hair.

"You must learn about yourself through your own power. Go on, imagine that you have a patient in front of you. How would you heal her?"

As her words sunk in, the breath of a cool breeze drifted softly up from this void, as though something was down there. My curiosity reared its annoying head yet again. Very hesitantly, I knelt a little closer to the edge, hearing small clumps of earth and stone crumble from the edges of the chasm, down into the nothingness. No sound came of the rubble hitting a base, so this was clearly not a hole dug by a garden shovel. I looked back at them both behind me, and two reassuring nods urged me on as I clung at the cold edges of earth.

With my head turned away so I couldn't see what might jump up at me, I placed my arm inside. I felt for the energy around me, connecting to that tingle in my belly that zipped up and down my spine when I connected to the Earth's energy. Grasping for anything and everything that was light and positive in the air around me, I willed it downward through my right hand. It was more difficult than usual, as I currently battled against pressure, fear, and pain. I had never felt pain before when I had dispersed energy from me into something else. The effort I was putting myself through exaggerated the now resident agony in my face and back. I was also distracted by the intense energy force I felt pulsing from Brennan. It was immensely strong, like someone tapping on the back of my head. It clouded my mind.

"Come on, Soph, just relax. You can do this, princess," he encouraged.

I clenched my burning eyes shut a little harder and concentrated. *Deep breath in, slow breath out. Repeat.* Recalling what Jaz and Cael had been through, if I could find some answers for them through all this, then I damn well was going to gather as much strength as I could. The thrumming ache in my head banged on harder with that thought, and a sting coursed up and down my spine with more ferocity than ever. I struggled to ignore this and focused harder. Sweat trickled from my temples. Finally, feeling the warm buzz of the earth's positive field, I sucked it in metaphorically, as though one would draw fluid up a straw. High on the energy, I relaxed a moment with my eyes closed, letting the power run through me. Then I set it free, allowing it to flush down and out of my hand.

I was flung back by an unexpected and powerful jolt. Nan helped me up from the floor, dusting me off motherly as she did so.

"See? Look what you have done, Sophia." She pointed to the ground.

The intense blackness was gone. A phosphorescent tunnel with a spiral staircase trailed vertically and endlessly down. The walls sparkled. The dark shiny stone was pinpricked with golden flecks. Its unexpected beauty resembled deep space. There was a mirage of slightly unnatural movement to the scene that should have appeared static. It was like looking at something through water.

Nan hugged me from behind, whispering into my ear. "Well done, Sophia. You are growing ever more powerful by the minute. You are indeed Quickening. Follow me."

"I'm what, Nan?"

"Call me Enl'iel, dear. I am no more your Nan than you are mine. The

Quickening is the jumpstart Cael most likely ignited within you when you were exposed to the imminent threat of that beast at the hospital."

"Is that thing gone?" I asked, clueless and terrified.

"Try not to worry, for now you are safe here with us. Let's get going, I'll explain it all when we are within the Library." This was far from reassuring.

She began descending first, reaching out for me to follow, when I asked, "Hang on, how are you going to get down, Brennan? With your crutches?"

"Oh, don't worry, Soph. I've been working on another form of crutch." As those words were spoken, he threw his crutches to the ground with a thud and leaned heavily onto the edges of the old workbench. His knuckles were white with the effort.

"Are you sure you're ready to try this?" asked Enl'iel. *It was going to take time to get used to that name.*

"Only been practicing every day for half a millennia!" he puffed through gritted teeth and effort.

Clearly that was a joke, I hoped.

"Stand back with Enl'iel, Soph. This could get a little outta hand," he said as he began to tremble from head to foot.

My entire body prickled and tingled again as an immense static heat filled the tiny space. It seemed to be coming from Brennan, who was now breathless with effort. With one hand on the bench, he ripped at his shirt, shredding it to pieces in a mad rush to remove it. His weakened legs held firm, just enough to keep him upright as he struggled away at whatever he was going through. His golden skin seemed to glow from within. He pulsed brighter with each passing second. My head felt like balls were bouncing off of the inside of my skull. There was a rhythmic thump, like the intense pounding of a heavy metal music concert ramming right into your chest. Some kind of light spluttered from his back. It flashed on and off, sporadically, like sparklers firing up and dying repeatedly. *Flashing?* I thought to myself. *All of those flashes I'd seen coming from his home over the years?* More unspoken questions tugged at me.

He groaned a little. I let go of Enl'iel's hand in an attempt to help him somehow. I faltered as he warned, "Stand back. You'll get hurt if you get too close." His breath was ragged, his chest heaved.

I backed up to Enl'iel again and stood with her down on the first couple of steps of the passageway. She looked concerned, but didn't move to intervene. She drew in her breath with expectation. Her knuckles were clenched around her necklace. At this point, Brennan's back suddenly lit up like the glow from a nuclear bomb blast. I instinctively shielded my eyes from the glare. Enl'iel just looked on with an expression of adoration.

Brennan suddenly flung his arms out with his fingers stretched wide. He threw his head back and rose up into the air. Literally off the ground. He hung there motionless, his back turned for a moment or so, in suspended animation.

I was speechless as I gaped back and forth between him and Enl'iel. She was clearly not shocked, rather more enraptured. *"Oh, love of my soul,"* she whispered. She too, seemed to glow from within.

I turned back to Brennan to see that his back was covered with the same inflammatory pattern as mine. Light emanated from the raised welts. No longer intermittent sparks, but rather a soft and warm glow pulsed out of small flaps of skin, like the gills of a fish. It was ethereal. It was beautiful. It was freaking me out. I'd absentmindedly edged forward, back up the steps. I couldn't help myself—I was drawn to him. Mesmerised, standing below, looking up at him and barely able to breathe, I brushed my fingers gently through the light across his back. A rush of visions surged through my mind, visions that spoke a single word: *family.*

He's like me—I'm like him! What the hell is he, and what the hell am I?

He turned around at my touch and was a sight to behold. He was simply stunning. Soft white energy glowed bright from behind him. It shone upward and out behind his back. His blonde hair had turned to a cool white, but the real spectacle was his eyes—they were amazing. Still blue, but they moved like unearthly swirling, sparkling opalescent gems. Their sheer beauty captivated me.

Enl'iel whispered softly behind me. "Behold this sight, my dear Sophia. This is a great Watcher of A'vean, your kindred and your protector." Abruptly she was no nonsense once more, calling sharply, "Enough showing off, Brennan!" as though this display was not in the slightest bit extraordinary.

"This is spectacular. I've not had my energy flow like this for far too long. By the heavens, it feels fantastic. It's like stretching for the first time in forever. *Ahhhhh!*" he groaned with pleasure, a wide smile spreading across his face. "I've been in a box for five hundred years, and now I'm free." He flexed all of his limbs, as though seeing them for the first time. The veins in his right arm glowed unnaturally, but it was his face that had my attention now. Along his right cheek and temple, he bore the same birthmark as me, and it glowed. I was speechless as I touched my hand to my own cheek, painful as it was.

The light energy behind him began undulating like the slow flapping of wings. He looked at me with those incredible eyes and smiled again. He glided smoothly over to me and pointed to the stairwell. "After you, princess."

We descended, to where and what, I hadn't a clue.

Chapter Fourteen

There was an uneasy quiet about the house in the minutes since Enl'iel and the others left for the Library. Esme was seated in an old Louis XIV chair. It was in need of a good refurbishment, but she liked the well-worn dip in the seat that her padded behind sunk nicely into. She was feeling restless—the air about her wasn't right. The tiny hairs behind her neck were straining in an effort to alert her senses. She was wise enough to know not to ignore these signs. She pulled her brown bag closer to her feet; it was never far from her reach. Digging around inside, she found what she was looking for. She held a thick sheaf of sage, strapped together with a length of brown twine. A sprinkling of cedar wood shavings and it was ready. She already had some lavender hanging above every doorway. The spiritual presence she felt was heavy and wicked, like the night before. A few repellent aromas might settle it down until the others returned. She was merely a human with a deep sixth sense; she could no more control a Daimon than a hurricane.

"Oh, for th' lov o', where are me matches? Always forgettin' them things!" she said to no one but herself. Easing her old bones up out of the chair, she padded heavily to the kitchen, humming to herself to break the tension she was feeling. Picking up a pack from the windowsill, she felt the fluffy caresses of Pumpkin around her ankles, purring like a jack hammer. "You lookin' for a snack, eh? Let me see," she opened the refrigerator. "Here ya go, a little slice o' cheese. *Mmmm*, don't you go tellin' Sophia, then. I'll be in trouble for fattenin' yer up too much again. He he!" she laughed to herself. It was nature that kept her going. It had no agenda. Animals were real, no lies or pretences. They gave you what they had honestly, and asked for nothing more than a snack and a rub on the belly in return.

People, well, they were so entrapped in what they thought they wanted that they weaved webs of deception and lies that led to nothing good. She always trusted nature, but was forever guarded with people. Their layers of falsity made them vulnerable to the spirits, both good and bad. *Like lambs to the slaughter, they were.*

As she plopped back down with a rather unladylike *thump*, Jasmine stirred.

Hmmm, she thought, *that's not right*. Enl'iel should have kept her out cold until she got back. Esme quickly set about lighting her sage to get the aroma wafting through the room sooner rather than later. Each strike she made with a match though, resulted in nothing but a burnt stick and no flame. There were only a dozen or so matches left in the package. She kept striking with no success. With the last one left, her hands were now trembling and her eyes wide with fear as she looked around the room. She knew now that something was working purposefully against her. Ever so carefully, she flicked the shard of wood quickly along the matchbox one last time and success, a lovely yellow flame illuminated her fingers. Grabbing the sage from her lap, she lowered the flame to light the dried herbs, and as distinct as if someone were right by her side, she heard and felt the blow of a cold breath. It doused the flame before it could reach a single fibre. She jumped in her seat, dropped the sage to the floor, and clasped her hands tightly to the arms of the chair as she looked wide-eyed all around her.

"You go leave us alone, ya hear? You're not welcome in this home. Go! Get out, get away from here!" Beads of sweat sprouted over her heavy brows. She looked over to Jasmine and rose to check if she was warm enough. Poor sweet Jasmine had been cold as ice, but stinking like a smoke house when she was found by Alfie. The girl felt fine now, but a fresh drop of blood was trickling out of her left eye. Esme picked up a damp cloth from the tea table nearby and dabbed it away.

"You leave her alone, you evil beasts. Go back to where you belong. Pick on somethin' your own size. She ain't no help to ya. Oh Jesus, Mary and Joseph, protect us," she spluttered to herself, drawing a half-hearted sign of the cross over her chest. She was raised a Christian, but had not practiced the faith for decades. However, in moments of extreme fear, she'd sometimes revert to a quick, panicked prayer out of habit.

The girl began mumbling incoherently in her sleep as her eyes twitched rapidly under closed lids. She ground her teeth in a manner that further set

Esme's nerves on edge. While tucking the blanket more securely around Jasmine's shoulders, the cat reappeared upon the back rest of the sofa and began growling and hissing. Its hackles were vertical and ears flat against his head. He spat, his paw raised threateningly with claws aimed for the sleeping girl. In the first movement she'd made since she'd been put to sleep, Jasmine's head lolled over towards the cat. A groan came from within her, like she was in pain. The orange ball of fur jumped suddenly, screeching as it went flying off of the sofa and up the stairs in a blur.

"*Ooo*, this ain't good, girl. You hang on in there with me. I know it's near you. Don't let it in, sweet pea. You a strong one. I know you been through a lot in your life, you be strong for me now, eh? I could do with a little help right about now. Old Esme is way outta depth here!" She looked about desperately, hoping for signs that anyone was returning. But there was just her and Jasmine and something else.

Leaning up out of the chair, she reached forward to dab Jasmine's eye again, as much to comfort herself as the girl. As she did so, Jasmine rolled her head back towards Esme with an unnatural flop. The old woman fell backwards in shock onto the floorboards. Her hand flung to her heart as pain seared down her arm. Her breath was shallow, her lungs unable to inflate. She crawled up onto her hands and knees and unwillingly made eye contact with the face staring back at her.

Motionless, Jasmine was still as a corpse, silent and tucked in snugly. Her head, facing Esme's agonised form, was glaring at her. It was wordless, expressionless, but with eyes wide open and as black as tar.

"You—leh—her—alo," was all the kindly old woman could spit out.

Esme knew it was the same spirit she'd felt in Sophia's room last night. It was here before her, attached to Jasmine, and it was murdering her in cold blood.

Chapter Fifteen

I moved in a velvety, dreamlike state. Slow and fluid, one step at a time. Right, left, then right again. It felt like I was leaving the old me behind as I descended down into the earth, becoming a girl that I didn't yet know. With my hands trailing along the jagged walls, my entire body hummed. The tingling travelled up through my fingertips and into my veins. When this energised blood hit my heart, the elemental force exploded back out with every pounding beat like the rush of a drugged high, piercing every cell in my body. I honestly felt like I might take flight, just like Brennan.

The steep abyss teased vertigo out of me every time I looked down. There was no railing to grasp onto so I dug my hands into any outcropping of glistening, rocky wall on either side to keep steady. I felt sure I was going to tumble forward to my death at any moment. This was clearly no problem for the guy flapping behind me, however. That whole Brennan experience was filed away as yet another thing I would ask about later.

The darkness deep below felt alive, beckoning for my entry. Every so often, Enl'iel placed a hand upon a still darkened wall and it would illuminate as it had above. She looked back each time with an encouraging smile. My apprehension must have been evident in my snail's pace progression.

"Keep up, Sophia. We are nearly there."

"I'm right behind you." I answered.

"Move it along, ladies. It's a little cramped back here," added Brennan

It was in this twilight glow as she encouraged me along that I first noticed she too had a small, twirling trail of white marks just at the edge of her right eye. It was much smaller than mine. It glowed when she smiled at me. *How had she hidden that from me?*

Eventually, both feet hit solid ground with relief. A large arched doorway greeted us immediately at the landing. Ornately carved columns proudly presented an equally ornate, vintage-looking gate. It appeared as large as the doorway of a church cathedral and arched up toward a distant ceiling. Blackness lay beyond the metal bars. An engraved plaque sat in the middle of it all. The edges of the plaque were surrounded by metallic engravings of fire, wind, water, and earth. In the centre of the plaque was a diamond with five squares set inside it. The craftsmanship was impressive, even in its rusted state. I examined the artwork as a cool breeze wafted through from beyond the bars. There was a deep silence here. There was no evidence of life, other than the three of us.

"Sophia, would you like to use the key again?" Enl'iel pointed toward the gate and stepped aside.

A keyhole shaped the same as the door above embellished the right edge. I took the key again without hesitation. With more effort this time than I expected to use, it opened the lock with a creaking, metallic crunch. It clearly had not been opened for many years as the lower end of the gate was covered with some kind of moss, and about a foot tall mound of dirt hid its base. This large, rusted door creaked open only with a heave and a push from all three of us.

"Where are we, Na—Enl'iel?' I asked.

"We are entering The Library of Antiquity. There are four of these sanctuaries left around the world. They are gathering places, learning institutions, homes, and safe havens for us. Places where we cannot be detected by unpleasant creatures, such as the kind you saw at the hospital."

Thank God for that, I thought. "Shouldn't we bring Ben and Jasmine here, too then? They saw that thing. Aren't they in danger?"

"If Kea can work her magic, then they will be just fine. Trust in us, Sophia. Just as you are going to have to trust in yourself," she answered cryptically.

How could I trust in myself? I couldn't trust that what I was seeing and doing was not some form of elaborate delusion. Perhaps I was still in the hospital after my run in with the patient gurney. It was easier to believe, but I knew it was just wishful thinking at this point.

Once through the gate, we walked the length of a short, high-ceilinged corridor, whose ambient crystalline light was the same calming hue as the stairwell. The floor appeared to have been tiled with large, perfectly aligned stones. The sheen of them bounced the light back up into our faces. They looked new, as though they had never been walked on, yet the place had an impressively ancient feeling to it. At the end of the corridor we came upon a smaller metal gate. It opened with a light push from Enl'iel.

I halted at this small opening as my hands grazed the bars of the gate. It was warm to the touch and appeared to be made of gold. It gleamed and hummed under my hand as I passed through it.

"Part of the security system," Brennan said. He was still unsettling me with the hovering thing. "Gold is a powerful conductor. We can use it to repel any unwelcome visitors."

"How does it work?" I asked, intrigued.

"I'm so glad you asked," he said as he flapped around in front of the gate. He stretched out his knuckles with a few popping sounds. "Let's pretend your friendly doctor from the hospital followed us down here," there was a gleam of excitement in his eyes.

"What? He could—I mean—is *it* going to come back for us?" I backed up, slamming my tender back into the rocky wall behind me, faint with panic.

"Brennan, look what you've done, trying to show off! No, Sophia, that evil creature does not know where this place is—none of them do. Brennan's security system has never been used to do anything other than to amuse himself!" Enl'iel assured me and gave him a scoffing glare.

"Sorry, Soph. She's right, but awfully boring, too. C'mon Enl'iel, let me show her a little fun." He looked at her with puppy dog eyes.

"You'll do it anyway," Enl'iel sighed behind me. I imagined her shaking her head in defeat.

"So true!" He blew her a kiss.

"So princess, just in case you want to know how to get rid of a door to door salesman, watch this."

He aimed his right hand towards the golden metal as a short burst of crackling lightning shot out from his palm. As it made contact, every bar on the gate seemed to absorb the energy with a sucking sound. It hummed like a million bees, then sent a massive shockwave of white light bursting through the other side, down the length of the corridor we had emerged from. If someone was on the opposite side of that gate, I was guessing they'd be toast, if that.

"Impressive?" he grinned, eyebrows raised questioningly as he waited for my reaction.

He was like a big kid playing with his toys. "Wait 'til you see our weapons room in the UK. It's even better!"

"Enough of that now, we are not here to play the fool," Enl'iel glared at him, with a wink and a smile attached to the end of it.

"Come, Sophia. Join us in our great Library." Enl'iel pulled me gently alongside her.

I gave Brennan a quick thumbs up for his trick, causing a massive smile to spread across his face. I smiled, despite myself and the situation I was in as I turned away to see what was ahead.

I found myself in the partially lit opening of a cavernous room. At a guess, it was the size of a football stadium, but it was hard to tell. The echo of our footsteps seemed to bounce back from quite a distance away. I could hear the sound of running water far off in the pitch darkness. The roof was so high up, I couldn't see where it ended.

Brennan gave me a gentle push from behind. "Don't be scared. Be *amazed*," he said comfortingly.

Before me was a multi-levelled room, lit faintly with strange candles along the walls. The three storeys I could see were connected with ornate staircases. On the second level were row upon row of neat, diamond-shaped storage spaces, crammed with books and what looked like scrolls of paper. A handful of white lights dashed among them, stopping and hovering for a time, and then darting off to another section.

"They are the Keepers of Knowledge. They collect, document, and protect both our history and the history of humanity," Enl'iel explained as I eyed the fascinating sight. They seemed so familiar.

Like my Fairies!

What caught my eye, though, were the incredible murals decorating the walls. They were mosaics that twinkled like a rainbow of stars. I ran my fingers along the lower ones, quickly realising that they were the rough-hewn cuts of gemstones and crystals of all varieties. Diamonds, quartz, rubies, lapis, and emeralds—an Aladdin's cave of wealth, woven into the fabric of the earthen walls as masterpieces.

I gazed around, awestruck. All manner of creature was represented up there. Birds, land animals, sea creatures, and people, too. In some of the images, the people looked like they were interacting with huge, ethereal beings surrounded by light. These figures appeared, as much as I didn't want to voice it out loud, just like Brennan.

"This is incredible!"

"This is *your* story, Soph," said Brennan. "The documents contained within these walls, and the murals up there, tell of our long history. They evolve and change as we do."

"*My* story?"

"Yes, Soph. This place will answer many of your questions."

"Who am I?"

Enl'iel placed her arm through my elbow, drawing me closer against her side. "Brennan, would you be so kind?" Enl'iel waved her arm around, indicating the general darkness surrounding us.

He elevated his body higher above our heads with the powerful force of light emanating behind him. It seemed to extend further out from his body the higher he flew. His square jawline was set firm in concentration. He raised his arms up and outward, and orbs of white, pulsing light appeared magically upon each palm. With an immense show of power, he smashed both hands together with a thunderous clap. Light sizzled and flickered from within his clasped palms as he seemed to work at moulding something. He then threw this mass of energy into the air above his head. Explosive fireworks lit up the roofline, revealing a gargantuan, rocky cavern. The sputtering sparks of light reflected off of a metallic-lined roof before retracting back into a massive white circle of light, hovering up in the nether reaches of this underground haven, like a subterranean sun.

"Not bad for an old timer, wouldn't you say?" Brennan hung there, hands on his hips, nodding smugly to himself with satisfaction.

"Let me tell you a story," Enl'iel began.

Chapter Sixteen

The drive to the market was mind-numbing. Trailing around after these humans, half-breeds, and hypocrites was so far beneath Nik'ael, that he almost considered it more enticing to face perpetual oblivion. All they did was worry about protecting her. *What about him and his kind? Weren't they as worthy of absolution? Had they not suffered an eternity on this forsaken hellhole for sins long since forgotten? Sins that these same brethren had indulged in? Sins that he himself had never partaken in!* He didn't buy it for a minute that they were not as aggrieved as he—they just chose to bide their time differently. When the time came, they would grip the same handle that will slit her throat. They too would hold the chalice to collect her blood. They were one and the same to him, travelling on different highways towards a mutual destination.

He needed to stop this little shopping expedition from returning too soon to the house at the bottom of the hill. Nik'ael's accomplice needed time down there. He needed to prepare, to get the Rogues in place, to be ready. Diversions needed to be put in place to secure the information he required, the vital clues he needed to finally get ahead in the game. How could he do this without being detected? Easy. He was a master of cloaking. He had perfected the art of being so close yet so invisible that I'el himself would not know he was underfoot.

As the black car crested the hill, leaving the local village, it shuddered.

The engine over-revved, draining the power. It sputtered and slowly ground to a halt as Kea eased it onto the blackened gravel by the edge of the road.

"Damn, I just had this thing serviced," she said, frustrated.

"Want me to have a look?" asked Ben.

"Sure, are you good with motors?"

"Yeah, not bad. I built my bike."

"Well, dive in, my friend. I'd like to get back with these things for your sister."

"There is no way Jaz will eat or drink any of that crap. She'll throw that green tea—hot and all—at someone, you know."

"Yeah, she sure is a tough nut, that one. I'd say the last twenty-four hours have been pretty hard on her. She was very defensive before. Something's off with her. I don't know what she remembers about the time the she was missing, but I'm worried about her. Would she talk to me about it, do you think?"

"That would be no! Leave her alone. As long as she's safe at home, that's all I care about. She'll talk if she wants to, but it certainly wouldn't be to someone she met five minutes ago. She doesn't know you from a tree stump, so don't try getting all BFF with her!"

Nik'ael was impressed with the exchange. He loved a good dispute, especially if it lead to a fist fight. Unfortunately bloody Kea had to keep it all too calm. Boring as Hell. Ha, how true that was!

"What about you, Ben? Remember much from yesterday?" She stood behind Ben as he leaned into the engine, a glowing hand out of his sight, hovering just behind his head as he was inspecting the oil dipstick.

Nik'ael smiled smugly to himself.

Ben flinched a little before he answered distractedly, "Besides feeling pissed off with that Doc for threatening Soph, not much. I'm not interested in a psych session though, so back off!"

Kea smiled to herself.

She was clueless. She thought she had the upper hand. Nik'ael felt intoxicated by the power of his subversive interference.

"There, I've tightened the spark plugs. They were too loose. Try it now." Ben shouted out from under the bonnet as Kea sat back in the driver's seat.

The car started easily, and they quickly set off for home.

Within minutes, it came to a rolling stop again. "What the—I thought you knew what you were doing, buddy?"

"Don't call me 'buddy,' and I do know what I'm doing! But you might notice that you don't have a toolbox or anything slightly helpful in the boot, so give me a break!" he snapped as he got out again. She popped the bonnet again.

This little scenario played out another five times as they attempted the drive back to the house. Nik'ael was loving every second of it. He'd send a covert burst of negative energy to the engine, Kea and Ben would get out and fiddle under the hood, becoming increasingly annoyed with each other. They'd head off again, but wouldn't you know it—*poof*—another breakdown. How very, very convenient.

Eventually, Kea and Ben had to concede defeat and wait for a roadside tow service. Lucky for Nik'ael, it was going to be a long wait on that winding, forested road. Time was now on his side.

Chapter
Seventeen

The sanctuary was gargantuan. It was so huge that *cave* seemed too insignificant of a word to describe it. The glowing orb that had somehow emerged from Brennan had lit up an expansive arena, with walls full to brimming with beautiful imagery. The floor was a mosaic of black stones impregnated with diamond-like decorations encrusted into the cracks that twinkled up at us like the constellations of the night sky.

The dazzling display drew my attention across the space to something in the distance. It seemed central to the whole cavern. Like a regal monarch, there stood a large pedestal with a huge green rock atop it. It threw off a dull, jade glow. From there I spotted six arched doorways that led out to some other unknown places. Above each doorway there was star. It glowed over the entrance to each dark tunnel.

"Look around you, take it all in," Enl'iel said with a touch of awe in her own voice.

"This is just breathtaking. Who made this place? It's incredible." I responded quietly.

"Let's start at the beginning, shall we?" Enl'iel answered.

She pointed up towards the east wall. There, an image depicted a triangular formation of stars against a night sky. The star at the peak was large and surrounded by licks of fire. Within it was an eye that sparkled iridescent blue with hints of every other colour spectrum weaving throughout it. Six smaller stars were underneath this one. As the pyramid of stars widened out towards the base, the stars became smaller and more numerous. Hundreds more stars at the base of the shape were cut in half.

"Sophia, this is a depiction of The Beginning. These stars represent the collective inhabitants of a world known to us—and no one else—as A'vean. It is a planet impossibly far away from Earth. It is a place of immense beauty, rather Earth-like, but exponentially larger. Earth is but a blip on a radar compared to the immensity of A'vean. This is the home of the creators of all life throughout the universe, The Throne of I'el."

I was about to ask something, but she held up her hand for me to be quiet.

"Humans are the creations of the Council of I'el. The Council is a race of enlightened beings, of pure conscious energy that take no particular form. They have travelled the universe, creating life where there was none for years beyond the millions. All life that has been sparked from them share a piece of their energy—a soul—and that provides a connection to them eternally."

"Are you talking about God and Heaven?" I asked, immediately intrigued.

"Yes and no. Humans think of their creator as a God or Gods who reside in a Heaven. Heaven is an obvious derivative of A'vean, long forgotten mind you. The Creator is in fact more than one being. I'el was The First, the Prime Energy. He—and I'll use 'he' for ease of description—is everything and nothing, all at once. Neither male nor female, just a pure force, born from the great Singularity that exploded many hundreds of billions of years ago. I'el is the First of the Seven, and was the first of anything in this universe to obtain consciousness. He is the supreme and most powerful of the creators. His word is the final one on all matters. In the beginning, he was alone, so he cast six conscious energies from within himself, each responsible for a different function in the propagation of life across the universe. It is a natural compulsion for him to create life. Taking it is against his very being, and has only ever been done so under extreme circumstances. You can see him depicted here as the star at the peak of the pyramid. The eye represents our infinite connection with nature, the universe, and Him. The six stars below him are his brothers, Earth, Wind, Fire, Water, Light, and Dark."

I didn't realise that my mouth was hanging agape until her soft finger gently lifted my chin for me.

"What do all the other stars in the pyramid represent, then? Is there a whole race of these energy-beings?"

"Well, yes, Sophia, there are. They are organised into a system of cascading power and function. I'el being the Prime and most powerful, working all the way down to the bottom, which brings us to who we are."

I was starting to get that tingly feeling you have when you actually know the answer to something but refuse to admit it to yourself. *One more minute of normality, please?*

"We, and that includes you and I, are descendants of the energies of A'vean."

I turned slowly around, looking left and right, up and down. Drinking in all that my eyes could take. "*I'm an alien?*" I whispered to myself.

There was a cough, then "*Hmm-mmm,* ah, do I look like ET?" interjected Brennan.

"No, but if I'm one of them, I'm not human, right? So then what am I?"

"You're a miracle. An Earth-born Angel of A'vean, Soph," said Brennan. "You are just like me, but prettier—just!"

His humour was lost on me as memories of the hospital stairwell came flooding back. *I flew. Lightning shot out of my body. I flew—I damned-well flew.*

I leaned against the wall for a moment, bent over resting my hands on my thighs. "What's going on? Why have I never known any of this?" I slunk down to a crouch, grabbing my aching spinning head. Brennan helped me back up as Enl'iel grabbed my arm in hers again.

"Come, the pain will ease soon enough."

She rubbed my back and I instantly felt relief.

"You have not known for your own safety. You will come to understand why. This is a lot to take in, we understand, but the time has come for you to know and embrace your heritage. I wanted to tell you in a more controlled and calm manner, but we have been pushed by circumstance to move forward with an uncomfortable haste, and I am sorry for this. You are very precious, Sophia," she said, hugging me snuggly, placing her head on my shoulder for a brief moment.

Should I feel scared, angry, amazed, or honoured? I didn't understand any of it, my emotions were in warfare with each other. I wanted to feel angry at the deception, but I also needed to understand all of this too.

"Why did you call me the 'Earth-born Angel?'?" I asked this as I let my fingers graze along the wall, feeling the addictive zaps of power.

"Look at this mural, princess. I'll get to that to the whole 'Earth-born' thing in a minute," Brennan replied. "This here shows the Six, descending to Earth, sparking life into what was a violent and harsh world. You see those lifeless-looking people on the ground? That's the moment when they thrust the energy of I'el into primitive man, giving them souls, a kick-start to their evolution, and an eternal connection to A'vean." He pointed to the images, pausing as he looked at them with what looked like reminiscence, as though he had been there.

"Early humans were weak, though, and didn't learn well. Normally, there's a strict policy of non-interference. Life must be left to evolve in its own way. However, the Council, and particularly I'el, felt a deep compassion for the struggling race, whose image was a physical clone of their most favoured spiritual form. So, after a lot of debate over thousands of years, they voted on intervention, as all were growing deeply worried for the survival of this unique species. Humans were being picked off by predators, and underutilising the potential they had been given. To help, they sent the Order of Watchers to Earth to protect them and gently guide them so that they could flourish. I was one of those Watchers, Soph."

I looked at Brennan dubiously. "You're like—an Angel?"

"Well, I know I look like one, but I was part of this group who were originally known as Watchers in our own language. I was a warrior Seraph for a time, but I tired of the warring worlds, so I volunteered. Angels, in fact, are actually a rank or so above us, we've just been piled into the same club by humans. Can't complain, it's not a bad gig!"

"Brennan!" Enl'iel scoffed.

"Oh you love it!" he winked at her. She just shook her head. Ignoring this ridiculous banter, my mind was working overtime.

"Hang on, how old are you?" I asked nervously.

"Well, if I add in this, take off that, throw in the Dark Ages—*hmm*, I'd say I'm a spritely fifty thousand years young, or so. Don't think I look a day over 5000 though!" His smug humour was annoying.

"Now you're just messing with me. This can't be real! That would mean you're immortal!"

"That would be a yes. Us Watchers, Soph, descended from I'el himself, are powerful, but we are much less so than those of the Council and the higher orders of Angels. Yet, we are indeed immortal. It's kinda cool, but has its drawbacks, particularly if you're injured. We can endure illness and injury for thousands of years which isn't pretty. Just come through that as you can see," he pointed to his newly working legs. I know it's hard to believe princess, since last week I was just the guy in the wheelchair across the road. But now I'm recovered, I'm your own personal immortal wingman." His eyes lit up, a smile spreading across his face. "I crack myself up—*wingman!*" He shook his head, musing at his own joke as he flapped his wings at me.

"Brennan! Save your stand up set for later." Enl'iel chided again.

"Sorry." He continued, moving me along the east wall to another mural as I clung tighter to Enl'iel's arm. "So, energy doesn't disappear, it simply moves from one realm or form to another. Humans and other life forms have souls that move on to different states of being after their mortal death. They have no control over what becomes of their souls. However if that energy, like you and I, has a higher level of consciousness, then it is perpetually self-determined—

effectively, immortal." He had a perfectly matter of fact expression as though this was all too boringly normal.

Words failed to come to my mind. I felt wide-eyed like a child, as though listening to the most riveting bedtime story of all time. *It actually was the most riveting story of all time.*

"We were sent to guide mankind in quiet whispers and dreams, to protect them from themselves and the wild world they just scraped by in. Because of the frailty of the human body, we assumed the same form as them. Humans can't look at us in our true form and survive. We found this out the hard way. They spontaneously combusted from the intensity of our original state. Our light overwhelmed them, biologically and emotionally." He shook his head at the unpleasant memory.

"Oh God! That's awful! So, you disguised yourself so humans didn't catch on fire?" I somehow found my voice again.

"Yep. Even a small glimpse could blind someone instantly—it was no way to make friends. So we transformed ourselves to look and feel like humans. We all kind of liked the fleshy disguises, taking various sizes, shapes, and colours. See, up there, we're those streaks of light falling over the Earth, the ones with the rather creepy looking faces! Must have a word to those responsible about their artistic licence. Hmm!" He regarded the images, unimpressed.

Comet-like streaks were indeed cascading across the rocky scene. Only because Brennan pointed it out did I realise that they all had faces.

"So you've just hung around forever, you're immortal, and you can change form!" I couldn't believe I was going along with this. "So why have you been a paraplegic ever since I met you?" I asked.

"Oh, that was from a particularly nasty fight. I got myself a really good beating—nearly killed my body. It's taken me forever to heal. After our initial transmutation to the human form, we can't acquire a new body each time an old one is ruined. We need to look after our bodies carefully. If they're injured, we can heal them to a certain point. However, if they're irrevocably damaged, we must return to our original form. We aren't magicians! So, if we can't use our body anymore we ascend to the Sanctuary of Souls. I wasn't ready for retirement, so I've been healing myself for five hundred years. The Middle Ages were pretty nasty times. Lots of Daimons prancing about in the open, when humans were a more superstitious lot. That's not taking into consideration the violence the humans drummed up, either! Man, they're capable of some bad karma." His eyes were bright with the excitement of the story.

"*Oookay,*" was all I could respond with.

We moved on to the next mural as I tried to digest this information. *What was a Daimon?* I wasn't sure I really wanted to know.

"What can you make of this image, Sophia?" asked Enl'iel.

I didn't answer for a moment as I caught myself looking at her new, youthful complexion again. Her lineless face was a vision of immense beauty. Her long white hair settled neatly around her shoulders.

Dragging my stare away, I answered after I took a quick look. "Um, I see people looking like they are having a party. There's food, and I think wine, and, oh—um, some of them look like they are —"

"Intimate?"

"Uh, yes!" I answered, blushing.

"What do you notice about the couples?" she prompted.

It took me a few more glances to get over my coyness to realise what she was pushing me to figure out. "Oh my God, some are glowing from behind, like you Brennan. You and they—?"

I stopped for a second.

Finally, I looked at Brennan. "You're like, the fallen Angels from the Bible? You fell in love with humans, and were thrown out of Heaven?"

"Well, that just makes us sound bad! It wasn't quite as shallow as that, but to summarise it, yes, guilty as charged." He had his hands up in mock defence. He was so far from what I'd call angelic. Clearly, the poised, perfect beings sold by religious institutions missed the part where they could act like irreverent class clowns.

"It was a bad thing, Sophia. It has led to much suffering. It affected the Order of Watchers' ability to return home, and changed the course of human history forever—and not for the better. You should not be so flippant, Brennan. You're a part of this mess."

"Too true," he responded, a more serious note in his tone for a second, but then he reverted back to the clown.

He pulled Enl'iel away from me into a spin and an embrace, kissing her passionately on the lips.

"But, if we hadn't partied, then I would never have had you, and *that* would be a Shakespearean tragedy of epic proportions!" he crooned as he leaned over her and kissed her again. The mark on her face glowed.

"Yes, well—" she was blushing like a teenager, self-consciously straightening her top as she pulled herself from his arms. "Let's keep the pace going Romeo, we must return topside shortly. I have so much to show you, Sophia, we can discuss the more *colourful* history later," she cleared her throat as she uttered this. Brennan had gotten right under her skin. It was hard to suppress my grin.

The next picture showed the Watchers cowering on the ground below a bright light with a fiery, burning eye within it. They stood in front of a huge glowing doorway. They appeared to be reaching towards it, trying to get through.

Brennan continued the narration. "This is the day that the Order was cast out, and the portal to A'vean closed indefinitely. With this connection severed, we were stripped of a ton of our power. Our minds were instantly erased of immense chunks of our universal knowledge as punishment, including our native language. Only small portions of it remained. We managed to salvage what we remembered by teaching it to a developing ancient human civilisation called the Mycenaeans. That's where the Greek language evolved from. Modern Greek is the closest thing we have to our own language now. This is why you'll notice many references or adaptations of a Greek-like culture in our everyday life and history."

Who knew? Wow! I thought with an increased thrill. History had been my favourite subject in school. *How wrong had we been?*

In the next picture, there were five figures upon a hill by themselves.

"These are your enemies—*our* enemies—*The Unseen.* You'll hear them referred to as the Satans as well. The reason for that is that they've behaved like a race of vicious beings from Satanos, a planet long ago destroyed due the violence of its inhabitants. We refer them as 'The Unseen' because they act from the shadows, rarely seen but always causing havoc. When we were exiled from A'vean, these five brothers of ours were so enraged that they split from us. Unfortunately, over time, they've enlisted many more of us, the ones who were fed up with the isolation. The Unseen vowed to cause carnage to humans eternally as a punishment to the Council for cutting them off. They didn't believe we deserved such a blanket banishment," he explained. "And perhaps we didn't, but who am I to judge that?"

"What have these enemies done?" I asked. An instinctive revulsion at the mention of them gnawed at my gut.

"They've succeeded with their threat. Every war, every major disaster in human history, has been initiated or fuelled in some way by the Five Satans and their pack of devils. They've stolen from humans the memories of their origins by mimicking Gods. This action alone thrust humanity into religious wars and power struggles for millennia. They get a smug satisfaction from the confusion and misery they cause," he explained, shaking his head with sorrow as though he personally were at fault.

"So where do I fit into all of this? Are you a Watcher, too?" I asked Enl'iel.

"No, my dear, I am not a Watcher. I am Eudaimonian, a hybrid of a Watcher and a human. Some of us are born of two Eudaimonians, or of Watchers and Eudaimonians. Rarely, since the great fall, have Watchers mated with humans. Those who do are shunned by the Council of Eloi—they are our elders who try to keep us all on the right path. The same cannot be said for the Unseen, who interfere to this very day with humans in ways they should not. The Christian Bible calls us Nephilim, and we have been wrongly portrayed as evil. We may have all or none of the powers that a Watcher has. Those like myself who inherit many powers can live a very long time. Others can live a life as short as any average human. The weakest links are those who have the minor powers of clairvoyance and such. A little like Esme who has the smallest touch of our heritage coursing through her. Generally though, they would never even know of their true heritage, such is the weakness of their lineage. The stronger the bloodline we have to a Watcher, the more similar we are to it. Before you ask, I am not as old as Brennan. My mother was human, a beautiful, kind woman from rural England. I was born in Tewkesbury in the year 1784."

I did a quick mental calculation. "You're two hundred and thirty years old?"

"Yes, dear."

"And still looks twenty-one, don't you think, princess?"

"Are you ever serious?" I snapped at his offhandedness.

"No sense of humour, chill princess!" He pretended to look at something in the distance as I scowled at him. I considered what Enl'iel had just told me as I instantly felt guilty for being harsh with Brennan. "Sorry Brennan."

"All good, I'd be the same if I suddenly found out I was a human!" I rolled my eyes at him. I looked back to Enl'iel.

"So, if you said Watchers didn't breed with humans for thousands of years, then how are you here?" I bit my lip as the obvious immediately registered.

"I am who I am because I choose the path of light. I am not merely a product of my parentage. No more talk of this now." She pushed me along. It was crystal clear that this topic was off limits, at least for now.

"Now," she continued, "before the great flood twelve thousand years ago, I'el took aside one human he felt great admiration for, due to his unwavering diligence and devotion to whom this human believed to be his creator. He was a man of peace, humble and generous. I'el respected this deeply, as he lived piously in an increasingly savage world. Enoch is the only human ever to have been in the presence of I'el. He took him from the Earth, taught him the mysteries of the universe, and warned him of things that would come to pass. Most importantly, he gave Enoch a very important gift, the gift of salvation— for us and for humankind. Enoch became a prophet, and could see into the future. He wrote it all down and shared it with only one other. He left snippets with our most ancient ancestors as clues, with the strictest of instructions that none but the Earth-born Angel should decipher his messages and reopen the portal to A'vean. You, my dear, are the key to finding and unlocking the mysteries of Enoch. Enoch wrote of these in our long lost A'vean language, said to only be decipherable by you." Enl'iel continued as I pinched myself to wake up.

"You will see up there the angel carrying him back to Earth. This is the Archangel Uriel. Enoch returned with a prophecy that you would come to the Earth when the time was right. You would be created when the line of your heritage had once again merged into purity. Clues have been dropped down upon us for thousands of years. Visions have been received, but only by the most trusted. Our halls here are brimming with the information that we have collected about how to reconnect with the homeland. The snippets we have gathered can only be sewn together at the right time, by the right person. *Now is that time.* Hidden around the Earth are the pieces to the greatest puzzle of all time. You alone have the ability to help the Watchers read Enoch's words and find the answers to opening the Gate of A'vean." Enl'iel maintained a serene calm, despite her eyes sparkling a mix of fear and excitement.

I was stunned by the gravity of what she was saying. *Creators, angels, watchers, saviours!* "How do you know that I am this person?"

"Upon your birth, there were signs prophesized by Enoch as passed down by the leader of the Eloi council, Gedz'iel. He received visions from I'el. In the past, there were many hopeful births, but yours was the first to show each and every sign. On the night of your birth, our enemies rallied in full force—such was the power emitted by you. Your first cry was heard and felt in every corner of every dimension. The movement of the Unseen proved to us without a doubt that you were the One, as you drew them out of every hidden realm that they cower in."

I was overwhelmed beyond words. Fear pricked at me like a schoolyard bully, taunting me to run.

Enl'iel drew me from these thoughts as we walked past a large depiction of what was clearly the Great Flood, ark and all. The only thing I noticed in this scene was a bereft-looking figure, hovering over an ocean full of bodies. His head was in his hands and he appeared to be weeping, as droplets of tears were falling to the waves below. His image moved me. I felt an instant and deep sadness at this sight. There was a dark shadow lurking behind him.

"Who is this?" I asked.

"This is a depiction of the one and only Eudaimonian who was drawn into the clutches of the Unseen. His name is lost to history, but not his story," she said.

"What happened to him?"

"Well, he was almost as powerful as a Watcher, it is told. He oversaw a thriving village, caring for and protecting humans and Eudaimonians alike. The day the rains began to fall, he came home to find his entire village slaughtered, including his wife."

"Oh no! By whom?"

"Archangels, I'm afraid. It is said that they indeed attempted to cull the half-breeds in order to limit their survival on Earth. Only humans were meant to survive the great flood. An attempt to allow them to start again, unsullied."

"He was betrayed by his own kind! That's terrible." I felt so sad for him.

"Yeah, it was a pretty dark time, princess. But, he had us—he just chose the wrong path, bloody fool!"

I wanted to know more about this poor Eudaimonian, but I was moved quickly away. Clearly, it wasn't what I was meant to focus on.

The next image I was shown depicted a woman reclining on a bed, surrounded by glowing beings. There was a swaddled baby in her arms. A light beamed up into the atmosphere from the baby, and a starburst emitted from where this light hit the night sky. The entire scene rested upon a beautiful decoration of rubies. The gems swirled around, enveloping them in the same shape and form as my birthmark. I touched my face in silent recognition. A pattern of concentric circles sat below the bed. At the foot of the bed, there was a sorrowful man. The mother was also weeping. That seemed strange, as I would expect the birth of a child to be joyful.

"Who's this?" I pointed to the scene with the baby.

"This, my dear Sophia, is the day you were born," Enl'iel said quietly. "It was a day that allowed only brief joy. Unfortunately, your birth put you in immediate danger."

I instantly looked at my mother, intently and longingly. I reached up to touch the image. *What happened to you?*

Enl'iel pointed to another mural, past the mouth of a darkened tunnel. I forced myself onwards, grudgingly dragging my eyes away from my mother. This new mural showed a young girl with long, white hair and eyes equally white. She was surrounded by white comets of light. Outside of this barrier of light were arms, reaching out of nothingness, grabbing for her.

"This is me, isn't it?"

"Yes, dear. You have been hunted your entire life. You have been in constant danger, more so when you were younger. There has always been an army of scouts nearby you, keeping watch. If you think about it, you will remember them. Their presence is embedded in your subconscious. Did you not see one this past June?"

"You know about the attack at the club?" I asked, incredulous.

"I know all of your movements. That was our beautiful Cael who intervened when that Rogue attacked you," she explained.

I remembered that flash of light as I was running to the door. Something had knocked that foul man to the ground. Cael—poor, poor Cael. "He saved my life. I need to go to him, to try to help him." Guilt plagued me as I thought of him suffering alone.

"Cael will be fine with time. He has already been moved to a safe place. We never leave a soldier behind."

At that moment, a shudder rumbled through the ground. I put a hand to the wall to steady myself. Brennan and Enl'iel looked up sharply to one another.

"Sophia, you are safe here, but we need to return to the house. Promise us you will stay right here. Nothing can harm you in the Library, all right? The Keepers will be here for company and protection," Enl'iel instructed.

"What's going on?" I asked nervously.

"We'll be back shortly, princess. No time to explain right now, just stay put." Brennan answered as he placed is hand to the right side of his face, closed his eyes, and disappeared in a flash of light. I was somewhat startled, to put it mildly.

"You will learn that little trick too, before you know it, Sophia. Please promise me you will stay here?" Enl'iel begged.

"Okay," I relented, as she too disappeared in the same surreal flash of light.

Chapter
Eighteen

Alone in this cavern, I could have been the only person left in existence; such was the feeling of relative silence and solitude in the Library. Apart from those little orbs busying themselves on the levels above with a quiet hum, I was alone. I dared myself not to wonder what Enl'iel and Brennan rushed away for, as I didn't think I could take any more surprises today.

My mind was reeling. There was just too much to comprehend. Instead of trying to make sense of the unreal, I used the opportunity to look closer around the cavern. It was either that, or curl up in a ball and cry. I chose the former, deciding to undertake a baptism of fire into to this new existence.

I returned to the depiction of my birth again, running my fingers across the parts that I could reach. It struck a deep chord within me. *Who and where were my parents?* My entire life I'd been told that I had been taken in by Nan because my parents couldn't care for me. Jaz suggested more than once that they were probably kooks like hers, but now, who knew what or where they were. *Did they know about me and where I was? Who I was?*

Were they even alive?

There was another shudder below my feet, and a small spray of dust rained down. The little glowing Keepers responded to this by taking on a frenzied state, buzzing frantically along the upper levels. The shelving started to disappear behind a veil of darkness. It seemed to fall across them like drawing a curtain. I wiped grains of dirt from my eyes, coughing a couple of times as the unsettled dust swirled in the air. Everything suddenly felt very wrong. The throb I'd forgotten about returned to my back and head. The veins along my arms felt like poison ran through them. I rubbed them, trying to calm the discomfort and intuitive and unwanted fear. Despite the fact that I was deep within the Earth, this place was not frightening. It was whatever was going on up there that had my nerves on edge.

I refocused on the walls to distract myself. I studied the fall of the Watchers. They were cowering from the heavens, shielding their faces. It was a sorry sight. One stood out, a lone figure who was not cowering. This aura-shrouded male Watcher, stretched taught with muscles, was pulling at something from a hand reaching out from the ground. There was a circular object and a cylinder in his hand. The blackened hand arising from the earth was grasping at it. The fingers were clawed, and it was clearly trying to steal whatever the Watcher was holding onto. Unfortunately, the detail of the design was not clear enough to make out what this tug of war was about.

While I was intently studying this scene, I turned suddenly, as I thought I heard a whisper behind me. Of course I was alone, and even the Keepers had disappeared with the last rumble. I wished they would come back. Their light and hum had been strangely comforting. I turned back to the mosaic, but again, another whisper drifted into my ears. No—it was more than one whisper. Turning nervously, my eyes squinted into the farthest reaches of the cavern. I looked for the source of the voices. *Nothing.* A hum buzzed in the atmosphere as I once more noticed the massive stone in the middle. I was drawn immediately to it, like a bee to a spring flower.

Nearing the stone, I could more fully appreciate the magnitude of its size. I stood there a moment, dwarfed by the jade coloured chunk of opaque rock. It was the shape of Lady Liberty's flame. I guessed that its circumference would take at least three or four average peoples' arm lengths to stretch around it. The whispers were nearby now, so I walked around the rock. Nobody was there. Curiosity eclipsed fear. The concentric circles reappeared on the pedestal as a decorative edging, with an iridescent blue opal inlaid in the middle of each symbol. More of the birthmark-like swirls trailed down the supporting column, towards the base. At the bottom, the diamond with five squares appeared again also. There was a lot of symbolism that was completely foreign to me. The circles were waist height, and I found myself tracing the shapes with my fingers. My face and back warmed with a pleasant heat for a change, yet my eyes still burned. I let my hand trail upwards to the immense stone, and for no particular reason, I placed my palm flat upon it. I jerked back in surprise. The second my hand made contact with the beautiful rock, my head was filled with a million whispers. I leaned in and touched it again, listening more closely. Yes, the whispers were coming from it. I couldn't understand anything, but I could hear them making calm, soothing sounds. It sounded like having the radio tuned into every station at once. I pressed my ear to the tepid stone. The voices flooding my senses filled me with a surprising burst of happiness, like being lost and then suddenly found. My physical pain was momentarily replaced with a great, energising heat that emboldened me, stirring something deep in my subconsciousness.

The floor shook with another rumble, but this time it was followed by an immense clap of thunder that penetrated down from above, the effect of which I could feel thrum through my bones. Something was certainly not right. My palm was no longer in contact with the rock, yet I could still hear voices—desperate voices, screaming for help. I grasped my head, my eyes shut tight as they pierced through my mind. I could hear them as clearly as though they were in front of me. It was Jaz and Ben, screaming. They were in trouble. Jaz was up there, Ben and Enl'iel, too. They were all I had in this world, and they were up there without me. So as most stupid people in scary movies do, I did the exact opposite of what I was told. I ran for the golden gate and took the stairs two by two, swatting at the Keepers buzzing in my face who had re-appeared suddenly, seemingly trying to stop me from leaving. My determination outgunned their efforts, though my thighs burned from exertion the entire way up. When I slammed my way out of the shed, I immediately knew why I was told to stay where I was.

The sky overhead was heavy with strange, billowing dark clouds. A slight fog was wafting across the ground at knee height, and the air temperature had dropped unnaturally low for this time of year. My skin prickled with the coolness. From my vantage point on the downward slope of the land, I snuck up behind the stone embankment that separated the rest of the property from the back garden. I climbed the mossy stones carefully. As a child, I'd played endlessly on this wall, but right now with my bare feet, it was nearly impossible to get a foot or finger hold to hoist myself up by. Eventually, after as many slips as successes, my eyes peeked over the top row of stacked rock.

The sky was darkening to an eerie black whilst my home was alight with the blinding white blasts from an unseen battle within. Bright lightning flashes lit up the windows, and smoke snaked out through every crack and crevice. Much of the pine cladding was scorched, yet no flames were visible. The corrugated roof was peeled back like a tin of beans. A stench that bordered on putrid replaced the normally sweet bush aromas.

Screeching, thumping, clashing, crashing. A body flung through splintering glass from my bedroom window, falling to the ground with a thud. My eyes peeled wide with shock as I held my breath. While I clamped my hand on my mouth to cage in the scream dying to escape, I slipped back off the wall. My aching vision was beginning to blur at the edges. I rubbed at my eyes. *My contacts must need changing,* I thought. This was no time to have poor vision. If ever a girl needed to see what was going on, it was now.

I warily crept around to the stairs that led toward the lavender hedge and up to the back door. It took all my courage to push myself to crawl up those six steps, holding my breath with each movement. I stayed flat to the ground, like a lizard. Pushing a peek hole through the purple and green foliage, I saw a body laying a few metres away from me. It was spreadeagled, arms and legs askew in nauseating, awkward angles. The figure, clad in a gaping hospital gown—to my utter shock—stood straight back up. It used its hands to attempt to straighten its clearly broken neck. The head flopped sickeningly back onto its left shoulder as it barely hobbled back towards the house. I noticed the morgue toe-tag on its left foot as it dragged a mangled leg along the ground. Ripping the wire door from the hinges, it disappeared back into the kitchen.

I shrunk down into a tight ball behind the hedge, horrified. My heart was straining to burst through my ribcage. It was nearly impossible to panic in silence. I rubbed my hands over and over to quell their shaking. *What was happening to my family and friends in there? What the hell was that thing?* I gripped my face, as though hiding the sight of this unreal scene would make it stop. Black spots began to pepper my vision. The singeing pain in them was as intense as my back, like standing too close to a flaming bonfire. After all these years of perfect health, I was struggling with this immense backflip. Pain was what I cured, not felt.

I plucked gently at my eyes, removing my contacts and threw them to the ground. If ever I needed clear vision, it was now. The sudden glare was intense, but my eyes felt slightly better as soon as the flimsy, brown-tinted lenses were out. Within seconds, my sight was clearing. It was surreal. I'd been severely vision impaired all my life, but now surprisingly I could see perfectly well without assistance. I gently rubbed them and looked up at the sky. Through the overhead yellow wattle blossoms, the ominous clouds were so clear and three-dimensional, I could have plucked one down. Small snatches of azure sky hinted through cracks in the dark mass, serving as an intense backdrop. A bird of prey circled high above a potential victim. I could crisply see the subtle brown hues of its feathers. *Incredible.*

An explosion erupted from within the house just then, jolting me up into a defensive crouch. I kept my head strategically below the hedge. I noticed that even the bees had disappeared, and the birds had dulled their tunes. The chaos from within my home sounded distant through my heavy, exhaustive, panic-breathing. Peeking through again, I saw the same body fly back out through the kitchen window, amongst a hail of wood and glass. It writhed on the ground, a ball of orange flames licking the flesh from it as it continued to struggle back towards the house. At the base of the porch steps, it reached out a skeletal hand, grasping at the balustrade. It suddenly collapsed there into a pile of orange, glowing ash. A plume of black smoke rose from it as an unearthly howl pierced the air around me.

Against all my better instincts, I commando-crawled cautiously along the ground towards the house, under the protection of the lavender. The strong smell of it was the only thing that felt familiar. The coarse stone path scraped into my skin through my now tattered dress. My feet were red and sore, my fingernails ripped and bleeding. My plan was to get close enough to listen to what was going on in there. Then from that point, I had no plan.

This apparently was all about me, though the reasons still remained unclear to my utterly confused senses. Something wanted me in that hospital, and Cael was attacked after taking me out that night. *Was that dream in the hospital meant to be a warning?* The coincidence of seeing the circular imprint upon his palm in that vision and then all around the cavern was not lost on me. People had been laying their lives on the line to protect me from an unseen enemy for my whole life. I couldn't just lay here and let my loved ones suffer for me. Despite this, my basest instincts screamed at me to run. It was against this natural urge that I had to fight within myself to push forward. Whilst trying to bolster my bravado, I could hear voices shouting inaudible threats. A scream of, *"Get out of here!"* was the only thing I could make out. Another huge boom scared the last of the birds from the trees. Two bright streaks of light launched into the sky above me, disappearing up into the clouds.

An unsettling silence descended after that. I froze, listening. Not a sound came—the house and surrounding forest were dead silent. As I lay on my belly, holding my breath and shrouded from view, my blood ran ice cold and my skin crawled. A faint shadow appeared on the ground behind me. Gurgled, rapid panting accompanied this shadow. I flipped over in an instant, only to be met with another body in a white gown, glaring down at me with black eyes. Frothy, green drool dribbled down its chin. It was a woman, at least it had been, until recently. Unfortunately, I'd seen plenty of dead bodies in my line of work, and this was no living person. Pasty skin, white lips, and an odour that was all too familiar—cadaver.

Taking advantage of my shock and her stealth, she reached down and dug her filthy, jagged nails painfully into my ankle with a vicelike grip. The cold of her touch was horrifying. She began dragging me towards the house, pulling me kicking and screaming with ease. I raked my hands through the grass and rubble of the path, ripping back my nails to the skin. My ruby fingertips were desperately clutching at anything to halt her. Where was that lightning power when I needed it?

Changing tactics, I grasped for anything in my reach to defend myself. My arms were being pricked and sliced as I tried to pull at chunks of the woody lavender. Just short of the stairs near the pile of ash, I gripped a substantial fallen tree branch and struck at this thing with all of my strength.

I felt anger and fear together as one emotion. Survival mode had kicked into overdrive, and I was acting on autopilot. As this feeling permeated through my body, something snapped within me. The veins in my arms began to glow white, and a simmering energy infused into my muscles, giving me a surprising boost of strength. The branch became hot in my grip. With one huge thrust forward, I managed to knock her grip from me as I rammed the branch forward. It pierced upwards into her livid, bloodless back. She turned on me, a deep animal growl escaped her foul lips, and more putrid fluid drizzled from her mouth. She yanked the tip of the wood out of her back without a flinch, and a gaping, cauterized hole was left in its wake. The stench of burnt flesh permeated the air. I quickly jumped to my feet, backing away towards the hedge again in a crouch. Regaining my grip on the wooden weapon, I swung furiously, making contact numerous times but not stopping her attack.

Mid-swing, she managed a forceful fist into my face that knocked me backwards. I was momentarily dazed from the unexpected blow. She was grabbing for my legs again when a loud *thwack* sound caught my attention. Her head sailed silently from her body. It landed right next to me, bouncing once before rolling to a gruesome stop. Lifeless black eyes glared at me. The headless body fell to its knees and continued to move, clawing along the ground for a moment before suddenly going limp and disintegrating into another pile of ash.

I felt a rush of cold, screeching air speed past me, the force of it blowing my hair wildly around. Revolted, I jumped back, ready to run. In doing so, I accidently kicked the head with my bare foot before it too disintegrated. This skin-crawling encounter made me falter and slip back to the ground. When I looked back up, I saw a familiar face looking down at me.

"This is some crazy shit, Soph. Don't tell me that I never have your back!"

Chapter Nineteen

Jaz loomed over me, blood-tinged eyes wide with the high of an adrenaline rush. She held a large shovel dripping with black fluid.

"We've gotta get out of here!" she yelled through gritted teeth, under her breath. She glanced all around for the next threat, like prey in a lion's den.

I had to shield my eyes from the glare as I looked up at her. The sunless sky created a pinkish aura around her head, like a halo.

I grabbed for her. "Oh my God Jaz, are you okay?" I found it hard to focus on her as my head recovered from the stinging blow. I tasted blood. I inched back deeper into the bush to find a bit of shade from the strange glare. My eyes felt bizarre and sensitive with their new found acuity. There was a sudden bang from inside the house making us both startle. Jaz threw the shovel aside and quickly squatted next to me.

"Let's redefine *'okay'*. But for this nanosecond, yes, I'm okay." She squished down next to me, I could see her shivering as she checked all around again. I felt frozen in place. She turned and hugged me tight, a gesture that spoke of relief.

"Soph-,"She seemed about to say something else, but then yanked back her head and placed an unsteady hand on my face. She tilted my head left and right. "What—the—Hell?" she whispered slowly. She squinted her eyes, looking closer at me, reaching out to touch my right cheek. She leaned in closer, looking deep into my eyes. *"Oh my God!"* she whispered again.

I shrunk back, averting her gaze and touch.

"Soph, what's happening to you?"

"What do you mean?" I blinked rapidly, covering my face with my palm, scared of the answer.

"Your face, it's—and your eyes! Holy Hell, Soph your eyes—they're bright blue, and—" she rubbed at her own green eyes a little, as if to sharpen her sight, then looked closely into mine again. "Soph, your eyes are sparkling!"

I pressed both hands weakly to my temples and rubbed. "I don't know what's happing to me. My body feels like it's turning inside out. Everything hurts," I whispered back.

"Do you know that your face is glowing? Your cheek—you've got, I don't know, it looks like a tattoo!"

Not knowing how to respond, I just covered my face with both hands and cried a few of the backed-up tears that were begging to emerge. "I don't know how to explain it. Something awful and amazing is going on, and I'm terrified."

"Holy shit, when I said one day you'd shine, I wasn't expecting it to be literal." She let out a nervous laugh as she glanced back, checking for danger again. We both smiled awkwardly at that. She could make a joke out of anything. Despite her darkness, she brought light into my life.

I wiped the tears away with the back of my grimy hand and sniffed. "I can't believe you were in there." I indicated toward the house. "What's going? I think Enl—err—Nan and Brennan are still in there. Did you see them?" It was still and quiet now. Perhaps everything, whatever it was, had settled down. She responded in a hushed but panicked tone.

"All I know is that I woke up under an overturned couch with a killer migraine. There were a bunch of people shouting threats at each other. I saw some strange stuff, enough to make me wish I were in a coma, dreaming it. There were more of those things," she pointed with a shaky hand and disgusted expression to the ashy remains nearby. "They were attacking a woman who I've never seen before, and your neighbour—what's his name?"

"Brennan."

"Ah, yeah, he was like, *floating*. No shit, Soph, he was darting around the room, throwing damn Zeus-like bolts out of his hand!" Her pupils were dilated as she recounted this with ever increasing fervour. Shock and awe was clear in her wild-eyed expression. "I was trying to sneak out when one of those filthy things grabbed me. The woman zapped it into a bloody fireball and told me to run for the shed and not look back. I didn't need convincing. I was hiding around the side under a bush when I saw that one sneak up on you. I would have run for the hills otherwise, but I couldn't leave you."

I hugged her tight. "You saved my life, J." I glanced around the area once more. "Do you think we should go in? It's been quiet for a while now. I'm pretty sure Nan was in the house. I need to know she's safe."

"Hell no! No friggin' way! We absolutely don't go back in that hellhole, *ever*. I didn't see Nan in there, not that I was looking for anything other than an escape route. There was chaos everywhere. Damn-it Soph, we're going to have to check for her, aren't we?"

"I don't want to believe me, but I can't leave Nan behind. Besides I don't know what the hell to do without her!"

"God, why can't life catch me a break? I suppose it'd be some good karma to shovel another head off one of those things that attacked me in the hospital!" Jaz was eyeing the shovel by our feet.

"You remember what happened to you in the hospital?"

"Not goin' there, sister! Here," she grabbed the shovel again and passed it to me as she sniffed back rare tears, "I'll grab that rake from the garden. If we're going to die, I'm taking out one of those fuckers with me." We looked at each other, seeing who would cave first. We didn't, so with my mouth tightly set in determination I nodded silently in agreement. I was terrified. Jaz's visibly shaking body told me she was too.

As we made to move, a massive explosion resounded from within the house, and another creature flew up and out of the roof, turning to dust as it hit the open air. We looked at each other, grasped hands for courage, and were about to run for it when Jaz was suddenly ripped from beside me through the thick lavender. I followed immediately after as something powerful grabbed me from behind as well. I screamed, struggling fiercely, trying to smack at it. I'd quickly lost the shovel, having only my bare weapon-less hands to claw at it. Jaz swore with every foul word imaginable. I would have too, if only I could have found the spare breath, but my desperate screams were exhaustive. I'd lost my footing, and whatever it was, dragged me mercilessly along the rough ground, bumping me up the steps and into the house.

It was silent inside, other than the struggles that we were making for escape. I was banged about through the doorway and yanked into a totally trashed living room. Hanging half sideways, I could see that the curtains were ripped but partially drawn, which cast a creepy afternoon shadow across the room. Piles of ash dotted the floor. I think I was dragged through one, as stinking dust caked into the moist blood on my arms and hands. Part of today's newspaper was scattered across the floor. I noticed the headline, which read, *Morgue raided, bodies stolen!*

"Can I put this thing down now?" asked a demonic-sounding voice from above me. "It's going to make me puke. It stinks. Ugh, it's covered in that purple stuff." The vile creature retched as it said this. A splash of bloody fluid hit the ground near me, making me want to repeat the gesture.

"Yes, drop it there. You've done well." A fluid male voice responded.

With that, I was flung to the ground like a piece of garbage.

I slowly hoisted myself up onto my hands and knees and found two chubby feet in pink slippers in my immediate line of sight. A familiar floral kaftan greeted me next. When I raised my eyes to the face looking down on me, I fell backwards in shock. Esme looked down on me with a sickening grin. Her once soft face was pocked with missing chunks of flesh. Deep blue veins strained through the skin on her cheeks like writhing snakes, highlighting the depth of the blackness in her eyes.

"Don't look so sad, petal, it's me—only *better!*" she laughed, evil dripping from each deep, scratchy cackle. It wasn't her voice at all—it sounded male, and it was terrifying.

"What have you done to Esme?" my voice cracked through a scream. I didn't know who or what I was talking to.

"Well then, if you hadn't caused such an ordeal at the hospital, I wouldn't have needed to go to so much effort today. But as luck would have it, we've driven away your pathetic band of soldiers for a while, so lucky me—I have you all to myself!" She or it, laughed and banged a glowing forked weapon onto the floor.

I was mesmerized by the voice coming from what used to be my beautiful Esme.

"Thank you, my dear." It looked towards Jaz, who was upside down, hanging by her feet in the grip of the other creature. "You were a very agreeable hibernation vessel for my soldiers, though far too foul-mouthed. Modern ladies really are quite unsavoury these days, don't you think?" He cocked an eyebrow at me as though I'd give a damn about what he was saying. "I prefer a nice Victorian woman, well groomed, mannered, and very obedient. Much easier to deal with—in *all* activities." A sick laugh followed that disturbing innuendo.

"What the hell are you talking about, you mother f—?" Jaz tried to go on, but was cut off as she was kicked unconscious by the monster holding her. I screamed as blood trickled slowly from her temple.

"She really is so hard to warm to. I might feed her to the Rogues—they do love fresh blood." If cruelty were a species, it was standing before me incarnate.

"What do you want with me, whoever or whatever the hell you are? Leave my family alone! Do what you want with me, just don't hurt them." My bravery was forced, but it came from the heart.

"Your heart really is your weakness as they stated. What a divinely poetic weapon to use. She'll live, but only after we've taken that little trip I offered you yesterday. What do you say? You are a very special girl, Soph'ael."

"What did you call me?"

"Of course, they've told you nothing." The deepening male voice chuckled. "Makes you all the easier to manage. Why, that is your true name—Soph'ael, the Earth-born saviour. The healer of nature, the one who shall return us to our home and deliver us the retribution for which we are owed." With that, Esme picked me up roughly with a superhuman strength in one hand. I was raised painfully by one arm above her head. I could smell the odour of decomposition emanating from her, and I gagged. I was in so much pain, I couldn't even manage a small kick or hit in an effort to escape—not that I even thought it was possible. Instead, I just hung there as she glared at me. I matched the stare with a false sense of defiance.

"Whatever you think you're doing, or think you're going to get out of all of this, forget it. It won't happen." I had no idea what I was saying, but I had to say something.

She merely laughed at me and said, "You truly have no idea, do you?" She looked away from me and sighed. With a flick of her wrist, a swirling vortex of fire appeared in the floor beneath my feet. I felt myself heat up and burn from within again. I concentrated on that heat, blindly willing it out of myself. Believing that I might have some control over this power thing, I desperately urged it out of me.

"Uh-uh, don't try it. One wrong move from you, and her head will be ripped from her shoulders," he turned me towards Jaz, who was now upright, but held by her hair alone.

"Okay, okay!" I said, shoving my free palm out in defeat.

"Excellent choice, smart girl."

I looked down at the growing fiery hole beneath my dangling legs. The mesmerizing blue flames were punctuated by a blackness forming in the middle.

I was convinced this moment marked the end of my life.

Chapter Twenty

This was going so much better than Nik'ael had hoped. Separating her and those fools was far too easy. They had always underestimated the power of his distractions. This battle was a superfluous fight used to draw them away and get her alone, defenceless, so that he could assess her progress. It was more than his ignorant brothers could possibly manage.

A little voice mimicking, and she was putty in his hands. Her innocence and ignorance was profound. She was far from ready. She was too easily drawn from wherever their safe haven was. The sheep, as he liked to call them, had learned nothing over the past thousand or so years. They followed their hearts, not their brains—somewhat like his brothers. These do-good Watchers had no dignity in his eyes. It was further proof that they were not as worthy to return to face off with I'el. They would probably roll over at his feet like dogs.

These sanctuaries they hid away in frustrated him no end. To his knowledge, none of his comrades or lackeys had ever been able to infiltrate these secret places. If they had, this war would have been won so long ago. The battle would have just been a waiting game with them securely under his control. With his skills, he should have been able to hunt at least one sanctuary down, but they outmanoeuvred him at every turn. Nik'ael was a master of subduing his presence. But still, he was detected each and every time he got close by their damn Seraph-trained militia. They'd bred far and wide, and had eyes everywhere.

As always, he didn't involve himself personally in petty altercations such as the scene playing out in the small house on the mountain. He stood quietly back and observed as he let Belial and the Rogues do his dirty work. Take a rancid soul, plus a fresh corpse, and he had the almost perfect soldier. They were a handy, disposable army. Bereft human souls who were desperate for something else to cling to, an alternative to utter oblivion. They had no place to rest in the middle realm, being such as they were. With no afterlife to move on to, they became prisoners of the Empyrean dimension. They were the worst sinners of their species, hunted and tormented by bored Daimon for sport. You can't die when you're already dead, so the constant do-overs of different ways to die were unbearable for them. They could feel pain and fear, but never the release that death should provide.

Upon conscription to this cannon fodder infantry, they were promised something better than eternal suffering. They had no real choice. Again, fools as were all humans, they did their job and were blasted away anyway, which is what these dregs of creation deserved. He may be many things, but even he could not atone for the souls of child killers and abusers, wife beaters, and the like. These were all cowards, and he despised cowards. These pieces of filth were used at his will and received nothing in return. It was the absolution that they deserved.

The irony of humanity was that they didn't need the Unseen to guide them into destruction. For an eternity the Daimon had dabbled in human affairs, interfering in subtle ways to provoke nuisance and distress for their own amusement. Humans were ironically innately wired to destroy themselves in the name of power, desire, or religion. They were self-evolved devils in themselves yet it was the Unseen that they feared. What a joke. Nik'ael could have just sat back with his brothers from afar with a box of popcorn and watched the apocalyptic movie play out before their eyes. But it was the boredom of exile that drove them long after their initial, raw hatred had waned.

A few spare Rogues were kept around long term, those with strong constitutions who had proved more worth 'alive' so to speak. Older, more experienced ones were excellent for reconnaissance, as they knew their way around. The difficulty was that they had to be fed, and in modern times, letting them suck a human dry of their blood was getting profoundly more difficult to achieve covertly. Unfortunately, the odd human had to just disappear. Creativity was required to achieve this task. Without a decent feed every month, the corpses would seize up and desiccate—it was an ugly business. The positive in all of this was that each empty human provided a nice, fresh body for the ever-increasing population of feral human souls banging around in his realm. His face grimaced with revulsion at the thought of them.

Today though, with Belial—ever the guard dog—on hand, he could dispose of them all. He was rather impressed with the feisty girl decapitating that Rogue in the garden. He liked her. She'd make one hell of a Daimon if she could just keep her mouth shut. He'd sent Enl'iel and Brennan off on a wild goose chase just long enough for him to see this plan through. The mere suggestion that Sophia had run off into the forest, chased by Rogues, had them out of there without question. *Too stupid.*

That Kea, though, had been a problem. He'd forgotten how strong she was. He remembered her from so long ago. They had been friends once. Friends look out for one another. *Well, not always.* She'd managed to escape the deluge unharmed and fled elsewhere. *But what did she do to help her kindred?* She could have helped him, or at least called for help from others. They couldn't have fought the Archangels alone, but they could have at least healed as many of their own as they could and saved them from being washed away. His eyes squinted with hatred at the thought of her betrayal.

Ben was a handy character to have around—threatening him was key to his success. Keeping him nearby, but in constant danger left Sophia open to manipulation. She would never let anything happen to him. She had a deep friendship with him, and perhaps a hint of something more. It was a weakness worth exploiting. His heart quickened at the thought of such an advantage. The humans' overwhelming need to preserve life and love would ultimately be their undoing, and it was a convenient weapon to use against them.

Nik'ael watched in hiding as Belial talked the talk. He was not trustworthy, this one. He couldn't put his finger on it, but there was something about him that seemed off. Although—so far—he'd always done what he was told, successful or not.

The time was getting close. His mission had nearly come to the point where he needed it to be. The answers would soon be in his hands. *Hopefully.*

He looked at her as Belial held her aloft. A small, distant pull inside him made him falter. She wasn't ready. She was too weak. He—*no, she needed more time.* For the briefest moment, he wanted to smack Belial to the ground and rip him to pieces for touching her. *No one should touch her. She was so innocent. She was his.* He shook his head, clenching his fists into tight, painful balls of rage.

Sophia was *essential.* That was what he was supposed to think.

Chapter
Twenty-One

As I hung over the ever-widening abyss, I could hear someone screaming at me to hang on. My arm felt like it was about to wrench out of the socket, so I listened for that voice to divert my mind from the pain. I clamped my eyes shut, as I didn't want to see what was going to happen to me. The voice was getting louder in my head.

"Don't go, Sophia. Don't let him take you. I'm coming for you." It sounded familiar, like Kea's soft, melodic voice.

I opened my eyes just a crack. Esme's grotesque form was still at the end of the arm holding me up in the air. She grinned at me in a sickening way. "Pretty thing, aren't you? Such a shame." This was followed by a low, rumbling laugh.

Whilst my eyes were squinting open, I saw a flash of light and felt a blast of energy sizzle through the room behind Esme. A thud came from behind a wall. She turned, dangling me like a ragdoll. Her movements were jerky and unnatural, like a puppeteer working a marionette.

"Make a move, and I'll just crush her now. Then we'll all be exiled for eternity." The hate in this voice was palpable.

It was in fact Kea standing there in a defensive stance. Wings wide and bright, she was an incredible, ethereal sight. She scanned the room in a nanosecond, taking in the entirety of the scene. Tears slid down my face as my eyes tried to apologise for the pain and terror that my mere existence had caused.

"Put her down, Belial. I can see it's you. You know you don't mean that. You want out like we all do. What have you done to that poor, old woman?" Her face was a picture of disbelief and sadness. "Your actions condemn you, yet I know you do this against your true nature. Why do you continue this rebellious routine? You know you're not really one of them. You are just their lap dog, less than nothing to them. Re-join us, and you can atone for what you've done. Do you forget your past so easily? This is not you, I know it." Kea begged of him.

That distraction was all that was necessary for what came next. From the corner of my eye, I saw a tall shadow emerge from the front bedroom. It had something long in its hand.

While this Belial creature was engaged with Kea, a crunch and squelch thudded near my legs. I looked down just as a huge axe head swiftly pierced through the middle of Esme's body, stopping millimetres from my legs. I was dropped, falling down toward the swirling mass beneath me, only to be scooped up in Kea's arms and swiftly pulled aside to safety as she flew with lightning speed. As she did so, she fired a blast at the thing holding Jaz. The impact sent it into a scattering cloud of ash. The grey matter fluttered to the floor and covered Jaz's still unconscious form.

Unceremoniously, in the middle of the living room, stood the seizing form of what was left of my beloved Esme. She looked down in surprise at the thick blade protruding through her stomach from behind. Ben stood to the side, pale with shock. He was splattered with dark spots of clotted blood across his swollen and battered face. He stumbled back, releasing the axe's handle, letting it drop heavily to the floor. He reached out for a handhold on the window frame and slid slowly down to the floor.

"You bastard human!" Esme screamed at Ben, as her body began to shake uncontrollably. Her mouth gaped wide and her head fell backwards as she collapsed to the floor. Whilst writhing around in spasms, thick black smoke poured from within her mouth, nose, and ears, converging into the figure of the creature from the hospital. He looked as impressive as he did there, but exponentially more deadly. He shook himself out as he stretched casually, cracking his knuckles suggestively towards Kea and Ben, as if teasing them for a fight.

"Something is not right here. This was not the plan," he said to no one in particular. "I'm being toyed with. You," he pointed directly at me and bellowed. "You will have your day before too long, young lady. The time is near. I see the change is already upon you. There is no escaping your fate, pretty one."

A frenzied gale had built up in the room from the frightening hole in the floor. The curtains were ripped from the windows, sailing like ghosts around the room. This Belial creature stepped towards the fiery abyss to escape, knowing he had been outmanoeuvred. All of his backup soldiers were now nothing but miniscule specks of dust, fluttering around in the air, chasing the curtains. I made a move to grab Esme's body. He snapped his head in my direction and viciously kicked her, sending her falling into oblivion, down through the swirl of fire and darkness.

"No!" I screamed out with an emotional agony that was almost unbearable. I dared to get closer to the hole, reaching into the cold flames, but Kea swiftly pulled me back to safety behind her. She held me tight and close, trying to soothe what was an inconsolable pain. I cried for my beautiful spirit-mother and slid out of Kea's grasp to the floor. All I could do was curl up in a ball like a baby. Tears flowed heavily from my burning eyes. I hid from the hellish scene in front of me, covering my eyes with bloody, shaking hands.

He laughed vindictively and spoke one last time. "See you soon, Soph'ael. I promise it won't be long. *Tick tock, tick tock.*" Through the gaps of my fingers, I saw him launch himself feet first into the hole. It swallowed him up and extinguished itself with an ear-piercing *crack*, leaving nothing but a scorch mark on the floorboards.

Popping sounds and heat filled the room within seconds of this, and I knew without looking that Enl'iel and Brennan had returned. In the muffled background of my sobs, I heard Kea explain what had happened. I felt them draw nearer to me.

"Sophia, are you all right, dear?"

I ignored Enl'iel.

"Soph, it's me. You weren't meant to see any of that. I'm so sorry, princess." Brennan rubbed my back gently. I shook it off brusquely.

I couldn't look at them—any of them. I couldn't even move. How much pain could one heart take? Every beat sent emotional and physical agony through to my very core. Every atom ached with loss. I could just lay there forever and let myself drown in the exhaustive grief. After a while of hearing their frantic murmurings though, I knew I wasn't alone. I had more that could be taken from me—more love, more happiness, more lives. Curled up in a foetal position, I resolved to not lose another person that I loved. The fingers that were cocooning my face became rigid with anger. I let them slowly curl into tight, burning fists.

I lay there for a while longer, allowing the ball of fire that was building in my gut to grow. Where sadness had enveloped me, a new strength began to rise. I calmed my breathing to a slow and deep rhythm, letting this feeling unfurl its tendrils and spread. I rose onto my hands and knees, barely aware of someone calling my name. With my head bowed to the floor and eyes shut, I ceased to resist. I no longer bit back against the turmoil. I relaxed with a deep, calming breath. *Deep breath in, deep breath out, repeat.*

"Don't be scared my sweet girl, I'm here, you are safe," I could feel Enl'iel's presence, her soothing energy, yet my body screamed from within.

"I -, help-, please-," I couldn't catch a breath as Enl'iel called out.

"Kea, call for Koi, we will need him as soon as he can get here." I thought I heard Ben call my name. Enl'iel reminded me with that she was right by my side, but Brennan's alarming comment was the clearest in my mind.

"She's Quickening—give her some space. It's okay, Soph, let it happen. Let go. You'll be okay, I promise." His voice seemed distant, yet comforting.

I drew my breath in again, impossibly deep. I opened my eyes wide and without warning let out a primal scream. Light seemed to pour out of my mouth, illuminating the room. The force thrust me back on my heels, my arms flung wide. My scream seemed to go on forever. I felt a connection to something in the air surrounding me, like plugging myself into a socket. Something crackled across my skin. A million energies passed through me. Countless ghostly faces came in flashes. They were strangers, and yet they were also somehow familiar. And then I saw *Him*. His eyes were a swirling galaxy of every colour, and they looked deep into mine. An indescribable beauty, yet not of flesh, but of love. I knew Him, and He knew me. I tried to call out His name, to beg for help but I was mute, and He was gone.

The pain took over. I screamed like a trapped animal as my entire body lit up seemingly from within. Acid poured through every artery and vein. My spine cracked and crunched as it changed and contorted into a new design. My will to resist this change was long since dead, my understanding of normality no longer in my repertoire. My chest heaved forward as an immense thrust of energy burst from within. It was like electrocution in reverse. I was sending out the impulses. Each beat of my heart thundered in my head. Heat poured from my spine as a bright light enveloped me, forcing me to fall forward to the floor again—spent. The thud of my weight on the boards seemed to echo. I looked down at my arms; the bloody scratches flickered on my skin. I forced myself to sit back up and watch my hands so I could see the miracle. I gazed at them, looking for answers. Pulsing veins glowed and dulled rapidly across my palms in tune with my heartbeat. Each thrum lit up the vessels so that they shone through my skin, like rivers of white light. My limbs were heavy. These strange hands shimmered in and out of focus as I noticed the drying blood that crusted in the grooves was glowing iridescently. Specks of light swirled within the crimson detritus. I bent my head to the side, squinting, trying to make sense of what I was seeing. Broken fingernails nails and torn skin healed before my eyes.

The pain was slowly dissipating, being replaced by something else. The skin on my back now tingled in a more pleasant way, like having a warm blanket thrown across cool skin. My body started to feel light and weightless. My head was no longer aching, and the sting seemed gone from my eyes. A new sensation dawned upon me, and it felt like I now had an extra set of arms. I could feel myself waving these things, but they weren't exactly arms. I wanted to move them, but they felt stiff, as though they'd not been used for a long time. I waved them about. My entire body shifted along the floor. Surprised, I moved them harder. I travelled further along the floor. I had no idea what I was doing or why, but I knew in my bones that I needed to do this. I put as much effort into the movement as I could muster. Suddenly, I noticed that my legs were no longer dragging along the ground. I looked down at my feet as I felt myself rise up into the air.

I was hovering above the floor. I could feel the light pulsing behind me in tune with my heartbeat, keeping me steady and aloft. My new arms were wings of light that I seemed to have control of. I could make them move back and forth at will. I realised in that moment that I felt right, and that before this, I had actually never been normal, in a very surreal sense of the definition. All the pain was replaced by warmth and strength. My body was telling me who and what I was.

On that day I was reborn.

Chapter
Twenty-Two

Five faces looked up at me from below. Three wore smiles of joy, and two were visions of dumbstruck shock. Suddenly self-conscious, I faltered, and like a toddler losing her balance, I tumbled to the ground with an ungraceful *thud*.

"Take Ben and Jasmine to the Library. They are no longer safe here," Enl'iel spoke with urgency as both she and Brennan rushed to my side.

"Done," responded Kea. "All right, guys, come with me. You need to hang with us for a while," she reached for Jaz and Ben.

From behind the protective arms of Brennan and Enl'iel, I saw Jaz speechless for the first time ever. Her bloodied face was a picture of disbelief. Ben was staring at me with incredulity. His emerald eyes burned more intensely than ever, despite the growing swellings on his face.

They both wordlessly followed Kea out towards the back door of our destroyed home, casting a few wary glances back at me as they went.

I then was helped up to my feet by Enl'iel. "How are you feeling?" she asked quietly as she placed a kiss upon my still fiery cheek.

"Um," I had to think about the answer for a moment. I inspected my trembling hands, arms, and legs—*all normal and present*. Everything seemed intact. I hesitantly patted myself down, feeling for something, anything, out of place. The wing things seemed gone. *Was that my imagination?* The light had also disappeared. Everything was checked off my *'not about to imminently die list.'* Nothing seemed damaged, but there *was* something deep inside of me that felt very different. "I'm completely exhausted and freaked out. What's crazy though is that I seem to feel okay." My voice was jittery as tears threatened to emerge again.

"Perfect. That is how you should feel. No more pain. You are exactly how you were always meant to be," she soothed.

"*What happened to me? Exactly what am I?*" a whisper of a voice escaped my lips. I already knew the answer, but I needed to hear it spoken out loud.

I looked to Enl'iel, but Brennan responded instead. "You are bigger and better than both of us, Soph. You've just been through one hell of a metamorphosis. You've just transformed into a High Angel of the Kingdom of A'vean. You're the living proof of Enoch's prophecy. This makes you incredibly unique and ridiculously powerful. I'm slightly jealous actually."

That familiar wink tugged a whisper of a smile out of me, despite everything.

"We were interrupted in the middle of trying to tell you this. You were always going to go through this change on your twenty-first birthday. However, you have been in the presence of increasing and imminent danger as of late. It appears Cael has most definitely sent you into a Quickening to bring you to maturity more rapidly, for your own safety. Right now, though, we are going to get us *all* to safety. We have plenty of time to discuss specifics. Hold on, dear, we are going to take a different route back underground," Enl'iel said cryptically.

I was too mentally tired to ask any more questions.

In my exhausted silence, they both encircled me. Brennan let his own wings emerge to envelop us. They both touched a hand to their faces, which lit up like New York City at Christmas time. Before my sight had time to register much more, I felt myself get sucked backwards.

I felt no sense of being present in my body as darkness and air whipped past me. I could see only pinpricks of light at first. Then they became bigger, brighter, and denser, as though I was thrown into deep space, rolling through the Milky Way. I was neither warm nor cold. I sensed the presence of Brennan and Enl'iel nearby, but couldn't communicate with them.

I felt like I was moving fast, yet everything around me seemed to move slowly. The world was paradoxical in this dimension. The sensation of falling overwhelmed me, and it took a few moments before I realised that my feet had safely planted themselves back onto solid ground. Two warm bodies stood on either side of me, holding me up.

I opened my eyes as they both stepped back. They kept hold of my hands to keep me upright until my balance kicked in. We were back underground. The Keepers buzzed frantically around me, and it felt as though they were checking me out to make sure that I was okay.

I was about to speak, when Enl'iel chided me first. "What part of '*stay here*' did you not understand, Sophia?"

I was being reprimanded?

"I specifically asked you to stay here! Do you realise why now? You could have not only got yourself but others killed! You must listen to us, Sophia. You are a fish out of water, and you cannot possibly know how to protect yourself!"

"I'm sorry, but I heard Ben and Jaz screaming for me. I couldn't just hide down here and save my own skin while others were in trouble."

She stood back, glaring at me, but not with anger. She regarded me seriously, shaking her head slightly. A look of deep concern and possibly regret flickered across her features.

"Your compassion will be your undoing, young lady," she predicted ominously.

"Enl'iel—" Brennan tried to intervene, but she put up a hand to silence him.

"Saving your own skin is *exactly* what you need to do. That was Daimon trickery. You were fooled by a Daimon, and a strong one, too. You have grown up human, which means you have yet to be taught the nuances of detecting Daimon interference. Even I can be fooled, and I'm very skilled in this subject. It must have been mimicking their voices to lure you out. Clearly, this Daimon is familiar with your weakness for helping others. It means you've had one watching you for some time now." She acknowledged this with a look of concern in Brennan's direction. An immediate feeling of violation rolled through me—*I was being stalked*. I hugged my arms around myself in an attempt to soothe a new wave of fear and anger. I knew something had been outside *Miss Marple's* the other day. *Was that it?*

"Now," interrupted a new voice, along with the sound of clapping hands. "Where is this student of mine, and what kind of mess do I have to fix up?"

My eyes were immediately drawn to a huge, muscular man descending one of the ornate metal staircases. His chest was heavy with silvery scars as it flashed from within a loose, white karate-style Gi. He exuded power and intelligence.

Large, olive-toned hands clasped firmly around mine. More silver imperfections flashed across his knuckles. He drew my hands to his lips and placed a light, warming kiss upon each one. I flushed scarlet. His face was a perfect balance of Asian beauty. Behind a swirling white mark like my own on his cheek , intoxicating blue eyes sparkled at me, while thick, cropped white hair set him apart. He stood back and bowed before me.

"It is a supreme honour to meet you. I am Koi, your kindred and your teacher." He had the slightest hint of a foreign accent, but I couldn't place its exact origin. Perhaps it was a mix of a few influences.

Both Enl'iel and Brennan leaned forward, and each pressed their right cheek gently upon Koi's in greeting. A slight glow passed between them.

"Good to see you, Koi. Kea was quick to get in touch with you." Enl'iel hugged him warmly.

"I was already here, waiting. This one called me." He pointed to me.

I wordlessly gestured my surprise.

"You called me through the Zythros Stone, didn't you?"

Again, I was a face of confusion.

"Did you touch that stone over there?" Enl'iel pointed to the huge central pedestal.

Instantly feeling like a kid caught sneaking into something I shouldn't have, I meekly nodded. "Sorry, I couldn't help it. I felt drawn to it."

Koi laughed heartily. "You are an innocent, aren't you? I heard your thoughts when you touched it, and I knew that if you were down here, then it was time for me to come."

I must have looked as confused and exhausted as I felt, because Enl'iel responded with, "Let's get you some food and rest. Too much to take in for one day. That transference has sapped your last bit of strength. I'm sorry to put you through that before you were physically ready, but it was a matter of urgency, I'm afraid." With those words, I realised just how tired and starving I really was. My stomach growled instantly at the thought of food. *I hadn't eaten since yesterday.*

"I have something prepared for you," Koi spoke up as though reading my thoughts. "Follow me."

We entered a tunnel on the east side and as we walked, the same crystalline lighting instantly illuminated the passage. It was as though the Earth and rocks intrinsically responded to our presence. I noticed many rooms along the tunnel, each with a white wooden door.

We came to a stop in front of one of these doors, and Koi opened it for me. I entered a small room, decorated as a cosy bedroom. A small camp-style cot was off to one side, a knitted throw neatly tucked over it. Nan—*Enl'iel*—had been expecting me for some time, by the look of it. Despite myself, I giggled. Nervous energy poured from me.

"What is it?" she asked.

I pointed to the throw. She could get a little defensive about her hobby. "Well, I've had a lot of years to keep myself occupied, young lady!" She pretended to look offended.

"It's lovely—it's a piece of normal in a whole lot of crazy." I gave her a hug, one that I think she needed as she squeezed back tight and let it linger.

"This will all make sense soon, Sophia. Right now, we are in emergency mode, and unfortunately, a lot of your questions will need to wait until we have you safe. Please trust in me?" Her eyes were moist as she spoke these soft words.

I simply responded with another hug.

Turning back from her, I noticed a small table, a water decanter, and what looked like a shower cubicle. On the table was a steaming bowl of something, which had my mouth instantly watering.

"It's my very own Miso soup. Packed full of vegetables, just for you. I hope you enjoy it." Koi gestured with a bow and an outstretched arm for me to take a seat on the bed.

I almost ran to the table. The hot, sweet, and savoury liquid was incredible. My senses seemed heightened, as each vegetable and spice punched at my taste buds. I groaned with pleasure as I practically inhaled it.

The three of them talked amongst themselves while I devoured the meal. It was finished off with some sweet coconut rice. I sat back, exhaustion was an anaesthetic swirling through my veins. My head seemed to be encased in a ball of cotton, as everything sounded distant and muffled.

"I think I need to sleep." I leaned back on the pillow, suddenly lightheaded, with visions of the day's events crowding my mind for attention. *It was all too much*. I heard my intoxicated voice say a few goodnights as I helped myself into the comfy cot. I didn't notice them leave, just someone tucking me in and placing a kiss on my head.

Chapter
Twenty-Three

I jolted awake. A dreamless sleep had finally allowed my body to get some decent rest. Before I opened my eyes though, I could feel the presence of someone nearby. I detected the scent of spice and ash that was all too familiar. I rolled my head towards the sound of deep, controlled breathing and slowly blinked my eyes open. Ben was sitting there, hunched over on a chair, his face in his hands.

"Ben?"

He looked up, distress washing through his pained expression. His battered face was a sorry reminder of what he'd been through, and all because he was associated with me. I felt the sharp bite of guilt gnaw at me.

"Oh Ben, look at your poor face." My voice caught as I reached out to touch the wounds, but he flinched sharply back. I felt a momentary hurt.

"I'm okay, Soph." His voice was thin and haunted and guarded. "What about you? Are you all right?"

What should I say? *Hey I'm fine, and by the way, apparently I'm an Angel and I'm here to save the world or something!* Awkward, surreal and embarrassed were all fair descriptions of my feelings right then. I leaned up on my elbow, pulling the bed covers with me for support as I was grasping for what to say.

Finally, I spoke with a measured, tentative tone. "Well, I think I'm okay. Physically, that is. I don't think I can string the right words together to describe what's going on in my head right now, though. What happened yesterday, what I saw, and what I did—" I let that last thought trail off into nothing. I couldn't look him in the face. I felt so uncomfortable. Picking at my fingernails was suddenly a very interesting distraction.

"You mean when you flew in the air and shot lightning bolts from your body?" he finished for me, his tone strange. Our eyes couldn't meet for more than a quick glance. He focused on the floor and worked at a thread sticking out of his jeans. I examined every fingernail thoroughly. The edge to his voice and demeanour made me feel as though I'd offended him somehow.

"Well—yeah." I was stumped as to what I could really say, so I sat up and forced myself to look at him. He looked up too. He looked familiar, my friend who I adored, yet he felt very much a stranger. My back and head began aching again, and nausea nagged at me with a sudden viciousness. I swallowed it down as I grabbed his hand.

"You saved my life yesterday." I put my other hand on top and gripped firmer, as though I needed him to know I didn't want to let go, to lose him, that I was still me.

He remained silent as our hands warmed in each other's. He quietly regarded me, unblinking. His eyes darted across every inch of my face with what seemed to be conflict.

"You stopped that—*thing* from taking me. Thank you," I said as I recalled that the creature used to be Esme. I choked back a quiet gasp of grief at the thought.

"I murdered. For *you*," his voice trailed off as he pushed my hands away. He looked away again for a moment, then back to me and said with a surprising conviction, "I'd do it again—for you."

"Oh Ben!" My lips quivered. *What have I done?* I looked at him with love and fear and confusion as he sat hunched over again, running his hands roughly through his hair.

"I'm sorry. I'm so sorry that you and Jaz have been dragged into this madness, whatever it is. I'm sorry you've been forced to do such a horrible thing. And look at you," I tried to reach for him again, but he pushed my hand back. "You're injured because of me. If I could've protected you both from it, I would have. It's all just so ridiculous and surreal. I'm pinching myself every other second to see if I'm actually awake. I had no idea about any of this. I wouldn't believe it myself, if not for the fact that I'm living it. I can't even begin to explain any of it to you—I barely know what's going on myself. I was happy just being me. This is all happening to me—I'm not choosing to do it. I promise I'll do whatever it takes to make things right, and to keep you safe." I looked to him for reassurance, but found none.

He remained stony faced, looking at me again as though he was trying to peel back the layers of me to find an alternate truth. It was unnerving. It was so un-Ben.

I broke the tension by diverting the focus from me. "Is Jaz okay? Where is she?"

"She's fine. Still sleeping it all off," he answered. My relief at hearing this was overshadowed by his curt tone. He was so confusing. He looked at me with an intensity that appeared to be a war of love and disdain. His voice was cool and distant. He was hurting, and I was the reason.

Ignoring the coldness, I focused on him again, not myself. "And you? Look at your face! You must be in so much pain. Your face is so swollen!" This time when I reached out, he let me touch him. I sat up straight on the edge of the bed to get a closer look at his injuries. He was badly bruised over his cheekbones, with one of his eyes swollen half-shut. The bruising was an angry shade of deep purple. Our faces were mere inches apart now. I could feel his breath on my skin. It sent chills through me. Those emerald eyes were too intense to bear.

My fingers gently traced the edges of the bruising along his cheek and jaw. He didn't resist this time. His bottom lip was swollen as well and split in the middle. Dried blood crusted around the wound. I lightly grazed my thumb across it, and as I did, we both drew in a breath at the same time, and our eyes met. I felt so immensely drawn towards him in that very moment. I pulled my hand back, but he grabbed it back and placed my palm flat against his cheek. He leaned into it and closed his eyes, pressing his hand over mine. He took in a slow, deep breath, as though he was savouring this moment. I felt faint from the rush of my pulse. Electric zaps ripped up and down my arm from the point where our skin was in contact. We sat in silence like this for a few all too short seconds. He was the one to break the moment as he sat back and took his hand from mine. He looked down again.

I placed my left hand on his other cheek and whispered, "*Please, let me heal you.*" I didn't bother trying to explain what I meant by that.

There was turmoil again in his eyes as he looked up. He quietly nodded with the smallest inclination of his head, not questioning my request. I was surprised that he acquiesced, as he didn't know what I was capable of. I'd never revealed my healing craft to him before.

"Okay. Take a deep breath in and let it out slowly. Let yourself relax. I won't hurt you, I promise." He did as I said. Those pained eyes didn't leave mine.

I pushed his ebony hair out of the way and spread my fingers gently across his skin. My stomach lurched again. *Deep breath in, deep breath out, repeat.* I concentrated on the negative energy flowing through him. It was full and abundant, as though his injuries were more than skin deep. His skin was soft and warm and the connection sent a thrill through me. *I don't want to let you go.* His pulse quickened, in sync with mine. Suddenly extremely self-conscious, I looked away for a moment at the floating orb in the corner by the door and took in another deep, calming breath. *I can do this.* The jelly-like feeling in my stomach was easing. The strangeness of his proximity was highly distracting, however.

I turned back to him with determination. I pulled at this strong negative field within the cuts, scrapes, and swelling, drawing it out. I pulled it towards myself. The nausea in me lurched again, and I felt as though I might be sick. I had to swallow calmly through yet another slow breath and put it out of my mind. It wasn't easy—there was deep suffering within this boy. Surprise and guilt swam through me. I should have known that he was hurting. He was my lifelong my friend.

With a renewed vigour and compassion, I ignored all that my body was throwing at me. My fingertips tingled sharply as the attraction of the positive and negative energies collided between us. I could feel him tense up as the veins in my arms began to glow. I glanced at him as I repositioned my hands. His breaths were coming short and sharp through flared nostrils. I felt nervous and under pressure from his heavy, nervous stare. Heat emanated from my right temple. The current of power surging from me cast a glow of white against his face, giving him an ethereal radiance.

The negative current sucked into my hands and was replaced by the warmth of the positive infusing from me back through his skin. He drew a surprised breath in and groaned as he felt it surge into his flesh, his head fell back with the effect. As the last of the heat left my fingertips, I bowed my head in exhaustion as the glow in them dulled and the transfer ebbed from a burn to a tingle, then dissipated into nothing. I felt overwhelmed physically from this healing. It wasn't unusual to feel tired after a healing session, yet this time it was much more intense. As I raised my head, I found him still staring intently at me, the green of his eyes had deepened with unshed tears. He gently prodded at his face.

Ben's face had reformed to his previous visage and smoothed out—he was healed. *He was perfect.* His skin was once more unmarred and perfectly Ben, right down to the scar along his jaw. I wiped away a warm tear that had trickled down his cheek, his bottom lip trembling slightly. I could see his jaw tense and clench as he fought the emotion that was still torturing him. He reached up with one hand and shocked me as he traced the lines of my birthmark. His breathing was increasingly unsteady, and mine stopped altogether. As his fingertips lightly glided along the swirling lines, the act felt as intimate as any touch could. His skin barely grazed mine, yet it sent lurching rolls of emotion through me. If his gaze were any heavier, I felt that my heart might cease to beat. I couldn't tell or didn't want to know if it was fear, confusion, or something more.

He withdrew his hand suddenly and with such a speed that it was as though he'd been stung. He then grabbed both of my wrists with a firm but gentle grasp, never once taking his eyes from mine. I thought he was going to say something. He opened his mouth a number of times, but then thought better of it. This exchange seemed to hang in the air, ridiculously uncomfortable. He sighed deeply as he laid my hands back on my lap. He stood up, tall and broad. The corded muscles of his arms were tight, veins twirling along them like rivers as he clenched his fists compulsively. Ben looked down at me, his expression dark.

"Why couldn't you just be normal?" He left the room without another word.

I felt like a gutted fish.

Chapter
Twenty-Four

It tortured Nik'ael to see her like that with Ben. She loved Ben. He could feel it, even if Sophia couldn't acknowledge it. Ben loved her too, and had done so for many years, but he was weak and stupid, destined for a bad end. That stupid boy had suffered through the solitude of unrequited passion for years. Nik'ael watched in the shadows as Ben kept a platonic distance deliberately to hide his true feelings.

Finally, ever so patient, Nik'ael had been the one to penetrate into one of their hidden sanctuaries. The pleasure he received from his victory was overshadowed however by the complexity of emotion rolling through his dark heart and mind. He was once a peacemaker, a protector, and a lover. But for thousands of years he was a hater, vengeful, and at times, cruel. Now, at just the point where he was near the culmination of his mission, he was plagued by doubt. His energy rhythm was out of sync. Hiding in these tunnels was not helping things, either. He could feel the effects of the repellents they used to protect this place sapping at his strength. The chromious-lined ceiling was like an osmotic force, sucking the life from him. Sneaking around in the darkness, watching her, was becoming insufferable already.

Knocking Ben around had been a great release of his frustration. Feeling his power inflict damage across Ben's body was healing for him, in a way. His thoughts had been realigned, and his vigour renewed. But now, she'd healed him. Despite her own pain, she had put Ben before herself as she had always done. Her compassion and strength, her self-deprecation, gnawed at the distant him—the one that would have scooped her up in his arms and taken her away, protected her, loved her.

He screamed silently in his mind as he smashed his fist into the rock wall. He felt the bones break. The pain was a balm, not a burden.

He clasped his head in his good hand. *Why was he doubting everything? Why now?* Yesterday, he had been on a high as he lorded over the destruction at her house. He hated her—he *had* to hate her. It was his mission to hate her. Yet at every instance, her every selfless move tugged at him mercilessly.

Finally, he bolstered himself up. He had to get out for a while. He must stay away as much as possible and manage this from afar. He needed his vengeance, not just for himself, but for Neren'iel. The guilt swirled like a storm through him again as he touched his bracelet. She would never forgive him. He knew it. But he had to do it anyway.

Blood trickled down his wrist, and he wiped it carelessly away on his pants. The explosive pain was now an annoyance. He ran his other hand across the broken one and winced as he heard and felt the bones knit back together. He left one small bone unhealed. One piece of him would remain broken, so that the pain of each movement would remind him of the pain he and his loved ones had suffered. It would keep him on track. *Focused.* At least that's what he told himself. He could take his leave for a while to think. He would be back soon. The proximity of her was just too much. He blinked out without taking the chance to hesitate.

Chapter
Twenty-Five

Grief engulfed me as I sat there with my hands gripping tightly around the edges of the cot. I felt like I'd just lost something that I didn't realise I'd had. Tears blurred the wall I was staring at. Utter misery had swept through me since Ben had sideswiped me with that parting insult. I didn't understand his apparent anger towards me. I could accept shock and fear at what had occurred over the past twenty-four hours, but this angry Ben was not what I would have expected at all. He was usually the first to jump to my defence, to protect me. It didn't make sense. Perhaps he felt he needed protecting from me?

The light of the floating orb brightened the underground room more intensely at that moment, as though trying to catch my attention. Its surreal presence distracted me from my thoughts long enough to force my attention to the room around me. As I ran a hand through my hair, I looked around the little space, noticing a bowl of fruit and a booklet on the table by the bed with a neatly handwritten note.

Sophia,

When you wake, feel free to use the shower. It is a naturally warm thermal spring, enjoy. I have left you a change of clothes on the chair, and there is a backpack of belongings for you. I will be in shortly to collect you.

XOXO Enl'iel

The booklet was a passport. I opened the small blue document to find my photo and details inside. I'd never had a passport. Who knows how she got this one. Clearly we were going overseas, but to where? Were they even going to ask me if I wanted to leave? Who knew what was coming next, anything was possible. The impossible was, in fact, happening. Despite still feeling raw about Ben, I knew that my assaulted frame would drink in a shower. I found some toiletries, along with black cargo pants, a white t-shirt, and a black zip-up hoodie.

The shower cubicle was merely the rock walls and stone floor with a drain fashioned below them. I pushed the silver flip faucet sideways, and steaming water immediately flowed from overhead. Earthy, mineral smells punctuated the air. The temperature was perfect. I stood there, leaning against the natural rock cubicle under the hot stream, and relaxed.

Too much, too soon. That's all that I could think. My emotions were fighting against the tidal wave of change engulfing me so quickly that I could not catch a breath. I quelled the panic attack with some calming breaths and focused on scrubbing my hair squeaky clean. I had a million thoughts racing through my mind, it was hard to focus on one long enough to find an answer or logic to any of them.

What was to become of me from here? Was I going to die? Could I even die? Is everything I've ever known completely wrong? Is there a Heaven? What happens when people die if there's no entry to Heaven? Who were my parents? Where are they?

I shook my head with utter confusion and put my entire face under the steaming spray in an attempt to wash away the conflict. I massaged my temples and sighed out loud to myself, "God, help me—or whoever you are."

The warm water felt strange as it flowed down my back. I reached around and prodded at my re-designed spine. Knobbly prominences protruded out from under my skin, along the sides of my back. I could just feel the soft leaflets of skin that surrounded them. It was bizarre. It was like I was touching a stranger, yet feeling the sensation myself. I wasn't sure I could come to terms yet with this within the period of a day. My physical appearance had changed so dramatically. Like a science fiction movie, I had morphed somehow from Sophia Woodville, average twenty-year old girl with poor eyesight and a fear of spiders, to a lightning-throwing, flying being, with swirly blue eyes that could track an ant from outer space. It was all too unbelievable, but there it was.

After dressing and finding a rather handsome pair of Doc Martins to wear, I looked for a mirror to brush my hair. There wasn't one, but there was a brush and a hair clip near the passport. After I was done putting my hair up, I glanced down at myself. I looked about ready for boot camp. It was a mirror image of what Enl'iel had been wearing after she morphed out of dear old

Nan. The image of that still messed with my sense of reality.

As though she knew she was in my thoughts, there was a light knock at the door as Enl'iel entered.

"Good morning, Sophia. Did you sleep well?"

"Yes, thanks. I slept just fine," I answered, kind of blandly.

She sat on the cot and gestured for me to do the same. She picked up the brush and asked, "May I brush your hair?"

"If you'd like." I offered her the brush as I pulled the clip back out of my hair. As a child, she brushed my hair every night. A perfect hundred strokes before I went to sleep.

She began to speak as she brushed.

"This is an impossibly difficult situation, Sophia. What should have been a gradual and controlled unveiling of information and disclosure to you has been forced into an avalanche of chaos. I am so sorry that you have been assaulted, frightened and shocked by all that has come to pass over the past few days."

I quietly let her continue, not disagreeing with her assessment.

"Upon your twenty-first birthday, on December 31st, you would have entered this change naturally and I was just recently preparing to reveal it all to you. Unfortunately it has been thrust all too forcefully upon you and all of us. I would have informed you and eased you into the truth of your heritage more softly. You would have been trained carefully, over time. Now that option has been taken from us by those who wish to destroy, rather than work with us. The coming days and weeks are going to be confronting and challenging for you, dear, but I am and have always been your guide and protector. I will be with you, among others, to teach you and prepare you for what is to come."

"What exactly is it? What is to come? I've heard about opening up A'vean so everyone can return. What does it all mean, and why does it have to be me?"

"As I have begun to explain previously, Enoch received instructions from our prime creator, I'el, about how the gateway to A'vean could be reopened to those who had lost favour. Those fallen ones being your ancestors who were the protectors of humans. Do you recall this?"

"Yes, the fall of the Angels."

"Well, as the story was handed down through the generations, it was prophesied that at an undetermined time, there would be the birth of a descendant of A'vean on Earth that matched the level of purity in which such beings were first created. It would be then that the Gates of A'vean could be re-opened by that pure Angel alone. We were told that the prophecies, as handed down by Enoch through his hidden writings, are meant to provide the clues to what this person must do to achieve this goal. The clues will lead them to the gates on Earth—and eventually open them—so that those who wish to reunite with their homeland may do so. All of the human souls of measurable worth may also be released from the limbo of the middle realm and return to their origin."

"So, I have to go find some old books or something?"

"You must find and follow the writings of Enoch, which have been preserved for you and you alone to decipher."

"If you know that there are answers written somewhere, why hasn't someone read them before now?"

"It is said that only the Earth-born Angel's eyes may read the sacred words. No other could comprehend them. They contain our ancient language that is buried deep within you. None of the exiled can read these words, so there was no point in us trying to do that which we are incapable of. It is the punishment handed down from I'el. The answers have been here all along, scattered in secret places around the Earth. However, if the wrong person were to find them, the risk is that not only will they be unintelligible, the rumour is that the writings will all crumble to dust. So, my dear, you are absolutely irreplaceable."

"How will I know if I can do this? That I'm the right person? I'm just— me!"

"The knowledge to understand what has been set forth is within you, that I have no doubt of. You shall not be alone, but you alone must be the one to read the secret scrolls and activate the gate through the purity of your blood."

I reeled back at this and jumped up from the bed, backing up to the wall.

"What do you mean?" My heart was racing with fear. *What was I now, a sacrificial lamb?*

"What are you going to do to me?" I panicked and gripped at the wall behind me.

"Oh, no! No, no! Oh, I'm sorry, I've frightened you." She got up to walk to me, her hands held up in defence.

I put my own hand up and screamed, "Stay away from me!"

She backed off immediately. Her eyes were pleading. "Oh Sophia, I've chosen my words poorly. What I should have said was that a token of blood is required to unseal the scrolls of prophecy. A drop, my dear, sweet girl—just a drop. You will not be hurt. I'm sorry I frightened you. We would never allow you to be hurt. Indeed it is the Daimon that have got it all wrong. This is why they hunt you. They got wind of snippets of information, thousands of years ago, from Watchers who were lured by them to the dark ways. They have wrongly believed that the Earth-born is meant to be sacrificed in order to open the doorway, despite us trying to convince them otherwise. They have long forgotten that I'el sees no glory in sacrifice, especially in his name. Unfortunately, over time, they have in fact attacked those they suspected of being the One, and indeed have stolen and murdered them all for nothing. The Daimon have a bloodlust that prevents them from accepting that it is but a drop of blood from a pinprick that is required. They have accused us of falsifying the truth to deter them."

She reached out to me again. I eased up a bit, and my panic began to wane.

"We have protected you since the day of your birth because we knew you were the One, and we have not let you out of our sight, for they have circled around you like vultures for twenty years. You have never been alone. Do you not remember when you were attacked in the city?"

"I will never forget it!" I snapped.

"I told you Cael saved you that night. He has mirrored your movements every time you have ever left the house, for your entire life."

I relaxed a little more now. "So, the Daimon want to kill me because they have the wrong information, but you will protect me because you know the truth? Either way, I need to be used for someone else's purpose!"

"Sophia, I know this is impossibly difficult. But yes, to be blunt, you are the salvation for those wanting redemption with their Creator, and also for mankind itself. You can reawaken Humanity to the truth and provide them peace through a knowledge that has been long lost to them. This is a huge responsibility. I know it is difficult, but you know deep down that you are capable of this. You have always known you were special. I know you have always wanted to be the girl in the middle of the back row, the one that doesn't get noticed. However, you have been aware of your healing gift for a long time, which tells me that you have also always known that you were actually the girl meant for centre stage."

"You may be right, but it doesn't mean I want it. I knew I was different. I know that's why you didn't let me go to school until I was old enough to colour my hair and wear contacts. I knew I was completely weird to look at with pale hair and eyes." Memories flooded back of me begging to go to school, but Nan telling me I had to wait, that the children wouldn't understand my appearance and would be unkind to me. I remember being basically blind until the age of seven. When I was eleven, she taught me to wear contacts. Once I could wear them comfortably, I was allowed out to go to school. It dawned on me then and there how abnormal my childhood had actually been. *Now I knew why*. I was a freak who had to be hidden from the world until I could be appropriately disguised.

Enl'iel was close by me now. I didn't flinch when she gently took my hand. The small swirls about her right eye glowed faintly. I felt a calming warmth flow through me. She was safe—I knew that in my heart.

"Enough for now, my dear. We have a lot to get through today. You are a strong girl, Sophia. You can rise up to this, and you will do so with all of your kindred behind you. Now, let us go and eat. Many people have gathered to meet you. We will talk some more later. Too much is crowding that head of yours already. Just know that you are safe and loved, and we will all protect you." I nodded as she gestured for me to come with her, out the white door.

I followed her through the glistening tunnel towards the light coming from the main cavern. I wondered which door Jaz and Ben were behind. *Had I lost them?* When I entered the main cavern, I was amazed to find that many people were now present there. I stood back in the archway, wary to walk through such a crowd. Some were milling around the green stone, while others were huddled in groups chatting, drinking from long flutes, or nibbling from large fruit platters. Energy flowed strongly through the room. The heightened electrical field was almost visible, as I could see small wisps of multi-coloured tendrils of light snap through the air like the Aurora Borealis. Some of the people were boldly flapping their light wings, like one would use hand gestures in conversation. Others were more subdued. I noticed that they all wore variations of white clothing that allowed their wings to move freely. I stepped into the room hesitantly, and as though a siren went off, they all immediately turned to face me. I nearly died of embarrassment. Women and men all glared at me with awed surprise, as though looking upon something mythical. They all had the same white hair and piercing blue eyes. What differentiated them was an impressive display of cultural backgrounds. All variations of skin tone and body type stood before me with the cohesive stare of those amazing eyes.

"Sophia!" called Koi as he rushed from behind the jade stone. He was the only familiar face I could see. I drew my eyes from a stunning woman with white dreadlocks that radiated against glistening mocha skin.

"You're up! This is excellent." He placed a comforting hand on my shoulder. "How are you feeling? I understand you must be most exhausted, physically and emotionally?" He looked at me questioningly with a genuine concern in his bright eyes.

I glanced back towards Enl'iel. She excused herself after saying to Koi, "Sophia has just received some deeper insight into her purpose."

"That's an understatement," I said.

"Oh, I see. That calls for some decent tea and breakfast. Come," He directed me beyond the humming stone to a small outcropping of rock, where a cloth had been draped with a Japanese tea setting and fruit platter awaiting us. He poured me a dark brew, dropping in a large lump of sugar. I didn't even need to ask—he sensed that I needed it. I sat and took the hot cup, drinking it thankfully. I munched on a few strawberries before I spoke, trying not to notice all the staring faces behind me.

"Are we travelling? I found a passport by the bed." Next I grabbed a peach and bit into the cool, sweet flesh.

"Yes, this afternoon you will fly to London. We are retreating to our main Sanctuary in Strensham to train you in safety, among other things, before we start our quest."

"Quest? Is this what Enl'iel was referring to?" I asked.

"Yes, Sophia, it is." He gently took my empty cup from me with a warm smile. "Come, let us talk."

We walked towards the south wall of the cavern where new murals awaited. A hundred eyes were focused on me. People parted the way, bowing politely as I passed. It made me very uncomfortable. *This is just me, guys—I'm lazy, I throw phones, and I live in a room that's a pigsty!* Well, I used to.

"Look up, tell me what you see," he said, ignoring the others as though they weren't there.

I looked up to the wall and bit hard on my lip as I sucked in a shocked breath. There must be a point at which the constant barrage of insults to reality would render me numb. I was wishing for this sooner rather than later. There, high upon the rock, were depictions that were clearly of me in the present. I could see my rainbow hair, glistening through the gemstones that inlaid the wall. I was up there, riding on my horse. I was there leaning over some ill person in a bed, laying my hands on them, healing them. I was there shielding my eyes from an outstretched hand with a picture of a concentric circle on the palm. I was standing over the horned Daimon as he retreated down a hole in the ground. A white aura surrounded my whole body in every picture.

Lastly, I could see myself floating in the air, surrounded by wings of light, reaching outward. It was confronting and frankly, I felt embarrassed, again. Dead bodies were laying at my feet in this image. They appeared to be gnarled and grisly, with leathered skin and claws for hands. I concluded they must be the bad guys. I held in one hand a cylinder, and in the other, a large disk. Behind me shone an iridescent, blue oval eye. I could only just stare more deeply at these pictures, which I'm pretty sure weren't there yesterday. It slowly dawned on me as I scanned the wall that in each picture, there was also a black shadow behind me.

"What is all this?" I asked as a little Keeper zoomed around me, tickling at my hair.

"This, Sophia, is a brief reflection of your life up to this point. Does it seem familiar?" He cocked an eyebrow in question.

"Yes, I see me in everything—and that there," I pointed to where I faced off the creature in my house, "that's what happened yesterday! How can that be?" Before he responded, I noticed the last picture of me again. My hair was pure white in it. Instantly, I reached around behind my neck. My hand held onto a thick lock of pure white, not a hint of pink or blue. "Oh my God!"

"Sophia, worry not. This is just an effect of the Awakening you went through. The power that courses through you and all of us whitens our hair. In time, you will learn the art of camouflage, if that is what you wish." He chuckled to himself. "You are the most powerful being in this world, and you are shocked by your hair!" He laughed warmly some more.

I looked at him questioningly. The hair colour was not the issue so much as it was more like a revelation to me. Seeing that on the wall, and then physically acknowledging the change in myself was shocking. Everything was shocking.

"Oh, I've offended you. Forgive me." He bowed, clasping my hands in his.

"No, it's fine. I know you were just joking. I'm sorry. I suppose jokes aren't really registering. So much is going on—it's just too much at once."

"Yes, it is, but you are not alone—that is why I am here. I will guide you, teach you our ways, and help you harness the power that lurks just under your skin. Once you can control that with ease, you will feel emotionally in control as well." He spoke so wisely, yet looked so young. The youthful appearances of all of these new people didn't gel at all with their intensity and apparent longevity.

"How did these murals appear? They weren't here yesterday." The Keeper buzzed more excitedly about me.

"Ah, that is a story of pure amazement. However, I shall save that story for another time. Now, let's finish our first meal and get you ready for the Unsealing."

"What's that?" I asked, curious.

"I shall defer that answer to the lovely Enl'iel." He bowed and stood back as Enl'iel returned with a plate of pastries. I took two without thought; my hunger was immense.

"Sit with me a while, Sophia. Share your first meal with me. Afterwards, you will start your journey, and ours. Today, you will unseal the Scroll Chamber."

Chapter
Twenty-Six

Yeqon smirked with grim satisfaction as he looked down upon the deeply slumbering young man. His captive's breathing was rhythmic and calm, Yeqon was in total control, just the way he liked it. The sounds of fire crackling in the blackened hearth interrupted an otherwise dead silence. The time was near for his coming of age. After this, he would be less a burden and more an asset. He had been stubborn to train. Defiance ran through him like a life force, yet he had grown into a powerful and obedient servant—in the end.

The fearsome male sat upon a stone bench near the head of the bed. He stretched out his long legs and crossed them at his ankles. Orange light from the hearth licked across his knee-high boots. He could not lean back comfortably, as his horns gouged into the wall behind him. He was seriously getting tired of these things. They were amusing centuries ago, especially for scaring the life out of religious zealots and the ignoramuses he had the misfortune of meeting. On the rare occasion that he chose to leave this realm these days, they sorely disappointed his vindictive nature. Modern man was too informed, and surprisingly now grew rather partial to a little Daimon worship. Toying with them was no fun when they believed you were just a great Halloween costume, or the living deity of their offbeat cult.

As he contemplated removing his horns, the door to the bedchamber creaked open, making the sleeping boy stir. Yeqon placed a large palm across the boy's brow, sending his brain back into the waves of a deep, delta sleep.

"Your Grace," said Nik'ael as he entered, bowing deeply.

"How goes your mission? Belial informs me that she has awakened." Yeqon looked Nik'ael up and down, surveying him for any signs of betrayal. Belial had bored him to death through a tirade of complaints about being uninformed about all of their plans. Nik'ael's plans, as it turned out. Belial was none too impressed with the events in the house on the mountain, thinking he'd failed again. Belial was an unwilling but powerful pawn who wanted to be a King. It made him wonder why Nik'ael worked around Belial and not with him on this occasion.

"It is proceeding well. She has indeed awakened, but she is weak and immensely ignorant," Nik'ael responded, fidgeting obsessively with his bracelet in a way that annoyed Yeqon. "I am pleased to inform you that I have finally penetrated one of their sanctuaries. I believe I am within the grasp of all that we need."

"Excellent, bring her to us immediately," commanded Yeqon, as he stood tall and foreboding. He rubbed his hands together with anticipation.

"Forgive me, but I believe it may be best to leave her with them a little longer. I do not believe she will be able to access the prophetic writings outside of their watch. She is green and nervous. She knows nothing of her heritage, and has no knowledge of what it is she would be looking for. They know many pieces of the puzzle already. She will learn from them what we do not know, and then we can take her, strong and knowledgeable, but sensitive to our persuasive ways. I know her, after all these years. I believe her energy will be too unstable if we were to force her to search under duress." He bowed and took a protective step backwards as he dared to speak this.

Yeqon stood taller, a menacing expression glimmering across his handsome face. His dark eyes glistened with intellect. "You presume to question my authority, boy? My understanding of the situation? How long have I dwelt among the worlds? I am of the first incarnation. I am spawn of the first six. *You*—you are a nothing, born from human garbage." He spat these words like venom. Nik'ael shrank back, cowering slightly. He revelled in biting hard at others. He swelled with power when others feared him.

"Please, Lord Yeqon, I mean no disrespect. I respect your great wisdom and longevity. Your lineage to I'el precedes you." He bowed more deeply again. "However, we have but one chance to use her. If we destroy her in our haste, we will be lost here eternally, with no key or knowledge or power upon which to use it. We have awaited this moment for so long. I humbly suggest that we let them use their energies to prepare her and build her up to her strongest potential. When we do take her, she will be malleable, knowledgeable, yet still breakable. We need her physically and intellectually strong, not emotionally." Another careful bow of submission.

Yeqon paced back and forth, kicking up dust as his eyes darted between the sleeping boy and Nik'ael. His patience was thin and his temper frail. The pressure from the others grew with every passing day. He did not want to seem weak. Yet, this loyal servant spoke some truth. If they were to accidently destroy her in their haste, that would mean certain annihilation for them all. All hope would be lost, and his driving force was nothing but vengeance. He would have it, and he would have it at any cost, even his pride.

Of all his kindred, Nik'ael was the only one ever able to get close enough to discovering the secrets of The Watchers and Eudaimonia. He was impressed and irked at the same time that a half-cast had done what he could not. Nik'ael was the first to detect the birth of The Earth-born, and his skills at camouflage were unsurpassed. He was able to get closer than any of them ever had without detection. Nik'ael's power was unheard of. His sire had been strong, his mother also of great lineage. Part Watcher and Eudaimonian of the first commission to Earth made him more powerful than even the boy himself understood. That was knowledge he would never share with Nik'ael, lest he think he was an equal of the Five. He knew though that he should at least consider his opinion.

"I will speak of this to my brothers. If they concur, then we shall wait. Until then stay as close as you can. By any means, discover the place of the scriptures—we need them as well as her. The very moment she is of sound condition, you shall personally deliver her to me, at my feet, where she shall bow to me and beg for her mortal life." He cast a glance back at the boy. "Much as he did," he said with a slight chuckle.

"As you wish. May I ask how the boy fares?" Nik'ael inquired.

"He does what he is told. That's is all that is required of him." Yeqon brushed off any further discussion about the slumbering boy by turning his back on Nik'ael and walking back to his seat. He picked up a flute roughly hewn from a leg bone and drank the draught within. He belched with satisfaction. Looking back at his kinsman standing by the door, he added. "Young one, you trouble me. There is conflict in your aura. Do you suffer a faltering in your loyalties?" He raised his eyebrows questioningly, daring Nik'ael to answer incorrectly.

"I am un-yielding in my loyalty. Have I not served you since the deluge with the utmost conviction? I betray only myself in that I am weary. I long to be rid of this wretched existence. I yearn to draw the force out of those who have cast us aside and murdered our families. Anger boils beneath my skin like an inferno." He bowed once more.

"Be gone then. Go chase down this wench. I am wearying too of this forsaken situation. Remove all obstacles, be they human or A'vean. Let blood run free and plentiful, like a raging river. All the more for the Rogues to feast upon." He let out a deep rumbling laugh.

"Get out!" He shot a blast of black smoke from his left hand that landed just short of Nik'ael's feet, making him jump backwards.

Yeqon was alone again in the room as the door creaked closed. The sound of sleep filled the silence, coming from the boy resting beside him.

"I will have pleasure killing you one day, boy. Great pleasure."

Chapter
Twenty-Seven

I waited with Enl'iel by the large stone that I now knew to be called the Zythros stone. Its name translated to *Whispering Stone*, and was like an angelic internet. All you had to do was place a hand on it, and you could communicate with any Watcher or Eudaimonian anywhere on the planet. She had done just that. She'd called on someone to come to the Library for this Unsealing ceremony.

"Today you will perform an ancient and long-awaited ritual. It cannot be done by anyone other than yourself, though again, you will not be alone. We will guide you. The first scripture of Enoch lies somewhere beneath our feet, long ago interred for safety by the Archangel Uriel. Just now, I have called upon His Grace, Gedz'iel. He is a benevolent Watcher who did not fall foul of I'el, but chose to stay among us to protect and guide those who were left behind after the great fall. He is widely admired for his compassion and sacrifice. For his great service, Enoch and Uriel took him into their council and shared enough with him that he may guide the Earth-born Angel on her quest whenever she should arrive." Panic was banging at the door again.

"I don't know if I can do this Nan, oh, sorry, Enl'iel. See, I can't even remember your name!" I face palmed with frustration.

"Hush, you are too harsh with yourself. Take a breath and relax, we are all here to help."

"But what if it's just not me? Can't this wait a couple of days so that I can get my head around what's happening?" Until two days ago, I was ordinary, average. I'd never even finished a crossword, let alone solved a puzzle that could determine the fate of a whole race. Self-doubt eroded my courage with each passing minute.

"Sophia, our hand is forced. We do not have the luxury of time to ease you into this. I'm sorry for that. You do, however, have the answers coursing through you. You have nothing to doubt. Draw strength from me, Sophia, as you can from us all. She soothed me with her familiar voice and soft eyes. Still, this was immense, and my faith in myself was not.

"I haven't seen Jaz yet, is she okay? I saw Ben this morning, but I haven't seen her? If I have to do this thing now, can she come with me at least?" I asked.

"They are both perfectly fine. However, they cannot be here for the Unsealing, as it leaves them open to subversion. The less they know and see, the better. They could be tortured or possessed to gain our secret knowledge, which would lead our enemies straight to us. Poor Jasmine has already suffered such a violation. They are comfortable and safe for now. You will see them at the airport when we leave for London." She seemed distracted as she spoke, and searched impatiently around the room for someone. I wondered if Jaz was as offended by what I'd become as Ben apparently was. I couldn't handle being shut out by both of them. If ever I needed her wisecracking, crass attitude, it was now. She could break the intensity and fear that I wore like a heavy cloak with one lash of her tongue.

"Why do we have to catch a plane? Can't we do that thing you did before and teleport, or whatever you call it?" I asked.

"Oh no! Goodness! That was for an emergency only. Your body is too weak to do that again and over such a distance. It could render you unconscious for months. It would certainly kill Jasmine and Ben. Human bodies cannot transfer like ours. Sadly, that too has been learned the hard way." I grimaced at the unpleasant thought as Enl'iel nodded knowingly at me, her expression sympathetic to me naivety.

A general murmur of excitement broke through the crowd at that moment. Up ahead, I could see people bowing and stepping aside as they had done with me. *Who could this be?* A crew-cut of white hair emerged above the others. Being generally very tall people, the fact that I could see the approaching person's head above the crowd meant that he was a Goliath in height. I felt that now familiar rush and tingle run through me as I did when I was surrounded by those who were like me—good *and* bad. This one was incredibly strong, as though a powerful energy surge had entered the room. I rubbed at the pins and needles in my arms.

"Excellent. They have returned. Sophia, you are about to meet the most revered of our kindred, a Watcher of immense longevity and wisdom. He will guide you through the Unsealing," she whispered in my ear.

The crowd directly in front of me parted, revealing Kea and Brennan, who both winked at me as they stood aside. In silent splendour, stood Gedz'iel, muscles stretched out like mountain ranges under the bare, golden skin of his chest. He wore nothing more than loose white pants. He took my breath away, not only from physical attraction, but because his sheer presence seemed to fill every corner of the room. He had an aura of superiority that made me feel small and insignificant. All without saying a word, just by being present.

His huge wings emanated a hum that echoed throughout the cavern. His face carried the stoic expression of a regal king, yet it was not warm, nor pleased to see me. The excitement that bubbled underneath my skin died a quick death when he spoke.

"This is she?" With his arms clasped behind him he did not even bother to point in my direction, he merely looked me up and down.

"She is small and weak. Are you sure this is the One?" he addressed Enl'iel as I burned with the humiliation of being inspected like livestock.

She bowed to him. "Welcome, Gedz'iel. We are honoured by your presence. I assure you that Sophia, also known as Soph'ael, daughter of Sarun'iel and Rik'ael, is indeed the Earth-born amongst us. Upon her birth, all of the prophesised signs were present. She has not transitioned through the Right of Sevens, and her markings are such that she could be no other. She has been ceaselessly hunted from the moment she drew her first breath. She awakened through a Quickening just this evening past, which is almost unheard of. Soph'ael appears to possess every gift that a native of A'vean would have, something a hybrid could never achieve. I defer to your assessment." She bowed again.

As she said this, she spoke to me in my mind. "*Do not fear Gedz'iel, dear, he will not harm you.*" All I could focus on were the names she spoke. My parents' names. I had never heard them before. *Did that mean they were alive?* My head swooned from the surprise, and I staggered a little, but managed to right myself.

"Are you ill, child? You seem unable to stand. Come, let me look at you." His deep voice commanded, rather than requested.

I tentatively took the few paces to him only with an encouraging push from Enl'iel. I was dwarfed by his size, and I had never been particularly vertically-challenged. His eyes mesmerised me immediately. Not only did they glisten with that familiar bright, sparkly blue that we all appeared to share, but his irises actually swirled with constant movement. Pink, yellow, and green flickered in and out from the black circle of his pupil, and it was almost impossible for me to take my eyes from his.

He reached out to me and placed a hand either side of my face. I reeled backwards, instantly blinded by an intense light and burning heat. It felt like only a second had passed, and it was over. Yet when I opened my eyes, I was surprised to find myself floating in the air with the sound of shocked voices beneath me. I looked down to find Gedz'iel flat out on the ground, unconscious.

As had happened before, I fell to the ground in surprise, having no control over this flying business. Enl'iel gathered me up as Brennan and Kea attended to the quickly rousing Gedz'iel.

"What have I done?" I asked, horrified. It was clear by the way everyone was looking at me that I was somehow responsible for the collapsed Watcher.

Through the excited background chatter, Brennan called to me. "Well, that's one hell of a way to prove who you are, Soph!"

"What did I do?" I asked again, looking at Enl'iel, whose face was trying to mask a smile of vindication as Gedz'iel stood up looking markedly more annoyed.

"You rendered him unconscious when he tried to read your aura. You defended yourself in reflex, just like yesterday. Your strength has shone right through." She squeezed my shoulders for assurance that this was a positive thing.

My attention was still only on the massive figure who again loomed over me.

"Your manners are sorely lacking for proper protocol. I see your human upbringing has left you ignorant of our customs. May I suggest that next time you are addressing a superior, you refrain from attacking him?" His expression had not changed, and it bordered somewhere between serious and deadly.

"Please forg—"

"Silence, young one, you need not apologise. You have caused neither offense, nor injury. Your outburst has however, has shown me first-hand the power that runs through you. No one else could overcome me with such speed and vigour as you have done. I see in your eyes that you bare the mark of I'el. Only a pure, full-spirited energy descended directly of the Prime Creator could exhibit such intensity in their mortal eyes at such a young age. The power of E'lan, the universal energy, shines deep within them already." I recalled that name, E'lan, from my distant memories as the word Nan had used to describe the energy that was the foundation of our healing ability. Small fragments of my past were standing out as the red flags of who I really was. Gedz'iel gently turned me to face the silent crowd. A sea of expectant faces. "Look at the way this legacy of I'el yearns to reveal itself. Soon her eyes shall turn, as do his." He almost smiled as he looked around the cavern, gently turning my chin this way and that, exhibiting my apparent amazingness. As he released me, I touched my own eyes in wonder. I assumed he was referring to the freaky sparkling blue that my eyes had morphed into. The socially unacceptable milky hue seemed a mere unpleasant memory now. He seemed to rise taller again, his wings extending further and his arms wide in gesture.

He addressed everyone then. "Behold, my kindred, the Earth-born angel of A'vean indeed stands before us. Finally, you are rewarded for your loyalty and patience. Only in your good deeds could this child be offered to you as salvation. Only in your repentance and abstinence from further temptation would I'el allow her to grace the Earth. We must all rise to this and pledge upon our very souls to protect and honour her, so that she may achieve her purpose and therefore your chance to once more attain the rapture of A'vean. Both Watchers and Eudaimonia, you are all bound by blood and spirit to follow that path set forth by Enoch through the word of the mighty I'el. We shall guide Soph'ael and fend off the threat of the Unseen at all costs, so that she may succeed in her quest." He paused momentarily, assessing the enamoured silent faces.

"For those of you who may be tempted, hear me and fear me now. If you, as others have, fall victim to the pleas and temptations of the Unseen, and in any way interfere with or place the Earth-born in peril, you shall suffer immediate and severe consequences. Be wary, my brothers and sisters, as the Unseen and their foul minions are more cunning than ever at manipulation and false promises. I sense even now that one is all too near us. Be on your guard. Do not let your weariness or desperation allow you to fall victim to them. The truth lies here." He pointed to me, and I took a step back, overwhelmed.

"Who among you recalls the fate of Mal'ael?" He turned his broad shoulders to face a distant wall and threw a ball of light out towards a darkened corner. The bright orb hung high in the air and highlighted a horrific scene. A watcher lay underneath the fearsome Gedz'iel whose hand was delved into the prostrate man's chest. The scene next to him showed Gedz'iel with a long, twisting snake of light hanging from his fist, as the dead corpse of the Watcher lay below.

"Mal'ael, once a strong and wise soldier, fell victim to the seduction of Anjou'elle. His alliance under her spell caused the destruction of much human life and allowed the Unseen to infiltrate the safe haven of Deryinkuyu after the great flood. He paid for this with the annihilation of his soul. This is now the most critical time—you choose to fight with us, or you choose Mal'ael's fate!" He bellowed the last of this vignette across the expansive space. The room was pin-drop silent as he looked around at every face, satisfied that his message had been well absorbed. "Now, Bren'ael, my old friend, where is the Chromious key?"

I remained in a state of complicit silence. I had nothing to contribute to the unfolding situation other than dumbstruck awe. I didn't know the questions to ask about a scenario that made no sense, so I stood in quiet wonder and simply watched. Brennan seemed to cringe as he was called forward by his apparent true name. He quickly brushed it off though, and from a brown satchel he produced the key I'd used to unlock the door in the floor of the shed. He handed it to Gedz'iel, who turned back to me and spoke.

"Soph'ael, daughter of Sarun'iel and Rik'ael, child of I'el, born of mortal flesh in purity and perfection, I present you with the Chromious key."

I thought he was about to pass it to me as he bent forward, however, instead he began to push the ends of the key together, crushing it in on itself. His palms lit up, as was so commonplace around here. The key glowed white as he pushed it, squashing it slowly in upon itself. Buzzing and hissing crackled from between his hands with the force and energy he was exerting on the piece of metal. The room remained silent, other than the sound of some falling rubble in the distance. Distracted by this, I looked up, and with my dramatically improved eyesight, I caught a glimpse of two faces peering out from around one of the furthest tunnels. I could tell without doubt that it was Ben and Jaz. They weren't meant to be seeing this, for their own safety, but I wasn't about to let anyone know that they were there, so I quickly averted my eyes back to Gedz'iel, just as both of his hands moved flat against each other.

"Soph'ael, this is the key to the Prime Scroll Chamber. Take it and begin your journey—*our* journey." He handed me the metal object with a reverence that seemed beneath him. I looked down into my hands and found not the large swirling key I'd used before, but a platinum coloured disc that was identical to the concentric circles that were repeated throughout this cavern, the same as Cael had shown me in the vision.

I was about ask what I had to do when the disc began to burn, and I was hit with sudden and vivid visions. My mind was assaulted with rapid flashes of symbols, stones, light, and dark. Images of engravings and blood dripping down rocky walls. I should have been frightened, but I wasn't. What I did feel was *enlightened*. My eyes flew open. I knew what I had to do. Clarity just descended upon me. I just somehow knew exactly what I needed to do right then and there.

I turned and walked to the Zythros stone. I paced slowly around its circumference, inspecting it. I stopped when I found what I was looking for. I briefly looked up to see Enl'iel nod in support, that I was doing the right thing. *Deep breath in, deep breath out, repeat.* Turning back, I noticed one of the concentric circle engravings was larger than the others, and had just the slightest depression in it. I turned the circle over in my hands, rubbing my fingers lightly across the circular pattern and then without hesitation, pressed it up against the rock. It fit snuggly into the space. I watched and waited. I looked behind me at all of the expectant faces. Every pair of eyes were glued to me with anticipation, as though their horse was metres away from the finish line in a one-horse race, and all of their bets were on me.

I looked back to the disc and contemplated it for a moment. As though a magnetic pull existed between it and myself, I reached forward and pushed the circle against the stone. My hand instantly lit up—the pressure of my skin on the disc caused it to glow insanely bright. A rumble of grinding stone vibrated underfoot, and a slight tremor unsettled the floor. Energy flowed back and forth through the disc, myself, and the now glowing and pulsating Zythros stone. Voices filled my head, urging me on, welcoming me, but also warning me of danger. For some reason, I pushed harder at the disc, and the entire stone monument heaved forward. The disc sunk away deep into the pedestal, as the Zythros stone ground its way noisily away from my feet. As it slowly revealed an opening in the floor, the stones underneath slid in and out to create a staircase. The echo of grinding stones bounced back through the cavern as they continued to move and clunk into place in the deep darkness. As the rumbling ceased and the Zythros stone stood still once more, I looked down at the staircase that disappeared into pitch darkness.

Another dark hole in the ground. Fabulous!

Chapter
Twenty-Eight

Suffice to say, I was not impressed with going down another dark hole, but something strangely innate told me that it was safe to do so, here at least. Gedz'iel threw a light orb down the stairwell to illuminate the way, and I followed as he took the lead. I was secretly looking forward to learning how to throw out one of those babies - it seemed like a pretty handy skill. I glanced back briefly at Enl'iel. Uneasiness caused my entire body to shiver. She urged me on with a smile, yet her eyes, warm and comforting, spoke of a motherly concern.

I followed him. Enl'icl, Kca, Koi, and Brennan came next, along with a handful of the little Keepers. I could feel everyone's excitement ignite the air. I glanced back at the group, seeing their faces set with determination. Brennan winked every time he caught me look back, his face always warm with a broad smile. Dripping water and mouldy, wet earth were an unwelcome assault to the senses as we descended cautiously. The air was freezing, yet it didn't seem to bother my now permanently fiery skin. The way ahead was lit by Gedz'iel's powerful glow. His wings never dulled, yet the walls stayed dark and dirty, unlike the bright tunnel that led us to the main cavern of the Library. It wasn't pretty down here, the energy was far less inviting. Gedz'iel didn't speak, as we followed on silently.

In the quiet, all I could hear besides the dripping was the hum of his wings and the sound of his loose pants flapping against his ankles as he walked. I dared to think of something to say, but no words were brave enough tease my mouth open. The stairs wound down steeper, and we had to jump across a small crevasse where some stairs had apparently fallen away, deep into the earth. *What the hell am I doing? I'm not Lara Croft!*

The stairwell was a tight squeeze, which I found ironic, as we were all so tall. It seemed an understated hiding space to access when it was meant for us. It had more of a Hobbit feel to it. I picked out clumps of dirt from my hair as it fell sporadically from the unsupported roof. Thankfully, the stairs levelled out quickly and finished in a small chamber carved out of a vertical sheet of rock. There was little effort put into this place, other than roughly hewn indentations in the walls where hundreds of small orbs burned away the darkness. It smelled of lavender and cedar.

The floor was muddy and unpleasant underfoot. The wall was covered with numerous roughly engraved writings in its centre. The pretty lettering initially looked completely unintelligible to me. A mish-mash of symbols that appeared a hybrid of Greek and Arabic, with swirls and dots, nothing akin to the English language. Gedz'iel spoke for the first time, dulling his light as he did so.

"Soph'ael, can you read the inscription?"

I stepped forward in the dim light and peered closely at the unfamiliar characters. It seemed to be a passage, perhaps a prayer, I wasn't certain. It was set into three stanzas, three lines in each. Initially, panic set in as it looked like gibberish. I began to sweat, my nerves rattled. I looked back at the three of them for help.

"Young one, do not panic. Do not doubt. Look with your spirit, not with your eyes," Gedz'iel encouraged me with his first hint of kindness.

I refocused on the wall, tracing my fingers over each and every grainy character. The rough and rocky interface was cool, but my fingers burned and glowed as they touched each engraving. I stood back and looked again from afar. Something inside me told me to close my eyes, to look no more upon the words. I did as my instinct instructed.

After a few nervous moments, something began to happen. The sounds and smells of the cave dwindled away into nothingness. The blackness behind my eyelids was replaced with an ever-brightening light. My heart fluttered with excitement. In my mind's eye, I could see an elderly man dressed in a Biblical-style linen tunic, seated upon a rock. He leaned earnestly over a parchment, writing with a stick fashioned into a quill. He dipped it methodically into an inkwell.

He looked up to me and smiled. "Welcome, dear child, I have awaited your arrival a long while."

He then picked up the parchment he'd been labouring over and turned it around, holding it up for me to see.

"Read," he instructed.

I looked at the words, and in an instant they were clear to me, as though they were written in English. With my eyes shut tight in concentration, I recounted them out loud from the vision I was seeing.

> *"Ten by seven years thereafter, the East is reborn through death*
> *Mine words shall guide thee*
> *Thy blood shall wash upon this wall*
> *Caress thy palm with crystal blade*
> *The fifth element shall fill with thy flowing spirit*
> *And the mysteries of I'el shall be revealed*
> *North, South, East, West,*
> *Thy light within shall guide the way*
> *Great child of I'el, beware thy heart."*

I opened my eyes with a start as I finished speaking. I turned to everyone and asked, "Did you hear that? Did I make sense?"

"Not to me. It sounded like A'vean, but I couldn't quite get it. It's been a long time since I've heard it in its pure form. The old neurons just don't seem to jiggy-up with the old language these days. It's like trying to watch T.V through static. Damn!" exclaimed Brennan as he tapped his temple, his face a picture of frustration.

"Same here," Kea added.

"What do you mean? I saw it in English in my mind and read it aloud, didn't I?"

"Soph, you spoke in another language. You spoke the lost language," Brennan responded, looking rather proud.

Gedz'iel interjected. "Soph'ael, you have spoken the true language of A'vean, inscribed by Enoch, as taught to him by I'el. Only you, at this time, are able to understand and speak this tongue, as we remain blocked from the universal connection. Only you possess the elemental ability to channel our ancient words. Please, will you repeat it in English? Trust yourself, it will come naturally," his eyes warmed with encouragement as he nodded for me to continue.

There was no point in allowing myself to be shocked by this—it was a waste of effort in this upside down world of mine. I looked to the wall and repeated the words, concentrating hard to make sure it came out exactly as I had said it just moments before. I repeated it twice more, slowly, so they all could think on it. After a few minutes of silence, Enl'iel spoke up.

"I believe it refers to the time in which Sophia was meant to reach the scroll. The year she awakened. If we go by today, 2014 then it is certainly accurate. Ten by seven years ago, I assume refers to seventy years ago, and the rebirth of the East. What happened seventy years ago to the East? The end of the human World War Two. Japan was decimated in 1945 by the Hiroshima and Nagasaki bombings. This is a country that indeed has been reborn into a modern and peaceful region," she explained as she inclined her head towards Koi, who nodded in response.

"Indeed, my earthbound homeland has rebirthed." Koi acknowledged.

"It has also long been known that you are to offer a small token of blood as assurance of your lineage. Ignore that washing the wall in blood rubbish. Enoch clearly was overdramatizing!" Enl'iel furrowed her brows in thought. "It's how and where you place this token that we must ascertain." She concluded, as Gedz'iel gave her a nod of approval. I was kind of impressed with her flippant rebuke of Enoch's poetic licence.

I studied the chamber we were inside along with everyone else. The inscription I had just read out was the only thing of interest, other than being surrounded by hundreds of repetitive symbols gouged into the rock. Nothing jumped out and said, *deposit blood sample here and press enter.* That would have been so much easier.

Gedz'iel spoke once more. "Young one, the answers are right in front of you. Invisible, yet in plain sight. We must consider Enoch's words carefully, as they will hold the clues for what is required of you." It struck me that he spoke so formally, like he was from a different time. Like Koi, his accent was hard to pin down. Perhaps a slight Middle Eastern lilt, but I couldn't be sure.

I looked back to the wall. "Could you guys please help me? I'm not even sure where to begin." A room full of nods reassured me.

We studied the wall for a time. Each of us mulled over this and that, offering then retracting suggestions. We prodded and poked at the engravings. The wall was symmetrically decorated around the script, and all of the symbols mirrored each other. Circles and diamond shapes, with swirling curls like raging waves that swept across the bottom of the wall. Some symbols were faint, while others had been hewn deeper into the rock. The wall was moist and glistened with dampness. *Or was that something else?*

"I need some light. Can I pick up one of those things?" I pointed to the orbs.

"Indeed." Gedz'iel immediately passed one to me. He rested it carefully on my palm. It tickled but felt like nothing other than a warm feather. It remained frustratingly dark though, without Gedz'iel's impressive light show. The orb shined just enough though, that I noticed the tiniest glimpse of gemstones embedded within the rock, as hints of glistening jewels winked at me when the light fell across them at just the right angle.

"If I could get a little more light, I could see better. These things are way too dull." I said. I looked expectantly towards them all, hoping for one of them to flip on their switches.

"First lesson, Soph'ael: cast your own aura out to light your way." Gedz'iel instructed me. "Does the great passage not say to let the light shine from within? I believe Enoch has instructed you to reveal your aura to light the way forward."

"I was kind of hoping you guys could help with that. I'd love to light up on demand, but I have *no* clue how that works. Apparently it just likes to randomly surprise me!"

"Despite your sorry lack of upbringing Soph'ael, it is as natural as drawing a breath to cast an aura." I heard a muted tut-tutting from an offended Enl'iel behind me.

"How? I don't understand how?"

"You heal?" Gedz'iel asked.

"Yes."

"Then you know how to draw and repel energy. It is the same with an aura. As you repel energy, it opens up space in the particulate matter around you, and your true form can emerge—your aura. Until recently you have performed a mere trick with your hands. Now, you are truly one of us. You must and you *will* rise up to who you are. You will learn to utilise this new power with your entire body. Even I can feel the energy coursing through you. Harness that strength Soph'ael."

I found only a small voice to answer him.

"I understand what you're saying. I feel stronger and more connected to the elements than before, but I just don't know how to control anything. It's not like you've given me much of a chance to learn," I grumbled in annoyance. His expression turned to one of barely masked impatience. My stomach churned. He was pissed, and I really didn't like the idea of someone like that cracking it with me. Note to self—keep whinging to a minimum and preferably not in front the head honcho of the Watchers! I gave Gedz'iel my absolute full attention.

"When we heal, in our mind's eye we can see energy flow in and out. We focus on our hands until we allow the release of that energy. It is not difficult. It is the same concept Soph'ael, just focusing on your entire form instead of merely your hands." He'd taken a step closer, looming over me in a way that made me feel small and insignificant.

"Enl'iel?" I looked to her for even the smallest clue. His mere proximity overwhelmed me. I knew he was trying to help but his demeanour clouded my mind to the point that I couldn't think straight.

"Take your time Sophia, listen to your instincts, you know what to do. Don't be frightened," she answered. She really was taking a back seat and throwing me to the lions. I felt justifiably crappy at her too. Gedz'iel grabbed my shoulders, turning my attention back to him. I looked up into his eyes. There was a softness in them, concern perhaps, but his expression was still cool and hard.

"You have unfurled your pterugia three times now. Perhaps if you do this it will assist you. The sensation is the same and your aura will emerge along with them as a natural consequence. Now, release your pterugia." He took a step back, arms folded and with an expectant look on his face.

"Um—unfurl my *what*?"

"They're the flappy things, princess. Your wings," whispered Brennan from somewhere behind.

"Oh, right, *pterugia*. Okay. I have no idea how to do that!" I threw my hands in the air in defeat. *Good one Soph!* In one minute flat I'd already broken my previous promise to self to not complain in front of said, scary Watcher. I kicked myself on the inside.

Gedz'iel snapped. "Has she been taught nothing of her heritage?" His mark glowed as muscles flexed impatiently across his chest.

"Your Grace…" Enl'iel began, but he interrupted her as he appeared to quickly calm down. He put his palm up to silence Enl'iel. His expression softened from annoyance to contemplation.

"No. My expectations are unreasonable. No more could be expected of her. Take no offence Enl'iel. You have carried your cause well. Perhaps I'm too intimidating for the girl. Ke'arel, you help the young learn when they emerge from stasis. Help Soph'ael," he ordered.

"With honour," Kea replied with a bow.

"Right, Soph, you can to do this. Piece of cake." She stood in front of me with her hands on my shoulders. She winked at me just like Brennan had.

"Close your eyes. I want to you to pretend that you are about to do a healing. Close your mind to everything but the buzz and heat in your back, not your hands. Concentrate on that energy swirling through your gut, trying to get out."

I did this easily, as it was what I always felt before I did a healing, apart from the weird back sensation. The second my eyes closed, the tickle and burn in my spine eclipsed all else and my stomach churned.

"Okay," I nodded, "Now what?"

"Now, imagine that energy wanting to burst out of you, and, like a raging waterfall, let it go. Let it run and spread far and wide down your back and out of your body. Picture pure, white light. The more you think of it, the more your mind and spirit connect. Before long, that connection will become so strong that it will be a reflex, just like breathing."

I concentrated on her words. There was a lot riding on me here, so it wasn't easy to be calm and stay focused. *Deep breath in, deep breath out, repeat.* I pictured that warm, white light that came so easily to my hands, travelling up my arms and down into my spine. Remembering how threats had triggered my other supernatural episodes, I thought of Ben and Jaz and how I wanted to protect them. This fanned the small fire of rage which smouldered in the pit of my stomach. I thought of Esme and that fire burned brighter. My body responded with an instant temperature spike, as my spine tingled and tensed. A small sweat emerged across my temples. I wanted to stretch—I felt balled up, like a knot. Like letting a rubber band snap, that pent-up energy suddenly released itself from my spine and I willed it to relax and melt away. As I did so, my entire body burned like a furnace. I could feel a shift occur within me.

"Yes! Yes, that's it, Soph. You did it, you're a natural!" Kea cheered.

I opened my eyes to find the room ablaze with a bright bioluminescence. I looked down at myself to see a soft light emanating from every exposed piece of my skin. The pulse points on my wrists rhythmically threw out a hypnotic glow. Every corner was of the room was revealed from the darkness, like a sports stadium lit up at night. Everyone was bathed in this soft light, and their facial markings seemed to glow with camaraderie. I turned my head side to side and saw on both sides of me large, self-limiting wings of light gently encasing my shoulders. It made me feel huge and powerful. I felt that same urge to move them as I had yesterday, and so I did. It wasn't the best idea, as they propelled me forward with such a sudden lurch that I was flung straight into Gedz'iel, who caught me in his massive arms.

"*Hmm*—some instruction is required here, I believe," he said this with the hint of an amused smile. "Refrain from exercising your pterugia for now. Still yourself, and use their light to guide you. You learn quickly though, well done. I am pleased. Your aura is strong." He propped me back on my feet, and faced me towards the wall. *Well done me.*

"That'll teach you for showing off!" Brennan quipped with a chuckle.

"There's a time and a place you know!" I glared at him.

"My bad," he said with a shrug.

I returned my attention to the wall. I felt all too well the pressure to figure out this puzzle and was now slightly giddy with the sudden light show my body was putting on. I examined the rocky edifice for a long while. All of the symbols popped out at me, but then just blurred into meaningless decoration. My confidence waned after many long minutes of intense study, and my eyes tired, forcing my vision into a trance-like stare. It was surprisingly this brief state of absence that did it. As my eyes glazed over, the light burning off me cast a shadow across the wall in such a way that it revealed that there, hidden within the mass of symbols, was a cross-like formation, with arms that ended in points. It revealed itself like magic, from floor to ceiling and left to right.

The words of Enoch were centred in the middle of this previously hidden cross. The twinkling of gemstones was evident only in certain shapes, and they lit the way, delineating the cross as though a guiding path to what I was seeking. Only the light cast from myself brought out this ethereal quality, showing me where I should look next.

The cross was comprised of the same repetitive pattern of symbols. Diamonds, with five squares inside them. The only significant difference was that at the end of each bar of the cross, on the point, the symbol was slightly larger. It reminded me of the face of a compass.

A compass!

"Wow, can you guys see what I see?" I asked of the crowd, slightly awestruck at the sparkling vision.

"Yes, Soph'ael, they are illuminated through you. The Earth speaks to us through your light," answered Gedz'iel.

"It kinda looks like a compass to me," I said unconvincingly.

"Soph, you're a genius! North, South, East, and West, the directions that were hinted at in the passage. It's a freaking compass!" Brennan exclaimed as he slapped me across the back like I'd just scored a goal on the field.

"But how does this help? If it's telling us which way to go, it doesn't make any sense. We can't go in any of these directions unless we head back up!" I was stumped.

"Perhaps it pertains to the location of something within this chamber?" offered Enl'iel.

I thought on it further. Gedz'iel ran his hand across the symbols hopefully. "Hmmm, I wonder—"

"What do you see, your Grace?" asked Koi.

"We are in the southern lands." Gedz'iel knelt and inspected the bottom symbol of the vertical bar. The light and shadows cast across his muscular back revealed silvery scars etched up and down his spine. I wondered how he got those. "I believe this is where we should focus." He gestured for me to look too as I quickly averted my gaze from his back.

The rough-hewn symbol initially didn't look any more interesting than the others. Gedz'iel probed at it with his fingers, running them along all of its ridges and indentations, and finally over the cracked rock surrounding it. The gems sparkled under his touch, but nothing more interesting than that appeared.

"May I?" I asked, not sure if I should touch it also.

"Please, do as your spirit wills you. I am a mere guide for you." He stood up and backed away.

I knelt as he had and reached my hand out, touching the symbols above the bottom one first. They glowed, heated, and emitted a small vibration. I let my hand run down to the bottom diamond, and repeated the same tactile exploration. For a moment, it just vibrated as the others had. Then, without warning, the five small squares within it glowed white and bright, as though lights had turned on from within the rock.

"Look, do you see this?" I blurted out excitedly to no one in particular.

I could feel the anxious energies behind me. A magnetic force seemed to draw my hand towards the symbol. With a suddenness that I was clearly not prepared for, this force sucked my fingers to the wall. I had no time to resist. It pulled each finger awkwardly onto the five square pattern, as though they were pressing all the keys on a key pad at once.

A massive jolt fired up my arm, forcing my head to fly backwards with the kickback. It would have thrown me to the ground, but for the fact that my fingers seemed glued to the wall.

"By the Great I'el, I believe she is opening the chamber!" called out Gedz'iel.

"Help me! God, what do I do?" I screamed as I pulled wildly at my wrist. My hand was stuck firm.

The vibration shot through the entire room, rumbling the floor underneath me. Dirt rained down from overhead.

Enl'iel knelt by my side, shielding me from the debris. "Do not fear, you will not be harmed. Breathe calmly. I believe the elements are identifying you as the true Earth-born." She rubbed my static-filled hair, soothing me in a moment that I was sure had no standard textbook approach for reassurance.

"What if it doesn't—recognise me?" I yelled. I could barely catch my breath.

"Oh, it will, dear. It surely will!" she soothed.

Clearly lacking human tact, Gedz'iel also answered my question in a matter-of-fact tone. "It will disintegrate an imposter."

"Oh, fabulous!" I pulled harder at my hand in extreme panic. At the peak of my fear, I suddenly rolled backwards. I was released from the wall as an arc of lightning shot through the room. Everyone, including Gedz'iel, ducked as it bounced around the space and disappeared back through the centre of the cross with a cracking explosion. As I lay coughing on the dusty floor, any thoughts of seeing if I was injured were overrun by what happened next.

Chapter
Twenty-Nine

The wall rumbled from within. The bottom symbol that had held me hostage began to move, withdrawing itself slowly back into the rock face. All the other symbols making up the cross pattern did the same with a dragging, stone on stone grinding noise. Gasps of blessings to I'el came from the others behind me. I couldn't take my eyes from the sight, but I did scuttle backwards, not knowing what might happen next.

Once all of the symbols had receded, a dark cross-shaped opening was left ominously glaring back at me. I stood up cautiously to take a closer look, keeping what I hoped was a safe distance. The light from my wings were like high-beams, yet the recess must have been deep, as all I could see from within it was a black void. As we all approached it, another rumble began, causing us to jump back. More stone grinding followed, and then, one by one, every other symbol on the wall rapidly collapsed in on itself, like a block puzzle falling to pieces. Dust blew back at us through the deafening noise.

In the aftermath of the explosive rock fall, I found that we'd all managed to huddle together, with Gedz'iel surrounding us all protectively with his expansive wings. As the last of the dust haze settled, a soft wind blew in at us from within the now much larger opening, where the wall had stood only moments before.

"Oh, my God!" My skin tingled and my pulse pounded with excitement. A thrill ran through me as I carefully found some footfalls amongst the rubble. I inched my way to the opening, tentatively grasping the craggy edge. The stale breeze ruffled through my hair.

"I tell you, Indiana Jones couldn't have done any better," Brennan joked.

"Just call me Tomb Raider," I laughed back at him, remembering my earlier thoughts about entering this mysterious underground space.

"This is no time for mindless humour. We are at the very crux of a momentous occasion for the children of A'vean. Appreciation for the reverence of this moment and this place should be heeded. You should know better, Bren'ael. You are an ancient and should appreciate the customs of your people with more respect." Gedz'iel's tone was scathing.

Ouch. That was a decent lashing.

"Forgive me, Gedz'iel. My years have been long in the human world, and I have acquired many of their appalling habits," he bowed respectfully, but I could see his barely-hidden smirk of amusement.

"I'm sorry." I couldn't quite meet Gedz'iel's eyes. I dared not smile, despite desperately wanting to.

"Hmmm, worry not. There is a time for enjoying the comforts of human frivolity, but now is not one of them." He turned away, dismissing us both. "Follow me," he stepped through the gaping back hole and disappeared. We moved quickly-Brennan, then me and Koi, who placed a reassuring hand on my shoulder. Kea and Enl'iel filed in last.

Our auras and wing-lights combined to light the way out as we moved through the cold tunnel. However, I noticed that Enl'iel remained in relative darkness. It occurred to me then that she must not have wings. I recalled her telling me that the Eudaimonia could have many or none of the Watchers' traits. Perhaps wings were the one thing she was missing.

The musty air clung uncomfortably to me as we walked through the damp, earthen tunnel. Gems of all kinds glistened along the walls. The floor underneath was hard, packed earth, with crunchy gravel underfoot. Brennan stopped suddenly and put his hand up for me to stop too. Gedz'iel had also halted, staring at a light that had appeared up ahead.

An agonised moan followed, making me jump nearly out of my skin.

"*What was that?*" I whispered.

"I have no idea," answered Brennan, concern shadowed his face. "It doesn't sound too inviting, though."

"Let's continue," Enl'iel urged. She gently nudged my back, and we proceeded forward, following a cautiously paced Gedz'iel, who crunched slowly along the path and into a new chamber on the left.

We turned the corner to find another orb-lit room. We halted again behind Gedz'iel, who was unmoving as he looked at something in the small space. The moaning intensified. I bristled, wondering what the source of this dreadful sound was. It abruptly stopped which seemed even more frightening. Gedz'iel put up a hand, as though to stop us from moving any further. I had zero desire to get any closer, although I shifted sideways so that I could at least peek around from behind Brennan to get a better view. There, hovering in a corner, was a ghostly figure with its back to us. Its head was downcast; it was silent, floating gently up and down. It began to flicker like a dying light bulb and then let out an almighty scream, causing me to plug my ears with my fingers. It then turned to us, revealing a ghastly pale face with dark, sunken eyes and a black, gaping mouth. It glared at us momentarily, then collapsed into itself becoming a streak of light, like a shooting star. The light darted out and around Gedz'iel, and he did not move or make a sound. It zipped up and down him, shrieking wildly. Shockingly, it pushed itself right through his chest, emerging from his back. He grabbed at his heart, dropped to his knees, and moaned. Despite myself and the poltergeist thing, I moved to help him, but Brennan held me back with a shake of his head. Gedz'iel put up a hand to stop any interference and seemed to recover quickly, gathering himself up onto his feet again. The spectre turned its attention to us and sped rapidly around us, screaming a terrifying, high-pitched squeal. It corralled us in an ever-tightening circle. Curses of warning were yelled in our faces as we gathered our backs together, not wanting to take an eye off of the frightful thing. Horrific images of mangled faces popped in and out of the spectre. It seemed to be trying to terrify us. It succeeded with me, while the others seemed cautious but unaffected.

Kea called to it softly. "Oh no, you poor, poor thing." It stopped the circling instantly at that and hovered over her head. Rainbow streaks of light emerged from within it. Then it snapped back into a tight, floating orb. A new shape emerged fluidly from the orb, elongating vertically and filling out into a translucent human form. Her wings ebbed slowly as she floated silently in front of us. Long, pale hair flowed down over white robes that were punctuated by a silver and gold armoured breastplate. She wore similar wristbands and an impressive sword on her side. She looked every bit a Grecian Goddess of war.

"This is Andr'eal. She has guarded this place from the time of Enoch." Gedz'iel spoke quietly as he reached a hand to her.

"Be still, my love. Come, the pain is over," he soothed. His face was an unexpected picture of longing as he caught a breath and swallowed, as if to supress tears. She regarded him with beautiful but disbelieving blue eyes. He didn't remove his gaze from her as he continued to speak to us.

"Her penance for repeated liaising with humans, teaching them elemental magic, was to either be banished to the Unseen Realm, or to stand sentry guard of the Prime Scroll chamber. She chose this; perhaps a greater punishment." His voice was thick as she glided cautiously forward to him and took his hands in hers.

My heart instantly ached for her. In her human visage, she looked a pitiful soul. Beauty and grace glowed through her, yet utter desolation emanated from within, almost as tangible as if she were flesh and blood. She was as wounded as anyone could ever be.

She spoke in a haunting voice as she gazed up at Gedz'iel. "Husband, I beg thee to free me from this confinement. Look about you—I have protected this place well. Nothing has passed by me, the great words remain secure."

I think we all jolted with surprise at her revelation. *She was Gedz'iel's wife?*

She spoke again. "I feel her presence." She looked about at us all, then drifted to me. She tilted her head as she inspected me with a pained smile. "The Earth-born is finally here." She ran her spectral hand across my cheek, leaving a chill on the skin. "Welcome, saviour of the children of A'vean." She kneeled before me and begged, "Please grant me release?"

I looked to Gedz'iel. I didn't know what to say.

"Beloved, you have suffered greatly. I have suffered with you—your absence has been a torture to my heart." His voice faltered, tears streamed silently down his dignified face. "I see you have fought well." He moved towards her again and as he did so, he kicked at something on the ground with his bare foot. A skull rolled to a stop just short of my feet. I realised with disgust that it was not gravel that we had been trampling on but bones, thousands of them.

"Come," he said.

Andr'eal glided back to him and they embraced briefly. I could see that he didn't want to let her go as she returned to me.

"I am at your service, Earth-born," she bowed.

"Please, don't do that, and just call me Sophia." I felt that familiar flame of embarrassment burn my cheeks with the over-the-top attention.

She inclined her head in acknowledgement. "I have fought the Daimon to preserve the scroll for you, Sophia. I hope I have pleased you."

"You've fought here all on your own?" I asked. "I thought this place was unknown?"

"It was, but there have been some among the kindred who have turned to the Unseen and other enemies just as vile. We have been betrayed. Look about you—I have been forced under duress to annihilate my own people." She pointed to what I had thought were more crystals by the base of the walls, but realised that they were parts of skeletal remains.

"Oh my God!" I knelt down by one. The site was grisly yet I felt drawn to run my hand along the smooth clear, skeleton. Enl'iel knelt next to me.

"When a Watcher or powerful Eudaimonian ascends, they leave a diamond skeleton behind. The particles of carbon in human flesh, over thousands of years, eventually fuse, like coal under great pressure, into remains such as this."

"How did they get down here? We had to go through all that back there just to get in here. I thought I was the only one who could access this place?" I turned back, speaking to the forlorn figure, huddling into Gedz'iel's side.

"They came through the earthen walls. The Rogues and the Afflicted, they have blasted through many a time. The Rogues clawed through with their rotting fingers. You must hunt down the betrayers." She pointed to the many greying human bone fragments scattered around. Gedz'iel growled like a wild animal.

"Traitors!" he mumbled with disgust.

"I have patched the walls at least once a century, until this one just passed. Not one attacker has succeeded in escape to tell the tale of what lay within my prison. I have not faced an intrusion in 150 years, although I believe my sense of time has somewhat faded."

"Who are the Afflicted?" I asked, inwardly wincing as she called this place her prison.

"You are indeed blessed if you are yet to meet an Afflicted being. They are Flourishing ones who have fallen victim to the heinous effects of Thanratos," she bowed again as she addressed me.

"What's that?" I asked.

"Dearest Sophia, it is the powdered bones of the mortal remains of a Watcher. The Afflicted ingest this substance to invigorate themselves. It does not bode well for their health, however. They lose their sensibilities and behave like savage beasts, desperate to obtain more and more. Our enemies use this to their advantage and bribe them with Thanratos dust to perform heinous acts. Watchers and Eudaimonians have been hunted to their mortal deaths purely so the enemy could obtain their earthly remains. Thanratos is immensely rare and powerful. I have fought many a battle protecting my own bones from falling into their hands. She pointed to a darkened corner and threw an illuminating orb that lit it up.

I gasped at what I saw, "This is—or was—*you*?"

"Please?" she gestured me towards the grisly corner. I heard Gedz'iel draw a sharp breath of shock at the sight, yet he maintained a dignified silence and stature. There, propped up against the wall, was a perfectly preserved diamond skeleton. It sparkled like a newly cut gem, a work of art as beautiful as it was disturbing. The ribcage was covered in the same armoured breastplate that she wore in spirit form. Intricate carvings were etched all over it, including that same swirl of our common facial markings.

"This was me. I was badly injured in an encounter a few thousand years ago, and with no one to help heal me, I had to ascend from my human form permanently." I was horrified—*what a dreadful existence.* I was learning that despite their goodwill and intent, the Watchers could be just as brutal as their enemies when threatened. The evidence of her victories sparkled directly underfoot.

I felt physically ill for her inhumane fate, and was immediately determined to get what we came for and set this poor spirit free. "Okay then, let's do this," I said. "What do I need to do? Let's get you out of this place."

She glowed with anticipation. "You have read the scripture henceforth from the entry chamber?"

"Yes, and unfortunately it seems you need some of my blood."

"That is so."

With that she leaned down and snapped off one of her skeletal rib bones with a glass-like *crack*. She ran it through her palm, lighting it up until it glowed lava red. As the glow died down, she opened her pale, translucent palm and offered it up to me. There lying across it was a razor sharp, diamond dagger.

Chapter Thirty

I carefully took the sparkling weapon that Andr'eal offered me. It looked more beautiful than dangerous, just like a Daimon. It was still hot, the heat warmed my palm, but left no mark. I turned it over a couple of times, admiring its beauty. I found it was every bit a weapon. The glistening blade was so smoothly and finely finished, it's potential to maim was blatantly evident. The handle was heavy and felt surprisingly comfortable in my palm. It was also engraved with words that spiralled neatly around the heavy grip. Without hesitation I surprised myself as I read them aloud.

"*Child of A'vean, a drop by thine own hand shall engage the fifth element.*"

Andr'eal spoke. "Blood drawn by your hand alone shall see the prophecy fulfilled. By force or vexation, it shall come to naught. But a drop from thy palm upon this stone shall reveal the Prime Scroll." She then pointed me in the direction of an unassuming, vertical rock protruding up from the floor. It had no point of interest, no decoration. It would be something you would walk past, unnoticed.

I looked back to the others for reassurance. They'd all taken a step back, clearly unable to help me now as they watched and waited to see the outcome. Their faces were tight with concern. A slight nod from Enl'iel and Koi encouraged me. Brennan gave me a thumbs up. I turned back to the stone. I prodded all around it with my fingertips. Nothing really seemed to point me in any particular direction until I noticed a small, unassuming indentation on the top. A thin channel ran from its edge and sloped downwards to the floor. There was nothing on the floor below that I could see. I was confused and mulled over this spot until Andr'eal seemed to understand my confusion as to what to do next. She placed her palm over the indentation and mimicked the swiping action of slicing at her hand.

I gulped. The thought was easier than the act. To slice my own flesh deliberately made my belly quiver. Again, resorting to some calming breaths, I closed my eyes for a moment to gather some courage. As I did so, I was confronted with the image of Esme being brutalised by Belial, and my anger surged forward. I took a step closer to the rock and without hesitation used that anguish for Esme. I sliced quickly across the base of my palm, wincing with the sting. I watched with ghoulish fascination as my surprisingly dark and sparkly blood flowed freely onto the rock. As the pool of crimson filled the concave space, it began flowing down the channel. Andr'eal then placed her ghostly palm over my bleeding one and instantly cauterized the wound.

"Thank you," I smiled, returning my attention quickly to the blood flowing smoothly over the stone receptacle. It dribbled down and out of the channel luxuriously onto the dusty floor. Small clouds of dirt puffed into the air where the shimmering droplets hit the ground. I gazed at the scene, which seemed to occur in slow motion. The expectation of something magnificent happening made the moment drag out painfully. The soft drips hit the floor, one by one, in the cool silence. As the flow ceased and there was nothing but a congealing mass of my blood on the ground, I began to quietly panic that perhaps I did it wrong, or even that I was not in fact the person they were waiting for.

That thought was eradicated with a deep, thunderous *boom* throughout the chamber. It shook dust and debris up into my face from the ground. I swiped it out of my eyes as a tremendous breeze blew up from apparently nowhere. Bone fragments and rock rose up around us. I protected my face with my forearm from the sharp projectiles flying around, but then it settled as quickly as it had begun.

The miniature tornado had disturbed the remains on the ground and exposed another diamond pattern carved into the floor beneath the stone receptacle. It must have been buried beneath the dust. Within the diamond, sitting in the middle square was the drying pool of sparkling blood. *Just like Cael's blood*, I recalled.

A cracking sound broke the brief silence as the rock split vertically up the middle, then crumbled away noisily to the ground. In its wake lay a long, rectangular box, half-buried in the grey rubble. It was ornate, but tarnished. I knelt down and picked it up, polishing it with the sleeve of my hoody. It was covered in swirls and concentric circles, and was surprisingly light for its size.

It hummed and warmed in my hands. The quickening pulse in my temple seared through my birthmark. A distorted reflection of my face beamed back at me in the few un-tarnished patches where I had just polished. My eyes swirled with colour, and the more intensely I looked, the more my irises glowed with colourful bursts amongst the blue background.

How could this be me? I'm just a normal girl—well, I was just a normal girl.

My reverie was cut short by a momentary vision that felt as real as the ground underneath me. A large eye, a single eye, appeared before me, blue and swirling. It was the most beautiful supernova-like burst of colour—warm and inviting. A voice spoke from somewhere around this vision, deep and soothing, yet commanding.

"Daughter of A'vean, beware. Thy heart is thy strength and thy weakness." In a split second, the image was gone, and I was back to staring at my reflection in the metal box.

Another rumble underfoot came, and a rain of rubble pelted my head. Powerful arms grabbed me from behind. "We must go, Soph'ael, the chamber is about to collapse!" Gedz'iel picked me up, the box clutched tightly to my chest as he flew with immense speed back through the passages towards the staircase. I felt my aura dull right down in his close proximity. The safety of his grip seemed to cause my entire body to relax, to the point that I nearly felt ordinary again—nearly. The walls were crumbling fast, and the deafening sound of grinding and crashing rocks made it impossible to hear where the others were. I hoped they were right behind us. I closed my eyes and wondered what in the world could come next. In my head, I heard a familiar voice. *Knew you could do it, princess.*

Gedz'iel's grip was strong, and his speed had us flying up and out of the hole under the Zythros stone in what felt like seconds. The room was full of people wearing expressions of great anticipation. Enl'iel was safely in Brennan's arms as they flew up and out behind us, with Koi and Kea at the rear. The large stone was already moving back over the gaping hole with a slow grind, shutting out the plume of dust spewing up from underneath. I was gently placed to the ground and checked over thoroughly by Enl'iel. My hoody fell to the ground as she turned me around, apparently burned from my wings. She did a quick creative knot to stop my t-shirt doing the same. *Now that could become a problem!*

"Well, you seem to be in one piece," she said with a relieved sigh as she rubbed gently over the fading white scar on my palm and dusted off my face. "You have done well, dear. Very well. Emse would be so very proud of you," A small tear slid down her face as she leaned forward and placed her right cheek to mine, a gesture she had never before done to me. I'd witnessed it between her and Koi, though. It was like a kiss, warm, reassuring, and full of love. "I love you, dear child. Do not, under any circumstances, believe otherwise."

I felt arms envelop me as Brennan hugged me from behind. "You're a star! Seriously, my own brilliance dulls in your presence!"

"Bren'ael, I fear you have been too long in the human world. Your conceit is unbecoming," Gedz'iel said dismissively as he drew my attention to him. "I commend and praise you, Soph'ael." He thanked me quietly and did the cheek-kiss thing. He then turned to the awaiting crowd. "Dear kindred, the Earth-born has begun a chain reaction that henceforth cannot be undone." A cheer arose as wings emerged and flapped in celebration. "We must leave immediately to protect and train her further before we begin the search for the Kaladai."

I wondered what this new thing was he referred to. I leaned heavily on Enl'iel as I listened and wondered, absolutely spent.

"What's a Kaladai?" I asked her.

It is the last of the keys for the great portal to A'vean dear, it is the only thing that will open the gate," she replied. Overwhelmed, I listened to Gedz'iel as he continued.

"Let you all return to your homes to await further instruction. You shall be called upon when the time is nigh. Ready your scouts and prepare for battle. Those who have yet to complete the Right of Sevens must be kept within the sanctuaries. Any human kindred must also be warned and armed well if they wish to join us."

As the crowd began to disperse, the Zythros stone suddenly began to pulse like the beat of a rhythmic drum.

"Oh bless the Heavens, a Keeper is coming!" exclaimed someone. Before I had a chance to wonder what they meant, a beam of light shot up from the point on the stone. It hit the roof briefly then vanished. There in its wake was a lonely little orb, a small Keeper. It blinked on and off, hovering above us. A group of Keepers zoomed out from the shadows, circled it and then whisked it away. It was all over in a matter of seconds.

A chorus of, "Blessed be A'vean" rang out as the entire crowd blinked out one by one in a mass of white, streaking light, heading back to wherever they came from.

"That, my dear, is how Keepers are born. When there is sufficient positive energy flowing through and around a Zythros stone, it generates the life of a Keeper. It is a great joy," Enl'iel explained.

Gedz'iel moved as though to leave, breaking yet another moment of amazement. "I shall return within the week. I must seek counsel with the Eloi. I shall also take Andr'eal to the Sanctuary of Souls. Her confinement is complete. Peace and comfort await her there." Andr'eal was close to his side, lovingly cuddled into him as he stroked her ethereal hair that floated like a halo in the breezeless room. Her translucent arms enveloped his chest, never wanting to separate from him again.

"Enl'iel, keep her well protected until she arrives in the Northern lands. I have Keepers and scouts at the ready to follow you. Jud'ael shall greet you in London." I heard Brennan quietly curse to himself at the mention of this name. "Beware of these humans you keep—they are a liability. Keep them under control. Soph'ael, learn your craft through the teachings of Koi, strengthen your body as well as your elemental energy, for at this time you are weak and vulnerable. Most importantly, strengthen your mind. Without self-belief, there is no benefit in physical or elemental strength, as your enemies will exploit any weakness of constitution." With that, he bid us all farewell with the same cheek-on-cheek gesture and disappeared in a blinding streak of light.

Leaning heavily on her arm, I asked Enl'iel, "So, we are going to London?"

"Yes, dear—immediately. Koi has prepared appropriate transportation, since you cannot travel safely by transference yet."

She guided me quickly away and up one of the swirling metal staircases leading to the second level. I was agonisingly tired, and my legs barely had the energy to make it up each step. As I ascended, I saw the artists responsible for the murals. Buzzing frantically over a spare piece of wall, the little Keepers were drawing crystalline colours from within the earth, creating a new image. It was no shock now, after everything that already had happened, that I saw my image revealing itself. A diamond dagger lay in one hand and a bleeding wound spread across my other. It was both surreal and phenomenally impressive. As we disappeared into a dark corridor, I asked Enl'iel, "Can you explain transference to me?"

"Certainly. It is how we move within the realms of the Earth, utilising portals in the atmosphere. We dissolve into the ether and reappear at the destination of our choice. Before the fall, Watchers could move throughout the entire universe *and* the Earth. Now, they and we alike are limited to the realms within the Earth. With practise, you too will be able to do this easily. But at the moment, your body is still growing and recovering from your awakening. It will take time, but it will come." Like the impressive light orbs, I thought that would be a pretty cool trick to have up my sleeve.

We quickly arrived at a large, wooden door and pushed through it. Kea, Koi, and Brennan were already inside the small room at the base of another staircase. Also there, seated on the floor with a bag on each of their laps, were Jaz and Ben. They both glared at me. I felt weighed down by their sombre expressions. After what happened with Ben, who knew how Jaz was feeling about me? I self-consciously glanced away from them, knowing they were still watching me.

"Up these stairs is a waiting vehicle that will transport you to the airport. A private jet will be ready for take-off. We will be shadowed by scouts—our military, so to speak. You will be safe," Koi spoke authoritatively. "Let us depart." He motioned the group up the stairs, smiling at me as I passed by. "You have done well Sophia. I very much look forward to training you." He gave my arm a reassuring squeeze as he led the way.

I looked back at my best friends briefly as I went up ahead of them.

Had I lost them as I accepted my new destiny?

Chapter
Thirty-One

It was early afternoon as we drove in a limousine, of all things. Where the money was coming from, I couldn't imagine. *A private jet, too?* Those forty-five minutes were supremely uncomfortable as my friends sat opposite me, wordless and avoiding all eye contact. Each time we stopped at a red light, the lack of anything to focus on out the window made their silence all the more unbearable. How inverted my world had become in a few short days. This new reality was hitting me full force like a sucker punch, and it didn't feel nice at all. I fiddled nervously with the back pack I'd been given that contained the shiny box, wondering what was inside its ancient facade.

As we arrived, we drove directly onto the tarmac like celebrities. We were met by well-dressed male and female crew standing by the entrance stairs. Enl'iel and Koi greeted them before they acknowledged me. Both of the pilots briefly flashed their eyes a bright, sparkling blue, but then they returned to their average brownish hues. *An impressive, covert greeting.* I was kind of blown away by this completely awesome trick. It was hard to keep my face from looking like a gobsmacked kid.

Kea and Brennan ushered Ben and Jaz into their seats, and then we were off within minutes, with none of the fuss that flying commercial entailed. Brennan made his way over to me whilst Enl'iel spoke quietly with my friends.

"Hey, princess. How are you doing? Big day—big couple of days, huh?" His Aussie accent was suddenly more muted, less discernible.

I contemplated his question for a moment as I watched the ground drop away through the tiny window. "I'm—I don't know. It's like I'm being swept up and away on a tidal wave. I can't go back, I realise that, so I suppose I just have to ride it forward, blindly." I replied as I leaned back against the beige leather seat, my eyes heavy. "I'm overwhelmed, Brennan." I rubbed my temples, grimacing in an effort to put everything in place.

"Yeah, it's been full on, but it'll all fall into place. Don't you worry princess. Your million questions will slowly be answered. Just know one thing—I've got your back." He said this as he gently squeezed my hand.

"Yeah. I thought my friends did, too." My eyes slowly succumbed to sleep as I gazed at the soft white clouds that rolled like a stormy ocean. The last things I saw before I drifted off were white orbs zipping around the wing in various formations, accompanying us like a military detail.

I awoke to the sound of the plane landing. The thud of the wheels hitting the ground jerked me forward, forcing my eyes wide open. I looked around to get my bearings. Something jabbed into my leg as I leaned forward to pick up my backpack. I fished around in the leg pocket of my cargos to find the sparkling, diamond dagger hiding in there. I couldn't recall putting it there, or why. *Would I need it again? How much blood would I be spilling?*

"We're home, finally. Man, I've missed this place." Brennan was unbuckling his belt enthusiastically, looking around with the anticipation of a kid at Disneyland. "I'd much prefer to wing it next time, though, so hurry up and learn to fly, princess. It's much more convenient," he smiled.

"We're here already?" I asked through a wide yawn. "I thought this must be a stopover!"

Brennan was stretching out his huge frame. His biceps flexed with a jaw-dropping pop as he casually ran his hands through his hair. Those scars on his upper arms peaked out from under his sleeve. His legs were now as strong as though they had never been injured at all. Strength oozed from his every pore.

"You were playing sleeping beauty for twenty hours straight!" He placed a quick kiss on my forehead before he headed for the door. Ben followed him, but didn't even look at me. That sinking feeling re-emerged. Jaz at least glanced back at me as she followed them. She gave me a half smile like she wanted to say something, but then thought better of it. She looked exhausted. I followed them down the stairs with my backpack slung over my shoulder. The chest contained within it hummed ever so slightly. It was as though it was communicating to me and I wondered if anyone else was aware of its presence like I was. The knife banged back and forth against my leg as I paced along. I continued to wonder about these mysterious items. The Kaladai, the scroll and god, or whoever, knew what else was coming. According to Enl'iel, we couldn't open the scroll until Gedz'iel returned. The mystery would remain just that for a while longer still.

In Heathrow, the seven of us went through customs. I had my passport at the ready, but was waved through with a quick stamp and another flash of sparkling blue eyes by a woman who was all business and no conversation.

"What's with all the eyes flashing?" I asked quietly. "Do they all do that?" I wondered if Ben and Jaz had noticed and been even more freaked out.

"It's our private acknowledgement of one another in the human world. We have our kind everywhere. Some are Watchers, but most are Eudaimonian. It's how we navigate quietly around the globe. In all areas, from healthcare, to government, transport, housing and sustenance, we are present. We exist this way to keep ourselves invisible, as well as to keep our ears to the ground to pick up any fluctuations in Daimon activity. Did you ever once notice that I have never carried a purse, or money?" Enl'iel asked with a coy expression.

"Actually—no! How did we get by in Australia? How did we pay our way?" I inquired, rather surprised at this immensely obvious oversight. I had money from work, but couldn't recall ever once seeing her whip out an ATM card.

"The *network*, dear. The network provides all that we need." She smiled an all knowing smile.

After a long walk through the huge terminal complex, we reached a bustling taxi rank brimming with compact black cabs. The smell of Christmas-scented coffee lured me to a nearby coffee cart. A flash of blue eyes ensued from the barista, and I had an intoxicating espresso with a hint of cinnamon within seconds. I immediately loved this network. The cool, wintery air and hot coffee quickly pushed away the last wisps of sleep. A light drizzle was falling as another limousine was loaded with the few small bags we had brought along with us.

"You guys certainly know how to travel!" I commented to Enl'iel as she gestured for me to enter first. She laughed lightly, a sweet trill that was bright and youthful.

A colossal man was standing by the open doors, looking very uncomfortable in a black corporate suit. He was twisting at his shoulders and stretching his neck tie, as though trying to escape its confines. He threw me a look of *hurry the hell up* as I clambered in the back. He unnecessarily shoved Brennan in behind me, causing him to glow and growl with anger. Brennan turned to get back out, but Enl'iel pulled at his arm and shook her head, giving him a soft, lingering kiss on his cheek.

"Don't you mind him, you and I have more important catching up to do than you and Jude!" Brennan seemed to immediately melt and forget about the driver smugly grinning outside. This must have been the Jud'ael guy they were talking about back home. Brennan's reaction to him matched the sigh of disgust he let slip when his name was mentioned.

The ride was much like the first one, initially. Silence came from Jaz and Ben until after we pulled off the M4 near Reading for them to grab a drink and bathroom break. When Jaz got back in, she sat next to me and passed me something from her pocket. It was a picture of Shadow and Grey, with a note. I read the quickly scrawled script.

> *Dear sweet girl.*
> *Don't you be worrying about your mutt and bag o' bones horse. I'll keep them fed and fat for you.*
> *You take care and come back to us,*
> *Alfie and Joan*

A tear sprung in one eye.

"Thanks, Jaz."

She reached out and squeezed my hand.

"Sorry for being a complete cow to you. I honestly couldn't string together enough dirty words yesterday but—" she squeezed my hand a little tighter, "I realised after having my hissy fit that you're the one who's probably got the most to be pissed-off about right now. All of this freaky crap is happening to you! I'm a terrible bestie for sulking—I'm sorry. I don't know what the freak is going on, but I do know there are lot people—or whatever—looking out for you," She glanced over at Enl'iel then hugged me briefly, pulling back when Ben got back into the car. His presence obviously caused her a conflict of loyalty, as he was clearly still ignoring me. She made a move to go and sit with him, but whispered to me first. "*Anyway, I can't go sulking for too long—you need to intro me to that God who's driving this thing!*" Clearly she was coping okay, because her hormones were back on, firing at all cylinders. Relief slid through me as she sat back next to Ben, whispering to him here and there, seemingly telling him off as he scowled in the opposite direction.

I barely noticed the rest of the long drive, only picking out the turn off sign to Birmingham and the Midlands along the motorway.

With scouts zapping continuously around the car for the rest of the trip, it was hard to see much outside. I wondered how they weren't visible to the general public, motoring along beside us. We turned off the main road onto a small one wide enough for only one car. Naked trees made a skeletal, overhanging tunnel as we drove toward a sandstone church to the left, atop a hill. We pulled into a gravel driveway beside the church that was surrounded by crumbling, snow-capped gravestones and turned down towards an impressive, whitewashed Tudor manor. A large stone sat proudly at the head of the driveway, engraved with the name, *The Old Priory*. The car pulled to a stop next to a side entrance. Before I could get out, I noticed a serene, elderly woman bustling out of an arched door, hastily rubbing her hands on her apron. She was immediately fussing and smiling, cuddling into Jude, Kea, Koi, Brennan and finally Enl'iel. She was followed out by a man, who of course was as stunning as the rest of them.

I stepped out, Ben and Jaz followed quietly behind me.

"Oh, me! Oh, for the love of the Heavens! Look at her! She's a true beauty. Welcome, child. Welcome to the Old Priory." With that, the old woman hugged me warm and tight. She smelled of flour and vanilla, and she reminded me all too much of Esme with her ample bosom and motherly warmth. She held me at arm's length and surveyed me carefully. That's when I noticed it. Her eyes were clouded over—she was blind, yet she looked me over every bit as thoroughly as anyone could. *How could she possibly know what I looked like?*

Her soft, wrinkled hand caressed my face, feeling about over my birthmark. Although she was a stranger, it felt very familiar, so I didn't stop her. She felt down my arms and grabbed my hands. "Child, you are long awaited, long loved, and forevermore so. You mind, I'll be looking after you here. Hmm, you could do with a little fattenin' up though! All skin and bone! You call on me at any time. You may call me Eilir, my dear. Oh me, that rhymed! Ha ha! May the blessings of A'vean be upon you!" She giggled charmingly.

After a dozen or so kisses covered every part of my face, she ushered me back over to Enl'iel. She greeted Jaz with same enthusiasm, but singled out Ben.

"Ah, we have a troubled soul here, I see. Buck up, young man. No time for self-indulgence. On with you, then. Let's fill your belly. You might have a different outlook once you have one of me cakes in you." He couldn't have been further from impressed with the look of annoyance he threw her way. "And that kind of attitude young man will get you nowhere with me! Hmmm!" I was sure I heard someone giggle, then clear their throat.

Eilir had her hands on her hips and her mouth pursed, challenging him to answer her back.

"Don't trouble yourself Eilir. I'll sort his attitude out. I'll take these two to get settled. Send down some of your best, please? It's been a long, tasteless drought without your cooking," Kea said as she gently pushed Jaz and Ben away from the house, towards the church.

Eilir blushed, "Oh me, by the Heavens, I do love her! Come on with you now Soph'ael, the kettle's boiled." With that, she turned and ambled into the manor with a warm chuckle, her floor-length skirt rustling with her haste.

The silent man followed right behind her in bare feet and simple white linen pants, just like the rest of the Watchers.

Enl'iel ushered me into a small living room decked out with well-worn leather sofas and floor rugs. There was a musty, well lived in smell to it. It was pleasantly homey.

"Eilir is our resident cook, although she is much more than that. It was a surprise to us all that a mere human could ever teach us anything. All our young look to her as a wise, guiding light. We can't possibly do without her. You'll grow to love her so. We will stop here a short while in the main house before we go down to the sanctuary. Would you care for a shower to freshen up, Sophia? Eilir has a change of clothes for you already prepared."

"Yes, thanks. That'd be great." I was still in my grimy, smelly clothes and felt foul. I thought on the old woman as I followed Enl'iel through the ancient house. "Um, Enl'iel, how can Eilir see me? Her eyes look as though they are blind." I inquired, maintaining as much tact as possible.

"Yes, dear, it is so. It is a long story, but Eilir was blinded by accident a long time ago in an unfortunate chance encounter with a Watcher. He was horrified by what he had done, and took her in. Unable to repair her sight, he has cared for her ever since. Over the years, she has been taught the second sight, she can see without her eyes. Dash'iel, over there, is the Watcher responsible. He has cared for her with unfailing devotion for over three hundred years. I'm sure she'll tell you about it. She loves recounting how she met him," she explained with a wistful look.

"Three hundred years! How could she live that long?"

She guided me up the narrow, floral carpeted stairway to the bathroom as she explained.

"He has healed and rejuvenated her with the elements in order to keep her well. Unfortunately, the human body has its limitations, and she is now nearing the end of her time on Earth. He does not leave her side. It is no secret to anyone that he has loved her for all these years and she, him. Unconsummated love, mind you, as our laws do not allow for such relationships to occur. The Council of Eloi would banish Dash'iel if he were ever to involve himself with a human in such a manner. They have lived side by side, in love, with a chasm between them. It is both beautiful and devastating." She finished this reverie with a deep sigh, as though she would allow the relationship to have flourished if it were up to her.

"That's so cruel. Couldn't they have been given permission? Why make them suffer like that?" I asked as I entered the bathroom. She turned on the shower for me and set down a towel and soap from a small cupboard.

"Sophia, love and lust are what have led to this whole predicament in the first place. There is, unfortunately, no tolerance for it. We will call for you on the half hour for tea, and then we shall retreat to the sanctuary. Enjoy your shower, dear."

I stepped into the tiny shower stall in the small, aqua room. A round porthole window allowed a view down the length of the property to the small river in the distance. A blue barge bobbed by a dock. As I scrubbed my hair I looked on and wondered what the pain of forbidden love might feel like.

Chapter
Thirty-Two

The second I was dressed in the clothes that mysteriously appeared whilst I was showering. Just as I was pulling on the slim fitting white tee over a crisply ironed pair of matching cargos, Eilir came knocking at the door.

"Tea, child? I have a lovely brew awaiting you downstairs in my parlour."

"Yes, thank you. I'll be there in a few minutes," I answered as I pulled my grimy Docs back on. I heard her patter off, humming happily as she went.

I looked at myself in the small mirror, still shocked by the white hair and bright blue eyes. I knew it was me, but it just didn't look like me. Thankfully, the birthmark had settled and was now a silvery colour, like a long-faded scar. I couldn't help but run a finger along it. It was no longer raised, and it tingled when I touched it. I was buried somewhere deep inside this strange reflection.

Tea was actually a banquet of sweet and savoury delights. They were awaiting me in a pokey little kitchen, on a small table that fit snugly under the angle of the staircase.

Dash'iel, yet to speak, pulled out a chair for me to sit, like a proper gentleman. I took the offer, still shy as usual, not used to this kind of treatment. As I sat, he kneeled next to me. He leaned forward and placed his right cheek upon mine, and a warm buzz of energy passed between us. It was such a personal and close form of greeting. It would take time feeling comfortable with it.

"It is indeed an honour to meet you, Soph'ael. I am at your service." His voice was deep and formal, but his smile lent a boyish charm to the youthful twinkle in his eyes.

"Thank you, I'm honoured to meet you too. All of you," I responded as I looked at both he and Eilir. Dash'iel smiled, then stood and left with a bow and a chaste kiss placed upon Eilir's hand. She beamed at him in a way that cast aside the years of her age, to the point that I could almost see a young girl, madly in love.

"He is quite the catch, don't you think, dear Soph'ael?" she quipped.

I was getting quite confused with interchanging of my name. "Please, call me Sophia. And yes, he is very handsome, Eilir," I answered to her utter delight. "Your tea and food are delicious, too. What are these amazing things?" I said as I held up a small, sweet pastry bursting with juicy currants.

"Oh me, it's an Eccles cake. So delightful, aren't they? Can you believe they used to be illegal, because they had a drop o' the drink in them? Oh, what a waste! I cook them for all of my special guests! Once you are quite settled and I can snatch a small square of time, I shall teach you to make them, if you like. I never was able to have my own babes, so it would be such a treat!" She clapped the tips of her fingers together with delight.

"Well, I could eat them all day, Eilir," I responded through my last sweet mouthful. She waved at me with a coy look of mock embarrassment and tottered over to the sink to scrub a dish.

"Eilir, I shall take Sophia to the Sanctuary now. There's precious little time, and much to do. Shall I send you up some help for dinner? I believe there are a few young ones that are in need of a firm hand today. I am quite sure you must have some pots requiring hard labour?"

"Oh me, yes, I do indeed. Send those little scoundrels up, and I'll have them sorted in no time!"

"Excellent, and thank you for your delicious treats. Such a delight to the palate."

"Oh, my sweet Enl'iel, nothing but the best for you, dear lady. Now off with you then, I've got tea to prepare." She grabbed a pair of scissors and began snipping some herbs by the open back door as she sang sweetly to herself.

"Come, Sophia. Koi is awaiting you. We must commence your training today."

We left the main house and headed for the church. Up the small incline of the driveway, we entered the overgrown graveyard through an aged iron gate. The bell tower to the left was in desperate need of repair. Crumbling around the edges and pock-marked, yet it was still a thing of beauty. A small plaque by the door proudly decreed that it was built in the year 1000 AD.

A medieval, musty air hit me as we entered the church. The large heavy doors protested the intrusion with an annoyed screech. Ancient wooden pews sat lonely and dusty under the vaulted roof. Gilt-framed gothic depictions of Jesus and the Twelve Apostles framed a small altar. Enl'iel guided me to the back of the building, through the aisle to a small nave. Here, the burial tombs of people long dead adorned the walls. A woman named Catherine, buried alongside her husband, Alfred, in the 1500's rested in the right wall. A marble effigy of the couple laying supine with their hands in prayer lay below an oval plaque that told of their story in Middle English. I couldn't understand anything other than the names and dates. Below our feet a bronze medieval knight was carved into the pale stone. It jumped out against the worn tiling surrounding it.

"Are you ready, Sophia?"

"No. Not at all!"

"I promise, everything will be alright. You will see that soon enough. Destiny is so often out of our control, but how we travel that path is very much a choice." Enl'iel then placed her hand upon the right cheek of the marble effigy of Catherine. It began to glow as the twirls and curls of a mark emerged like magic upon the cheek of the static object.

As this happened, the soldier underfoot rumbled slightly, and I stepped back as the image descended into the ground and slid off to the side. It revealed another underground staircase, more brightly lit than the others, at least. *How many dark holes could I visit in one week?* This was becoming scarily normal.

"Come now, Sophia. You have many kindred to meet, and much to learn. Once you enter the sanctuary, you must not leave without one of us, as you are yet to know how to use the mark of A'vean to control the opening. Until you have mastered the art of transference, this is your only way in or out," she explained. "In your current state, being stranded outside would be immensely dangerous."

"What's the mark of A'vean?" I queried.

"That, my dear, is the 'birthmark' upon your face. All those with a strong elemental connection to A'vean bare this symbol, to some degree. Some are more pronounced than others. As you will discover, it provides us with an ability to connect with one another, and to control the elements around us as our spirit flows through it." All my life I'd been looking at that scar, a part of the real me after all, but hadn't realised it.

The entrance was dusty, appearing rarely used, yet I saw fresh foot prints in the thick grey layer down the first few steps as I descended into the warm, underground ground passage.

"The others brought Jaz and Ben through earlier to settle them in. I understand this is very hard on them, especially Ben. He has a troubled soul, that poor boy," she said.

"I'm really worried about him. I'm worried for them both. They've had such difficult lives. I'm scared this will all be too much, and that I'll lose them. Or worse, they'll get hurt."

"Give them time, they will come around. Neither have had the security of stable families for so long that they lack trust in anyone but themselves. They will slowly realise that they have that in us. I have put in a word so that Ben will have his mind occupied. They will be safe here, and I know you will not lose their friendship forever, dear. Be patient." She walked on ahead and left me to think of him the entire journey down. His cold behaviour still stung like a fresh face slap.

We arrived at a landing with a white doorway—at least I thought that's what it was—until she walked straight through it. Enl'iel's hand peeked back through and beckoned to me. I followed her through this veil of light, and every cell of my body buzzed as I did so. Beyond it was nothing short of amazing.

What the Library of Antiquity was to record keeping, this Sanctuary was to urban living. I'd entered a secret, underground world. Multiple levels spanned out around a central shaft that descended to what looked like an endless depth. It was pleasantly warm and bustling with activity. The perimeter was dotted with numerous doorways and corridors, embellished by ornate, wrought iron balustrading. The walls were thick, with lush greenery that bloomed with huge, unusual white flowers, which lent a surprising freshness to the air. Orbs of light bobbed at various points, providing almost daylight brightness. Everywhere I looked there were people. They were walking, flying, talking, and bustling to and fro. Ordinary things were going on, like adults carrying children and '*workman*' pushing trolleys of goods. Some sat reading books on a bench by an underground waterfall. White-haired children ran around squealing, their parents chasing after them. Teenagers huddled in a far corner, laughing and glancing suspiciously around, as though they were up to something. It looked every bit a thriving, albeit hidden, society. This display of ridiculously normal activity played out like it would in any ordinary town. Apart from the flying, the floating lights and the fact that, well, they weren't human!

"Wow!" was all I could manage to say.

"It is amazing, isn't it? This is the Katoika Sanctuary, a home to all. This is a place for any of our kindred who do not wish to live in the human world, and even those who do, but wish for a little respite of the soul from the madness above. It is also the chief training venue for everything from schooling our youngsters to training our military."

"You have an army?"

"Indeed. The Watchers were an army Sophia. They all volunteered for the Earth mission from various ranks from all over the universe. It was very much the 'must have' ticket of the time. If only they knew what was to come. Fortunately all those military skills have come into their own with the never-ending war with the Daimon."

Amazed, I followed her along a paved path around the cylindrical space and down a set of sparkling stone stairs. A number of people acknowledged us with a polite incline of their head, accompanied with a brief flash of their mark of A'vean. One woman embraced Enl'iel with the customary cheek-kiss as I had come to think of it. She had a small child with her who walked boldly up to me.

"You're pretty, are you a Watcher? Do you have big pterugia? What's your favourite colour?" she asked in rapid succession in a cute, high-pitched voice.

I knelt down, looking into to her opaque eyes. Her little fingers reached out to feel the curves of my face. She squinted hard, trying to see me more clearly as I replied, "Well now, that is a lot of questions. Let me see? My favourite colour is pink," she squealed with delight at this. "I'm not sure how big my wi—*pterugia* are, and if being a Watcher meant I could hang out with you, then I certainly hope I am one!"

She squealed with excitement, "Mama! Mama, look at the pretty lady. She wants to be my friend!" She flung herself around my neck, trying to reach up to do the cheek thing. I obliged as her little cheek, with its tiny swirls of white, emitted spurts of light that tickled my skin. My own mark responded with a warm glow that smothered her face. "Ooh, Mama, she gave me a *biiig* kiss!"

"Enough now, Av'ael. This is a very important guest, please don't bother her," she said apologetically as she bowed in front of me. I tried to reassure her that it was perfectly fine, but she grabbed Av'ael's hand and gently tugged her away. "We mustn't keep them, my sweet." The mother acknowledged me again with a swift bow then whisked away. The little girl waved frantically at me as she disappeared down another staircase.

"How cute!" I said as I waved back. "She has the second sight, too, like Eilir?" I asked.

"Yes, all Eudaimonians are born with it. It is truly an experience when we see with our eyes for the first time. The first sight is a time of great celebration. You will see a lot more of that kind of attention from the children. You are— for want of a better human term—somewhat of a celebrity!"

"Oh, no! No, I don't want that! I can't stand being the centre of attention," I complained as she ignored me, leading us left down another sparkling corridor. It was lit by glowing orbs every ten or so paces. I was almost immediately distracted by an ornate sign carved into a doorway to the right that read, *Stasis, please enter and exit quietly*. A woman appeared ahead of us and entered the room carrying a tray brimming with herbs and steaming liquids as we passed.

"What's in there?" I asked. My brain was crammed, full to bursting with everything new that was throwing itself at me. I wanted and needed to absorb everything. I felt a pang of guilt with the growing excitement as I remembered the fear Jaz and Ben must be feeling. The pull was too strong though. "Please, may I see?"

"Of course, I think you will feel quite at home here, actually," she answered with a look of satisfaction.

Enl'iel took a step back and gently pushed the door open, a finger to her lips miming quietness. I found myself in a hospital-like room, filled with small, neat beds. The familiar essence of sage, lavender, and cedar filled the air as the aromas smoked dreamily from golden lanterns hanging from the ceiling. There was no modern equipment here. It was as far from my accustomed hospital ward as it could ever be. It appeared every bit a Middle Ages mock-up, apart from the shiny, decorative metallic sheets that served as wall coverings. They reminded me of the old, pressed metal ceiling in *Miss Marple's*. The room was dominated by a long, wooden preparation table that ran down the centre. This was adorned with mortar bowls that contained powders in various states of preparation. Herbs hung in abundance in various stages of the drying process whilst clear bottles steeped pungent-smelling tonics, giving the air a heady note. Medicines were being pounded at by numerous women and men with long, herb-entwined plaits flowing down their backs. Loose white linen tunics adorned their tall statures, which were accented by expressions of deep and silent concentration.

The cots were occupied by a handful of sleeping bodies.

"Sophia, this is the room of stasis. It is a healing room and also a safe haven for our children. All Eudaimonian children come here at some point as they pass through three stages of development called the Right of Sevens. You met dear Av'ael who is four and still sight impaired. At birth, we are blind, and by age seven our eyesight has fully developed. Around the thirteenth year, we all enter a natural hibernation phase for one full year as our bodies go through the metamorphic changes that bring out the gifts and powers inherited from our bloodlines. These gifts only come to fruition through a state of inertia, as it is extremely painful—something you well know. The fact that you went through this change over a matter of days is what sets you apart."

My God! I didn't feel pity for myself, but rather relief that these children didn't have to suffer as I had. She continued with this fascinating history lesson as I listened on in silent wonder.

"They are tended to by our Alchemae, who keep the children's mortal flesh healthy whilst they sleep." She indicated the busy men and women who were measuring, mixing and distilling at the preparation table. "Our young ones are incredibly vulnerable in this state and cannot protect themselves. Many a young Eudaimonian has been brutally picked off by Rogues and Daimon for sport in the past. That is why they all pass through this safe haven to endure the change. At twenty-one, we go through the final transition. If we are to develop Pterugia and hone any new skills, it will happen then. This unfortunately can be *the* most painful process, thank the heavens it is brief."

I gazed at the loving attention a young girl was receiving as a woman laid moistened leaves along her inflamed spine. Small, fernlike patterns blazed across her skin, just like mine. I was glad she was unconscious for this process.

My eyes were then drawn to the rear of the room, where a sheet of white, pulsing light hummed from floor to ceiling. A male passed through it a number of times.

"What's behind there?" I felt drawn to it.

"You could say that is our Intensive Care Unit. Come, it may ease your soul to see inside."

I followed, feeling that familiar thrum of energy reverberate through my back—I sensed pain that wasn't mine.

As I passed though the tingly white shield of light, I gasped with surprise. There, prostrate upon a large bed, was Cael. He lay covered in sweet smelling poultices, hiding the horrific wounds on his back.

"*Oh, Cael!*" I whispered. I rushed to him and knelt by his side.

Surprisingly, he responded to my presence as he turned to my whispered call. Heavily drugged eyes opened a fraction, revealing a hint of gleaming blue. He smiled weakly.

"Now I know I shall heal, for seeing you well." He closed his eyes. He lay quiet and peaceful.

"Will he be okay?" I choked back tears of guilt.

"He will in time, a long time. Unless he chooses to ascend," she replied as she placed a kiss upon his head.

"*Ascend?*" I asked as I also placed a kiss upon his cheek and held his hand before we moved away.

"Like my dear Brennan, Cael's wings were partly ripped from him, leaving his mortal body gravely ill. He can recover, but it may take years. Ten, twenty, or even hundreds, like Brennan. Or, if he so chooses, he can ascend his spirit and leave his body behind, like sweet Andr'eal," she explained solemnly.

"You mean die?" I asked, grasping my mouth in shock. The thought twisted through my insides.

"No, dear. We are immortal spirits who can exist consciously without an organic body. He would simply move to the Cavern of Souls and await the time of rapture. The very same rapture that you will hopefully bring about for us, sooner rather than later. You may visit with him anytime, if you wish. I sense it has already restored some of his strength to see you so well. Now though, it is time to meet with Koi. We have such little time now that you are known and awakened. Time is now a precious commodity we dare not toy with. Despite your fatigue, you must begin your training immediately."

Chapter
Thirty-Three

Belial took his punishment with the honour and bravery that any soldier of worth would. He was beaten almost to the point of descendence into the pits of Hell. Any thoughts of a mortal death releasing him to the peace of the Sanctuary of Souls were long ago lost. He was a hairsbreadth away from joining the A'vean filth that lived below the cracked Empyrean earth, alongside the human garbage. Plum blood poured from his split lips and swollen eyes. His wings were dull, and a horn had cracked painfully in half.

"You have betrayed us with your failures. You could have proceeded without his permission! You are pure-born after all! Do you not have your own mind? You committed yourself to us, yet so often return with the pathetic excuses of failure," Yeqon blasted him once more with a lava-hot crack of light. The blow finally brought Belial to his knees.

"How did you fail? How?" Yeqon screamed inches from his face, making him wince. He resented that deeply.

"She was awakening before you! The portal was open, and you allowed someone to destroy your mortal vessel!" His hand was now wrenched around Belial's neck. The strain of anger drained all the beauty from him. He was as ugly on the outside as his blackened heart in that moment.

"*Master*," he breathed raggedly through his injuries. "I was betrayed— someone works against us."

"Excuses, excuses. Meanwhile, another eternity flies by while we rot here. What was Nik'ael doing? Didn't you have a plan?"

"Yes, M-master," he coughed and spluttered. Yeqon eased his hand slightly. "He cleared the house for me—but, I'm not certain, I think Nik'ael may have changed the plan."

"Liar!" Yeqon knew of Nik'ael's own ideas. He pressed Belial hard to test him, to dig out anything Nik'ael may have failed to divulge. He needed the release of a decent fight, and Belial was an easy target. His brothers were lathering on the pressure. He needed to appear in control. "You simply failed, after he had done all the ground work. You had her in your grasp. Either way, you should have brought her to me! Be damned Nik'ael's ideas!" He threw Belial to the ground, at the feet of the other four imposing figures. "I grow weary of Nik'ael's procrastinating. No more. We attack *now*. We will hunt them down, wear them out, until their blood pours such that we could sail the Earth upon it!"

Yeqon's spies had informed him that the girl had been taken into hiding for training. Despite Nik'ael's arguments, Yeqon believed now that she would become too strong, too quickly after much heated discussion with his brothers. This latest failure tipped Yeqon over the edge. Lashing out like this, pointlessly, showed that he was under pressure to maintain control. He appeared weak now, and weakness meant vulnerability.

"Pineme, summon Nik'ael. He is to cease his mission and join us immediately in bringing that wench in. She will not resist us once we have her in our possession. I shall enter that filthy Earthen realm myself, if need be!" He spat at the ground in disgust at the thought, his spittle sizzling on the scorched ground. "Clearly we cannot rely on anyone other than ourselves to discharge that which has been commanded. As for you, Belial, you shall have time to think on your insufficiencies. You should have overcome her. Despite everything, she should be at my feet this very moment. A little stay in the pits should clear your mind whilst you heal." He smiled vindictively.

"No! Please, Master!" Belial was shamed by such begging, though he persisted whilst on his knees, like a pathetic dog.

No discussion was entered into. The red glow of Yeqon's trident rammed into the ground, opening a great chasm. Piercing screams escaped into the humid air. Yeqon laughed with pleasure at the display. The others joined in his amusement, stamping their feet and weapons on the ground rhythmically and chanting foul curses at the beleaguered Belial.

Belial looked on and begged one last time. "Please—no!" He looked up into their chiselled faces as he clawed at the ground. The broken horn fell from his head. They were enjoying his suffering, whilst Yeqon asserted his power before them. *Scum, they were nothing more. How stupid he had been to join them*. He was done with them. They would rue the day they cursed him to the Pits.

"Join your equals in the bowels of the Pits. You may learn something there," Yeqon bellowed.

Unceremoniously, Belial was shoved with various weapons by the Five into the chasm. He went to join the six hundred and sixty-six tortured yet obedient demonic A'vean souls. He fell. He fell far and deep, the screams of the imprisoned Daimon army more painful than any corporeal beating.

Chapter
Thirty-Four

Smooth, gemstone-dotted corridors led us deeper into the subterranean labyrinth. The smell of peppermint and a door slightly ajar made me pause and double back. I followed my senses through the heavy wooden door and was rewarded with the sight of that dragon-tattooed arm holding up a *Darkest Goth* mag. The *slop-slap* of chewing accompanied the quick flicking of pages.

"Jaz!" She sat up as I ran to her armchair. "You okay?" I asked.

She answered by throwing me a Mentos, which I playfully caught in my mouth as it fell. We both laughed.

"Despite feeling like I'm buried alive and being confined unless 'safely escorted' by my glowing guard," she eyeballed the handsome but silent sentry standing by the doorway, "I suppose you could say I'm living the life! They feed me, all be it vegetable slop, bring me trashy mags, and would you believe there's even a flat screen in this place? Look, it's possessed! No electrical connections! Ha!" I did look, and it was working—how, I had no clue. *Dr Phil* was running quietly in the background. It was her favourite show because the 'screwballs' she saw on it made her feel '*somewhat normal*'. I always got that—normal, that safe old feeling. I wondered how normal she was feeling right then. A quick look around showed me she was decked out in a quite comfy little room. Despite the bare earth walls, it was full of colourful floor rugs and furniture and a huge, four-poster bed.

"How wasted is that baby?" she said as she saw me eyeing its luxurious linen.

"Jaz! You're appalling!"

"I know, it's a talent!" She winked her long lashes in my direction.

"So, how are you, angel-girl?" She looked me up and down as though she might find alien antennas.

"I suppose I'm okay. I'm alive aren't I?" I gave her a nervous smile. She seemed to be waiting for more. "I'm literally living minute by minute. I don't ever know what's around the next corner. But guess what? I found Cael! He's here, alive. Not in the best shape, but alive!" That had her sitting up.

"Really? I *so* thought he was a dead man. Can I see him? Be nice to stretch my legs, even with *Mr Personality* over there tailing me."

"I'll take you when I can. That's all right, isn't it, Enl'iel?" I asked, feeling her energy hanging heavily over my shoulder, anxious to get going.

"Yes, dear, that will be fine," she answered as Jaz eyed her suspiciously up and down.

"Where's Ben?" I felt like I'd been asking that question incessantly. She threw her mag down and took a sip of water.

"He's next door, and luckily for him, he has that hunky Jude dude as his personal bodyguard slash jailer—whatever they want to call it. He's taken him out for a bit of bro-mancing or something. He's especially crappy at the moment. I think they've gone to blow off some steam or something. Might pull his fat head in an inch or two! Don't worry about Ben, Soph. It's all about feeling out of control for him. Don't take it personally—he's barely talking to me, either."

"I'm sorry, it's all my fault."

"Your fault? His smart arse attitude is his own problem. Don't waste a neuron on him Soph." She popped another mint in her mouth. "You reckon he likes peppermint?" She nodded at the guard. As my mouth hung open at her impressive ability to bounce back to her predatory man hunting, Enl'iel interrupted. She was none too pleased by the look on her face.

"Okay, okay. Enough now, you two can socialise later at first meal. Sophia, you must have your initial session of training with Koi. He is waiting. Jasmine, please, behave like a young lady?" She pulled me up gently and we left the room with Jaz staring at me, her smart-arsed look gone, one of worry replacing it.

A short walk and one long spiral staircase down deeper into the Earth, I found myself inside what I can only describe as the largest gym I'd ever seen. To be honest, I hadn't seen many, but I was sure this was the big Mama bear of them all. It was crammed full of weights, heavy, hanging hessian sacks, and running tracks. Metallic walls gleamed with medieval-style golden and silver weapons. They neatly adorned the walls in descending order of size and nastiness. There was nothing modern in sight. Impressive pieces of body armour hung majestically amongst the cache as well. It could have been a training stadium for an ancient Olympic games, though luckily without the nude athletes. *Unluckily if you were Jasmine.*

There were a number of people already there, the first of whom I saw were Jude and Ben. His head snapped up in my direction the moment I walked in. It felt like a siren went off whenever I entered a room. Apparently I couldn't make a discreet entrance. After a whispered word through clenched teeth from Jude, Ben inclined his head slightly towards me in an uncomfortable acknowledgment, then turned his back and pounded mercilessly into the innocent sack in front of him.

Koi manifested into physical form right in front of me with a pop of light, giving me a fright. Enl'iel took her leave, promising to pick me up later. She pecked at my cheek, the way she did when she was just my Nan. The lingering aroma of English breakfast tea hung in the air briefly after she was gone.

"My dear Sophia, it is an honour to begin your training. First and foremost, I wish you to know that this shall not come easily. Your mind must be as strong as your body. Clarity of the mind clears the body for strength and growth. You must move thoughtfully with your mind, not with the emotion of your heart. I was taught this concept eons ago, when I was a Seraph, like so many of us here. Fighting through the many worlds of the universe to maintain peace and order, this mantra has guided us well through many a challenge. I wish you to repeat it often, embedding the thought into your deepest self."

His words resonated with the warning from the vision of Enoch and I'el. *Beware my heart.*

Koi clapped away the moment, startling me again as I digested his speech.

"Please." He indicated to a neat pile of white clothing. "Change into your training attire, and we shall begin."

I did so in a small bathroom hewn from rock, alongside a row of natural spring showers. The steam of someone else showering clouded the air with a mineral, earthy tang.

I met Koi back in the arena wearing the white Karate-style pants and a white t-shirt with a gap in the back. Heavy but comfy new black combat boots replaced my Docs and had me looking half cadet, half ninja. I was painfully aware of Ben's eyes boring into me from behind, but I resisted the urge to look back as I heard him pounding away.

"Now, we shall begin. Your body has been neglected and unchallenged in your human life. Your recent transition will have left you in a physical aftershock. We must enhance your physical strength, alongside harnessing you elemental power. A little training each and every day, and you will be surprised by your own potential. You won't know yourself within the week. Finally, in time, the fun part—weapons!" There was a gleam in his eye as he said this, which suggested that he was a true soldier, a master and lover of his craft.

We began with a gentle jog around the perimeter to warm up. Ben's stare felt like a heavy blanket. But each time I lapped past him, he was looking the other way.

Why did it matter to me so much?

My love of jogging paid off with Koi being very impressed that I kept a steady and fast pace with him. We completed five huge laps of the track that was marked out by neatly recessed white stones. I was rewarded with a smile, a handful of almonds, and a refreshing mug of minted water. The run was followed by some weight training. At first, I balked at the dumbbells placed at my feet. They seemed too heavy for my lanky arms.

"Just think of them as cotton buds. That's all they are to you."

"Your faith is way too easily given, Koi." I said as I stretched my arms in preparation.

"I give none of myself unless it is fully deserved. *Try.* Trust in yourself, and try."

"Okay, but don't laugh when I bust an artery!"

I bent my knees, keeping my back straight, as Koi had shown me. My hands locked around the two grey weights. I faltered when I saw *40 kilograms* engraved on each one.

"Uh, no way—"

"Cotton buds!"

Cotton buds! Sure thing.

I closed my eyes and felt like an idiot. Then forced myself to imagine cotton buds. Big, heavy, metallic cotton buds. I yanked hard. Nothing but an embarrassing grunt happened.

"Shouldn't I try something just a little lighter first?" I whined.

"For what purpose? To convince yourself that you are capable of less? No. Pick them up, now." I gave him a jaw-drop of disbelief but received no sympathy. *Damn it, I was going to look like a fool.*

I took a deep breath and couldn't resist a quick look around. I was sure there'd be a crowd waiting for a good laugh. There wasn't, and luckily, Ben seemed to have disappeared along with Jude. I could hear clanging metal, but couldn't see them.

I gripped again and tried really hard. *Cotton buds, cotton buds, cotton buds.* I lifted. I felt nothing. About to complain again, Koi said, "Ah, there you are. Welcome to your new life, Sophia."

I opened my eyes to see that my arms were well above my head, with a weight suspended in each. It was as though they were feather dusters—practically weightless. *Cotton buds!*

"Holy crap! Sorry, I mean—how did I do that?" I let them down softly, like two pillows, and turned my hands over, looking at them for evidence of this amazing strength.

"It is the elemental power that courses through you. You are able to displace mass with a thought and energy surge." This little weight session continued for some time until Koi sensed the fatigue creeping into me. "Here, drink. Rest a moment."

Before I was at all ready he said, "Now, let's actually work! It is all very well and good to be strong and able to run, but what if you are running from something? What if something powerful and extremely fast were chasing you down? Whilst you are so green you must practise the defensive rather than the offensive. Are you ready to test those running skills?" he mused as he clicked his fingers. A red orb appeared with a sizzling *crack*. It hovered above him, malevolently humming and pulsing. I took a step backwards.

"This is a training orb. It will help you run faster, become stronger, and more nimble. Your reflexes will be honed. I want you to run again, but do not let the orb catch you. I will count to three, and then release it. Now, run!"

I didn't question him as the orb seemed to spring to life. It pulsed a brighter red and seemed only to stay still because Koi's palm coaxed it into submission. I ran. Within seconds, I felt a sharp sting as the orb struck my back. It was attacking me. I glanced back to see it weaving around the room emitting horrid stinging pulses in my direction. I pounded the ground as hard as I could but the evil thing was too fast.

"Run harder, Sophia! Think quickly, outmanoeuvre it!" Koi yelled from the distance. I ran harder, glancing back only to try to see its position. My breathing was beginning to labour with the panic of this new unknown entity in Crazyville. It zipped around me, zapping at me like a possessed lightning bolt. I only managed to go a couple hundred meters before it tripped me up and I fell to the ground, exhausted and bruised. It hung above me momentarily before gliding back to Koi who approached casually.

"What—the hell—was that?" I half yelled, trying to catch my breath. I was peeved. I didn't realise I was going to get electrocuted. Koi offered me a hand up, but I brushed him away and got up myself, rubbing at my sore arms and legs. I noticed Jude and Ben leaving in the distance as I rubbed the aches away. Ben was stock still, staring at me openly, until Jude unceremoniously shoved him out the door. It seemed Ben had met his match in brooding attitude and brute force.

Koi pulled my attention from the doorway. "Not impressive, yet neither disappointing."

"I assume that's a compliment?" I was even more annoyed. "Is that it? Is that what I have to do to train? Learn to run?"

"In part, for now. You will know when I am pleased." He turned his back and conjured more of the orbs from his palms. They danced around above him in a smooth synchronicity.

"This, Sophia, is just the beginning. When you are confronted by Rogues, as you are all too aware, they will be fast and merciless. If you come across a Daimon, speed, strength, and cunning are the least you will need until you are able to control your elemental power. I will bolster these strengths so that you may have at least a modest ability to protect yourself. Your training will be intense and harsh. There is little time before the Unseen and their foul hordes make their move. Your identity is known by the Daimon, your location will now be priority number one. Your safety will be near impossible to guarantee if you are unable—at the very minimum—to outrun an attack. This is why the Orbs are an unpleasant necessity." I digested this for a moment before nodding silently to him. I dusted myself off and readied myself to continue.

For the next hour or so, I ran and dodged those horrid red devils. I was sure that they actually enjoyed it. Finally, Koi gave me a reprieve and sent me to shower and change. I was dripping with sweat and aching in places I didn't know I had. The shower was bliss. My skin was a canvas of purple bruising, a surreal artwork of pain. A handmade lavender soap—just like back home— was conveniently left for me. The aroma was familiar and comforting. I found a change of clothes awaiting me when I emerged. It was one of the soft, white linen outfits that most of the Eudaimonians and Watchers seemed to wear. They were comfy and loose. The outfit was less karate and more yoga retreat. Jaz would surely give me hell when she saw me.

'First meal' was how they referred to brunch. Breakfast was more of a room service affair. I liked that idea a lot. At first meal, I sat with Koi in a massive hall on the highest level of the Sanctuary. Whilst he ate in a quiet contemplation, I watched those around me. People were coming and going from the buffet-style line. Eilir, fussing around over what to serve and when, slapped the hands of her young apprentices when they put things in the wrong places. Enl'iel sat at the far end of the large table with Brennan, they waved and smiled my way. My hunger, day by day, had grown to the point that my plate was filled with an unladylike amount of roasted vegetables. The physical changes of my awakening must have been sapping my energy because I never quite felt satisfied and was constantly looking for the next snack. I noted with relief though that everyone else seemed to have large portions, too. I immediately felt somewhat more connected to them. As I was sticky-nosing at other people, I noticed Ben sitting with Jude and Jaz a few tables away. While every pair of eyes in that room glanced secretly and sheepishly at me, the one pair that I wanted to look at me didn't. It was killing me. My desperation to attain his acknowledgement was consuming me. I needed to reconcile this unknown animosity oozing from him.

"How are you enjoying your meal, sweet girl?" Eilir asked as she appeared out of nowhere and piled delicious, freshly baked rolls in front of me.

"It's delicious, thank you. How in the world do you cater for all of these people?"

"Oh me, child, it's been many a year of practice, and a few good clips around the ears to the other cooks! I run a tight ship!" You could almost see a twinkle of pride in her dull eyes as she breezed away to chastise some poor kid.

"Well, aren't we Miss Popularity!" joked Jaz as she slipped in next to me. "Seriously though, do you have any sway on getting a steak down here? Do they *all* eat like you?" I laughed and elbowed her away. She was a balm that soothed my worries and kept me grounded. She, on the other hand, hid all of hers.

"Sorry but I think you're just going to have to force that salad down," I said with a smile.

"Hmph! And you think you're having a hard time!" She shoved some cucumber around with her fork as though it were a piece of poison. Irreverence was her calling card. I was about to ask her about Ben again, when to my utter disappointment, Koi interrupted.

"And now it's time for session two!" He announced with an amused smile. He stood up, waiting for me to follow as he greeted Brennan and a new guy as they approached our table. I'd just crossed the globe, taken a beating this morning, and they wanted a second torture session on day one. My look of appeal to Enl'iel down the other end was met with a sympathetic smile, but no intervention.

"See you later, Jaz."

"Not if I see you first. Be careful, Soph." She answered as Jude breezed silently by and took her back to Ben, who was also getting up to leave. He actually looked my way, so I waved tentatively. His jaw clenched, but he forced out a strained smile before they left together. *Why bother?* I thought to myself. Fake affection seemed worse than being ignored.

I followed Koi back downstairs reluctantly. I stopped him at all kinds of points of interest along the way to ask a myriad of questions, trying to delay the inevitable. Eventually we were back in the arena. *Damn!*

"This afternoon, we are going to focus on your elementals." Koi rearranged my top, which was apparently not sitting right. "You must keep your back clear, to avoid singeing too many outfits. Eilir is the resident seamstress too, you know. Even I fear her if I have not taken appropriate care of her '*hard and endless work*,' as she likes to put it." He raised is eyebrows in mock fear of Eilir's apparent drill sergeant wrath.

The clothing was cleverly designed so that it left the ferny leaflets free to allow the pterugia to emerge unhindered. It was mainly a concern for the women though, as barely any male ever seemed to wear a shirt down here. This was somewhat distracting, if I'm being honest. As we walked and I was thinking on this pulse-quickening topic, I noticed on Koi's left shoulder a collection of perfectly straight white lines. They looked like a barcode of scars. Brennan and the new guy breezed past us and I noted that they too had these same straight markings in the same place, just less of them.

"Calm yourself Sophia. I can feel your anxiety. It is your mind we are exercising this time, not your flesh." He clapped his hands together with anticipation and entered a new room off the main arena. "Come."

I found myself in a very different space. It was devoid of anything other than a single, large white orb, floating in the centre of the room.

"You now have the honour of being in the room of Enlightenment. Eudaimonian children who are so gifted, learn to use their elemental powers here from age fifteen. At twenty-one, if they develop pterugia, they will learn the power of flight here in safety and under strict guidance. I regret that you must learn so intensely and quickly, but that is a matter simply out of our hands."

"She'll be fine Koi. I've seen her in action," Brennan added with a thumbs up to me and way too much enthusiasm.

"That remains to be seen," Koi responded dryly.

The other guy remained silent, watching me in a rather overtly uncomfortable way. Brennan seemed to notice this and elbowed him hard in the ribs. He responded with an elbow back. *Weird!* I paid them minimal attention after that as I was drawn to the massive spectacle in the air.

This orb was truly impressive. It generated an energy that left a tangible and visible static in the air. Just like back at the library when it was full of people, I could see wisps of multi-coloured current snap and twist faintly above me. I felt my heart instinctively match its rhythmic pulsations.

"Sophia, Brennan will instruct you with your elemental powers. He is one of our most skilled with the orbs. His mastery of the power of E'lan is universally acknowledged. Indeed, you have witnessed his abilities already," Koi said as he waved his hand towards Brennan. "I will merely be here to observe."

"Can't believe you're finally here, Soph. You're going to love this," Brennan smiled his cheeky, boyish smile. He was annoyingly infectious. "This mother of an orb will help you learn how to control the elements, so that you can draw and repel the E'lan around you at will with a pretty impressive force. So far you've just reacted reflexively. Impressive, but not enough to cut it in the real world of the Daimon. This orb will teach you conscious control of that power. Had you been born on A'vean, this would have been as instinctual for you as it is to us. Watchers come into existence with full knowledge, while the Eudaimonia must be taught. I actually taught Enl'iel many years ago. She was a quick learner, just like you Soph. You need to be taught as though you grew up Eudaimonian. It'll be an honour to help you too, princess." Brennan finished with an unnecessary and over-exaggerated bow.

The other guy spoke up unexpectedly breaking his brooding appraisal of me. I'd noticed he'd been checking me out. It didn't really feel flattering the way he squinted his eyes as he glared in my direction with his arms crossed.

"She must be trained efficiently and quickly Brennan. The Militia are reporting more and more Rogues daily. The Daimon are ramping up infiltrations across the continents. There's no time to waste. Sophia, I'm Lorcan, First lieutenant of the 1st Seraph legion and brother to this smart mouth!" He broke with his sombre demeanour as he playfully punched Brennan away in the shoulder, giving away a half smile. *Okay.*

Surprised, I went to shake his hand, just as he bent in to do the kiss-thing, causing us to bump heads awkwardly. It was a rather embarrassing exchange. "Sorry, hi," I said quickly as I stood back.

"Oh, um, sorry, hi. Yeah, um, I know you're just getting used to our customs." He seemed equally embarrassed as a flush of scarlet hit his cheeks.

"Still great with the ladies there I see, bro," Brennan teased.

"Shove your pterugia up your—"

"Manners! You are representatives of A'vean and the great council. Act as such!" chided Koi.

They were both as human as any two brothers. I was in Wonderland. My world was a contradiction. I just hoped I didn't meet the Queen of Hearts anytime soon.

"Let's move on," exclaimed Koi as he threw a shot of energy at the feet of the two brothers who were jostling and mouthing rude remarks to each other. "Enough you two. Begin!"

Brennan and Lorcan pulled themselves together quickly after the scolding and took on a more adult air. Brennan began. "Okay Soph, the aim of this exercise is to look into the energy orb, to acknowledge its power, to feel it, to understand it, and invite it into you. Sounds poxy, I know, but trust me, you'll understand what I mean soon enough. Don't be scared, it can't harm you. You and the orb are essentially the same—both made of the purest form of energy. You just happen to be prettier!"

"Brennan!" Koi grumped. Lorcan laughed to himself. I was just standing there, a prisoner to their banter.

"Alright, alright! Just trying to chill the tension Koi. Calm down." Koi turned his back and moved a few paces away, I assume to refrain from zapping them with more fervour this time.

"Anyway, as you learn Soph, this will all become easier and more natural, until you barely even need to form a thought. The connection will be instant." Brennan finally concluded his less than polished intro to *How to be an Angel 101.*

"Okay, sounds less painful than this morning. How do I start?" I asked, immediately determined to make a better impression than on the running track.

"First, relax your mind. Calm your breathing, and let your thoughts melt away. Close your eyes and feel nothing but the energy, just like when you heal someone" he instructed.

I obliged.

"Okay. Wow! I can actually feel it. It's strong and really hot." I answered immediately, as my back began to warm.

"I think she's talking about me!" Brennan quipped to Lorcan.

"Belt up, bro!" Answered Lorcan, as he barely contained laughter.

"What the hell?" I said as I opened my eyes, losing the connection, to glare at them both.

"You are both asking for a one way ticket to Jude," Koi responded to them both with an angry growl.

They both raised their eye brows in mock fear, then apologised.

"Sorry Koi, sorry Soph." They said in unison.

"I can see why you idiots got yourselves in all this trouble!" I gave them my best dirty look.

"It's been a long time in hiding, drowning in boredom Soph. Sorry. This is actually very serious. I'm just letting off some steam. Come on. Let's get on with it then. Go on, try again." Brennan had a fairly convincing expression of deep concentration now. I relaxed a little and tried again.

"Okay, I can feel the energy again. What do I do now? It's really intense. It feels so different to before, back at home, I mean."

"It should feel different. Your body is now more attune to the pulse of the universe, so you should feel it potently within your whole body, not just your hands. You *are* the elements, Soph. Now, listen closely, and your heart should beat in rhythm with the pulsations." Brennan said, a more serious edge to his voice now.

Again, that was easy, since it had already happened the second I'd entered the room. My confidence was brimming. I nodded silently to him.

"Now, imagine that you are reaching your hand out, grasping at the light, and pulling it into you."

I did this—well, I tried. Within a split second, I was flung backwards to the ground, legs in the air. My face felt crimson with embarrassment, again.

"I thought this wasn't going to be painful?" I grumbled as I dusted myself off-again.

"Told you, brother—she may be the great Earth-born Angel, but man, that human world has screwed her up like a pretzel!" Lorcan laughed at me. *What the hell?* I snapped, unusual for me but I had just had enough of these two.

"Shut the hell up, you don't know me! You don't know what I've been through. Give me a break, will you?" I was completely pissed at this Lorcan guy. "If you're here to help, then help me! Otherwise, just get out!" I pointed sharply to the doorway and a small crack of light sputtered out of my fingers, as the A'vean mark singed my face with a burning anger.

"Ah, thank you, Lorcan. You have at least been of use in something. Hmmm." Koi still eyed Lorcan and Brennan up and down, disapprovingly. "You have proven my suspicion to be correct."

I looked at him, confused. "*What?*"

"Apologies, Sophia. I asked Lorcan to rile you. It is a skill he is proficient at. As is his brother." Lorcan muttered a whispered profanity, but then high-fived Brennan. I gaped at them both, ready to happily punch them out.

"I was worried that it was anger which drove you, and so it is. Remember, we must use our minds, not our hearts. You have much control to learn. I felt your anger in the scroll chamber just before your pterugia emerged." Koi explained.

"I was thinking of Esme. It seemed to help when I couldn't make anything happen." I answered him.

"Indeed. We all have struggled with this at some point, particularly after loss. We can work with this though. We just need to use that passion in a more controlled way. Please forgive Lorcan, no ill intent was meant."

I looked at the annoyingly gorgeous Watcher, "Sorry for yelling at you," I said rather half-heartedly. Their earlier juvenile behaviour still irritated me.

Lorcan shrugged, as though it was nothing. That angered me just as much. He offered a handshake, which I begrudgingly took. I didn't understand myself at the moment. I was never one to harbour anger, hold a grudge, or have a temper. That was the sole talent of Jaz. I was Sophia, the compassionate nurse of comfort and ease. *Not right now, though.*

Seemingly sensing my confusion and feelings of failure, Koi took my hand in his.

"Come now, you have been thrust into a new and dangerous world, one that must seem something akin to a nightmare. All in such a brief time, too. Despite us pressing the need for expediency that your awakening has brought forth, you must not be harsh on yourself. We all have weaknesses that sometimes surprise us. Look at these two for instance." He pointed to the brothers who looked up with surprise. "Eons of experience and still little more than children at times!" A couple of grumbles came from them, but they kept a self-preserving silence. "Insight is your greatest power, as with it you can address and overcome all such deficiencies. Now that you know this weakness exists, we can build on your strengths to harness the elements."

After the shaky start, we practiced a while longer. Brennan and Lorcan snapped out of their ridiculous behaviour under Koi's strict watch and pushed me to the limit. I was grilled over and over until I could stand my ground with the orb and take in at least a little of its power without an immediate kickback onto my butt. All but once I was thrown to the dusty ground at some point. I could, however, feel the connection grow each time. It felt a little less forced with every new attempt. I could feel my body wanting to draw in the power. It was believing it with my human-bred sense of reality that was the problem. The fact that I could feel my body wanting to respond soothed my bruised ego somewhat.

This little routine played out for the next three days. I slept, ate, and trained. I barely saw Jaz. Ben was a ghost. I visited with Cael, who was growing increasingly more lucid. On the fourth morning, after a particularly punishing session with the nasty red orbs, Lorcan appeared to announce word of Gedz'iel's arrival.

He was early. I wasn't ready.

But it was time to open the scroll.

Chapter
Thirty-Five

The shadowed figure lurked outside of the church in the cool, dusk air. The evening light hid him well enough amongst the barren trees. The light drizzle cooled his temper somewhat. The call in the recesses of his mind was driving him mad. It had begun hours ago, as a distant summons. Now it was a harrowing scream, laced with threats, beckoning him to return to the realm immediately. He ignored it and the throbbing headache it gave him. He was done. They were backing out of the plan of attack—he knew it. Yeqon was so power-hungry these days that he made decisions based on clawing the kingship into his grasp, rather than what was actually the right path to take for their mission. He knew he could only ignore them for so long before he was tracked down. This was a big risk, but he had to take it. His discovery was epic—he couldn't abandon it just to bolster Yeqon's gluttonous stupidity.

He couldn't believe he'd finally found the hub of their world. They knew it was in the Northern Hemisphere, near the ancient dead portals, but they had been hunted away ferociously, always outnumbered. Yeqon and the others were holding onto the six hundred and sixty-six worst of their kind for the right moment. Stolen from Tartarus before the portals were destroyed, he had kept them subdued, waiting until the time was right. They did not want to risk a crushing loss at the wrong time.

Nik'ael had managed to covertly follow her. He stayed only as close as he dared. Her power drew him in, like a moth to a flame. He could be as blind as that old Welsh woman in the main house and still find her. She lit up the air around her with an aura that he'd never seen before. Of all the Watchers he'd known, never had he seen such beauty. The colours and warmth and purity that surrounded her made him tense to the point that he needed to lash out, to strangle the life out of something, just to release the stress. The fracture in his hand reminded him of the need to control himself. The self-inflicted pain was a representation of all that he'd lost. The other beauty that had once been ripped from his heart.

It was harder now to stay concealed. The militia were everywhere, always on guard. Back in Australia, their obscurity at the tail end of the globe gave them a false sense of security. They were more lax. Here, it was as fortified as any place could be. It was dangerous to put out a call for back up—he'd have to ride it out until he could get himself close enough to find the kind of information that would make taking her worth it. He might be forced to use other means to support his one Daimon army. Despite what Yeqon claimed and demanded, if they took her before she knew enough, it would all be pointless. Yeqon was too stupid to understand this nuance—he was a murderous thug with little brains and too much power. *Who was he to judge, though?*

He again rubbed at the bracelet. It was well worn now. Some of the beads were half the size of when Neren'iel had made it, so impossibly long ago. Shame crashed through him like a tidal wave. He had betrayed his long dead wife in more than one way. What he'd turned into, and these endless thoughts. The longing thoughts of the Earth-born that he could not seem to repress. What would Neren'iel think of what he'd become? He already knew. She would be repulsed, horrified. He had shamed her memory through his every action. She would have forgiven her transgressors, whereas he could not. For a moment, he let his guard down and drew away, down to the small river. He let his true form emerge. It was a relief, like taking off ill-fitting clothes and slipping into comfortable ones.

He rubbed again at the bracelet. Counting the twenty-one brown cedar beads eased him somewhat. The itchy rash the cedar now gave him was annoying. As the allergy grew, he knew it to be a barometer of his darkness. She had given it to him when his final Right had come to completion. Twenty-one beads for twenty-one years of growth and knowledge. He remembered the celebration. The whole village had put on a massive feast, as was custom for the twenty-first year, no matter what powers emerged. The Eloi council had observed the ceremony, which was also customary. Back then, they were all equal—all family. That was until the slaughter at the hands of their own. Instantly, his anger seethed out of hibernation. His head ached and he cracked his knuckles until every last one popped loudly enough to scare the birds from the tree he hid within. It hurt, but also soothed him at the same time. The Avon River rushed wild and cold below, as did his heart.

The Earth-born was going to allow him to avenge those ancient atrocities. To avenge Neren'iel's murder. Despite what she would think of him, this had always been his single aim—to avenge her life. At what cost, though? *His eternal soul, no doubt.* He would end up in the pits of Tartarus, he knew that—*if he was lucky.* The spiral went so deep, there was no way out now.

Damn them. Damn *her.* He clenched his fists and returned to his previous form. He was going to have to be extra careful now. Those around her would fight to the death to protect her. *Let them.* He could handle that. He was irritated by the thought of her death, though. All of a sudden, it was an unpalatable thought. In the back of his mind, he was wondering how he could avoid that. Could he get from her what he needed without killing her? "Ahhh!" he banged at his head with clenched fists. He felt like he was going insane. Her blood was necessary, and he needed revenge. Yet her face haunted his dreams. *What was happening to him?* The wind blew hard, and a small chirp sounded beside him. He grabbed at the bird that landed too close and squeezed the life from it. *There.* That felt better.

Chapter
Thirty-Six

I quickly showered after being summoned. Enl'iel met me in the change room, dressed in a more formal version of the standard outfit. It was tastefully emblazed with golden swirls along the cowl neck of the top. The cut of the fabric was just that bit sharper, the white more intense. She wore no shoes as seemed the custom, unless you were training or heading outside. Her hair flowed luxuriously down her back, daintily entwined with a multitude of herbs. She was breathtaking, and as angelic as anyone could look. She swiftly healed the extensive bruising along my arms before she gave me a matching version of her outfit. "We do not dwell so much on fashion, but do adhere to some small tokens of formality when we have a meeting of importance. It is a small show of respect for our heritage," she responded to my unspoken question. My outfit bore the same golden embroidered swirls but had a little extra bling with a few clear gemstones woven through the gold. She must have seen my eyes gleam at the beauty of it. "That was Eilir's special touch, just for you," she said with a smile. "She is a sweet soul." The door opened at that and two Alchemae healers entered, baskets brimming with all things foliage. The females silently and expertly braided my hair with sweet smelling flowers and oils making me feel so pretty that I was left wondering where the ball was.

The walk down to meet Gedz'iel after my lengthy day of endurance was exhausting. The journey was so deep into the Earth that a set of orbs followed us to light the way through pitch-black corridors. The walls eventually became plain packed dirt. The metallic lining had stopped many stories back. I'd stopped counting after descending the tenth flight of stairs. It would've been quite handy to have gotten a handle on the flying trick already.

Brennan had caught up with us and echoed my thought about halfway down. "Get those wings out and start flapping, princess. You're a proper angel now. I don't like breaking a sweat like a human with all of this walking. It's not good for my pores!"

"You're such a tease, Brennan. Get on ahead and see if they are ready," scoffed Enl'iel playfully.

He obliged by springing his wings and flapping away in an instant, leaving nothing but a breeze in his wake.

We were greeted by Kea outside a set of large, dark wooden doors.

Again, she was dressed as we were. She appeared all the more stunning with her hair piled atop her head, a crown of lavender bringing out the intensity of her blue eyes. Everyone seemed to glow from within. The beauty of their auras came from somewhere deeper than their skin and shone through.

Her demeanour seemed surprisingly more formal as she greeted us.

"Enl'iel, blessings to you. Precious Soph'ael, may the blessings of A'vean be upon you," she inclined her head inviting us to enter. I simply said "Hello." It was a lacklustre effort but I was in a new culture, a new place, a new world.

I'd already got the feeling that there were strict protocols for behaviour in Gedz'iel's presence. I was relieved Jaz wasn't there—she'd flip the bird without a second thought. She would be the proverbial bull in a china shop.

I followed Kea through the impressive entrance, into a sort of drawing room of a forgotten era. Stiff, uncomfortable-looking furniture from a century or two ago was scattered over a myriad of Persian-looking floor rugs. A large, wingback chair sat proudly behind a huge desk off to one corner. Books in the thousands lined the walls.

A stone hearth was glowing brightly, lit by pulsing orbs in the place of real fire. The rest of the room was softly lit by sweetly scented candles and scattered orbs in the highest corners of the ceiling.

Sitting in that wingback chair was Gedz'iel, who in my opinion looked drawn and tired. He stood immediately upon seeing me, and mustered a small smile as he came forward to greet me. Five new faces stood behind him with a calm air. They appeared all of eighteen years of age, but even I could feel the ancient energy rolling off of them.

"Good evening, Soph'ael, or as I have been informed more than once, *Sophia,* as you prefer to be addressed. It is pleasing to see that you have arrived safe and well. I trust you have had a taxing few days, and have already begun training, so may I first thank you for the enormous strength and show of grace you have displayed." He bowed politely. The five others behind him nodded their heads in silent agreement.

"I would like to introduce you to the Council of Eloi. They are my peers, advisors, and kindred who are here to witness the reading of the Prime Scroll. We are all here to bear witness and make assurances that not even a whisper of the contents shall fall into the hands of the Daimon." Five pairs of sparkling cerulean eyes were glued to me throughout his speech. The huge, deeply bronzed men were dressed as Gedz'iel was in nothing but sleek white pants. They stood silently by him as he made the proper introductions.

"This is Theus, Matias, Serael, Amais, and Pathos." As they bowed to me in turn, their white A'vean markings lit up with an unparalleled brilliance. The backdrop of smooth earthy skin tones made the sight all the more beautiful.

I bowed in return, again not sure of the protocol.

"No, no!" spoke the surprisingly gravelly voice of Pathos. His aged tone did not match his appearance at all.

"You do not bow to us—you honour us with your presence. We are merely here to serve and protect you, your Grace." He bowed again, as did they all. The awkward flush of self-consciousness rose to my cheeks again. This was so not me.

Gedz'iel continued, "The Eloi are of the very first Watchers that were sent to the Earth. They are the last of original influx. They lived with the first functioning humans on the African plains. Being the oldest of our kind on this planet, their penance has been long endured. For this reason, I took them into my council to guide and protect other Watchers and their offspring. You will find no greater leadership or protection than here." He swept his arm across to indicate the five broad-chested men. "Now, time runs from us. Are you ready to open the scroll?"

"Yes—I think so. I will try my best." I struggled to find even a weak voice in the face of the task ahead of me, one that I really didn't understand. Its magnitude was well beyond me at this point. I looked back to Enl'iel for encouragement, and got it with a kiss blown from her palm in my direction.

"This is not about trying your best, Sophia. This is your birth right and destiny. Your spiritual connection to I'el alone will allow you to read that which we cannot. The words of Enoch were written strictly for your eyes only. Had they not been, we surely would have solved this ourselves instead of enduring such a banishment. Ours has been a curse of ignorance and the pain of abandonment. We have tirelessly protected what we do know whilst we awaited your birth." The glow of the orbs cast shadows across his face that brought out a different edge to him. The youthful strength gave way to a simmering anxiety beneath the surface. He looked almost human. His eyes were sharp and alert, burning for an end to it all.

"How long have you been waiting?" I ventured to ask.

"In excess of a hundred thousand years. Time has not moved swiftly either," he answered.

"What? That just sounds ..."

"Impossible? Yes it does and it has been almost impossible to endure at times," added Serael. "An eternity of nothingness alleviated only by sporadic wars with the Daimon," he concluded.

"So all this time you've tried to understand clues yourselves, yet you knew even if you had a breakthrough you still had to wait for me? That's just so cruel. Why would I'el make you suffer so much and so long?"

"Because our actions have caused exponentially more suffering among humans, and that is our shame," answered Pathos.

"How have you endured it? I can't imagine it at all." It was incomprehensible. I found it hard to believe that I was actually awake whilst hearing this impossible story.

"To pass our time we committed to helping humanity the way we were supposed to in the beginning. We whispered in their dreams, guiding them to their own self-evolution. We pulled together what we could recall of our ancient culture as best we could and passed it on to some of the earliest developing cultures so as to preserve our own memories. The risk of losing all that we knew of ourselves the longer we were cut off from A'vean was too great. We did not know how long we would suffer or how much of our history we could retain. The beneficiaries of this knowledge were the Mycenaean culture who became the progenitors of the ancient Greeks. That is why there are so many similarities in our vocabulary, the smallest snippets of our own ancient past stay alive every time a human speaks the Greek language.

"You created the Greek culture?"

"Not quite, as I said, we merely left suggestions in their subconscious. We simply embedded remnants of our knowledge into their developing culture. They lived and died under their own direction. They worshipped their own versions of Gods. They prospered and perished, paving the way for new cultures to emerge in that region. The rest, as it is said, is history," Pathos concluded, as Gedz'iel spoke again.

"You, on the other hand, were born with this knowledge coursing through you. You do not need to try your best, Sophia—it is *within* you, as you have already experienced when you retrieved the Prime scroll. Belief is all you need." He placed a warm hand on my shoulder, gently lifted my chin and stared intently at me. "You are not human, you are something so much greater. You must acknowledge this." With that, he broke the intense moment as he passed me the silver chest. It immediately vibrated under my touch. "It knows you. Answer its call. Open the chest, Sophia. I cannot—I have already tried. Please, make us wait no longer."

One of the five men—*Theus*, I believed—brought over a heavy chair and motioned for me to sit.

I settled the chest on my lap. It warmed as it continued its gentle hum, the sensation made my legs tremble. I slowly ran my hands over the pretty rectangular shape. They glowed and also began to tremble. The lid swirled with fine artistry. Curls of silver engraved every surface. The edging was thick with concentric circles that seemed expertly soldered on to give the chest an ornateness that belonged somewhere palatial. As my right hand passed over a small indentation on the front, I heard a soft click. The lid popped slightly ajar and I lifted it open. I could feel the eyes on me, the breaths that were being held. Even Gedz'iel seemed on the edge of his ancient seat.

Inside the box was a long, cylindrical tube. I picked it up gently, hoping it wouldn't disintegrate suddenly, like an ancient artefact. The heat of the bodies pressing in around me grew, as though they were at the precipice of a great moment and I was in the driver's seat.

The brown leathery tube was light and, not surprisingly, covered in swirling patterns. Unfamiliar letters scripted themselves along the swirls, which seemed to come alive as they moved across and around the tube. These words were strange to my eyes, but not to my heart, which was thrashing wildly inside. I felt like I had been jabbed with an adrenaline needle.

I ran my fingers over one of the sentences and read it out loud in a careful, measured voice. "*To propomenon phugein adunation.*" The words fell naturally from my lips. "It is impossible to escape what is destined." The translation just blurted out of me.

I repeated the phrase quietly a few times as I continued to turn the waxy leather slowly in my hands. "It's not like you haven't tried, Soph," I quipped to myself. Across one end, a time-blackened wax seal capped it off. On closer inspection, I was shocked to the core to see a name scrawled across it. In beautiful script was written, *Soph'ael.*

Sensing my surprise, everyone asked at once, "What is it?" Kea and Brennan were practically breathing down my neck.

Gedz'iel knelt in front of me and asked, "Something troubles you, what is it?"

"No, it's nothing—it's-it's just that my name is written across the seal!" I answered. Saying it out loud seemed even more preposterous than seeing it with my own eyes. The energy in the room immediately soared. Static crackled through the air, as everyone became agitated with the anticipation of what was to come. They now knew for sure that I really was the person that they had been waiting for. I knew, for the first time, that I was who they said I was.

"Do I just—?"

"Yes, Sophia. Break the seal," answered Gedz'iel.

I tried picking at it with my stubby fingernails, but it was rock hard, and they were no match for it. I twisted and pulled at it next. No one made a sound or move to help me. This was my puzzle to solve, apparently. I ran my fingers over and over it, looking for a crack or weak spot. I didn't want to damage it by being too rough. I stopped for a moment to think, fixating on the words that were written across the cylinder. *It is impossible to escape what is destined.* I repeated them over and over in my mind with my eyes closed until I suddenly felt something burning me. I hadn't realised that my hands had lit up. Melted wax drizzled through my fingers and down my leg, drying instantly in little clumps on the ground.

The collective intake of breaths heightened my own excitement. *I did it!*

I took a minute to let my hands dull and cool before I tipped the cylinder upside down, catching an aged, rolled up document. I stood back up and went to pass it to Gedz'iel, but he motioned for me to open it.

"No. You must read it," he instructed.

I walked to the desk, slowly unravelling the delicate parchment across it. I winced at the crinkling and crackling sounds as I opened it, terrified that it would rip or break apart. I pressed on though until I had beneath my hands a one-meter long document. Words were perfectly written on it in a careful hand, so neat and precise that it seemed almost impossible that it could have been done without the aid of a printer.

"Shall I just read it out loud?" I asked.

"Please," Gedz'iel responded, he stepped closer to me, the skin of our arms touching. The power rolling off of him seemed to transfer to me, giving me a jolt of confidence, clearing my head instantly of the last remnants of doubt.

I glanced down at the words, and began to read.

The Glory of A'vean shall dwell upon thee.
As I stood in awe at the foot of the great alabaster mountain, glistening among the range along the horizon, the mighty and most revered Great Lord spoke unto me of the dishonoured Watchers. It was benevolence he spoke of, unto mine ears alone, honoured and bound by veiled secrecy.
"Enoch, righteous man of men, come hither and hear mine words. Cast them to the furthest reaches of the Earth, until such time as the righteous and worthy are enabled, by purity of soul alone, to read unto themselves of the manner of their salvation from eternal torture and banishment."

Henceforth, the seven Archangels made worthless pleas for the Watchers of A'vean, for their absolution and forgiveness. The Glorious Throne thundered in rage. For a time, His wrath was wrought upon the Earth through flood and plague and ignorance for generation upon generation.

The progeny of lust suffered until such time as He sought out the Council and pronounced, "Nought have I shown mercy upon those Watchers who have henceforth disgraced and dishonoured themselves amongst man. They, who created abominations with the blood of women, have shamed all. Such as it is, suffering among them and mankind alike, has been great. The unnatural offspring have risen above their misery and flourished. So greatly and with such dignity have they endured execration that it yearns at my heart to offer absolution and peace, for are they not of my being? As they suffer in their ignorance, so do I. For unlike the Daimon, evil runs not through them like a purging fire. Thus, once more, all realms of A'vean may again be availed to Watcher and mankind alike. For such time that purity of soul and intent courses through the flesh and blood of a Watcher born of the Earth, legate of the disgraced, that the key to hence unlock the portal between Earth and A'vean will itself avail unto them."

"The blood of truth shall open the gates. The righteous of heart and soul may emerge unto the glory of the seven mountains, and dwell within the falling waters of eternal life. They may once more eat from the Tree of Life and walk with the Angels evermore."

"Be warned of he who draws blood with ill intent. Beware the wrath of the Titans of Tartarus that shall thunder upon you like a rain of fire, lest he test the gate with an unclean soul. The Earth-born Angel shall, of her will alone, draw of her blood to seek the wisdom lent unto the reverent and obedient Enoch. For only the pure and true may seek to understand that which will unlock eternal freedom and rapture at the foot of thy throne."

The great Lord called me forth, and blinded by His light, I bowed and fell submissive at His feet, for He was light and power, but could take the form of man if He so chose.

In mine ear He whispered unto me, "Hear my name and shout it from the highest mountains and deepest seas. I am

I'el, creator of all that is and ever will be. I give mercy unto those that preserve life, those that allow all to be as they were created without judgment or harassment. Aggress against me and know thy anger. Kill not your fellow man in my or any other name, for that which tortures man, tortures me. Show sorrow of the heart for your transgressions. Love of all that live among you, and thy heart will fill with love once more."

And so it came to pass that I'el told unto me the secrets of passage between A'vean and Earth. The accursed portal that was to be closed evermore was now, by design, free to be sought and open, but only by the most righteous One.

And to the Earth-born, a time predetermined, her birth shall be. The first place of pilgrimage shall be far. Mine words and devices you shall find to be corrupted. Trust not all who adore you. The Unseen shall harass, trick, and covet you.

Tread with caution through the quest you must endure. Strength shall come to you, but compassion, as your weakness, will render you anaemic in the eyes of evil.

The land upon which thy parents were born shall be your first passage. In yonder resting place of your father's mother lay the words of I'el. From the sprig of bloom did thy father descend. He, thy father, who shall be hunted by the lion and boar to protect you, has waited there, afore your birth and ever after. Through denial of birth right, he has protected you. Follow on in glory and strength of thy father and thy predecessors who sacrificed all for you. Your challenge is great, the weight upon thy shoulders immense.

Three chests of knowledge must be sought. They will lead you to the door of A'vean. All-seeing that I am, humbly through the Lord I'el, in mine eye I see treachery among the most exalted. Heed this warning that discord and malevolent forces shall interfere with mine works. The Kaladai shall be corrupted.

Paradoxes lie everywhere. Mere mortals shall redeem mine works.

The Devil will guide you, an Angel shall destroy you."

There was utter silence in the room as I finished reading. My head thundered. *Treachery*. It was not the most positive of revelations. It seemed to give and take all at once. The effort of translating the ancient text had been less natural than I was led to believe. I was stunned with myself that I had read these strange symbols out loud in English, as though I'd spoken the language every day of my life. The true A'vean language, the language of the Creator, ran through me as naturally as my blood flowed. In all that I'd read though, the one thing that clung to me was the reference to my father. *Was I finally going to find out about my parents? Who were they?* The skeleton in the closet that was my parents' identity seemed precariously close to revealing itself from the cobwebs of the past.

Were my parents alive, in any sense of the word? These Watchers and Eudaimonians were impossibly old—eternal. Therefore, my parents could still be around. *If so, where had they been, and why had they not made contact with me?* Overthinking again, I was becoming nauseated. *Deep breath in, deep breath out, repeat.*

Gedz'iel broke the silence, his voice solemn. "Well done, Sophia. You have begun what shall become our triumphant return home. Repatriation is more important to us than you could ever imagine. I honour your courage and belief in yourself, though I sense that belief still wavers. Be patient. It shall evolve and strengthen every day."

Everything suddenly felt suffocating. Gedz'iel blurred, the air felt thick and every sound exaggerated. Brennan breathed too heavily behind me. Enl'iel noisily twirled a wad of her hair around her fingers. Kea's bracelets were clanging like cymbals. I could hear every sound as though it was plugged into an amplifier. The thudding of my own rapid heartbeat pulled it all together into an irritating symphony in my mind. I barely tolerated the booming of Gedz'iel's voice.

"There is much to consider within this scroll. The references to traitors disturbs me greatly. Return home all of you. Consider Enoch's' words with the wisdom of your years. Assist Sophia in unravelling their hidden meaning. Be on high alert for anything that may cast doubt upon *any* of us. This pains me to even put into words. May we stitch our story together in fullness without malevolent interference, especially from within," he bowed towards me, as did everyone else.

"Please don't do that. You don't need to do that." I was mortified by the excessive attention.

"Accept who you are, Sophia. We honour and protect you," he replied, as the others mumbled their agreement.

Thrum, thrum, thrum.

The resting place of my father's mother.

Thrum, thrum, thrum.

Kaladai, Portal, key.

These words wove themselves through my mind amid all the noise.

"Enl'iel, she is weary. She is yet to attain psynostris. Take her and administer a resting tisane. Our time is short, and her strength must be rallied. She *must* be strong. I fear taking her out into the world with the threat that awaits us. There is a worrying movement in the Underworld. Some Afflicted have been picked up from the underground in Central London. They are preparing for something, and we too must be prepared. Have Koi intensify her training— we must stay ahead of the Daimon. Arm the humans."

Thrum, thrum, thrum,

Psypnostris, my father's, mother, my father's mother

Thrum, thrum, thrum.

With that, Gedz'iel and his five companions flashed out of existence. The room was silent, but it was still chaotic in my head, and the noise followed me like the after effects of a rock concert as I made my way silently back to my bed.

Chapter
Thirty-Seven

Sleep was torturous. I tossed and turned, tangling the sheets around my thrashing limbs. Vivid dreams of clawing hands, screams, and burning flames licking at my feet, terrified me to near wakefulness. Eyes—black eyes, green, red, orange and blues eyes—flashed at me, pinning me to the bed. A beating drum thundered through the room, vibrating up through the bed, resounding painfully in my head. A presence was near me, hovering over me, touching me. The beating drum pounded harder as a hand caressed my face. "*Mine,*" was whispered into my thoughts. For an eternity, my eyelids rebelled against me and refused to open as I screamed at myself to wake up. This presence was heavy, and lingered as it ran what felt like fingers slowly down my arm and held onto my hand. *Was it here to hurt me?* It didn't feel like it, yet it was certainly not welcome to violate my personal space. I continued to scream wildly at myself to wake, as this dream-invader left me numb and limp with the fear of its intentions.

Finally, my body listened to my mind, and my eyes flung wide open, scanning every atom of space surrounding me. It was still and dark with a quiet and intensity that only the night brings. Within seconds, my pupils had adjusted to the dimness of the space, and my body froze just as it had in slumber. The soft glow of my mark illuminated something. A shadow hovered silently, unearthly, inches above me. It had been there all along, not just in my dream. Dark and featureless, it was cloaked in a malevolent red-ish aura that my newly sharpened sight could not seem to penetrate. Wings that spanned far into the room gently flapped. Red and orange sparks flew silently from them with each movement, floating away and disappearing into nothingness. To my own surprise, despite the rigid state of my limbs, I felt no malice from it towards me. The shock of its reality was what was keeping me quiet and still. I realised almost instantly that this dark visitor was not angry or dangerous in that moment, and that it was not here to hurt me. *At least for now*. It was sad, deeply sad— *desperately* sad, with a loneliness that left a hollow pit in my own stomach. Despite myself, I felt compassion for it, overwhelmed with an annoyingly incessant need to help. As these thoughts passed through my mind, it reached out a silhouetted hand and gently caressed my face with a hot palm. At this point I realised that the drumming, though still present in the background, had dulled considerably and was replaced with my heart thrashing against my ribs.

I spoke tentatively, hoping that kindness would be returned. "Who are you?" No answer came, but it did draw its hand quickly away. "Do you need help?" This time, it responded by gliding slowly away until it stood by the doorway, its head hung low and wings retracting into nothing more than a mild glow behind its back. It was clearly a male by the sheer width of his shoulders. The muscled arms were far from hidden by its veiled disguise. "Who are you?" I asked one last time, just as a wave of nausea punched me out of nowhere. That question was obviously too much, as it vanished in an instant in a sparkling display of red and orange fireworks, leaving a sulphurous odour behind which brought the nausea on worse. This gave me a fright, and I pulled the blankets up to my chin, glancing around the room for more intruders. After I was satisfied I was alone, I sat up and took a sip of water from the tall glass by the bed, suddenly feeling extremely parched. Unnerved by the incident and the darkness, I called to the dormant orb by the doorway to light up. It responded by bathing the room in a soft and comforting glow, alleviating the thickness of the atmosphere. It was a handy trick Brennan had shown me. Apparently, he was the master of these things. I fought the urge to call for help. For some reason I felt like I needed to keep this to myself. After a lot of contemplation and no conclusions about the creepy apparition, I eventually drifted back into another fitful sleep.

By the morning, I was achy and exhausted when Brennan, Jaz and Ben came by to pick me up for training. I didn't even have time for a shower to dull my pounding head before Jaz palmed me an apple and an Eccles cake, saying that she was allowed to watch me 'kick some butt' in training this morning. Ben followed on silently down the corridors and staircases, broody as usual. He was looking gaunt, almost haunted. He appeared unwell, but seemed to still have a strong energy. This place was not good for him. He was an independent spirit who had never dealt well with being told what to do. I bet if he hadn't been surrounded by supernatural beings he would have been out of here days ago. I felt on the edge of saying something to him a number of times, but forced myself into silence each time. Jaz on the other hand, despite her regular bitching, was looking amazing. For the first time in years her face was clean of the heavy makeup. We had no chance to bring personal things with us due to our sudden departure, so she was forced to go *eau naturel*. She looked fresh and youthful this way. *If only she saw her natural beauty, inside and out, as I did.*

"You look like crap Soph, no sleep huh?" was Brennan's way of saying good morning.

"Well thanks. That's the way to a girl's heart! No, I didn't sleep well at all. Even if I did, I seem to feel constantly exhausted anyway," I said.

"Ah, that'll pass princess. You're adjusting. Sometime soon you'll need far less sleep. When you reach psynostris, you'll feel a whole lot better."

"Gedz'iel mentioned that word last night. What is it? Not more pain?"

"Nah, it's actually awesome. Psynostris refers to wakefulness. We need minimal sleep. A rest every few days is all it takes to keep the blood and bones going. In our natural state we never sleep, not required. Very handy when you want to party," he joked.

"I can't imagine that at all. No sleep?"

"Too true. Just a few hours a week. It will come to you soon enough, probably the second you clock over to twenty one."

"Wow, I want me a piece of that magic! Could you imagine it Soph? Non stop all-nighters!" Jaz piped in.

"Yes, but the trade-off Jaz is that you have to play like us and fight the Daimon and plenty of other nasties," Brennan toyed with her.

"Oh, you can shove that then. I'll stick with bed and a hot guy instead," she quipped

"Jaz!" I said

"Oh you love it!" she answered, not too far off the mark.

"So, princess, I thought these two happy Gilmores could come watch you train today. They've been cooped up so long, they've forgotten how to smile!" Jaz elbowed him and told him to shut it, but thankfully did so with a playful edge. For some reason, when she was tense, so was I. When she relaxed, I softened too.

"If you play nice, I'll go grab Lorcan and some scouts and take you all skyward this evening for a little fresh air. We might not see sun, but at least it will be out of here, and hopefully we can have a little fun. What do you say, kids?"

"I'm not a kid, angel-boy," snapped Ben.

"Angel-boy! Nice work man!" retorted Brennan.

"You're behaving like a kid, bro. Say sorry, you jerk!" Jaz snapped at him with a slap on his shoulder.

"Nah, no harm Jaz. It's cool. Takes more than that to rattle me. Dude, we're on the same side. Want to get out of this place tonight? Have a break from all these weirdos down here?" Brennan mused at him.

I didn't realise it was even an option to leave. We were all silent with the surprise of the opportunity as we stared at Brennan, mouths open.

"Anyone going to join me? Do I have to have my own, lonely pity party out in the big wide human world?" Brennan gestured his hands wide, almost comically with his eyebrows raised.

Brennan was just too damn light sometimes. The gravity of what was going on seemed a little lost on him. But perhaps it was just his way of getting through yet another day of very long existence.

I suddenly answered with an enthusiastic 'yes please' for all of us, hoping to catch a break from this underground world. I needed to breathe some fresh air. I wanted to run. I wanted my muscles to burn and ache, not from being chased by orbs, but the freedom that running through the hills and trees allowed. When I ran, I usually contemplated my worries, and boy, I had a few big ones now. From the moment I saw Cael in St Xavier's, to this very second, I had been propelled through a whirlwind of chaos. There was no time for questions, no time to say, *No thank you, I'll check out of this option.* I quietly coveted the chance to allow the twisting in my guts to unravel by releasing the pent-up stress that I was loath to share with Jaz and Ben. Not that Ben seemed interested in me at all. Despite his behaviour, my hurt had calmed a little and I understood the stress he must be feeling. I looked at him, just catching him glance away from me. He wanted to talk. I'd try to be patient and let him come to me in his own time. Still, I craved for one of our nights in, where we would just talk for hours during movie marathons.

"I'll do anything to get out of this place. It's like being buried alive," Ben finally ground out the words, like they were glass in his mouth.

Brennan reached for a high-five, but was left with fresh air from Ben so he looked to Jaz, who obliged. "I'm in, thank God. Can we go shopping? I'd kill for volume pump mascara and a steak sandwich, extra rare!" She added that last part with a nudge in my side to tease me.

"I'm sure that if you promise to control that temper of yours, I can talk Her Majesty into allowing a shopping trip. Behave, Jaz, okay?" Brennan responded as we took the final staircase down into the training room. She twisted her hair around a finger and looked innocently at him, as though she had no idea what he could mean.

"Her Majesty?" I asked

"Enl'iel, princess. She's the head honcho. Her word is *the* word around here when Gedz'iel isn't in. Even has Koi in a tail spin at times!" He answered as he pushed through the heavy doors, revealing a handful of red orbs. They hovered in the air, waiting for me with what I just knew was glee.

I swallowed the last of my pastry as I eyed them cautiously. Koi was in the centre of the room as Jaz whispered, "*Holy crap, what are those things?*"

"Sit back and watch. You'll be glad you're spectating, trust me." I answered as I buffed up my courage and walked in with as much attitude as I could muster. I wasn't ready for yet another pounding. Jude was over to one side with a young girl, bashing the life out of a wooden dummy with a nasty-looking silver and gold weapon. Lorcan was standing behind him and gestured to me, but when I responded, he called out, "Not you, Ben! Send him over for some fun." I turned to tell him, but he was jogging over already, a surprising smirk on his face. He had the look he got when he had an old motorcycle to pull apart and repair from scratch. Jaz was already chatting with a flame-haired human girl in fighting gear. I watched Jaz as her attention was frequently diverted to ogling Jude. How her wild hormones still raged in this situation was an absolute mystery.

The orbs escorted me over to Koi, and the anticipation of failure had broken out into an early sweat down my back.

"Good Morning, Sophia. I trust you slept well? *Hmmm*, no? I sense you have not. Your mind is troubled. Is there anything I can do?" he asked as he cheek kissed me.

"No, I'm fine," I lied. "Just nervous. I want to do better today," I said truthfully.

"And so you shall. You have improved each and every day." He laughed as he gently patted me on the back.

Brennan walked past us as he headed over to where Jude was and said, "You'll be okay, Soph. More of the same, but this time you actually have to beat them!" he winked annoyingly at me.

"Hope you're not betting your life savings on it," I called back at him.

"Just our eternal salvation, Earth-born!" an eaves-dropping Jude shouted from fifty feet away as he sliced clean through the middle of the dummy.

"That is far from helpful, Jude. She learns quickly, her energy is immensely strong. It's her self-confidence and trust in her own abilities that needs more attention. That kind of comment is counterproductive!" Koi snapped.

"Apologies, Master Koi. I'm sorry, Sophia. That was uncalled for."

"I love a man who can apologise," cooed Jaz from the sidelines. I scowled at her as Jude bowed in contrition, immediately turning from me and asking Ben, "Want to have some fun, human?" as he handed Ben a dangerous-looking sword that was nearly as long as he was tall.

"Hell yeah!" Ben pumped one fist into the other with more life than he'd shown in days. He was bug-eyed as he gingerly handled the massive weapon. He turned it over, the sheen of it flashing across his sallow complexion. I wasn't sure that it was a good idea, but if it helped him out of the funk he was in, it couldn't be all bad. I looked briefly back at Jaz. She dropped the apple she'd been gnawing on as she gawked at Jude with unabashed lust when he removed his sweaty shirt, preparing for another slashing session. This would only end in disaster. She was looking at him the way human guys drooled over her. It was evident that she was non-existent to him, not to mention that she didn't know about the non-fraternisation clause between our species.

The orb session was actually not as bad as expected this time around. It started off a bit shaky, with my butt being zapped black and blue within minutes, but then something just clicked. The third time I ran from them, I realised that if I concentrated on the energy pulse rhythmically thrumming through me, I could draw on the instinctual anger of being attacked as this energy surged. These regular beats of E'lan running through my veins were hypnotic, drawing me away from my erratic emotions into a brief place of calm. Because I knew I was safe and not at risk of death in this controlled environment, I could take the time to allow this calmness to harness the anger into something I could control. Whilst dodging a close shave to my face as I reached the halfway point of the circuit, I surprised the orbs by tumbling forward into a tight ball, spun around and landed on my knees, facing them. In a flash, I thrust out my hands and threw a burst of white-hot arc of light their way, as easy as if I'd pitched a baseball. Two were both hit with this one powerful blast from my hands. They illuminated into a bright white colour, stretched out into long, thin vertical lines of light, and then just blipped out of existence.

"Oh no! Did I kill them?" I panicked immediately, but was met with applause and laughter.

"Sophia, well done. You have caused no harm. These training orbs are not alive, so to speak. They are useful energy pulses that we create, and have no sentient sense of self or the ability to feel pain, fear, or discomfort. They have fulfilled their purpose, and you have used them perfectly. I am beyond impressed with your progress in such a brief time. Your innate abilities are surging through you like reflexes. Within the week, I believe we shall be able to inform Gedz'iel that it will be safe enough for you to venture out from the security of this sanctuary." He had walked over to where I was still kneeling on the ground in surprise and relief. He offered his hands to hoist me up, and I noticed then the pale white tattoos across his fingers as they grasped my hands. I'd originally thought they were scars, but I could now see that they were letters. *Love* was tattooed across the knuckles of one hand, and *Hate* across the other.

"Interesting choice of words on your hands Koi?" I questioned through recovering breaths of fatigue.

"Ah yes, they are a reminder to me of the intertwining of the two most powerful emotional energies. Love and hate are really the same feeling. They both have immense power to cause pain and heartache, but they come from completely different points of contention. It is easy to confuse the two, and the Daimon like to use their intensity against anyone they can. These tattoos remind me of a time when I was very near to losing myself. I look upon them to remember. It is important to keep the two emotions separated, as when they become blurred—like a lover scorned—there can only be an undesirable outcome." He glowed as he told me this, his fervour only enhancing his beauty. But his eyes told a different story, as though the words recalled pain. I wondered what he had been through. *Had he lost a love? Had he been the spurned lover?* He ran a hand though his short hair. "Now, we continue."

Koi pushed me harder after that. Each time he produced a red orb I managed to bring it down, but not without racking up a few more bruises. Lorcan had come to join in, watching my steady progress with an intense interest.

After I had banished what felt like the hundredth orb, Koi invited Lorcan to instruct me in physical combat. I was a little alarmed at this, to say the least. Not to mention exhausted. When I began to protest, Koi explained why.

"You will not always be running from and fighting the foul zombie creations that are the Rogues, Sophia. You will come across a Daimon or two sooner than you'd care to. And it may not be conveniently after you have rested, either. Indeed, attaining the state of psynostris would be better sooner than later for you. Encountering Belial was not a pleasant experience for you, I'm sure, and he certainly chose to attack when your defences were lowest." He mused, eyebrows raised. "As you can well appreciate, a Damion's strength in all elements and reflexes are far superior to Rogues. Lorcan, will you instruct Sophia in a physical training battle, as you do with all the newly awakened?"

"Of course, Master Koi," he bowed respectfully. He cleared his throat as he fiddled about a moment, smoothing out his already perfectly smooth training pants. He seemed nervous. His broad, bare chest moved in and out with measured, deep breaths. His boyish face seemed flushed with nerves as he smiled briefly at me, revealing charming dimples on his cheeks. He was a Watcher, a powerful being, but he seemed more a bumbling teenager in that moment. With the previous smart-mouthing forgiven, I tried to help him out of the extreme awkwardness he was exuding.

"I'm pretty nervous, Lorcan. You'll explain exactly what I'm meant to do? I've never even had a self-defence class before!"

"She's a crap fighter, kicked her arse in high school!" Jaz called out with a whoop. She paled as Koi approached and had a word to her. I giggled to myself.

Lorcan seemed to relax when I smiled. "It's an honour to teach you, Sophia. This will be a breeze for you after what I've seen today. Your human upbringing doesn't seem to have scarred you too much." I didn't share his optimism as he motioned for me to walk by his side. We headed to a doorway across the running track, past Ben and Jude, who stopped briefly to watch us. Jude swiftly pulled Ben's attention back again with a swat across his back with the flat edge of a sword and a growl. Ben responded with a well-placed expletive retort. I wasn't so sure this was what Ben and his moodiness needed—roughhousing with Jude—who was clearly his own personal fan club.

Through a darkened doorway that was lit spontaneously with well-timed orbs as we entered, we arrived in another, smaller room, dug out of the cool earth. It was dim, and would've been pitch dark but for the faint glow of Angelic light illuminating from the millions of crystals pin-pricking the walls. The orb light refracted this ethereal glow throughout the space. The room was a train wreck of debris, as though a building had collapsed there long ago. Partial stone edifices lay in various states of decay, creating a maze of tunnels and hidey-holes. Shards of clay pots were scattered everywhere. Barely-there wooden beams lay criss-crossed over some of the remains. It was an archaeological mess and delight, all in one.

"What is this place?" I asked in awe.

"It's an old Roman city, more than two thousand years old, I think, and looking its age, I'd say. It's dark and pokey, great for hiding in. We use this place to teach battlefield stealth and hone both physical and elemental reflexes. It's kind of like laser force, but you actually get hurt here—sometimes. But *you* won't, I'm sure! Watch out, though, you'll still find the odd skull rolling around the floor!" That little gem gave me a chill.

"You know laser force?" I was surprised by this information even more than the impressive remains.

"You think we don't get out much? I often head into the human world. Laser force is wicked! Don't mind a game of football either, when I can fit it in. You like the game?"

"Not really to play, but I followed Australia when they were in the World Cup. Ben loves soccer. I've had more than my share of 3am games to watch over popcorn with him."

"Well, he can't be as big a tosser as I thought he was if he's into the world game! Oh, sorry," he said as I raised a brow at the insult to Ben.

"It's okay. He's being an idiot at the moment."

"That's putting it mildly. Anyway, there's more to being a Watcher on this outpost of a planet than slashing Daimon and protecting beautiful—*um*—" he immediately flushed, coughed, and mumbled something in another language, then walked on ahead, trying to ignore what he had just said. Awkward was the standard in my life now, apparently. I pretended I didn't notice what he said, not wanting to make him feel any more embarrassed. I did enjoy the warm feeling the compliment gave me though.

"All right, Sophia-" he began, his voice finding a deeper, thicker English lilt.

"Just call me Soph," I interrupted. I hoped the familiarity might break the suffocating tension now oozing from him.

"Right, okay, *um*—Soph, how this normally plays out is similar to fighting the orbs. We use the ruins as an obstacle course, and the objective is for you to steer clear of me and actually hunt me down without me catching you first." He pointed to a half-collapsed stone doorway with the Roman numeral XII carved above it. "We start at door twelve because—well, we just do. Not sure why." He smiled and raised his perfectly sculpted white eyebrows charmingly. "Since you don't know how to dull your energy too well yet, I want you just to pretend to attack me. Aim at the ground near my feet. Please don't actually zap me—you might just kill me!" he chuckled. I didn't follow suit. It wasn't an amusing thought, knowing that I could accidently kill one of them. The anxiety in me surged, causing my back to burn and head to ache. That old friend called '*run for the hills*' tried to emerge, but I managed to ignore it, but only just.

"I *will* zap you though, like an orb. No mercy! "A devious smile spread across his face. I could almost have been sucked in by his boyish charm if he wasn't describing his intention of attacking me. "So, if you can catch me off guard, you need to engage me in physical combat. Wrestle with me, kick, punch, scratch—anything. Don't be afraid to hurt me with your fists—this is what I'm trained for. Sometimes we can't—for various reasons—use the elements of E'lan, so we have to be prepared to fight however we can, and physical strength is always on our side. This is also why we carry weapons if we know we are going into combat—everything helps. Daimons are proficient hand-to-hand fighters. They also have some nasty weapons, so we need to keep pace with whatever force they will use against us. Haven't you ever wondered where humans got the inspiration for weapons in the first place?"

"Not really," I said.

"Look no further than Yeqon and Lilith, there's a match made in Hell! We've always used weapons on the more violent places across the worlds but they were never intended for here." He shook his head in disgust, pausing a moment before continuing on. "Unfortunately, Daimon often like to play with their victims for their own sadistic amusement. They even keep some in their own realm to hunt for sport. That's a place you never want to end up in. They won't necessarily kill you immediately, so you must know how to fight with whatever resources you have, whether that be your energy, your fists, a chromious blade, or a rock on the ground. I know you haven't trained like this before, so this will be a sort of 'get to know you session' in order for me to see what you're capable of, and where we'll need to focus."

"I have no idea how to fight. I've barely ever swatted a fly! I suppose, like everything else at the moment, I'll just see what my bizarre instincts happen to dish out!"

"That's the way—positive thinking. As long as you don't dish out a life-ending blast, I'll be pretty chuffed. Now, I'm giving you two minutes to hide. Then I'm going to hunt you while you hunt me. The winner gets the other's Eccles cake from Eilir tomorrow! Fair?" His unusual twang was playful now and completely broke the tension I was feeling. Although a fish out of water, I was safe here, despite the less than pleasant training methods. I took a cue from his casualness.

"No way! I'd rather give you my PIN number—those things are too damn good!" I took off at a run through doorway twelve, smiling to myself as the sound of his friendly jibes about who the winner would be, faded into the distance.

Chapter
Thirty-Eight

The hunt was on.

I squatted behind a stack of huge, earthenware urns in the middle of the *warzone* as Lorcan had called it. It was almost pitch black in the tunnels, so I let a little warmth enter my face to emit a small glow from my A'vean birthmark. It was becoming easier each time to draw this energy up to my face. I didn't need to visualize it, just a slight twitch to my cheek seemed to be all it took to draw it up and out. At least *that* was going well. It was deadly silent but for the distant clanging of Ben and Jude playing with those awful weapons.

Drawing on every suspense movie I'd ever seen, I kept my back to the walls and edged ever so slowly on tiptoe around the corners of the decrepit walls. My soft glow cast deep shadows across ancient graffiti and artwork etched into the long forgotten remains. The ground was uneven, covered in buried debris. I remembered Lorcan's quip about skulls, and tried to imagine it was only pottery shards that I was cracking through. The vile memory of the Prime scroll chamber prevented me believing it was merely rubble underfoot. A rush spread through my chest as I felt my way around the labyrinth. It was actually exciting, like playing a grown up game of hide and seek.

The sound of splintering wood had me double back to where I'd started. I thought I heard a mumbled expletive and felt a rise in the static in the air. I could sense Lorcan's energy nearby. My cheeks warmed as my mark lit up brighter, and my hands tingled with the thrill. I felt like a lioness waiting to pounce. Some new, deep-seated instinct threatened to emerge. *Deep breath in, deep breath out, repeat.* My glow dulled compliantly so that I didn't give my position away. A smile broadened on my face. I edged carefully around a huge, mouldy wooden beam, ready to strike, only to find a little glowing orb bouncing around. *Was that left by Lorcan to tease me?* I turned back, nearly tripping over a decayed wheel. The static in the air weakened as he retreated. He was hunting me, not the reverse. This was *his* game. I needed to change that. I stopped a moment and closed my eyes. I took another trademark deep breath and let my mind relax. I reached out with my senses to feel the energies around me, like Koi had been teaching me with the giant orb. To my left was a cool calmness, and to my immediate right there was a quiet sizzle of electrons. I moved silently that way, one side step at a time, and it became stronger. My skin prickled as I was becoming more accustomed to when my own kind were near. My face flared up unexpectedly.

I stopped again and tried to calm this unintended beacon. I visualised a gushing waterfall, only my power was the water falling over the cliff face, away and down into a deep lake below. I let that elemental energy flow away as I willed myself invisible. My face and hands settled relatively quickly, my body was cool, still and quiet. Each time it was easier than the last. My confidence blossomed a little.

I was so deep in the ruins now, not a wisp of light was present. I crept closer to the buzzing, and I could feel him nearby. I could hear rapid yet controlled breaths. *Could he sense me?* He didn't seem to be moving from his position. I was squatting behind two large stones, heart pounding and holding my breath. The air was alive. I peeked around the corner and that was my mistake. He was there, he saw me, and threw a nasty sting of light that bit my hand before I jumped back into the darkness.

That made me mad. He laughed. I rushed back around just as Lorcan was retreating. I kept pace with him, my agility, jumping and ducking around the mess of obstacles both surprised and delighted me. It spurred me on. Like a flash of lightning, he zipped in and out through the corners and corridors and mess. He glowed, revealing himself, as though he wanted me to catch him. He was toying with me. Making it easy for me to find him. That made me mad, too. I wanted to show him that I could do it without his help, so I stopped and ran the other way. I felt him stop, too. I think that confused him—he thought I would take the easy option. They all thought I was too human, too weak. Perhaps it was true for now, but not forever. My university lecturers thought I was too introverted to succeed as a nurse. I rose to that challenge, and I would rise to this one.

I quickly did a quiet circle back past the two big stones, over to where I thought he had stopped. He was there. I could feel his energy from behind the crumbling, damp walls. I managed to keep my own energy so low that I felt darker than the veil of blackness surrounding me—he wouldn't be expecting that. Despite the excitement of the chase, I maintained a calm control. My waterfall was working, and I let it keep flowing through my mind. The static buzz was teasing my hair on end as I edged up to another toppled doorway that led out of the tunnel I was hiding in. I could hear him breathing softly, mere paces away. I was nearly jumping out of my own skin with the thrill of catching him first. I counted quietly to three, then sprang from around the corner, straight into Lorcan's back. He yelped in surprise as we toppled to the ground. I had him face down for a just second before he flipped me over. I was flung a few feet away where I slammed hard into an unforgiving rock.

"So, we're playing dirty?" I puffed, as I pulled myself up.

"As hard as you want it!" he said as he threw a thin bolt of light at me. I dodged it just in time, as sharp stone pellets blew out from the disintegrated rock behind me. I lunged forward. He met me head on, and his martial arts skills quickly outmanoeuvred my girly kicks and punches until I was flung down hard. My back ached painfully as I came to rest across a beam of wood.

"*Ow*, that hurts!" I yelped. He hesitated a moment, which is when I swiped a foot out and tripped him up, bringing him crashing down on top of me. Dust puffed up, making me cough and splutter. Once it settled, I wiped my eyes with my free hand to see his face staring intently at mine, mere inches away. His eyes swirled, studying me whilst I was pinned beneath him. Our breaths were rapid as we tried to catch them. I wriggled and squirmed, but he was too heavy. His thick arms imprisoned me.

"You're more impressive, more naturally gifted than I could have ever imagined. I didn't expect you to be able to hunt me. You dulled your energy signature to invisibility. You are indeed an Angel of the highest order." His breath was warm, sweet and soft. The pulse in his neck quickened. He shifted slightly, so that his weight was not so heavy on me.

"Are you going to let me up?" I asked, feeling suddenly self-conscious of his lingering proximity.

He didn't answer, he just stared silently at me. This unexpected awkward moment made me babble, a skill I actually was proficient at. "You know, I think I've earned that Eccles cake."

"Indeed," he said softly.

"I'll share if you let me up right now."

"Only a pastry?" he asked in a husky tone.

My heart froze.

"Um, —Lorcan, I'm tired. Please, let me up." I wriggled my other arm free, but he moved to grab both of my hands and pinned them back by my sides. His mark glowed strongly; it swirled all the way across his forehead and down to the edge of the right side of his jaw. He just stared at me, taking in my face with his ethereal eyes, his head tilting subtly left and right.

"Lorcan, please stop. You're making me feel uncomfortable. Please, let me up!" I pleaded. The fun had just been sabotaged.

That seemed to snap him out of whatever this moment was to him. He pushed up wordlessly and turned his back to me.

"Lorcan, sorry—" I began.

"You've nothing to be sorry for. Go get changed, you'll need to have Enl'iel attend your wounds." His tone was flat. He walked away through the mess we had made, into the dark shadows towards the main arena without looking back.

Why were guys so difficult?

I was a tad black and blue now, with a nice welt across my hand thanks to Lorcan, who had vanished. *What a wuss.* I shook my head and laughed a little at the ridiculousness of it. Was he embarrassed or annoyed? Who knew? If only guys, angelic or not, would actually communicate! I was left all alone to ponder the aftermath of his hormonal outburst as I had to find my own way out of the maze and back into the central arena. Clanging echoed off to the left. Jaz remained just inside the main entry watching Jude and Ben still go at it with swords that looked like they could kill at a hundred paces. *Nice.* Otherwise it was empty but for Koi who, with a look of deep concern, immediately took me back to the Stasis room for healing. He counselled me on my progress as we walked.

"I hear you fought well. You have minimal injuries, this is commendable with an opponent such as Lorcan. He informs me you exceeded his expectations. You are becoming exponentially stronger by the day. Just a few sessions down, and already you are able to begin the process of controlling your elemental power. Lorcan was very impressed with you."

"He said that?" I asked, rather surprised after the—*incident.*

"Indeed, Sophia. He informed me that you hunted him with stealth. Your fighting technique needs more finesse, but he said you are much stronger and more resourceful than you realise. He will continue to train you every morning and evening from now on," he finished. My hair bristled a little. That was going to be comfortable. *Not.*

We pushed through the Stasis room door to find Enl'iel readying a bed with some poultices, bottles of things I didn't recognise, and a tall glass of water. I gulped it down before saying hello. The room was not as full as the first time I visited, but I noticed the white veil of energy still blanketing Cael's bed down the back.

"Oh my word, look at you! Master Koi, a little gentler, please? You're every other colour than skin!" she exclaimed.

"Ah, the cost of learning, and learning well. The orbs and Lorcan might consider themselves less fortunate on this occasion, my dear Enl'iel. She has performed impeccably today for one so unsure of herself," he leaned in and bid me goodbye with a bow and a kiss to my hands.

As a pretty female Alchemae brought a cup of herbal tea for me to sip, I looked down at my swollen, fingers. They were cut and scorched. I felt achy and sore all over. It even hurt to sit. *This was barely injured according to Koi?* I stared intently at my crimson, chipped finger nails as exhaustion set in. Enl'iel spoke soothingly as she dropped essences of this and that all over me.

"Stop doubting yourself, Sophia. A week ago, this was but a fairy tale to you, and look at you now. With barely any introduction, you have fought off our orbs and matched wits with our best trainer. You have read the ancient language, and begun to unlock the secrets of Enoch. You have defended yourself against both Daimon and Rogue. Imagine where you will be a week from now! Acknowledge your successes, believe in yourself, and confront your challenges was grace and fortitude. When you thought yourself a mere mortal, you exuded an enviable confidence in your ability to heal. You have that and much, much more now." She poured her energy into my aching palms as she spoke, instantly relieving the pain.

"I know what you're saying is true. I can feel the changes in me. And today, I did feel more in control, I kind of enjoyed it actually." She smiled at this revelation.

"I'm just so uncomfortable with all of the attention and people acting so weird around me. I miss normalcy, I miss my friends." I sounded like a whining child, but I was too tired to care.

"There is no more 'normal' in your vocabulary and I'm sorry for that. However, you will adapt—you *must*. Accept that your kindred revere you. You are precious to us all. As for Ben, I know that's who you are referring to—"

And now Lorcan, I thought quietly.

"He will come around. I know his behaviour is hurting you, but you must understand that his human sensibilities and masculine stubbornness are a brick wall in front of his common sense at present. Give it time. He loves you, and he will open his heart to you again," she soothed.

My cheeks burned when she said that he *loved* me. *What did she mean by that?* She was already distracted with preparing me a plum tea while I read too much into her offhanded statement. He couldn't love me, well, especially not now. I thought of Koi's tattoos and unrequited love and then mentally slapped myself around. *Stop it Soph!*

"Now, finish this, and then take a shower. I see Koi did not let you refresh after training!" She screwed her nose up a little. I must have stunk like a men's locker room. "Afterwards, I believe Brennan is taking you, Jasmine, and Ben up and out of the Sanctuary for some fresh air? You will enjoy that, but stay cl—"

She didn't finish her sentence as the door burst open. Ben was shoved through the door, with Jude right behind him. His left arm held high in the air by Jude, who was trying to stem the flow of blood cascading down his arm. Jaz was close behind them, cursing at Jude with all of her extra special expletive words for apparently causing this injury. Brennan was trying to hold her back.

"Hands off, freak!" she screeched at him as she struggled in his grip.

I jumped up at the sight. "What happened?" I visually assessed Ben for any other injuries. His aura was dark with anger. He was holding his breath, on and off, almost gasping. He was tense with pain. All my aches were suddenly distant memories.

"I'm fine, Soph. It's just a scratch." He spluttered, out of the blue, obviously seeing my look of concern. The sound of my name coming from his lips made my heart skip a beat. I immediately helped him sit on my bed, whilst Enl'iel called on the same Alchemae for a multitude of herbs, lotions, and bandages.

"This behemoth brute sliced my brother! Almost in friggin' half!" Jaz poked at Jude with her finger, jamming it hard enough into his back that he stepped forward out of her way.

"Will someone stop this howling human before I silence her myself? My ears are about to bleed! He has a scratch, that's all." he growled in her direction, making her back off slightly. She gave Jude her filthiest look as she garnered a renewed tenacity and shoved him away from Ben, taking over the task of maintaining pressure on his arm to stem the flow.

"You cut my brother! I don't care who or what you are, just back the hell off!" She then gave her complete attention to Ben and helped as Enl'iel and I inspected the wound. It was deep and gaping, far from a scratch. I was immediately alarmed.

"It was my fault, sis. Leave him alone. I insisted on using the weapons. I forgot how strong these—uh, these *guys* are. I forgot they aren't normal," he explained.

Jaz's renewed accusing glare had Jude smugly back off towards the door. He matched her glare with a frightening scowl, unflinching. *Now there was a match made in Hell.*

"Jude?" Enl'iel questioned him with her own look of annoyance.

"Apologies, human. Steady on with the insults, though," he said in an overtly forced, softer voice, far beneath the might of his presence. His face brimmed with annoyance, which told me that apologies were not his forte. I felt Ben bristle when he referred to him as 'human', but he kept himself quiet.

The strain of pain over-ruled his need to continue a pointless interspecies war of insults.

"Whose idea was it to let Ben near the weapons? *Hmm*?" Enl'iel questioned Jude and Brennan further, each of whom were looking at each other accusingly. It was like two bulls in a paddock pawing the ground at each other, daring each other to cave and drop the other one in it.

Lorcan entered the room at that moment of standoff, adding to the delightful feeling of discomfort surging on the air. I felt instantly awkward as he averted his eyes from mine. I concentrated on dabbing at Ben's wound with some gauze as tea tree and calendula essences were dropped into the gash. Ben winced slightly, barely restraining a groan. Lorcan had put his hands up in defensive innocence to Enl'iel's questioning whilst Jude surprisingly acquiesced. "I have dishonoured us all with my lack of judgement." Enl'iel chastised him further with a few choice words as he took his leave, mumbling something about heading to London to check on the troops that were stationed there.

"Don't go far Jude, you will be needed here," she called after him as he slammed the door behind him.

"Brennan, you're not off the hook. Don't look so vindicated. You are just as much to blame," she snapped.

"But," He thought of eluding the truth but then conceded "Ah, it was fun while it lasted though, wasn't it buddy?" He was such a juvenile.

"I'm not your God-damned buddy!" Ben grimaced as he lashed out at Brennan through gritted teeth.

"Shhh, calm down Ben or you'll make the wound reopen," I soothed.

I snuck a covert look at his face. We were so close, yet I felt poles apart from him. Ashes and spice tinted the salty sweat pouring from him.

His wound would, under normal circumstances, need surgery and an impressive number of stitches. It would still take some time to heal, but I knew we could do it. As Enl'iel dropped the last essence in, some of his blood dripped down onto her hands. She paused a moment, looking so concerned that I panicked quietly to myself. She looked off in the distance momentarily, seemingly in thought.

"Lith'eal, please, would you fetch me some more bandages?" she called to another Alchemae in the back as I wiped the blood spatter from Ben's face and neck with a damp gauze pad. My fingers accidently touched the scar on his cheek. He jerked back, nearly opening the wound up again just as Jaz had started bandaging it. "Don't!" he snapped at me.

I was shocked by his ridiculous anger. I lost it right there and then.

"What? What the hell is your problem, Ben? You've been an iceman to me for days! When is this going to stop? I'm sorry about what's happened.

I'm sorry my life has turned into a freak show, but believe me, it's certainly not been my choice. I'm sorry you've been dragged into it. Don't you think I'd much rather be home right now, hanging out with you guys like we used to? Like *normal*? Don't you think I want everything to be normal, too? Well, it's not, is it? So just get the hell over yourself! I'm just trying to help you. Stop being an idiot!" I huffed and looked away as I caught a barely hidden smile creep into the corner of Enl'iel's mouth.

"You tell him, Soph. God, you've got a thick head, Ben. Grow the hell up! You're being such a dick!" Jaz will forever be my fan club.

Enl'iel cleared her throat as she tried to ignore Jaz's colourful language, whilst Ben just glared at the floor with thin, tight lips.

"Apologise to Sophia, human, or next time I'll take to you with my own sword, and with purpose," growled Lorcan. I'd forgotten he was even there. "Her wounds may not be of the flesh, but they run deeper than yours. Apologise, now!" he seemed bigger and scarier as he let his wings unfurl like an angry gorilla puffing out his chest.

"Okay, okay, fine. Back off!" He looked meekly at me, not apologetic, though—more conflicted. "Sorry, Soph. Just give me some space and time okay? It's not you, it's me."

"*Oh my God*! I can't believe you just said that, Ben! It's like *the* worst breakup speech in history, and you guys aren't even—hang on, *are* you two?" Jaz's eyes were nearly out of her head with intrigue.

At the same exact moment, both Ben and I belted out a firm "*No!*"

His over-enthusiastic denial had started the blood seeping again through his half wrapped bandage. His face paled. Enl'iel was reinspecting it with a deepening furrow of her brow. I was already tense again with concern, Jaz's statement long lost on me now.

"What is it? You look so worried." I asked as she unwrapped it again. She stalled a moment then called for a eucalyptus and lavender poultice. "It's just deeper than I thought, dear. Ben, I know you are frightened, but will you allow us to heal you with our elemental energy? The blade that struck you can often fester flesh very quickly. It is created of a substance that affects not only the flesh, but also the spirit. I sense your energy to be very low, which is perhaps why this wound is so unpleasant. Do we have your permission? It will not hurt, I promise." Her face was pained with concern as she held his hand tight in her own. Jaz poked him in the back.

"Use a brain cell and let them help you." She poked him one more time for good measure.

He scowled her way then nodded his assent quietly. Both Enl'iel and I immediately laid our hands across the oozing wound. I felt him hold his breath and tense. Jaz was wrapping up the briefly used, bloody bandage, as our hands began to illuminate. She scuttled in closer to him, watching us with intrigue with her eyes wide. We began to let our joint energy flow into his arm. I concentrated deeply, as the negative energy oozing from him was intense. I drew it up and cast it out of me. The wound began to knit together. He winced and groaned slightly, making me falter.

"Concentrate," Enl'iel urged. Her intensity was incredible, her concentration unparalleled. I heard Jaz draw in a breath as she watched the wound fuse almost completely back together. We stopped when there was just a small, one centimetre gap to allow any fluids to drain out. Sweat poured down his gaunt face. It wasn't meant to hurt, but he seemed drained to exhaustion. I wondered about these weapons and the power they had.

"Wrap that clean bandage over the small wound that is left Jasmine," Enl'iel instructed.

"It's okay, bro, all done. Hang in there." Jasmine wiped his brow lovingly, then bandaged the small wound close to his elbow. Her voice was gentle as she helped him through this moment of pain. She kissed him on the cheek, as he leaned into her and sighed.

"Now, Jasmine, dear. Bandage over that small wound with this fresh gauze, twice a day. Would you like to monitor it for me? You are a capable young nurse," she asked.

"Sure, of course." She faltered a moment. "Hang on! Your voice, it's so familiar. You sound just like-but no, you can't be! You're not, but—but *how*?" Jaz squinted with a confused and suspicious glare at Enl'iel as she finished the last few wraps of the bandage.

"Watch, dear," Enl'iel said as she briefly flashed her old 'Nan' visage at Jaz.

Jaz nearly jumped out of her skin, just as she fastened the bandage securely. "Holy mother of—seriously? Nan? What the—?"

Enl'iel smiled quietly to herself with sweet amusement.

"I only just found out myself, Jaz. I'm shocked, too, and I lived with her!" I said.

"Concealment is one of my many talents," Enl'iel said with a girlish shrug.

Jaz gave her a tweak on her arm just to make sure was actually real.

"You guys take freaky to a whole new level. Funny, I was wondering what happened to Nan. I didn't want to ask you, you know, in case she'd been…"

"I'm here and perfectly well," answered Enl'iel. Jaz' face was enamoured, she seemed absolutely gobsmacked and impressed all at once.

"Impressive, very bloody impressive!" Jaz said with a satisfied nod.

"This is getting more entertaining by the minute. Are we finished here?" asked Ben dryly, apparently unaffected by this new and paranormal development.

"Indeed we are, Ben. You need to get out of here for a while, get some fresh air, and perhaps some decent manners back into you. Brennan is going to take you all topside. However, it will only happen if you rest first. I will bring you some analgesia shortly. Please inform me if you are in pain Ben, you do not have to endure pain whilst you are in my care. Now, freshen up, eat, rest and then have a nice break. But, do as you are instructed—*all of you*—for your own safety and ours, or you shall not be allowed out again." She got up and took the tray of used medicinal jars to the central table, then disappeared behind the veil of light concealing Cael.

Brennan took the other two away to rest and get ready, Lorcan followed behind them. I was just leaving for the showers when Enl'iel called me back, emerging from Cael's isolation zone. "Wait a moment, Sophia," she said calmly, "take this." She passed me a bracelet with a white pearl-like oval stone inlaid into a silver setting. "Gedz'iel returns tonight to send you on your quest. You need all the help you can muster before you begin this journey. I do not know what lies before you. This, dear, is part of your Soul Stone. It is but a remanent of the one your parents gave you upon your birth. When children of our kind are born, they receive a Soul Stone to protect and soothe them. It is a gift from the spirits of the Cavern of Souls, the most ancient and revered sanctuary on Earth. These stones are a gift to celebrate a birth. Unfortunately, because of who you were, there was much haste and panic after your birth, and your stone was lost—bar this small piece that snapped off. I was to give it to you at your twenty-first reception, but circumstance has not afforded us that luxury. You will notice that all of the young children carry them around to soothe and protect themselves from negative energy." I recalled immediately that little Av'ael had held one in her hand, but it had been the size of a glowing plum.

"Please, give this other one to Jasmine. It is but a small cutting of my own stone. It may calm her unruly anger. Her soul is damaged, and I can only hope that one day peace will enter her heart and blot out the darkness." She placed in my palm another delicate bracelet with a tiny, asymmetrical wedge of stone set in it. "Please, tell her it is a token gift from me, nothing more. Lord I'el forbid that she accept help from anyone or anything!" she added with a resigned shake of her head. She fiddled with her own Soul Stone necklace as she spoke. It was a habit she had done for as long as I could remember, usually when she was worried about something. "Off you go now, enjoy your small slice of freedom while you can," she disappeared back through the veil to Cael.

I looked around the Stasis room briefly before I left, only now noticing the glowing Soul Stones laying upon the chests of each slumbering teenager. I turned to leave just as I heard a slight commotion. Glancing back, I noticed a young girl surrounded by what I assumed were her parents. She was waking from her hibernation, it seemed. There were tears of joy, hugs, and laughter. The word *reception* was mentioned, as an Alchemae began to assess her condition. I felt like I was eavesdropping on an intimate moment, so I slipped from the room, wondering how different things may have been if my parents had been in my life.

Chapter
Thirty-Nine

reshly showered with a single silver braid running down over my shoulder, I made my way through the bustling mass of people, thankfully unrecognised this time. Anonymity suited me. I could have been in the downtown area of Melbourne, Sydney, or even New York—the hustle and bustle of the subterranean population was surprisingly similar. As I finally made it back to the central entry level, I noticed for the first time, a floating platform one storey above us, just hovering there, as though it were in space with no gravity. It looked like a chunk of earth had been dug out and tossed up there. Old roots hung down like scraggly hair as it gently bobbed up and down. I stepped back as far as the surrounding wall would allow in order to crane my neck up to see what it was. There were flashing lights appearing and disappearing atop it, and a faint, warm glow was emanating from it. As I wondered at this new marvel, I felt a tug at my leg.

"Hello, pretty Sophia. What you looking at?"

I glanced down to see little Av'ael, her dull eyes glued intently on me.

"Well hi there, little one. I was just wondering what the floating rock up there is?"

"Oh, that's our *sys—syth—* Zitos stone! I'm not allowed up there until I'm twenty-one. Are you allowed there? Mama told me it's pink!"

"Well, I haven't seen it yet, but I hope to soon. And if it is pink, I'll be sure to tell you."

She squealed excitedly at this and ran off to her mother, who was calling her away. *So there was one of these here, too.* Noting all of the flashing energies coming and going up there, I assumed that was how they entered and exited without using the church. I eyed it a while longer, then made my way to the *Sophia* exit, translated as *the door for those unable to control their powers.*

"Hey, Elsa!" called Jaz, who had decided I looked like the Snow Queen now that I had white hair.

"Oh, you just kill me Jaz, so funny!" I smirked, wishing for my rainbow locks back. Brennan laughed, Lorcan stared, and Ben looked anywhere but at me. Two new faces giggled at the comment, and I rolled my eyes. *What and who now?*

"*Excusez-moi*, Sophia, but it is a compliment. You are very pretty, as is Elsa. *Bonjour*, I am Kristen, and zis is my brother, Thomas," said a gorgeous, olive-skinned girl about my age. Her brother was the polar opposite in appearance—pale, blue-eyed, and golden blond. I snuck a quick look at their eyes and could see instantly that they were human. I put my hand out to shake, and Kristen laughed. "Brennan, 'aven't you taught her 'ow to greet someone properly? Does it take a mere 'uman to do it?" She leaned in and did the cheek-kiss, although with her, there was an absence of any elemental connection. No buzz, just the warmth of her skin on mine. Her hazel eyes sparkled with kindness and strength as she stood back, and I felt her to be an instant friend.

Thomas followed suit. "It's an honour to meet you, and will be an honour to protect and serve you," he said in a smooth, more understated French accent.

"There now. What other Angelic customs must we teach 'er?" teased Kristen.

"Yes, yes, pull your head in, *l'enfant*," Brennan answered.

"Ooh, you 'ave been practising your French, *formidable!*" Kristen responded.

"Don't get too excited *Petite Fleur*, it's one word at a time, sweet pea." Then he turned back to me. "Princess, these two balls of Parisian cheek are part of our extended family. They are descendants of the humans who took refuge with us after the great flood, and pledged their allegiance to us. We protect them, train them, and they in turn, serve us in many ways, particularly reconnaissance in the human world. They are invaluable, even with their rather large egos."

"Huh! Will you listen to 'im? I learn from zee master!" Kristen replied as she playfully swatted his bare bicep.

Both Kristen and Thomas then extended an arm and bowed to me with huge grins, revealing long bows and a quiver of arrows on their backs. It was all very *Robin Hood*. I wondered why guns weren't an added accessory to the expansive cache, all these ancient weapons seemed understated in the modern world. As if reading my mind, or the fact that I was caught staring at his munitions Thomas disclosed, "They are silent, deadly and do not attract human attention. Could you imagine the commotion if we fired an Uzi every time we saw a Rogue?" *Okay, fair point.*

"And, they don't necessarily knock them down. Every weapon outside our elemental energy must be chromious lined or tipped. It brings them down every time. Plain old metal just doesn't cut it," added Brennan.

"Okay, Ben and Jasmine, you guys will stick with Kristen and Thomas. They will guard you, along with Kea, into Tewkesbury, where you can shop, hang, or do whatever you want to for a couple of hours. Stock up on whatever you need—I don't know when you'll get another opportunity. Stay close, and do everything they say," Brennan warned with an uncharacteristic seriousness.

"*That* is the best thing I've heard in days. I seriously need me some makeup. No zombie-things around up there, though?" There was a sudden and real note of fear in Jaz's voice as she pointed to the ceiling.

"Jude has already secured the route with scouts. You should be perfectly fine. Just try to be on your best behaviour, okay? It took some quick talking to keep Jude here a little longer to help after what happened before. So Ben, keep your trap shut, at least around Jude! Jaz, you will be just fine, don't worry, mini princess," He gave her a brotherly peck on the top of her head. She blushed and surprisingly hugged him, perhaps a second longer than necessary. She craved love, this girl, but sought the wrong kind in all the wrong places. If only she'd accept more than just the type wanting to get up her skirt. When this rare moment of comfort for her with Brennan was over, he waved his hand across the veil of light that protected the entrance to the church, and the aged stone staircase was revealed once more.

"It's safe to go on through now. Don't ever try to sneak though the veil—your arse won't thank you for the sting," he laughed as he urged us along.

As I exited through the heavy church door with Lorcan and Brennan, Kea was already revving a dark coloured car for the others to drive them to town. I waved to Jaz as she gently held Ben's arm while he got into the car first. Unfortunately, it was late afternoon when we emerged, and being winter in the UK, it was already very dark out. It was disappointing that I wasn't going to see sunlight today. Just a smidge of sun on my face would have been bliss.

Jude reappeared briefly as they got in the car, ignoring Jaz with a practiced ease as he called in a few more scouts with a high-pitched whistle. "There's been a bit of Daimon activity in Birmingham—just want to bolster up a few more lead scouts to clear the way," he said to Brennan as he flashed out of sight, heading up the disappearing Jaguar with twenty or so dulled-down scouts zooming in formation on either side of the car as it wound away through the darkness.

"Okay princess, ready for a little R&R?" Brennan asked as he passed me a gorgeous pair of new running shoes. "Want to see if you can outrun a Watcher?"

"How did you know I like to run?"

"I am the best! But, I've also been your neighbour for your entire life, forget so soon? But we'll stick with the simple fact that I am the best."

I scoffed warmly at his ridiculously large ego as I strapped on those babies within two breaths. I took off after him down the narrow, paddock-lined road. We ran for a couple of kilometres before he jumped a wire fence and headed off south of the church, across a field of sleeping cows covered with a fine dusting of snow. A few beasts lazily raised a head to check us out, chewing away on a previous meal. I scrambled over the derelict fence while he jumped it like a pro, leaving me far behind.

The second I stepped onto this field, I felt a heavy thudding in my chest. A steady drumming, like the dream I'd had the other night. I felt pain that wasn't mine. Desperate screams fought for dominance in my head. It took my breath away for a second or two. Brennan shouted out something rude to me about my fitness from the distance. I shook my head as I leaned over resting on my thighs. The thudding continued heavily in my chest. I tried to brush it off and pushed myself onwards, attempting to ignore this uncomfortable intrusion. To distract myself, I recalled the passage of Enoch's words about my father. *Sprig of bloom, lions and boars*—whatever that meant. I hoped Gedz'iel knew what that mouthful of confusion was all about. As the thrumming continued, I wondered why Enoch couldn't have just said things plainly—but of course, that would have just made life way too simple. Mulling over those words distracted me enough that I'd caught up to Brennan quickly. I pumped my legs so hard that all I could hear was my own heartbeat as I drowned out the unwelcome sounds with exertion.

I pulled up behind Brennan, still marvelling at how he'd recovered. A few days ago, he was the paralysed photographer across the road, and now we were running cross-country together. Despite the incessant and covert noise intrusion, my body felt alive. The sting of burning muscles invigorated me, leaving me wanting more. My steady breaths puffed out white clouds into the freezing air as Brennan said, "Just down the hill and over the river is a surprise for you." He took off again, barefoot, like a flash.

We reached the small stretch of rushing water and made our way across to the other side on a conveniently located, very rickety rowboat. I wasn't sure how it even stayed afloat. There seemed more holes than wood on the floor. The thrumming was almost insane as we climbed up the other slippery bank in pitch darkness. At first I didn't say anything—there was enough drama going on. We walked down past a derelict outhouse of some sort toward another paddock lined with huge, white trimmed fir trees. I had to say something then, though. The screaming in my head was out of control.

"Can you hear that?" I asked.

"What, princess? Why are you yelling at me?"

"Sorry, am I? It's just so loud. That drumming sound? I'm sure I can hear someone calling for help or something. I don't know," I said, rubbing my cheek, which was threatening to sear right off my face. I couldn't let my power show outside, lest I attract something unpleasant, so I pushed the feeling as far back down as I could. It eased off the further we walked away from the old building.

"No, I don't hear it," he responded, concern replacing his smile. "I don't feel any negative elementals around here. The E'lan is stronger near the sanctuary so perhaps you are picking up on another Watcher in the vicinity. Strange—I can normally feel my kin if they're nearby. You are more powerful than me, though. Your antennas are probably picking up someone far off, clever little lady." He reached a hand out to me. I took it. "Stick close though, just in case princess. If anything happens to you, I'll have to deal with Enl'iel, and that is not a happy option, trust me!" We pushed through the line of thick firs as a misty rain fell, cooling off my still warm face. He pulled me closer, pointing out into the middle of a darkened paddock.

"Do you see it? This is your surprise. You have twenty minutes. Knock yourself out!" he gently pushed me forward as my eyes adjusted to the darkened space, revealing a sight that bought a well of tears to my eyes. A piece of normal stood there, swaying its long, grey mane. A stunning horse almost identical to Grey grazed lazily in the distance. He looked up suddenly and it felt like he was beckoning to me as he nodded his head up and down, stamping his hooves into the cold, hard earth. I gave one backward glance to Brennan, who waved me on, and then bent down to squeeze through the perfectly kept wooden perimeter fence. This amazing creature let out an attitude-filled whinny and pranced over to me like a supermodel. We met halfway, and like instant friends, he nuzzled into my shoulder, wriggling his upper lip, looking for a treat. I smelled that beautifully familiar, equine aroma. I hugged onto his muscular, Arabian neck and felt his warmth and strong heartbeat. If I'd closed my eyes, I could have been home. He shoved at me impatiently with his head.

"Okay, okay, you want to be friends?" He pawed at the snowy ground before ripping up a small mouthful of frozen grass that peeked out from between the white patches. "May I?" I asked, as I'd always done of Grey.

More hoof-stamping and swishing of his tail followed. Without another thought, I grabbed a luxurious handful of mane, swung up onto his wide back, and said, "Go for it!"

And he did. Straight into a full, bounding gallop around the large, misty field. He threw his head in that high-strung stallion kind of way, and I revelled in each loping lurch. Moonlight lit our path in a magical glow. With my legs squeezed tight against his ribs, I let go of his mane and threw back my head, letting the cold air rush past me, sending my hair wildly about. I felt instantly connected to him. I kept my eyes closed as he ran, and the longing became stronger and deeper by the second. Time slowed down, the air became thick, and the sounds around me slowed and deepened.

Home, I thought, *I just wanted to be home.* Suddenly, I thought I could hear someone urgently calling my name. *Who was it? What were they calling me for?* I was in heaven here. *Leave me alone.*

"Stop!" Was someone calling for me to stop? *No, I'm not finished yet.* The thundering hooves faded.

"Wait, Sophia. No! Stop!" I ignored these calls. I was going to enjoy every second of this tiny piece of normalcy, squeezing it out for as long as I could. The thrumming in my head was dissipating, the burning in my face had gone, and silence and peace surrounded me. My body tingled as the stallion took me away. Numbness overwhelmed me, a feeling I gladly accepted. Cool, warm, cool. Silence, blackness, stillness. The loping feeling suddenly stopped. I realised with a sense of confusion that the horse was no longer beneath me. I could no longer hear anything as something yanked me from within, backwards through a starry cosmos, away from the beautiful creature, away from safety, away from anywhere.

Chapter Forty

It had been for but the breadth of a hair that Nik'ael had not been discovered today. He was not sure that he could move around or even near the Sanctuary any longer. His care factor had taken a nosedive as his loyalties wavered more than they had in a thousand years. He had always struggled with his inner Daimon. Destruction was never quite as palatable to him as it was to the others who had switched alliances. Guilt had always gnawed at him after each and every terrible thing he had done.

He was at a crisis point—seeing her so close, yet so impossibly distant pulled at every fibre of his being. His fingers worked at those beads almost constantly now, the worry and frustration wearing them thin. Concealment and the proximity of all that chromious was near killing him as he watched the others drool over her, be near her, touch her. He had a death wish—he knew it. What more could he expect when deep down in his dark heart, it was not just Yeqon he was deceiving, but also himself?

He wanted Ben out of the way. His presence had an effect on her that had become far too distracting for both her and himself. He needed, for his own self-preservation, to remove Ben from the equation. Having Ben fawning privately over her so closely was impossible to deal with any longer. Perhaps then he could regain his perspective and lust for vengeance. It would hurt her, and that stung him. It would hurt Ben more, but he could live with that. Ben was nothing. This handy topside excursion had been exactly the chance he needed. Brennan and Enl'iel would be done-for once Gedz'iel found out that they'd let Sophia out of the sanctuary. He bristled with satisfaction at the thought of that smart mouthed Brennan getting zapped to this side of nowhere.

Without Sophia nearby just now, he could concentrate better, and deepened his cloaking as the scouts increased their presence tenfold upon approaching the small town. He stood outside the *Tewkesbury Bell Inn*, pressing into the wall and assessing the layout of the main street for escape routes and points of ambush. Leaning Tudor buildings still stood proud with heraldry flags lining the length of the main street. He remembered this place from the 1400's, whilst Richard was being tormented into doing things he didn't want to do by Anjou'elle and Neph'reus. Richard had fought hard, like a nobleman should, but he was hopelessly overpowered. He was no match for those evil vixens of the underworld. Nik'ael chuckled smugly. *Those were interesting times.* The aristocracy were so riddled with the perversion of Daimon influence back then. Even the rare good-hearted king could be a pawn for the Unseen and their stupid games with humans. He momentarily wondered to himself just where those two devilish women had gone. They hadn't made so much as an elemental blip on the radar for centuries. *Suspicious.*

As the scouts swarmed every dark corner, the village came alive after hours with the local half-breeds opening up the shops for their own kind. He almost admired their little network of bartering that spanned the globe. Never a thing was in want. Whilst humans starved for the simplest things, the Eudaimonians just gave each other whatever it was they needed, no matter the value. Perhaps if humans possessed less innate greed for material wealth, this world would not have been so easy to send to Hell. That was the irony he saw on Earth. Everyone was so scared of death and going to the wrong place, yet the real Hell was the one they'd created for themselves through war, greed, and oppression.

He called for Belial again as he shadowed Jasmine near the pharmacy. Belial never took more than a few minutes to respond yet he had ignored all three summons today. He knew that he'd scorned him back at the cottage on the mountain, but there was a purpose in that—though he'd not had the time to fill Belial in. Even so, he was but a guard dog, and not too smart. Like himself, Belial also had divided loyalties, it oozed from him, so he could never be sure how much he could be trusted.

Back when Belial's daughter was born—after a dalliance with a human woman—he'd almost lost his way, nearly running back into the arms of the Watchers. He'd actually fallen in love with the human and fathered two children with her. The first was a son, who had disappeared after the woman was locked away in Bedlam Asylum for being insane. The stupid woman had announced to medieval England that an Angel had fathered her child. She'd nearly burned at the stake for it. Belial searched for his son fruitlessly, on and off for years. He eventually rescued the woman in a midnight raid on that horrendous human institution and kept her alive and young for 300 more years. He had fathered another child with her, a daughter. The woman had finally gone truly mad from the mix of negative and positive elemental powers coursing through her. She ran off to the south and flung herself from the white cliffs into the ocean. The tragedy brought Belial to his knees. It was a love Nik'ael understood—he'd had that with Neren'iel. If it weren't for his own quick talking to draw Belial back into the fold, the brothers would have long ago thrown his butt into the depths of the Pits. Belial owed him, and he needed him to pay his debt right now.

He listened in the distance of his mind, while the humans dined at the kitschy, 1960's Chinese take-out. The laminate and chrome table was piled high with food, and Jasmine was glaring at Ben.

"Don't even say it!" she threatened him with a pointed chopstick.

"What? I just didn't think you ate that stuff," Ben answered with a tease.

"If you ever tell Soph that I like tofu, your lips will be as fat as your head!" She showed him her fist as she shovelled vegetables into her mouth. Nik'ael liked her a lot. She amused him no end.

As the group rose and left, he knew the time was near.

He smelled them before he saw them. While he was watching Jasmine back in the pharmacy, he sensed the slightly foul, metallic tang. Only his highly tuned hearing picked up the ragged, rapid panting coming from the shadows of the alley ways. It oozed from their pores. He knew this was the opportunity he needed to get rid of Ben, to create a bit of mayhem. It would make Sophia vulnerable, and possibly dangerous, but might also push her powers to the point that could bring this situation to a head. If he had more leverage of his own, then hopefully she would be putty in his hands and the brothers would have to sit up and acknowledge that his way was the correct way.

The chain around his neck hung heavily against him, not in weight, but in the oppression of his sensibilities. What he was about to do went against every grain of goodness left in him. *What little there was, anyway.* He'd seized the opportunity back in Melbourne. When the secret cavern below the library was collapsing in on itself, he had swooped in and out, gathering exactly what he'd been looking for. He was now a few chess-moves away from checkmating himself to a one-way ticket to Tartarus if he was ever caught by I'el. It was cannibalism—there was no way to pretty it up. It churned in his stomach, but he needed to do it. He fiddled with the bracelet, begging for forgiveness that was wholly undeserved.

The handful of bone-thin youths he'd seen slip down the lane towards the Avon Barges were his targets. Their deathly pale skin and fidgeting movements confirmed who they were. Addiction and toxins oozed from their ravaged bodies. Ragged clothes hung from their skeletal frames. Desperation shown in every fleeting glance they made up and down the street as they looked for a quick hit. They would be puppets for him; he would be their God whilst he was their supplier. While the others moved to shops further down the street towards the Abbey, he quickly darted down an alley behind a boarded up bakery. He took a breath, hesitated momentarily, then undid the concealed vial and sprinkled a few grains of the iridescent contents along the ground leading back to the pharmacy where the unsuspecting Jasmine was browsing somewhere in the vicinity of her brother. The smell of the Thanratos made him retch as he quickly went back into the strategic position that put him where the action would happen.

Jasmine was carrying a string bag filled with hair dye and wearing a new set of earbuds blasting Pachelbel's Canon when he heard the panting edge closer. It had taken them mere seconds to pick up the scent. Ben held a stack of auto magazines and a bag of mixed nuts that he was slowly chomping on. The Afflicted were mere feet away from them all, under a veil of shadows. He'd heard them licking the Angel bone dust off of the pavement, and it disgusted him. These vile leftovers of his own kind were but a means to an end on this occasion.

Within another thirty seconds, a few scouts had picked up the scent too. They zoomed in a panicked but controlled figure-eight around the unaware shoppers. Kea, instantly on alert, called out to everyone to head for the car. An immediate and exciting tinge of fear filled the air as people began to quickly scatter. Kristen and Thomas cocked their bows with an immediate and deadly-looking stance. Chromious arrows were held at the ready as their keen human eyes darted everywhere, looking for the enemy. Jasmine was initially oblivious to the scene, her face buried in a magazine and temporarily deafened by the music in her ears. Ben would be taken out, no question; the numbers were on Nik'ael's side tonight.

Fifteen Afflicted emerged from the damp shadows into plain sight. He acknowledged them with a subtle nod of his head and a flash of the vile around his neck. He found their leader—a tall, scrawny, white-haired woman who moved like a marionette. Her previously bright blue eyes were dulled to a sickly grey. He communicated telepathically with her to explain what he wanted and what they'd get in return for their compliance. She smiled wickedly, and her eyes gleamed in the lamplight as she licked her lips. Her group panted hysterically in turn. They hooted and hollered loudly, sounding like crazed soldiers heading in for the slaughter of battle. There was nothing remotely Eudaimonian left in these wretched beings, and even less was human. They were simply non-entities, stuck between two worlds but ultimately destined for nothingness.

He gave the word, and they attacked without hesitation. Elemental energy surged on the night breeze as the air crackled with electricity. The street lights flickered on and off, buzzing and hissing with the negative pulsations. Screaming like nails on metal, the Afflicted charged. Thomas and Kristen let fly with a barrage of well-aimed arrows. Christmas decorations exploded from the street poles as casualties. Red tinsel fluttered to the ground, symbolic of the blood about to be shed. Kristen, despite her small stature, took out two with a single arrow as it penetrated so forcefully that the same arrow still had enough power to kill another Afflicted attacker coming up behind the first. Kea was in full power. She threw out crackling bolts like a machine gun. The suburban Eudaimonians were cowards, quickly closing up shop and retreating instead of helping their own. *Typical,* he thought. Jude appeared briefly as he chased down two Afflicted back towards the river. Thomas took a pounding by a growling, towering male as Ben cowered in temporary safety behind him in front of a closed shopfront. Half bald with the fits of self-mutilation, the haggard Afflicted pounded into Thomas with iron-like fists. Thomas' combat training shone through, though. Even without the benefit of ethereal size and power, he was agile, strong, and cunning. With a slight, close-lipped smile, he flipped the male to the ground with a twist of his legs and put an arrow though its empty heart before it could blink. The arrow entered so forcefully the creature was pinned to the ground. Chromious metal descended these creatures instantly, just like a Rogue. Numerous bright balls of blue flame smouldered over the pavement, leaving nothing but a stinking pile of ash behind. Ben was slack-jawed at the horrific sight.

Nik'ael had once used these chromious weapons himself. He both admired and cursed them all at once.

Jasmine, with a hand over her mouth and eyes wide, had run to hide with Ben in the doorway, having finally noticed the fray. Mascara and lipstick tubes rolled across the road, resting in the wet gutter where she tossed her bags away. Her movement conveniently drew the attention of one of the Afflicted to Ben's position. The beast made a clicking noise and whistled. The last six made a beeline for Ben. Jasmine screamed wildly for help.

"Where the fuck is everyone? Help, help us!"

"Get down Jaz, get down!" Ben yelled at her.

Ben stood protectively in front of her, too foolhardy and macho to hide any longer. The dull sound of classical music drifted up from the side walk from the hastily discarded IPod, lending an eerie, distant soundtrack to the show. Ten more Afflicted emerged from across the street, attracted by the fight, engaging Kea, Thomas, and Kristen in battle. Jude took them out one by one from the other side of the street. The small force picked the foul creatures off quickly, but not before one of them got to Ben. It dragged at him with sharp, claw-like fingers.

"Ben! No! Help us!" Jasmine screamed. He'd never seen her cry in all the time she had befriended Sophia. He felt a twang of pity for her. She was gutsy and loyal,—qualities that some of his own kind could benefit from.

"Run Jaz, get out of here!" Ben put up a pathetic attempt at fighting off his assailant but he did not resist for long, knowing there was no chance of success. He was pale and grunting with the effort of self-preservation as he stood his ground momentarily in front of Jasmine. Always, he *always* protected his sister. They did not touch her, though. They had what they came for. She screamed and scratched and kicked at the thing that had a grip on her brother's shirt. Ben shoved her back with his elbow.

'Get back, run! Get away from these freaks! Go home!" he yelled at her. Ben glanced back at her solemnly, and his free hand pushed her harder, back into the doorway, out of harm's way.

Nik'ael listened as Ben screamed in frustration at her again, "Run, Jaz! "Remember," he faltered as he struggled, "I've always loved you, sis. No matter what happens, nothing will ever change that. Now get the hell outta here!"

He shoved her back again as she sprang forward to him, then let his legs slacken, allowing the thing to take him. Despite the barrage of energy pulses coming its way from Jude and Kea, it managed to drag Ben off through the mayhem, into the shadows, towards the river and into oblivion. Nik'ael's mission here was accomplished for now. He put a shaky hand to his head and transferred away to the maniacal screams of Jasmine assaulting his ears.

"No! Not my brother, no!"

Chapter Forty-One

Heaving breaths, wet and warm, ruffled my hair. Crisp air coated my skin in coolness. As I became more aware of my senses, I screwed my hands into fists. The crunching of dry leaves instead of cold snow disturbed the otherwise silent blackness around me. Through a veil of matted hair, I opened my eyes and lifted my face slightly, bringing a few leaves with it as they had plastered themselves to my face. The warm breath was on my neck now. I stayed prone, not sure what to do, not sure what had happened. I held my breath and just listened. Something flew overhead. A branch snapped in the undergrowth, alerting me to things lurking in the dark surrounds. I concentrated on the breathing, focusing on the rhythmic sound. It was soft and smooth, not particularly threatening. Despite the fact that it seemed to be safe, I let my face warm, just in case. My arms and back began to defensively burn of their own volition, preparing to pounce. My instincts seemed to kick in, whereas my common sense was yet to catch up.

A sudden sloppy lick to my arm quelled my racing heart in an instant. A whimper confirmed it as a paw pressed onto my arm. I looked up to see, of all things, Shadow.

"Shadow? How did you get here?" I sat up slowly, confused, clearing my eyes with a swipe of my forearm and checking myself for injuries. My face crinkled with the anticipation of gashes that, surprisingly, were not there. The dog nuzzled into my chest as it dawned on me that I was not where I thought I was.

"How did I get here?"

A descending full moon beamed across the landscape, highlighting softly swaying gumtrees. I was somehow back home. *How?* I found myself down the back of my property, laying by the small stream that had dried to its summery trickle. I sat up for a while amid the canine-licking fest, trying to fathom how I came to be here. Everything seemed surreal. The ground was cool and firm. A bat flew quietly overhead. The tepid wind was just audible as it brushed through the trees. Shadow's unwashed aroma was certainly unmistakeable. I cautiously stood, dusting myself clean of the prickly leaves and noticed a slight mist developing, which hid my feet from view.

"C'mon boy, keep me company." I scratched the top of his head as I took in the surroundings more thoroughly. Listening and feeling, instinctively with my increasingly sharp hearing and vision. "Stay close." My voice seemed too high-pitched with the uncertainty of simmering fear as I babbled away to my fluffy body guard. The energy on the air was all too wicked. Shadow pressed protectively into my legs as I walked, the glow from my face lighting the way through the dense bush. I was wobbly and unsure in my steps. Whatever happened had taken something from me.

I figured I had better get down to the Zythros stone to call for help, so I headed for the shed. That was my first mistake. Within seconds, Shadow had his hackles up. A deep growl rumbled from within him as he bared his teeth. He stood protectively between me and something up ahead in the dense undergrowth. Without thinking, I concentrated a little and let my face glow brighter to see what was there. That was my second mistake. Out of a woody clump of unkempt lavender scrambled a decomposing, one-armed Rogue. The foul thing was grunting incomprehensible threats in between apparent retches, as though it was ill. Fortunately—for my olfactory senses—the floral fragrance was strong in the air, as the bushes were full and aromatic with their summer blooms. As I backed up a few paces, a memory suddenly emerged of 'Nan' telling me as a child that lavender kept bad spirits away. *That's why I was surrounded in it and bathed in it daily*! Lavender made these horrid things ill.

Shadow lurched at the creature while it vomited black fluid uncontrollably. It flung him like a rag doll to the side, but not before the dog had pulled off the bottom half of its single, flailing arm. It was now thankfully unable to grasp at me as it suddenly lunged in my direction, teeth bared and eyes bulging. Its lack of arms gave me the split-second of time that I needed to draw enough elemental power from the air to throw a small but effective bolt at it, turning the monster into nothing more than a pile of stinking ash. The short amount of training with Koi and those awful orbs was starting to pay off when I actually needed it.

That success was mistake number three, though. Like a moth to a flame, my power surge was a beacon that caused the ground to rumble. Like snakes writhing underneath the surface, the ground moved unnaturally as horrendous, skeletal arms began clawing their way out. Faceless limbs grabbed at anything they could as they emerged with a frightening speed. Shadow rebounded, snapping and growling like a hellhound at everything he could that was trying to dig its way free. It was a sickening scene. I didn't know which way to move. Hands and faces were being ripped to bloody shreds by him, but they just kept rising, undeterred. I stamped on a few, making crunching sounds I would never forget. Fog rolled in thicker now, blanketing the ground, making it difficult to see the enemy. The stench returned in a foul domination of the sweet summer air. Shadow disappeared in the sudden whiteness. I called for him as I cautiously backed up, the ground rumbling yet again. I turned to run, and cold things grabbed at me. My wings emerged. They were useless though as they seemed to falter with the intense fear I was failing to overcome as I tried to run. I wriggled my shoulders as I fled, encouraging the damn things to do something. I didn't give up though and kept trying to fly. Unsurprisingly, I only managed to fling myself face first into the ground, landing eye-level with a skull with one dull, bloodshot eye glaring at me from under a bed of dried leaves. I punched at it furiously and blasted it at close range. Then I got up and ran as hard as I could, wings long forgotten. At least I knew that I could trust my legs to move fast. I screamed for Shadow, hearing his barks and yelps in the haze.

From somewhere in the darkness a frantic, screaming whinny rang out. Hooves thundered. Out of the trees ahead of me burst Grey, with Shadow in hot pursuit. They both laid into the attackers with teeth and thrashing legs. I took the unexpected opportunity to keep running, knowing that my only hope right now was to get to the shed and down into the cavern to use the stone to call for help. Something grabbed painfully around my ankle as I was mere paces away from the rear of the shed. It tripped me up. I could smell the sweet pond water, hearing the trickle of the little waterfall that ran down from the top of the garden as I seemed to fall in slow motion.

My head smacked against something hard as I fell. The warmth of the blood that trickled down my face brought on the reality of the danger in full force, sending my heart into overdrive. The panting and gurgles seemed frenzied now, as though the appearance of blood excited them. As I struggled with the iron grip, kicking at it with all my strength, I saw that I was surrounded by a handful Rogues in various states of decay. It was distressing to see that some were even children—young and old, male and female, of various races and ethnicities. It appeared that anyone could become a Rogue. The perpetrators of these horrors were beyond evil.

This split-second of sorrow was quickly washed away by the salivation of the one that held me. "*Just one bite!*" it gurgled though lips that barely moved, pushing the others into mass hysteria as it clawed further out of the ground. I threw a well-aimed bolt at it, taking out half of its head, but it held tight as brain matter fell sickeningly to the ground. My fight or flight mode was on and hot. My now frantically flapping wings luckily threw up a decent gust of dirt and leaves as I kicked at the left overs of this thing that had hold of me. The flying leaves and dirt caused enough of a distraction as they all spluttered and coughed that I could throw a few more bolts out unencumbered. I ashed one or two more as I finally kicked the head clean off the one gripping me. I scrambled away, coughing back the urge to throw up.

Shadow and Grey had worked their way up to me by kicking and snarling through the throng, holding the rest back. Seeing them under threat, with blood pouring from Grey's neck, caused a primal scream to surge from within me. Lava-hot, the energy oozed from every pore of my body. I was glowing from head to foot, ashing anything that touched me or them. I screamed for Grey and Shadow to run, fearing for their lives. Despite my apparent superpowers, more foul things kept emerging from every square foot of ground, they didn't fear me. *How many had been lying in wait, and for how long?* The thought was horrifying.

A yelp from behind had me glance back as I was now mere feet from the peeling green door. Despite being Ms Earth-born Saviour, I was clumsy and tripped over myself, only to come face-to-face with another corpse that took a handful of my hair, burning his flesh as he touched me, but he didn't let go. I yanked back just as a set of hooves came thundering down around my head with a precision that stamped the burning, gurgling face back down to where it came from.

"*Hurry, Earth-born!*" the command was implanted privately into my head. I flipped over to see Grey standing over me, and all seventeen hands of him looked down at me with eyes that were—*knowing*. In a brief lull of quiet, I sat back, panting with the exertion of the fight and looked up at the strangely calm horse. Shadow reappeared and licked my muddied face. His breath stank of garbage and his teeth were stained with dark, clotted blood. "Good boy, thank you," I kissed his muzzle.

After a quick glance to check on the progress of the Rogues up the slope, I heard another command. "*Run, leave this place!*" I looked up at Grey again, and for reasons I couldn't explain I thought the voice was coming from him. He stamped his feet as though to maintain my attention as he shook his head, then his whole body. His entire body simultaneously shimmered and blurred in and out of focus. As he reappeared, crisp and clear, I almost forgot what I'd just been running from. He had changed form, from a stormy grey to a solid, shiny black, with a lustrous white mane and tail. Swirling blue eyes looked down at me as wings of light, just like mine, slowly flapped from near his withers. With a swish of his tail, in my mind I heard, "*Jump on. I shall get you to safety. The ground here is alive with evil.*" He shook his head with impatience and pawed at the ground. I didn't hesitate as I heard the gurgle of new things nearby. I grabbed hold of his white mane and swung myself up, easily done with a surprisingly helpful flap of my own wings. "*Hold on,*" he communicated to me. With a sudden lurch, we were skyward, flying away into the dawn light, away from danger, and further away from what I knew as reality.

Grey—*whoever or whatever he was*—flew smoothly over the landscape. This left the creatures on the ground confused and they receded back within the ground and undergrowth. Eyeing the ground below to make sure it was now safe, he circled back to the old shed as I clung tightly to him. He, too, knew that's where I needed to be. He landed softly near the door and withdrew his wings. He nudged me forward with his soft muzzle. "*Run, Earth-born! Run fast to the Zythros stone.*" He turned and screamed as horses do, just as he faced the onslaught of the new wave of Rogues crashing mercilessly through the tree line. Shadow reappeared and launched at a woman who was raking craggy nails up and down her own bloodied thighs. Her white hospital gown was filthy and torn as she searched for a target. Grey reared up and charged, dispatching her into a fleshy mess as more came in for the attack. I stood frozen momentarily, one hand on the peeling green door. "*Go, my friend. I will hold them off for you. Run now!*"

I did what he said as the melee erupted into a screaming, bloody fervour. I ran inside to find that the wooden door had reappeared over the opening to the underground sanctuary. I knelt down to pull at it, immediately remembering that there was no handle, just the rusted keyhole—and the key to it was long gone. *How was I supposed to open it?* I punched at the door in frustration as I panicked. *Is nothing easy?* I searched frantically for something to wrench it open, digging through an assortment of rusted tools. I heard a surge of gurgled panting and an equine scream that made my blood run cold. I looked out the window, rubbing a hand across the grime. Grey was surrounded and being scratched at from all angles. Shadow bit at every decaying leg of the ever-increasing army. There must have been ten, maybe fifteen of them. There was no thought in it. I ran back outside, surprising them with my reappearance.

Grey snorted in annoyance and screamed in my mind, "*Leave! Now!*"

"I'm not leaving you to die, Grey!" I threw out as much energy as I could draw off the morning breeze. I took out three in one go, then flapped my wings to lighten the darkness and stir up the undergrowth again to cause more confusion. That, I *could* do. This light of mine also helped to singe what skin was left on a few others, leaving them nothing but horrific, mobile skeletons. I couldn't fly, but I could use these puppies to ash these devils away, bit by bit. I ran at the Rogues, taking them by surprise again, which made taking them out them all the easier. They seemed seriously stupid. They lacked combat skills and forward thinking. They didn't know what to do when I rushed them.

"Get away! *Argh!*" I yelled and screamed, madly waving my arms and wings, convincing myself that I could be intimidating. Some did back off. I felt cocky and brave, until I heard a yelp and a *crunch*. A huge male had picked up Shadow and bit into his neck. To my abject horror, it appeared to drink his blood, then throw him to the ground, limp. *Dead.* The beast roared and beat its chest with a crazed bloodlust and renewed strength. Blood dripped down its faced, onto its chest that bore a stitched, vertical surgical wound up the sternum. As one, Grey and I attacked. He turned his rump and booted off its filthy head, whilst I ashed it with minimal effort but great satisfaction.

I ignored the new rumblings underfoot as I ran to Shadow's lifeless from. Grey paraded a guard in front of me, daring anything else to advance as he arched his neck and stomped his huge white hooves. I knelt down, pulling the huge ball of fur onto my lap. His life force was gone, and nothing but the dissipating warmth of what was my most loyal friend remained. I hugged him tightly.

"No! No, my precious boy, no!" sobs choked me as I was blinded by hot tears. I screamed skyward, "*Why? Why do we have to go through all of this? Why can't you just come and help? Damn you!*"

My sacrilegious screams went unheard, but it helped emotionally to let it out. As I saw Grey through the blurring tears struggle to hold the next barrage back, I felt fiery anger consume me. *What more was I to face?* No time to adjust, to heal, or mourn. I burned with resentment.

I whispered to Shadow, "*Go on, boy. Find your place in the stars.*"

The new Rogues had wriggled fully free and were advancing too quickly. A kookaburra laughed nearby, as though the scene was all too funny. *I hated that bird.* I hugged Shadow briefly and laid him gently down. To prevent those things from getting at him again, I turned my face away as I incinerated his body, keeping him safe from further defilement. He became one with the earth immediately.

The air felt empty now, and so did I. Grey trotted back and placed his head over my shoulder and nudged me backwards to the shed. "*You are going to get yourself killed before you can save your kind if you do not do as instructed,*" he invaded my thoughts again.

I answered, teeth clamped firmly together, breathing slow and controlled. "I will not let another one of my loved ones die for me—including you, whoever you are!"

He spoke as we matched pace, slowly stepping backwards, mirroring the tempered pace of the Rogues, not making any sudden moves. They had slowed somewhat, as though now aware of the force they faced. *Soulless corpses that seemed worried about being killed*—the thought struck me as strange. They took a step forward for each two we retreated, silent footsteps making no sound other than their grotesque, bubbly breaths as we slowly circled round to the shed.

"*Sophia, I am your Grey, but I am also your guardian. When I arrived on Earth, my mission was to serve and protect those of A'vean. You were my final mission. So, as a soldier, if I have to die to protect my charge, you must accept this fact as do I. There is always a place for me upon the fields of A'vean, be it in body or spirit.*" He nuzzled warmly at my ear, then took a mouthful of my singed shirt, pulling me backwards. "*I will miss that four-legged flea farm. He was acceptable company.*" He snorted mournfully as he nosed me up to the shed door.

"Me too, Grey. Me too," I sighed, just as a loud *crack* behind us made me jump.

The Rogues screeched in what seemed like mass panic as we turned to find, of all people, Lorcan. He dusted himself off casually before he threw out a warning bolt of light, blasting away half a dozen Rogues in one go, causing the others to retreat a fair distance.

"Well then, if you were trying to run away, you need to brush up on some military stealth, Sophia. I could track your elemental signature from Jupiter. Very sloppy. Hansel and Gretel were more subtle." His tone was clipped, but not cold.

"What?" I was surprised to see him, grateful to see him, but also immediately pissed off. "Oh God, I'm sick of this! Just to let you know, I have no freaking idea how I got here!" I yelled, my own tone clocking in somewhere between furious and hysterical.

"Chillax will you? Keep stepping back slowly while they are unsure of themselves. I know this was not your doing, so to speak. You've accidently transferred yourself through emotional longing. Why you chose a Pegasian beast to fret over, I have no idea!"

Grey stamped his feet in disgust at the insult, but nudged me to Lorcan, who was backing up towards the door just like us. "*Go, Earth-born, he is a tracker. He has come to return you to safety.*"

"What about you?" I asked quietly, alarmed.

He responded by flapping his wings wide and bright, rising into the air. "*Don't you worry, my beautiful friend. I will be near, and we shall meet again soon. Thank you for the peppermints, by the way. I particularly loved the peppermints!*" With a kick of his hooves, he was gone in a flash, taking out three more Rogues in his wake before disappearing like a shooting star across the dawning sky.

"Always one for drama, that lot. Unfortunately, they have the annoying habit of being loyal and useful," he mumbled as he grabbed my hand.

"Let's get you back to England. I'd say after this, your life supply of Eccles cakes are mine!"

His humour was lost on me.

Lorcan kept close. Wings wide and pulsing, the four remaining Rogues retreated into the bushes, patting at their rapidly eroding flesh. He drew me into to his wide, bare chest, but as his wings began to envelop me, we were thrown off balance, falling to the ground on top of each other as the ground beneath us lurched like an earthquake had struck.

"Well, this is becoming a bit of a habit, don't you think?" He quipped as he looked down at me, all too close for comfort. I was full on about to smack him out when we were distracted simultaneously by the pond bubbling, as though suddenly at boiling point. In a nanosecond, he pulled me to my feet and shoved me back so hard that I fell straight through the green door, landing face first on the ground inside.

"Get down into the sanctuary now, Sophia!" he yelled just as something sharp flew past my head, so close that it nicked my ear. I pressed my sore earlobe and coughed the dirt from my mouth as my eyes found six huge, pulsing arrows of white energy embedded in the splintered wood on the back wall. Lorcan was yelling at something or someone and blasting crackling bolts in rapid succession. Inside, the shed walls flashed bright with each blast.

"Ha! He's sent one of his dogs in! Too weak to chase down a mere girl himself. Typical!" Lorcan berated someone. It was followed by a deep, seductive voice that drew me to the small window again, hunched over with just my eyes peeking over the sill.

"Your insults mean nothing to me. Yeqon cares little for anything other than her blood. As a loyal servant, I am more than happy to oblige whilst he attends to other leverage." This new, huge male loomed intimidatingly. His ashen hair blew in the breeze of his grey wings. A large band of Rogues emerged wet and rotten from the pond behind, flanking either side of him. *What leverage was he referring to?* Something deep within me twinged. *A warning, but for what?*

"You were more fun 20,000 years ago, Pineme. Get bored?"

Lorcan took a step back, which accidently drew the focus of this Devil in disguise to the window. For a nanosecond, he saw me. In that paradoxically long, drawn out moment, his dark eyes bored into mine with zero emotion. He drew up his bow and shot six more arrows in my direction. I threw myself to the ground, landing on the door in the floor as glass shattered everywhere.

A metre-long fiery bolt had wedged itself deep into the ground. The force that it took to get it into the concrete-hard dirt floor, must have taken immense strength. The earth sizzled around it.

"You fool! If you kill her she's no good to anyone!"

"I believe we only need her blood,"

"You have no idea what you need, idiots!" Lorcan retorted.

"We need her to get vengeance and that is all," Pineme's voice was deceptively calm.

"Run, Sophia! Get to the stone, get down there now!" Lorcan commanded with the same calm as the evil one. Cracking and popping filled the air once more as I raked at the handle-less door.

I still had no key for the lock. I pulled and pushed at the damned door from every possible angle. The groaning of the newly advancing Rogues had quickly made me frantic. I kicked at it, punched it, and tried to dig it open with my bare hands. Nothing worked. I could tell Lorcan was hopelessly outgunned as I saw him slowly edging closer to the door through the shabby reflection from a square of polished tin on the wall. As my fear grew, so did the heat in my body, and my wings unfurled wider of their own volition. A bolt of energy was fired inside, reflecting off of the tin and blasting upwards, blowing the roof clean off.

I screamed at Lorcan, "I can't get in! It won't open!"

He was now fighting from the doorway. His size was such that I could see his wingspan and feet, but not his shoulders from my vantage point.

"Bollocks, Sophia! You know exactly how to open it. Whatever you did to get into that Scroll chamber is what you need to do now! *Hurry*!" I heard him groan as he took a shot and stumbled. "Don't even think of it, just get out of here!" he warned as I moved to see how injured he might be.

I turned back, just as another flurry of arrows flung past him, one slicing down my arm. I grabbed at the wound, the glistening blood trickling quickly down to my fingertips.

Blood.

Blood!

That was it.

I crawled to the door and let the crimson droplets fall, one drop at a time, onto the rusted lock. Instantly, a resonating *boom* shook the ground. The wood shimmered and hazed away until it evaporated into nothing but a dark void.

"I'm in, Lorcan! I did it!" I screamed through the frenzied cacophony of Rogues now scratching at every side of the shed. One had climbed the side and was peering down at me from where the roof had been.

"Go! Run for your life, I'll meet you there! Run!" he called laboriously.

I threw myself down those stairs, missing three or four at a time as I heard the Rogues overhead. Lorcan couldn't hold them all back alone, not to mention a Daimon as well. I could hear the echoes of these foul creations falling over each other to get to me. The gurgles and groans were tormenting as I fell and slipped down a flight or two at a time. I tried a few awkward flaps of my wings. They worked for a second, until I smacked myself clumsily into a wall. I tried to run, fly, and run some more with limited success. When I finally reached the golden gate, I slammed it shut quickly as I saw the filthy creatures scrambling around the corner from the stairwell, each one for himself, trying to get to me first. The gate had no lock. *How could I keep them out by myself?* I was frantic, grabbing at my head for an idea. The murals pressed in on me. They were judging me, telling me that I was the wrong person for this. I was weak—they'd made a mistake. *Normal. Boring. Average.* Their jewelled eyes bore down on me as I imagined these words.

"No!" I yelled back, "I'm not!"

Then it struck me. "Brennan, you gorgeous genius!" I called out loud as the eyes went back to blank, stony stares.

I flung out my right arm, channelling all of the anger, hurt, and fear towards the gate. I also let in for the first time, some self-confidence. "I can do this!"

My mark raged, but this time it felt fantastic—empowering even. The burn up my spine was like wine to my tastebuds.

"Burn, you evil bastards!"

The elemental burst that shot from me was so strong that it flung me backwards, like the kickback from a shotgun. I watched as the energy hit the golden bars. A hum instantly followed, vibrating the metallic barrier like a giant harp playing a deafening tune. The decomposing hands reaching through the bars smouldered, and they began to retreat slowly back, unaware of what was coming. Like a sonic boom, a solid white, atomic light lit up the corridor. Within seconds it was all over. The dust settled, and there was nothing but silence and the sickening smell of burnt flesh left behind.

Brennan's security system had actually worked. *If only that self-indulgent show-off had been there to see it.*

I looked around the huge space, alone. I nearly threw up as I suddenly realised that Lorcan had been following me. For a moment, I thought I must've incinerated him, too, until a light tap on my shoulder reassured me otherwise.

Behind me, with an expression of awe on his face, he quietly said, "You really are the One!"

With that said, he enveloped me in his wings and transferred us home.

Chapter
Forty-Two

As Lorcan's wings retracted, I sensed an immediate and panicked urgency in the Sanctuary as everyone in the main area ran. I looked down from above as they carried bags, pulled children hurriedly along, and wheeled those in Stasis down to the deepest levels. Even the greenery reacted, with the large, white flowers closing as if in self- preservation. I watched the frenzied scene below from where I'd arrived, next to the pink version of the Zythros stone. The monolith was alive, vibrating with the sounds of a million voices humming within it.

My head snapped around as my name was called sharply from behind me.

"Sophia! If you were not so valuable, you would be in the highest order of trouble with the Eloi council right now, much like Brennan is! Come now, we are in crisis!" Enl'iel was wearing white training gear, complete with armour across her chest. There were pacing footprints in the dust on the floating deck. She must have been waiting for me anxiously.

Her reaction both surprised and worried me. Her expression was stony, and seemed almost foreign to her face.

"Bring her down!" she ordered. Lorcan flew me down to the first level, landing amongst the hustle and bustle by the door to the main corridor that led to all of the lowest levels. Enl'iel transferred down with ease.

"Go search for Brennan. Tell him that he had better be ready before Gedz'iel or I get there. Go on, now!"

Lorcan disappeared in the customary flash of light. Without so much as an 'Are you okay?' from Enl'iel, I was dragged in an uncomfortable silence—apart from her huffing and puffing—until we had descended to the stuffy library in the depths of nowhere.

Awaiting us was the council of Eloi, silently surrounding Gedz'iel, who languished casually against the desk, arms folded. They were still and emotionless on the outside, but their auras were fiery. All six of them had their wings spread wide. Like Enl'iel, they were dressed in battle armour. Their hips were heavy with weapons. Kea, Jude and Koi stepped back as Gedz'iel surveyed all present.

"Welcome back, Earth-born. You have caused quite the stir—you and young Bren'ael." He cocked his head to the left, where I saw Brennan slouched down in a winged chair. He looked like a teenager stuck in detention after school. He smiled weakly at me.

Gedz'iel rose from his position slowly and methodically, grazing his short hair on the orb-powered pendant light above. His armour clanged menacingly. He looked to Enl'iel.

"You of all people should have known better," He cut her silent before she could respond by turning his back on her. He faced me.

"Foolish choices. All of you!" There was a group cringe as his cool temper brought us all to attention. "Relaxation outing! At a time such as this? You, Sophia, have no business being above ground where the enemy slither in every crevice and under every rock! Fools, the lot of you!" He turned his back on us all then, breathing slow and deep as if to maintain control of his anger. He leaned heavily on the edge of the desk. It would have felt easier if he had just balled us out. The calmness of his voice, cool and sharp, was gut-wrenching.

"I—" I began to explain myself, but was immediately cut off by his sharp tone. It seemed more deeply punctuated with that common, indistinct European accent most of them seemed to have, especially in his heightened state of anger.

"It matters not how or why you did what you did. The fact is that the act of your transference has caused waves around the globe. The energy signature you left was so strong and unrefined that it has alerted and drawn up all manner of evil to the surface. They are close enough to us now that they may as well knock on the front door!" he finally bellowed the last part. Sarcasm didn't suit him. He must have been furious to reduce himself to it. "We are all but compromised now because of your inability to control your emotions. We have been forced to dispatch the strongest among us as sentries and scouts. Our weakest are hiding in the lowest chambers. Our young ones in Stasis, the next generation, are our most vulnerable."

He paced back and forth, glared at Brennan, and then beckoned Koi and Kea over. They spoke briefly in whispers. Koi shook his head many times before bowing and stepping away. Kea seemed to also plead a case with him before taking a step back and standing by my side, giving me a reassuring rub on my shoulder. Just her touch was enough to ease my anxiety.

"I'm sorry, but I don't know how I did that. One minute I was riding a horse, and the next, I was face-down in my old backyard!"

"And because of it, our hand has been forced! Lorcan nearly paid with his mortal life, hunting you down. We are ill-prepared to search for the prophecy of Enoch, but we must move forward prematurely, due to your stupidity." His tone was now dripping with anger. "You should have foreseen this, Bren'ael. You've lived by her side for twenty years. Your softness is a weakness, as is hers!" Gedz'iel didn't hold back the insults as he stared the supplicant Brennan down.

My attempted apology had clearly fallen on deaf ears. Not a soul, not even Brennan supported me. I gritted my teeth and balled my fists. *How could I have known I had the power to do this?* In the blink of an eye, they'd expected me to absorb a lifetime's worth of knowledge and training. Without question and drowning in fear, I had followed this freaky twist in my life. I'd ridden a rollercoaster of shock and awe, allowing nature and trust in those around me to take over. Absolute trust is what I gave them. The least they could have done was cut me a little slack. Two weeks ago, I'd been working the early shift and window-shopping for Christmas presents in the village, and now I didn't even recognize myself in the mirror. My face had become red hot with my impassioned thoughts.

"Sophia, calm yourself down," Enl'iel said in the least motherly tone I'd ever heard from her.

"Calm down?" I yelled. My eyes burned with fury as I looked around the room. "I've questioned nothing! Not a damn thing! I've accepted everything you've thrown at me. I've been terrified, attacked, injured, and through no fault of my own, I mess up! If I hadn't been kept in the dark for the last twenty years, I might've had just a little bit more preparation for such an occasion as this! Whose fault is that, huh? *Not* mine! A little truth more than five minutes before my body whacked out on me, and I might not feel like I'm on a suicide mission, blindfolded!" I kicked the chair beside me in anger. To my surprise and delight, my newly emergent strength had it sail clear across the room, smashing into pieces against the far wall.

With nothing left to say, I shoved past a room full of shocked silence, slamming the heavy door so hard that it left a crack right up the middle. I didn't care. I was beyond pissed. I ran through the corridors, ignoring the call of my name. Up a level or two, I stretched my wings that had popped out again without an invitation. I pumped them a few times before ramming into some poor sod laden with boxes as he came around a corner. I apologised and quickly helped him up, then ran the rest of the way. At first I just ran randomly to blow off some steam, then an idea came to me.

Exhausted, I slammed the door shut and leaned back against it, breathing out my anger. My trembling hands glowed strong and bright as I rubbed them across my face, clearing my eyes of unwelcome tears. *Enough crying.*

The room was quiet and empty except for them. *Yes!* I thought. The red orbs hung in the far corner of the training room, their glow reflected across the array of weaponry hanging along the far wall. I flicked my hair back over my shoulders and shook out my arms. Before any common sense could take over, I called out, "C'mon you little bastards, give me your best shot!"

They just hovered in frustrating ignorance.

"C'mon, attack me! Do it!" I screamed at them, flailing my arms and egging them on. Still nothing. I stamped my foot in anger and threw out a small, sputtering shot of energy. It landed just below them, refracting off the wall, down into the ground. Just that act itself felt good, releasing some tension and anger. I looked at my hand a moment, turning it back and forth. I marvelled at what it could do. Then I looked back up, surprised to find that the orbs had disappeared.

A sudden static energy teased at my hair. I turned slowly, only to see that the bunch of red nasties had snuck up right behind me. Clearly, my tantrum had finally got their attention. It didn't feel such a good idea now that they were looming ominously over me, though. I took a step backwards in a moment of hesitation. But then my lingering anger overcame the self-doubt enough that I stuck out my chin arrogantly and taunted, "Bring it on!"

I was under siege immediately. All five launched their nasty stings at me as I ran, ducked, and rolled like Koi had taught me. I came out of a roll roughly after copping a blast to my heel. I shot a stinging rebuke back that knocked one orb out of existence. Their hum intensified as I darted around behind the wooden training dummies. Dodging in and out of them, I avoided most—but not all—assaults. My heart raced with exhilaration. My wings felt increasingly strong and purposeful. They grew brighter as my confidence soared. I was still a little dizzy, feeling drunk from the transfer, but I was mad on the buzz.

The remaining orbs grouped together, then formed into an arrow pattern. They chased me down through the dummies and out into the open. They were fast and methodical, with robot-like precision. My body stung all over. Despite this, I stood my ground and gritted through the pain as I doubled-backed to the dummies and headed deeper underground, descending to the ancient ruins that I'd trained in with Lorcan. I managed a few flaps, and had actually become airborne for a short time. My unsteadiness was a surprising bonus here. Their accurate attacks flew by me as I wobbled wildly all over the place. This advantage gave me enough time to hide behind the door of an ancient home. It was dark and musty inside. Unfortunately, the orbs found me within seconds, and zoomed straight in through a sliver of space between a crushed window frame. They surrounded me in the far corner by an upturned urn. An eerie red glow spilled across the tight space. For some reason though, they'd stopped firing at me. In a move I didn't anticipate, they collectively threw out what seemed to be shackles made of a fiery, red energy, and bound my arms to the wall. As much as I struggled, I couldn't move.

"That's not fair! You're fighting dirty! Let me go!" I yelled as I struggled.

"What in I'el's name is going on in here?" Koi ripped the door from the last of its hinges and stormed in like a thundercloud. The orbs retreated, and my shackles immediately dissipated into thin air.

"Thank you," he acknowledged to them as they buzzed away.

Covered top to toe in dirt, fresh blood and bruises atop the old, I looked away as Koi and the entire group from the meeting room entered the small, dark space. They all looked relieved, some looked immediately annoyed. Koi glared at me, his eyes turning an icy blue as they pierced mine. His mark glowed vibrantly, pulsating like a vein, throbbing with anger.

"Are you trying to get yourself killed, Sophia? These orbs are capable of dealing a deathblow if they sense a security breach. You're lucky they recognised who you are and called to me. Foolish child!"

My cheeks blazed. I couldn't look at any of them. I was annoyed and humiliated, all at once.

"We all understand the immensity of the stress you are under. You have lost your dear friend Esme, may her mortal soul one day rest on the plains of A'vean." He swiped a palm across his mark and raised his hand, palm up, as did they all. I took it as a gesture of respect. "You have faced terrible creatures and dire circumstances whilst discovering who you truly are. But are you so naïve to think that we would not support you in this? You are not alone. The pressure is high, but the bond here is deep. Running off like a human child having a tantrum is beneath you, Sophia. You are a sensitive soul—this show of aggression is surprising. I thought better of your inner strength."

The unexpected lecture stung more than the orb's zaps.

"You know *nothing* about how I feel! You were born knowing who and what you are. I've had it flung in my face, out of the blue!" I pushed off the wall, rubbing at the bruising down my arms. "I've gone along with you all without question. I've not made even a ripple of fuss. I haven't been able to mourn Esme, not even offer her a proper funeral. Besides seeing all that I have, I now come to find out that I have parents somewhere, but nobody tells me who or where they are. I have powers that I can't control because

I was kept in the dark my whole life. So, until I get a few answers, you all can decipher that damned scroll yourselves!" I shoved past the still shocked group and marched back to the main arena, stopping to lean against the wall of golden swords.

I couldn't believe I'd blurted all of that out, but I was seething. It seemed that the more this power emerged, the more untapped anger arose in me as well. I had always been calm and level-headed. This transition was turning me into someone I didn't like. Every pulse pounded as I tried to calm down. It seemed when faced with a real threat, it was the rawest emotion that fired me up. My wings were just settling back down when Enl'iel approached, placing a hand to my shoulder. I jerked away.

"You should have told me earlier, Enl'iel. I would have had more time to adjust. I thought I knew you, I thought I knew a lot of things, but my entire life's been a lie."

"I know, Sophia. I am very sorry for that. I understand how you must feel. We did what was best for your physical safety, but perhaps not your emotional wellbeing," she responded calmly. "We shall give you the answers you need as best we can. We all seek answers, and we can learn these together. We are all one of spirit and family, Sophia."

I refused to look at her as I turned my back and peered at my distorted reflection in a golden blade.

"Sophia, come now, we must move forward. I sympathise with your plight, but for the sake of our survival and our home world, you must push these emotions aside." Gedz'iel's deep voice preceded him as he took my hand in his and turned me gently around. He tilted my sullen face so I was forced to look at him. I didn't dare resist.

"I feel your pain—I truly feel it as my own. It is a burden shared by us all. You are like a daughter to us, as we have all watched and protected you for all of your precious life. Unfortunately, we do not have the luxury of time at present, as the Unseen are on the move. We are both the hunters and the hunted now. We must rise against them with the first strike. If they were to use their spies to get ahead of us, to compromise our path to the portal—if that happens, I cannot guarantee we could protect humankind from whatever they plan. If somehow they were to open the portal, anything could come though. It is a gateway to the universe, Sophia. It is a wide, vast, and densely populated universe. If they were to get their hands on you, they would force you—one way or another—to do their bidding. Come now, help us, help yourself, and help the humans, who we were sent here to protect."

Gedz'iel took a step back, giving me space to think. All of their eyes were on me. I didn't want to listen to him, but it all made annoying sense. Even Brennan looked on, giving me a reassuring nod. They were all now so irritatingly calm that I just gave in as Gedz'iel led me from the training room. My hand felt warm and safe in his. I relaxed enough to ask a question in a more level-headed tone.

"Will you tell me everything? Not in a day or a week, but now?"

Gedz'iel stopped a moment by the heavy doors before we re-entered the library.

He placed his large hands on my shoulders and looked down at me. I was barely a foot shorter than his imposing stature, yet I still felt small. He leaned down and placed his glowing mark to mine. "A *K'ufili*—a kiss for my kindred. A gesture of love and oneness." I instantly felt a warmth stirring inside of my chest. It was a calming feeling, not like the build-up of an energy surge. I was immediately more relaxed.

"Sophia, you think yourself so insignificant. Ordinary, to put it in your own words. Well, inside that *ordinary* girl is something extraordinary. I regret that you have been blocked from discovering this gift through your concealment. In time you will come to see how inexplicably un-ordinary you are." He held my face in his hands, rubbing his thumb gently across my cheek, like a wise, old magi, disguised in youthful beauty. "Be at peace with who you are," he said, followed by another K'ufili as we re-entered the library.

My instant thought was, *But ordinary was good and safe.* It was my motto, and I didn't want to let go of that. *Could I be ordinary and extraordinary at the same time, like an A-list Hollywood star who had it all, but chose to live a simple, unimposing life away from the limelight?* It seemed an unlikely and almost conceited thought, not at all how I thought of myself.

"Enl'iel, her mind troubles her still. Perhaps you might give her a small measure of comfort before we proceed any further?" Gedz'iel beckoned her over.

"Of course," she answered, her eyes downcast and not meeting mine. The sting of his chastisement was still evident in her demure tone. The glisten of a tear on her cheek tugged at my heart. Guilt trampled my lingering anger.

She took my hands in hers. "Sophia, I want you to close your eyes and concentrate on nothing but a moment of pure joy," she instructed.

I regarded her briefly, wondering how I could conjure up anything even remotely jovial at that moment.

"Please, dear—trust me." Her eyes were unashamedly moist now. She hurt as I did. I melted and finally closed my eyes.

She placed her hands on either side of my face. "Now, think of this special moment. Think of it, and nothing else."

I searched my memories for something that couldn't be tainted with sadness, a time that was pure, innocent, and happy. It came surprisingly without effort. I recalled the day I sat with a five-year old girl in the Paediatric

Ward. She had just beaten leukaemia. Whilst her parents cried with joy in the corridor with the doctors, she sat with me and brushed my hair into rainbow plaits and ponytails.

"Nurse Sophie, are you a real fairy? I think you are. Do you know the tooth fairy? Does she sparkle like you do? You always sparkle when you visit."

She'd asked me a million questions that afternoon as we played hairdressers.

Had that innocent child seen something in me that I didn't see myself?

I suddenly became aware that I was smiling as I felt a shiver rush through me. My eyes popped open as I sucked in a sharp breath.

"What did you do to me?" I asked in a slightly accusatory tone.

"Look, dear! Look!" She guided me to an oval-shaped, bevelled mirror by the doorway. I could hear a lot of hushed murmuring behind me. I looked at the image reflecting back at me.

"Oh my God, Nan—sorry, *Enl'iel*—how did you do that?"

The reflection showed a much more familiar face—comforting and ordinary. It was me, *just* me, with my rainbow hair beautifully restored.

"It will only last as long as your power is kept within. You will soon learn the art of concealment in time, as we all do. For now, I gift it to you." She kissed me *K'ufili*-style and led me back to Gedz'iel.

"And there she is, my old princess!" Brennan practically shouted from the sidelines.

"Does this help?" Gedz'iel asked.

"Actually, as stupid as it seems, this hair does make me feel a whole lot better. I feel like me again." I answered, as I ran my hands though the multi-coloured mane. "I remember when Jaz first put the bright green through it. School wasn't impressed," I giggled to myself.

"I am pleased to hear this. Now tell me, what it is that you wish to know?" Gedz'iel asked.

His immediate compliance boosted my feeling of security. I began to feel that perhaps I really was part of something here, and not just an outsider dragged in to be used and cast aside.

I could only think of one pressing thing to ask.

"Who and where are my parents? Also, I want Jaz and Ben with me. Besides this," I gripped a fistful of hair as evidence, "they are all that's left of my old life. They are the only people who I trust to have never lied to me. I need my friends." I thought I'd asked politely, but I could literally feel the hurt of the insult to Enl'iel. It hurt me as much as it hurt her as I heard the intake of a short, sharp breath of shock from where she stood behind me.

"Very well," he answered just as the doors cracked open. Eilir entered, humming as she busied herself with setting up tea and cakes. "Not now, Eilir," Gedz'iel said, firmly but kindly.

"Oh, pish posh, you won't be savin' *anybody* on an empty stomach! Now, eat and drink, before it gets cold." She *tut-tutted* to herself as she shoved a cup under Gedz'iel's nose. He took it gently and kissed her cheek, as did they all. It appeared that they truly adored her. I noticed her limp had worsened. Dash was ever her shadow, helping her walk, despite being slapped away by her when he tried to do too much.

Gedz'iel put his cup down after drinking it like a shot of espresso. "Soph'ael—Sophia, tonight we hope to discover the location of the next piece of the puzzle, but we must unravel Enoch's clue first. You have made a valid request, and along with my brothers," he indicated the five Eloi members, "I believe it is of no service to any of us to keep anything hidden from you now." He made me take a seat then. The light orbs suddenly seemed loud and irritating. This unexpected moment was almost too much.

"Your mother is a Eudaimonian of great lineage. She, Sarun'iel, has links going back to the time of Adam and Lilith. She gave birth to you and another child twenty years ago."

I fell back deeper into the chair. "Another child? I have a sibling?"

"Yes, a twin brother. So powerful was the elemental signature that emerged from your first cries that Daimon gathered from far and wide. All manner of evil crawled from their cesspits and hunted your parents down. Your family were unaware of exactly who or what you were—until it was too late. They had been living amongst 'the Hidden,' Eudaimonia who wish to live as humans. They use little or none of their gifted A'vean powers. This made them invisible to us until that night. Their unpreparedness allowed them to be overwhelmed by an ambush under the cover of darkness. Thinking quickly, your mother caused a diversion, running off with a bundle of blankets into the woods whilst hiding you away with the midwife. Your father ran with your brother. As far as we know, your father was overwhelmed by the Daimon, and your brother was either captured or killed. He has never spoken of what happened. The midwife saw this unfold from her hiding place beneath the cottage, through a cellar window where she hid with you.

"After a time, your father returned to the cottage with the body of your mother, who had lost her mortal life protecting you. " I physically shuddered when I heard this and braced the edge of the chair.

"Your father has not been seen since that night. It is believed, with no evidence of his ascendance, that he has searched the world for your brother after sending you away to safety with the midwife. That very midwife stands before you today." Enl'iel discretely acknowledged this revelation with a bow of her head. Tears welled in my eyes.

"You knew them? What was my father's name?" I asked quietly, my eyes boring imploringly into hers.

"Yes, Sophia, I knew them briefly. They were kind and gentle. They lived simply. In hundreds of years, they had never conceived a child, so when you and your brother were born, their joy was unimaginable. Your father's name is Rik'ael, but around the village, he was known simply as Richard of Woodville," she answered.

I was floored. I had a brother, a blood relative, and possibly a still living father. My heart then lurched again in grief for the mother I would never know. A mother who gave her life for the survival of her children. I was blinded by my rapidly welling up eyes.

"You said my mother *is*—as though she's still alive!" I blurted out.

"Indeed. She continues to exist somewhere in the Cavern of Souls. Her immortal spirit has been in mourning within the stones of the Earth for twenty years," answered Gedz'iel solemnly, before he continued. "We have searched for your father, and your brother, too. They unfortunately have left no trail behind, even for our best trackers, such as Lorcan. We have, thus far, failed to entreat your mother from her place of mourning—her despair runs far too deep and she remains well hidden. Lorcan was dispatched just this past hour to Peru to appeal to her, begging for any information she may have."

"I, I can't think! I—err,—can I see Ben and Jaz now, please? "I asked. I needed my friends to help me make sense of all of this.

Silence engulfed the musty room. The orbs seemed to glow even brighter. The smell of earl grey tea and vanilla sponge intensified, and hearts beat more rapidly all around. I could see coloured auras surrounding everyone, but some were brighter than others. Gedz'iel's was golden. The council of Eloi, who stood silently behind him, were bathed in pinks and blues. Pathos had licks of orange around his head. Everyone else was surrounded with a spectrum of rainbow light. I could feel the tension radiating as the assorted auras flickered erratically. Only Gedz'iel and the council remained calm and static. I felt feelings that were not my own next. *Fear, regret, anger*. It was like I was tapping into them all. The silence was achingly long as I studied each face around the room. Brennan was picking his nails with a small dagger by the hearth, head down. Enl'iel looked back at me with sorrowful eyes. Kea motioned my attention back to Gedz'iel.

"That is not possible right now, I'm afraid. I'm sorry, Sophia. Jasmine is recovering from shock in the newly relocated Stasis room. Unfortunately, whilst you transferred, there was an attack. She witnessed young Ben abducted by a horde of Afflicted—I am sure at the behest of a Daimon. I am much aggrieved to tell you this."

"What?" barely a whisper, my voice was almost eclipsed from the shock.

If I could have sunk down any lower, I would've disappeared into the fabric of the chair. An emotional numbness had set in at this latest news. I wasn't mad or sad or anything other than cold with emotional paralysis. I ran my finger across the armrest, tracing it along the dark, sculpted wood. It was smooth until the bump at the end, like my life had been, up until recently. For a moment, I just sat there and took in the room. It was filled with paintings from all eras and styles, yet my eyes were drawn to a familiar, concentric circle in a modern-looking painting directly ahead of my chair. Silver and gold circles overlapped each other against a black backdrop, and these swirling patterns absorbed me. I thought I heard my name, and then felt a pressure on my shoulder. The circles danced, enticing me in. One seemed to grow and pulse wildly before it emerged from the confines of its silver frame. I ignored the others, which were snapping in and out of the picture in turn. The large one was pinpricked by a small light. Soon, the light grew into a swirling mass of pink, blue, and gold-flecked hues that swirled and sparkled.

An eye—*His eye*—burned down upon me once more.

Silence.

Chapter
Forty-Three

I was shaken from the trance by Brennan. "Princess, come back now."

I blinked as Gedz'iel knelt in front of me with Matias and Theus. Serael remained back at the desk with Amais and Pathos.

He looked intently at me, his warm hand steady upon my glowing, trembling one.

"She has connected with I'el, may he forever be blessed. Her eyes turn as his." He touched his hand to his mark, looked to the ceiling, and raised his palm. It was the same sentiment I'd seen frequently over the past few days, whenever I'el was mentioned. I was still numb as I watched his reverent gesture. The tinkering of china, as Eilir waddled past with a butler's trolley, registered somewhere in the distance.

"I get it," I said after a few moments as my head space cleared.

I slowly stood up, and they all backed away, while everyone else held his or her attention achingly rapt on my next move. I turned and looked at each and every face as my pulse thundered. Intense expressions met my gaze, all brimming with anticipation. They simply looked on silently, patiently.

"I get it. I understand now, somehow." I furrowed my brow as I heard myself. The words kept coming, I just didn't know from where. I paced a little in front of the hearth. "I know what I am. I am more than a key. I feel some kind of link between this world and his." A surge of energy swirled around me as I felt the warmth of their smiles brighten the room. "Whatever happened just now has left something behind, like some kind of strength or connection. I don't know, it's just something, I don't feel the same." I ran my hands through my hair nervously, feeling ridiculous as I said these things, but also knowing that they were absolutely true and needed to be acknowledged out loud. "I know I have to embrace this and fulfil a purpose, no matter what the human in me says." I spoke to no one and everyone, perhaps more to myself.

I rubbed my eyes, they felt strange. There was an ache in the back of them. I walked back to the mirror and looked. My irises were a more intense blue than before. They sparkled and seemed to be moving—yes, the blue turned clockwise. *What the?* They were swirling, a biological cosmos coursing around my pupils. It was terrifying, exciting, and grounding, all at once. It cemented in me the acknowledgment to myself of what I was, and pushed back the last of my lingering doubts.

I rubbed across the Soul stone bracelet for strength. "I will serve you and do my best to save you all. However, you need to do something for me. I won't rest until I find Ben and hunt down anything or anyone that has hurt my family." Thoughts of Esme brought tears back to my eyes again. "I need you all to promise me that we will see this through together, and seek justice for all those who have been hurt. We serve each other, we are one and the same, or we are nothing."

I was quietly taken aback at my own sudden arrogance. I was always a follower, and yet here I was, demanding vengeance and servitude. Had I not been so high on energy at that point, I may well have run out and hidden in embarrassment.

Everyone inclined his or her head as I finished speaking. Their marks all glowed in perfect acquiescence.

"Sophia, you indeed are the daughter of I'el. You finally feel our eternal connection of oneness. We work and live as one and so in turn, your needs are our needs. We will seek that which is important to you as it now is important to us." Gedz'iel said.

"Thankyou." I turned to Enl'iel.

"Is Jaz going to be okay?" I asked.

"Yes, she will recover. She is shocked, but comfortable, and has received calming tisanes to help her rest while her emotional wounds ease. Gedz'iel has deployed scouts to search for Ben. Kristen and Thomas captured two Afflicted, and Jude is interrogating them as we speak," she responded.

I grabbed the last steaming cup of coffee from Eilir's trolley as she waddled by with perfect timing. I gulped it down. Hot and sweet, with a touch of bitter at the end, which befitted how I felt. Warm and comforted, but disgruntled to the core about the hand dealt to me.

Eilir beamed and passed me an Eccles cake. "Eat up, sweet pea, you can't be doing great things on an empty stomach now, can you?" I took the sweet pastry and leaned down to kiss her grey head. I couldn't stomach it right now, but I took a small bite to please the sweet old woman.

"Oh me, I love this one. Now, Dash, go get yourself some decent fightin' clothes on. I suspect you'll be needed here, rather than by my side." She gestured him out the door with an authoritative few flicks of her hand.

"Eilir, no! I will stay with you, as always." He responded, placing a loving arm around her shoulders. She leaned into him and patted at his chest. This gentle giant alleviated, for a moment, the evident strain that walking was having on her.

"Oh, go on with yer! We both know the time has come for you to stand with your brothers and sisters again. You've looked after me long enough. No more 'o this guilt. You've given me a longer 'an happier life than I ever would 'o had if I hadn't run into you that night. Never has a woman been gladder to be blinded by a man!" She laughed heartily. "You go on now, I'll be here waitin' for you. Always 'ave been, you know that." She fumbled around with her apron and dabbed at her unseeing eyes.

"She speaks the truth, Dash'iel. It is time to put personal needs and regrets behind and stand with us. You have cared well for this gentle soul. Dearest Eilir, I will see to it that you are relieved of your duties as required, and rested," Gedz'iel instructed. He placed a glowing palm across Eilir's spine, giving her aged body an instant and visible relief from her pain.

"Yes, your Grace, I understand," responded Dash, as Eilir pushed at him to let her go. He took up a post with Brennan and Kea by the hearth. The glow of the fiery light gave away the strain of pain in his face at the sacrifice.

"Let us move on now, please?" Gedz'iel guided me back to the desk. It was time to be strong and grown up. The scroll lay open across the desk. *Deep breath in, deep breath out, repeat.*

"We have awaited you many a millennia. I honour you and offer you my unwavering service." Matias took my hand and bowed, then offered me a *K'ufili* kiss. I accepted and the spark that passed between us, emboldened me with a jolt. "My gift to you, Soph'ael—courage." He stepped back as he pushed the scroll towards me.

"Okay, here we go," I said, more to myself.

I ran my fingers across the cracked, stiff script. The words seemed to swim across the page and jump out at me. The harder I stared, the more three-dimensional they became, as though I could pluck them from the air. I picked up the tea-coloured sheet, inspecting every inch. I read through it slowly to myself, lingering over the reference to my parents. *The resting place of your father's mother.* This was where we needed to go. *But who was my father? Rik'ael was a name but where did that lead us?*

"So, Lorcan is trying to connect with my mother's spirit?" It felt weird saying that.

"Yes, Sophia. Hopefully, she will extrude herself from the crystals to speak with him," Matias replied.

"*Extrude* herself?"

"She dwells, as do others, within the crystalline walls of the Cavern of Souls. A place of safety and contemplation for those of us who have ascended the human form, but cannot return to A'vean," he answered.

I placed the delicate paper back down, gently smoothing it out as I did so. It crackled like dried leaves, but thankfully remained intact.

"Clearly my father is key in this passage. How could no one know how to track him or his family? You knew him once, Enl'iel. Don't you know even one of his family members who could maybe help?" I asked.

"I knew Rik'ael, who, as I said, went by the human name of Richard, for only the briefest of times. I knew nothing of his past—he was very secretive. Your parents chose to live a hidden life as Gedz'iel explained. They only contacted me for your birth, as the one thing we must come together for is a new birth. A human cannot deliver a child for a Eudaimonian, as the energy the birth exerts could very well kill them at the worst, and blind them at the least." She gestured toward Eilir as evidence. "I knew him a mere few hours, it is the only reason we even know his name. He is a ghost to us. Your mother's lineage though, when we briefly re-discovered her, was indeed a surprise. Her line is well respected. It appears her love for him drove her underground and out of our lives long ago." she answered.

"Okay, well what about my name, Woodville? If he gave me that name, it must have been for a reason, to link me with my heritage. Should we follow that lead and see if we can track him down? Can't we Google his name or something?"

A cough-masked laugh echoed from someone in the room. Pathos broke the stony-faced silence that the Eloi had perfected and chuckled at my comment.

"You think that's funny? I don't hear *you* making any useful suggestions!" I snapped. There was a touch of Jaz running through me today.

"Indeed, Pathos, show some respect. She learns more of our ways every minute. Sophia, we are never documented in a traceable way, as the humans are. We have called for Rik'ael across all the realms in and around the Earth, with no response," Gedz'iel said. "He has never been known to anyone in our community before, and this is why it is so difficult to trace his lineage. It is as though he arrived out of thin air. Such is the problem with the Hidden—if we don't know them, we cannot find them, and if we cannot find them, we most certainly cannot help them. Perhaps there is more in the scroll that we are not seeing. Can you read it once more?" he asked.

I nodded and looked over it again. I read aloud the section pertaining to my father.

"It just makes no sense," I said.

"We are all here for this exact reason. You translate and we will decipher. Not everything weighs solely upon you, Sophia," Gedz'iel answered.

"Thank goodness for that, we'd be hear for another century."

"More truth in that than I care to entertain, princess!" jibed Brennan with another annoying wink. I gave him a dirty look.

"Read that section about the boar again, please?" Gedz'iel instructed.

As I again mentioned the reference to the boar and the bull, Eilir, who was stacking cups, slapped her hand across her knee and clucked out loud with a whoop and a laugh. "Oh me! You are all so big and 'ansome, but lacking the sight!" She tapped at her temple, smiling to herself. "It's right in front of yer pretty faces. Don't yer all read the books? Lordy, yer lived through our entire 'istory, and blimey you've near well influenced 'alf of what's gone on! Yer should've picked it right up!" She chuckled again as she re-tied her apron and shook her head at her own amusement.

"Eilir, what are you talking about?" asked Dash with surprise.

"Oh my love, it's 'er name! 'Er name is the clue. I may be mere peasant-born, but I've had a good deal 'o years to pass the time with books. Woodville and sprig 'o bloom is what gave it away. Sprig of Bloom is the Frenchy word for Plantagenet, an' Woodville, well that's the name 'o the lass that married the 'ansome King Edward the fourth. 'E was one those Plantagenet kings. Elizabeth Woodville 'ad many a bairn, Sophia's father must be one of them. Queen Elizabeth, she was always rumoured to have a touch of magic about her. A Queen of England, ha ha! That's her dear old Gran!" She pointed straight at me.

None of what she said at all registered. It was too confusing, too ridiculous. So, in Sophia tradition I focused on something completely irrelevant.

"Eilir, don't think me rude, or that I'm questioning you, but how do you read books?" I asked, completely unable to digest what she had just blurted out.

"Why, dear, Dash reads them to me, sweet pea, Think he's read me every book ever put to the press!" she answered. I was hanging onto her every word as she continued.

"Oh, me, sweet Sophia, your 'o the line 'o the Kings of England! Oh me! The Plantagenet kings! That last bit about the boar, that's old mad King Richard's standard. So then, who was 'ol Richard hunting down, as the script says? I wonder? Could it 'ave been yer dear old pa? If he were as powerful as any 'o this lot here, I'd say he was all too valuable. A good reason to be hunted by the old boar, Richard!" She chuckled away, her Welsh drawl becoming thicker and more enchanting as her memories flowed through. She was delighting in helping us, it seemed. We all silently took in her massive revelation as she patted down her grey skirt and lace apron. The irony of a room full of immortal beings and a blind, elderly human apparently cracking the case wide open wasn't lost on anyone as we all regarded her with open admiration.

"But why would my father be hunted down by a human king? If he was brought up Hidden or human, as I was, who would know about him?"

The Eloi named Amais spoke next. "Master Gedz'iel, Sophia, may I?" Gedz'iel nodded, so he proceeded. "I believe Eilir speaks some truth. I recall being present for a reception of youths in the human fifteenth century. Master, you were away at the sanctuary in Peru. We were called upon numerous times during this period of festivity to deal with a number of Daimon infestations within the human aristocracy. Do you recall Neph'reus and Anjou'elle?" All in the room, other than Eilir and I, reacted immediately with disgusted acknowledgment. "At that time, they were known to be hunting amongst areas suspected to be settlements for the Hidden. They were looking for anyone who could even remotely be considered the Earth-born. They had their dogs sniffing around for energy signals in every valley and forest. There were rumours at the time that the British royal lines had Eudaimonian blood running through them. For years, she preyed on the royal families, trying to get close.

Anjou'elle drove King Richard mad with her infestation of his mind. What reward she received from Yeqon, I could not guess, but I knew then there was more to that particular act than the mere passing of time for her. With Richard, she pushed a decent human into a crazed monster. Matias and I were called to the chamber of Edward the fourth on the eve of his death by Jacquett'ael who only then revealed herself to be the mother of Queen Elizabeth. That enlightened us to the hidden Eudaimonian heritage of Queen Elizabeth and King Edward. By the time we arrived though, he was far too ravaged. His pterugia were gone—he had been ambushed in the night. He ascended well before his time. He was a strong kindred, who had fought well to protect his family. There was the pungent stink of Daimon in his chamber, leaving no doubt that one or both of those vixens had been there. This is when Elizabeth went into hiding with her children, knowing that her true self was no longer a secret. Until that moment they had lived quietly. Hidden in plain sight in the ruling ranks of mankind. Her sons and daughters were now targets. It was just prior to the Great Undoing of the Unseen, when we managed to push every known Daimon back into the Empyrean realm. It all makes perfect sense now. Elizabeth must have secreted away her most powerful child. That must have been Rik'ael, Richard, your father. Her name before she was married to Edward had been Elizabeth Woodville, your name, Sophia. It was about the time King Richard became unstable. He was obsessed with Elizabeth's' sons. Now, we know why. Anjou'elle and Neph'reus knew something of her son's power and wanted to circumvent nature. Perhaps to possess your father until he revealed himself as the Earth-born or fathered the Earth-born. "

Gulp!

"This makes it all fall into place. There seemed to be no sense in what they were doing at the time. The word back then was that they were just toying with the humans for amusement. It was always their calling card," Brennan added.

"They had intel, they had a plan, and they very nearly got what they needed," said Kea.

"Yes, yes, that's it! Oh me! Her father musta' been one of the princes, you know Dash, the princes in the tower! Old King Richard wanted those boys good and proper, but everyone thought it was to save his crown. There was always the rumour though that the boys got away. *Hmm*—I wonder?" Eilir commented. Everyone was almost on tip-toe with the anticipation. The revelation had energised us all. The room glowed and snapped with the spike in elemental energy.

This was powerful stuff. I recalled reading about the Princes in the Tower in high school history. They were supposedly murdered by King Richard the third. *Could they really have been Eudaimonian? Could one of those much-discussed children be my father? Could he have somehow escaped and survived?*

"So, my father escaped his possessed uncle and found his way into the Hidden society of Eudaimonians?"

"Ooh, she's smart as a whip!" cooed Eilir.

"If I may, Eilir, dear sweet lady, you are in fact a most amazing soul. You have pulled together the facts for us in a most incredible way." Amais placated her ego until she blossomed with rosy cheeks.

"Eilir, you are as amazing today as the day I met you," Dash whispered as he helped her to a seat. My ears were attune to the smallest of sounds, and the love in his voice had a life of its own.

Amais took his place back with the Eloi, behind Gedz'iel who white-knuckled the back of a chair with a look of great contemplation. "Brennan, you know what to do?"

"Consider it done," he answered!" I looked back at the hearth to see him hugging into Enl'iel. He kissed her cheek, then her lips, then walked over to me, placing a quick peck on my head. "I've always called you 'princess.' Who knew it was for real? Ha! Now we know exactly where to go. Time to get this party started!" He then stood straight as a soldier, assuming an unfamiliar seriousness.

"Your Grace, I'll take my leave with Koi to gather the ranks. I'll arm the humans and send out decoys. Recall Lorcan, and send him my way as soon as he returns. We could use the battle smarts of a decent Seraph and tracker. He can lead the human infantry with Jude. Jude may join us when his interrogation of the Afflicted is complete." He bowed and let his mark glow brightly. "Sophia, you must head to the armoury. We leave for Windsor tonight." He ordered, no smile, no jokes, just a stiff nod.

I wondered why we were suddenly heading to Windsor, but the room was moving before I could ask more questions.

Gedz'iel finally took control of the strangely escalating situation. "The council and I shall go to the perimeter of the Empyrean realm to secure extra sentries. We must prevent as many leaks as we can. I feel a shift in the elements. We have no time to waste. Move with caution and haste. Sophia, listen to your elders, use you resources. Your powers grow ever stronger, and you must remember that you are not in the least alone. Rely on your kindred where you can. Enl'iel, guide her with a firm hand until she reaches maturity, whilst she remains unstable." With that, both he and the Eloi blinked out of the room in a brief flash, leaving me frozen, like a deer in headlights. I could still feel the heat of their auras long after they had gone. Everything began moving in fast forward. The energy in the room was high. Heartbeats raced with anticipation. It felt like a hybrid of excitement and fear. Enl'iel and Kea beckoned me to follow them out the door. A human resident with red hair helped Eilir out and down the corridor in another direction. I could hear her protestations of not needing an escort echo back at me. I quickly grabbed Enoch's scroll and stuffed it back in its cylinder and into my right leg pocket. The diamond dagger had taken up permanent residence in the left one.

Before I could blink, I was back in the huge training room, where armoury of all styles was being handed out to a roomful of people. The multinational, variously sized human contingent of hundreds, were standing in orderly ranks, assembled by the door to the room of ancient ruins. Whilst they jostled with an electric excitement, they were being handed quivers, swords, and shields. Once armed, a cord with a glowing stone was placed around each neck. The lofty Watchers and Eudaimonia were arming up with the impressive Chromious arrows and golden swords. I was thrust toward a woman with hair plaited and entwined with lavender and other herbs. In fact, I noticed that *all* of the Watchers and Eudaimonia were now sporting the same fey-like hair, as though they'd just stepped from a fairy-tale forest. A breastplate was tightly secured to me as an unseen stylist-assailant yanked at my hair and threaded it full of herbs as it, too, was newly plaited down my back. I turned to find that my hairdresser was Kea.

"All the protection you can get, honey. The Daimon hate the smell and positive energy of cedar and lavender as you should well know by now. It makes them so sick that they can't hide or maintain their disgustingly clever guises. That's one thing you'll learn—Daimon are quite the masters at concealment. You can easily think you're seeing a perfectly harmless human, when you're actually face to face with your worst nightmare. I've been fooled before." She pulled down the string sleeve of her scoop-backed top to reveal a jagged, silvery scar that cut through a few of her energy leaflets where her wings emerged. "Note to self, if someone starts gagging for no reason, back off, or blast them to Hell. Literally! Otherwise, you're very likely get your pterugia ripped out." She winked at me, and then moved on to help someone else.

"Sophia, front and centre!"

Kea spun me around, pushing me in Brennan's direction as he called me to join him on a stone platform under more infamous red orbs. I moved stiffly in the heavy gear up the steps to join him. He drew the attention of the masses by thumping his chest plate with his sword a few times. The metallic clang immediately drew the crowd into attentive silence. I felt a thousand eyes on me as he began to speak with a presidential impact. He didn't sound the least bit like himself.

"The time is upon us that we finally begin the journey home. The Earth-born saviour is here to serve us as we serve her. Our singular aim is to escort her, protect her and fight alongside her as she clears the path to A'vean. The Daimon scourge every realm, every corner and continent. Crush them. Descend as many as you can so that Tartarus may have fuel to burn for eternity. Fight like the Seraph that you are today my kindred, like the warriors you have always been." A roar of approval came from the Eudaimonians and Watchers. "If we are forced to ascend in order to protect Sophia, then we must commit to this now. If she succeeds, we shall be reunited back home, where we belong. We will once again be afforded the luxury to move through the universe at will, no longer a prisoner in this small, forgotten galaxy." More cheering. "We rally together as the kindred that we are. Enough of us have ascended for no good reason, other than a scuffle with bored Daimon. If we are to dwell in the foundations of the Earth, then let it at least have a reason and purpose. We continue today what has already begun. We continue today our path to freedom!"

The final roar shook the room, as weaponry banged rhythmically against shields and armour plating. Wings lit up the naturally dark space. The well-trained humans looked down with perfect timing to protect their vision from the stunning but dangerous display.

"This is our Saviour. Never was there a more precious being on the Earth. We honour her for who she is, with our unconditional protection and guidance." Another huge roar erupted, as weapons were raised and orbs were flung from the hands of Watchers and Eudaimonia. The humans in the back, headed up by Kristen and Thomas, were no less enthusiastic. They now wore metal helmets, their eyes protected from the glare by a film of black. They too jabbed swords and shields in the air. Gold and silver flashes reflected throughout the cavern. I could feel the nervous energy and hear a thousand heartbeats drumming in my head. For the first time I didn't feel that familiar twist in my guts that the embarrassment of excessive attention drew. I felt bolstered, strengthened by the comradery. I think I actually smiled.

Koi appeared next to me and spoke. "My kindred, two Daimon and a hoard of Rogues have been seen within this county. We move, *now*. You all have your orders. Cover every square foot to flush them out and away from Windsor." He left the platform. I followed him to the bottom of the stairs where he met Lorcan, who'd arrived back from his search.

My mother, did he find my mother? I tried to follow Koi, but Brennan grabbed my arm.

"Not now, princess. I know what you want, but we need to focus on one thing at a time. Lorcan has his orders, too." With that, Brennan pulled me back up the stairs and raised his sword-baring arm, along with the other, and created an enormous orb, the biggest one I'd ever seen.

"Upon the orb, as it dulls, we transfer out. This mass movement will cause enough distraction and confusion among the Daimon and Rogues that Sophia should be able to safely reach her destination, undetected. To our beloved sons and daughters of the Earth, take caution and heed your leaders. Waste not a drop of your blood, if you can help it. Conceal yourselves so you may move unheeded, unnoticed. We thank you for your unwavering support of us, mere visitors to your home." He stabbed his sword to the roof. "*Nike*— to victory!" he shouted, like some mythical hero.

The orb pulsed, as though it was counting down. As it pulsed, I saw the Watchers and Eudaimonians alter their appearances. Hair, skin, and eye colours morphed from one thing to another. It suddenly looked like a room at the United Nations, except that they were all wearing the same outfits. The men in loose, white linen pants, bare chests covered with armour plating. The women wore the same pants, but also had equally loose, string-sleeved white tops, featuring deeply scooped backs. At the exact same time they all shimmered slightly and these fighting clothes disappeared under a veil of concealment, leaving them looking like they were dressed in street clothes. "Wow!" I gaped at the magic of it.

""I'll teach you that someday, Princess," he whispered in my ear.

After counting ten pulses, the orb dulled to almost transparency, and everyone—with the exception of me, my small contingent, and the humans—blinked out, en-masse. Brennan was left behind, staring down at me, his glistening chest plate heaving from the thrill of what was to come. "Let's go, princess. We've got a Queen to dig up!"

The neighbour from across the road seemed a mere memory.

Chapter
Forty-Four

I waited under a large oak tree, branches heavy with fresh snow, as the human legion was led away in groups of twenty by Jude and Lorcan. That familiar drumming returned to my head the moment I set foot outside and I could've sworn those distant screams for help were haunting the furthest parts of my mind. I blinked it all away as I watched what was happening in front of me.

An unarmed group of humans handed out street clothes to the others to cover their fighting gear. There were several mini-buses parked up the gravel drive towards the Tudor house. They were emblazoned with *Gloustershire Tourist Co.,* a clever way to send out people in many directions without raising suspicion. Kristen and Thomas escorted them, appearing to be in some position of leadership. Koi, Kea, Brennan, and I left in a black Jag. Enl'iel stayed behind as caretaker of Jaz and the others who were in Stasis and the otherwise vulnerable.

"I feel kind of ridiculous, dressed like a Roman soldier and riding in a Jag," I mused at Brennan as I plucked at the uncomfortable outfit. Humour seemed inappropriate, but I was hoping for a little stress relief. The air was suffocating with tension.

He smiled. "I'll have you know it's actually the inspiration given to the ancient Greeks—let's not let the Italian's think they have all the fashion kudos!" His trademark smile and wink flashed brightly again. "These clothes protect us. They allow us to move quickly without disturbing our pterugia and this armour damned well saves a lot of us from ascending these flimsy bodies. The ancient human empires quite liked our style. Where's the fashion sense gone these days? Skinny jeans just don't cut it when you're trying to roundhouse a Daimon!"

He mimicked a karate style move with his hands. I raised an eyebrow and laughed. He laughed too.

"Point taken though, princess. These days, we look more like a costume party with nowhere to go!"

Then he plucked at his loose pants. "Luckily, this particular car is Chromious lined—better to ride in virtual invisibility to the Daimon than walk around, dressed in this getup. If not a Daimon, we'd probably be attacked by the local lads looking like this!" Brennan winked again. There was another hint of the irreverent neighbour I once knew.

"You don't do serious much do you, Brennan?"

"Serious? Who needs serious, unless it's absolutely necessary? That, back there in the cavern? That was to muster some courage and cohesion. That's what I used to do. I was a marshal, who'd rally the troops. Lorcan and Jude would train them for wars in other worlds. I'll let you in on a secret Soph. There are so many effed up places across the universe, there's little enough time for fun, so I'll take humour over angst any day."

"Here, have a drink." He passed me a chilled water bottle.

"Close your eyes for a bit. We'll have to take the long route just in case, but hopefully we should be left alone. The Daimon and Rogues should be too distracted with the energy signatures blasting across the northern lands right about now." He pointed to the dimming horizon as another day ended. Through the setting sun, I could see faint blasts of light wafting across the sky.

"And there you go, like bees to honey!"

"Won't that put others at risk who live in those places?" I asked. Guilt ravaged me.

"Nah, don't worry. They've all headed to wastelands, moors, remote shorelines—"

"We never place innocents at risk, if it can be helped, Sophia." Koi interjected, emerging from a contemplative silence on the other side of Brennan. "Except for you, my dear girl. It is unfortunate that what you are requires so much risk. I am most regretful for this." He inclined his head in apology.

"It's okay, Koi. I know it's not your doing. It's not anyone's doing. I suppose I could blame fate if I need to point the finger, but what's the point. It's happening and I can't stop it. I trust you guys to help me. It is what it is!" I sighed in defeat as I answered him, reaching over Brennan's lap to pat his hand. In a rare move, Koi actually smiled. A warm, handsome—*beautiful*—smile. I felt his pulse relax with relief as though I had taken a burden of guilt from him.

We drove for quite a long time, but I couldn't rest. Sleep was not my friend. My rhythms were so disrupted. Spending so much time underground and barely seeing the sun was messing with any possibility of quality rest, not to mention the world-saving burden weighing heavily on my shoulders. When I did try to close my eyes, I couldn't switch off the sounds. *Voices, heartbeats, breathing.* Every day it seemed I was more in tune with frequencies that no human could or probably should hear. I nibbled on some crackers to quell the growl in my stomach as I read the scroll again. *The resting place of your father's mother.* Everything had happened so quickly, from me reading the unreadable scroll, to Eilir making the connection and the mad rush to leave, that I'd had no time to ask what was to happen next.

"Koi, how do you know we need to head to Windsor?"

"Ah. Well, there is a story to that. As the truth revealed itself through our precious Eilir, all of the pieces fell together in an instant. We are all too familiar with the happenings during the time of King Edward the fourth, and his brother, Richard. The Daimon were rife in England during their reign. We all knew these monarchs well. Elizabeth's mother, Jacquett'ael, is a very powerful Eudaimonian. She chose to live in hiding once she bore children, as a means to protect them from Daimon. However, she was forced to come out of hiding when her children and grandchildren were harassed incessantly. The elemental powers of Elizabeth Woodville's children were known to be particularly strong. We entreated Elizabeth to join us once Edward had ascended, to live in the caverns, but she felt her children had a higher purpose on Earth. She felt they could make a difference in the lives of humans by leading them in peace, through their own aristocracy. She was outnumbered and overpowered, however. Both Jacquett'ael and Elizabeth called on us numerous times to intervene when Anjou'elle and Neph'reus failed to retreat. Neph'reus is a woman you never want to meet and Anjou'elle is an Empath who can sense the powers and vulnerabilities of others. She was using the all too vulnerable Richard to get to his brother's children. She managed to kill off a few of Edwards young to simply absorb their power! She and Neph'reus, have coveted the lack of connection with A'vean. The chaos they've caused for no other reason than boredom, is a list too long to recount. They are just as dangerous as any Daimon you could ever come across, especially as their motives have never quite been clear. They have not been seen or heard from since that time long ago. This could be a good or a bad thing—I do not know which yet. Silence can be both golden and deadly."

"Do these women want me, too?"

"I would say they are equally as dangerous to you. Would they want you for the Unseen or themselves? That I am unsure of. They have used many a soul as a pawn to bargain with in the past. We only hope their long standing absence means they have been descended and you will never cross their path." he answered.

Great. This was a fantastic twist.

"So, the Windsor connection?"

"Forgive me, I tend to over-elaborate. I thought perhaps some background might bring more sense to your understanding of things. This revelation about your parentage has brought great clarity. It pulls everything together. Because we knew Queen Elizabeth Woodville prior to her ascension, we know exactly where to look for her, your grandmother. She was buried upon her mortal death at Windsor Castle."

I was simply dumbfounded. I now found myself entwined in one of history's greatest love stories and betrayals. It was so bizarre. King Edward the fourth married a commoner, Elizabeth. It was a story of star-crossed lovers, all too familiar to the first Watchers who fell in love with humans. From all of this, my father was born. He must be Richard of Shrewsbury who was supposedly one of the twins in the tower who disappeared and was never seen again, feared murdered by the usurping Richard the third. *Or so it seemed.* The rest was history. He must have changed his name as he went into hiding only using the Woodville name to connect me to my lineage when I was born. I sat in the car, over five hundred years later, marvelling at this almost ridiculously unbelievable revelation.

The drive to Windsor castle took a couple of hours. We took some back road detours in case we were being followed. Since I remained wide-awake, I received a brief history of the English monarchy from Brennan, who felt the need to contribute to my understanding of all the monarchs as he sang their names in a ridiculous but funny rhyming song. After a time, we all quieted and I gazed into the shimmery beauty of my diamond dagger as I contemplated my links to royalty. *Ordinary*—I was so far removed from that comfy old friend, I couldn't even remember what it felt like anymore.

We finally pulled up to a quiet backstreet in Eton, just near the river. Tourists were still out in numbers, snapping the iconic academic district. The long, Union Jack-lined street featured old shopfronts with stiff garish clothing in the windows, leading the way to the impressive castle facade. *There was nothing like this back home.* We all covered up in thick winter coats to conceal our clothing and blend in with the crowds as we exited the car. Kea slapped a woollen hat on my head, tucking my long plait up in it. They all altered their appearance slightly, taking on various eye colours and warming their hair to blonde. I was vastly jealous and impressed.

"Try to keep those baby blues low key. Don't want to draw too much attention," she quipped. Other than shutting my eyes, I wasn't exactly sure how I could do that, so I kept my stare fleeting, never looking at anyone or anything for too long.

One of our tourist buses pulled up behind us. Kristen and Thomas took the humans ahead of us to scout around the area. Unused cameras dangled from their necks whilst weapons hid at the ready, concealed under their heavy street clothes.

I felt like I needed to be out front, taking charge and making decisions. But frankly, the only decision I had been capable of making was to accept and move forward with this curve ball in life. I had to follow the others' lead. I had no idea where to go or what to do.

"The standard is down—her Highness is not in. This makes things a little easier," Kea commented.

"How so?" I asked as we turned the corner out of a small road and onto the street directly opposite the main castle gate.

"Fewer guards to deal with, Soph. We'll wait a little longer, until the tourists die down. Then we duck in, break into St George's chapel, and meet your Grandmother. That's where Elizabeth is buried," she answered.

Kristen reappeared. "Everyone is deployed. We are ready when you are." She inclined her head, then turned away and pretended to snap photos along the cobblestone street.

"In here, Soph. Let's grab a drink while we wait," called Kea as I drew my gaze from the impressive thousand year old castle. We entered the *Whitehorse and Wagon* pub, which sat opposite of the castle's exit gate. Just as we sat down in the window bench seats, Kristen traipsed back in with a satisfied smile.

"*Mademoiselle*, you look like the cat that caught the mouse," Brennan quipped.

"Oh! 'Ow well, you know me, *monsieur*! I 'ave just 'ad a very interesting little chat with zee guard over 'zere." She pointed to a portly officer who was looking around for someone, his mind clearly not on the job.

"'Zere is an old tunnel under 'zis pub that used to move supplies to 'zee castle. It 'as been backfilled, but you two boys can do your 'zing, no?"

"How did you find that out?" I asked.

"Oh, a little Parisian charm goes a long way, Sophia." She batted her lush lashes, stuck her head back out the door, and waved at the guard. He immediately blushed, acknowledging her ever so carefully whilst sucking in his belly, attempting to stand up taller. It was quite funny to see him gobsmacked by her, smoothing down his uniform and puffing out his chest like a proud pigeon.

"I couldn't charm a fly to a steak!" I joked, half believing it.

"Oh, it's not about 'ow you look or who you are. It's about making people feel good about 'zemselves. And you, Sophia, make people feel good without even knowing it. You just cannot see 'zis gift you 'ave. Now, I will talk with 'zis lovely barman while you 'zree find 'zee cellar. I will follow on soon." She sauntered over to the bar and had the young guy entranced in seconds, asking him to show her how to use her camera.

When he was well distracted, I followed them past the bar. I tucked a stray piece of hair back up under my hat and took some initiative. I asked a man with *Manager* on his name badge where the restrooms were. I thought that would cover us for heading out back in a group. I felt his heart quicken as I spoke, and I could hear the blood rush through his veins. I also felt the strange sensation of connectivity. I was compelled beyond self-control, to let my mark glow just slightly, with the smallest intake of breath to control it. A quick flash of blue in his eyes told me that he was my kindred. He nodded for me to go down the back hallway as he threw his clipboard over the bar. *Wow!* As we passed by towards the rear of the pub, he quickly put up the *closed* sign, announcing a plumbing problem to all the patrons and other staff.

"Well done, Sophia. Sometimes the smallest things bring the largest rewards. You are already able to sense your own kind—a great gift," Koi commended me in a whisper.

I suddenly realised that I'd used elementals in public, but before I could panic, Koi hushed me with a finger to his lips. "It was but a mere blip. I did not even notice." He patted my shoulder reassuringly as we moved on.

The manager followed us and introduced himself as "Stev'ael," then added, "Just call me Steve."

"The guard was correct, there *was* a tunnel under here five hundred years ago. But it was filled in—quite solidly, I'm afraid," Steve said as we descended creaking, wooden stairs into a keg-filled cellar.

"Are we safe using elementals down here?" I asked.

"Absolutely, unless there are any monsters lurking in the dark. Steve?" Brennan asked jokingly.

"All good here. Haven't seen a Daimon in years, not to mention the other filthy blighters."

"Excellent," I said, more to myself. I was pumping up and down on my feet. I threw off my jacket as did the others and stretched my arms. The armour felt less cumbersome but no less ridiculous. Nerves and excitement intertwined, revving me up into an internal frenzy. *Jaz would've loved this,* I thought. But then that made me think of Ben, and my excitement waned as my heart plummeted. The fact that he'd been taken by mind-altered monsters was just too awful to contemplate. My guts churned as I watched Koi inspect the solid wall of dirt behind a corroded medieval gate.

I'll find you, Ben. I promise.

Chapter
Forty-Five

"Sophia, I believe this is meant for you," Koi waved me over.

I held a dinner plate-sized padlock with a concentric circle engraved on its face.

"Seems I'm expected everywhere!" I sighed in resignation. The heavy, circular chunk of metal hummed as I immediately concentrated all my energy on it. The lock burned up red, then white hot, and the ensuing light caused a blinding flash. I looked back to see that the lock was disappointingly still intact.

"Interesting," Koi murmured as he inspected it more closely. He turned it a few times in his palm. "Chromious. It appears that it requires a different form of energy to release it."

"I don't,—oh." The dagger banged knowingly against my leg. I slid it out of the pocket into my immediately sweaty palm. Drawing my own blood, even a drop, was harder than I imagined.

"Just like in the scroll chamber, Koi?" *How much of this stuff was going to be spilled?*

"I believe so. Forgive us for the sacrifices you make," he bowed away after offering me a warm *K'ufili*.

"Hmmm," I huffed.

With the dagger in my right hand, I closed my eyes briefly, bit my lip, and jabbed the sharp end into my thumb. The sting was unpleasant but tolerable. A thick, iridescent drop sprung quickly. I let it dribble across the engraved portion of the lock. It languidly rolled through the indentations, filling up the concentric design in a ghoulish, sparkling display. Once the blood had filled the pattern, I waited and watched, as I pressed on my thumb to stem the bleeding. The moment it congealed, the same red and white heat lit up the room once more. When the light faded, the last of the lock was crumbling away onto the dirt floor. Brennan had the gate screeching open within seconds. We all stepped through, where we then faced the wall of solid, packed, freezing cold earth.

"'How will we get through, Master Koi?" I turned to see that Thomas and Kristen had appeared, with a number of human troops. Their stealth was impressive.

"Ah, Thomas, I trust you have finished the deployment?'

"*Oui.* We are covered in all directions. We can assist you here now if required."

"Thank you, Thomas. If you can, keep your group in and around this building, please."

"As you wish," he made a quick and sharp bow to Koi.

Thomas turned to Kristen and the small group, giving instructions. Kristen went back upstairs with the humans, whilst Thomas took up a sentry post halfway up the stairwell.

"How will we get through this?" I asked.

"We will use our collective energies to vaporise the blockage. Kea, Brennan?" Koi looked at them expectantly.

We stepped through the iron gate, our footsteps squelching in the muddy floor as we approached the wall of dirt.

"You two know what to do?" Koi asked Kea and Brennan.

"Sure do."

"Yep."

"Sophia, on my count, we are each going to focus a single energy pulse at the same time into the centre of the blockage. Timed well and given that there are four of us, this should clear the tunnel. Are you ready?"

"Yes, I think so."

"You *know* so," corrected Kea. "Positive thinking, kid."

I smiled at her optimism.

"I will count back from five. That should be enough time to draw your energy forth. Deep breaths, Sophia, and relax!" Koi instructed as he gave me one of his rare smiles.

"Okay," I nodded. I was already calming my mind and feeling for E'lan in the freezing air. It was there, vibrating steadily, invisible but as palpable as if it were a snug blanket wrapped around me.

He was counting.

"Five."

Deep breath in.

"Four."

Tingling in my arms.

"Three."

My body heats up and my wings unfurl.

"Two."

I draw it all in, accepting the power.

"One."

I exhaled.

Four arcs of lightning exploded from our palms and disappeared into the centre of the wall. The static blew our hair wildly and I could feel every small hair on my body stand to attention. For a moment afterwards it was eerily silent, until the dirt and rock imploded upon itself with a loud boom. I intuitively flapped my wings to blow the dust and debris away from me. Rocks rolled over my feet, and we all coughed a few times. Once it was all settled, I marvelled at the now clear passage.

"Now that's team work!" Brennan said as he retracted his wings. I tried to pull in mine with no effect. He saw me looking back at them in frustration. "Relax your shoulders, breath and will them in." I tried this. It worked somewhat as they collapsed slightly inwards but were stubbornly refusing to disappear completely.

"It'll come princess, don't you worry,"

"I'm not so sure about that," I eyed over my shoulders at the stubborn glowing appendages.

"Just do what I say," he said as he placed a warm hand across my spine. "Now, close your eyes and breathe in." I did. He rubbed down the length of my back and in an instant they had retreated.

"Impressive Brennan," Kea commented.

"I know!" he smirked as he pushed me towards Koi who was inspecting the inside of the tunnel.

"Look, we are near an ancient portal. The earth here has come to greet us." Koi pointed for us to look.

Before I stepped in to see what Koi was talking about, I couldn't help but notice all of the white scars down his wide back. Craggy, silvery lines criss-crossed around his pterugia openings. *Battle scars*, I feared, just like Gedz'iel. Other markings seemed to be ornate tattoos, the meanings of which I didn't know. They were as beautiful as they were mysterious.

I followed Koi's gaze. The tunnel was glistening with all manner of gemstones. It resembled twinkling Christmas lights at night.

"What is this?" I was nothing short of amazed as we made our way over the rubble, moving carefully along the tunnel. I ran my hand along the energised walls. Pins and needles instantly infused my fingertips.

"The earth here has seen our power before. It is alive and connected to us, which tells me that this may have once been one of the ancient, long-dead portals. One from the beginning of time," said Koi.

"Profound," said Kea.

"Awesome," said Brennan.

"Wow!" I said.

"The crystals are attracted to our power. They have, in essence, greeted us." Koi explained.

It was a stunning sight.

We made our way quickly though the glittering darkness, coming rather suddenly to a vertical ladder that we climbed up and out of through a heavy metal grate, into a circular room. It was damp, cold, and musty. The stone-stacked walls were ancient. There was nothing in the room, other than a well, sunken deep into the ground.

"Where are we?" I asked in a whisper.

"We are in the Keep," answered Thomas, who had followed secretly behind us.

"Why are you whispering?" Thomas asked me.

"I don't know," I answered. It just seemed a place one needed to whisper in.

Koi looked momentarily alarmed at his presence, but Thomas was quick to alleviate his worry.

"Master Koi, all is well. I took the liberty to follow on, in case I could assist you with any guards inside the castle grounds," he explained.

"Thank you, Thomas. And yes, we are in the Keep, the central stronghold of the castle. I believe we need to make our way out through the gardens and over the dry moat wall. St George's chapel is just outside, in that direction." He pointed the way, as though we could see it from our position behind thick stone walls. "Thomas is correct to be concerned about the human guards. We would not wish to be seen digging up a Queen. The attention would surely draw the Daimon, not to mention make us a few unneeded human enemies."

Digging up my own grandmother was a sickening idea to contemplate. I feared what I would find, but also equally feared the sacrilegious act. Yet, this was all predicted by Enoch. It must be the right thing to do, however unpleasant I found it. *Right?*

A glowing blue light caught my attention, distracting me from my ethical dilemma.

"Brennan! What are you doing?" whispered Kea. "You will draw attention with that thing! Turn it off!"

"Rubbish, it's just a phone! Actually, the smartphone is one of my favourite things that humans have invented." He held up the backlit device for us all to see. "Unless you guys can pull the blueprints for this place out of thin air, we're going to be fumbling around in that dark chapel among a hundred graves. Look here, thanks to Google, I've got the layout of the chapel, as well as the exact position of Edward and Elizabeth's burial chamber. Once we're there, we can be in and out quickly." Brennan flashed the phone to each of us individually to check out his find. Koi grumbled at it with a look of suspicion. Clearly he wasn't a tech head.

"You have a *Nokia*?" I asked in surprise. "I thought you guys knew everything! Well—almost everything."

"If that were the case, princess, we wouldn't need Enoch, you, or five hundred-year old bodies!"

Fair point.

"What do you say, Koi? Look, it's a clean run, in and out," Brennan appealed as he pointed to the screen, showing the exact position of the tombs.

"Indeed, that is most forward thinking of you, Brennan. The quicker we are in and out, the safer Sophia will be. But put that thing away now, lest we are detected by that light!"

"Master Koi, the exit doorway over there is monitored with a security system. It needs to be disengaged," Thomas reported.

"I've got it! Here, Soph, you check out the floor plan while I sort this." Brennan gave me the phone. The screen showed a black and white line drawing of the current burial places for both the recent and long-dead nobility within the chapel. A beeping alarm sound drew my attention as I watched Brennan break a sweat trying to disengage the alarm before it blared and announced our presence to the world outside. He gave it a few small power bursts at various points. All of a sudden a long, high-pitched squeal sounded for a few, breath-holding seconds. Then all went quiet, until an electronic *click* was heard as the door to the outside was unlocked.

"Damn! Those humans are getting more ingenious with those bloody things. That was almost embarrassing!" Brennan mused to himself.

We snuck out of the Keep ever so slowly. Not a glow, or even so much as a warm breath passed between us, so that the dark remained our friendly concealer. Thomas was shivering within seconds. Despite his heavy coat, the nearly freezing temperature was getting to him. He made no complaint, though, even when Brennan offered him his coat that he'd slung around his waist.

"It's just a costume for me man, here, take it."

"It's no problem. The cold keeps me focused."

Thomas seemed on high alert, his eyes darting everywhere, ready at any moment to pull a weapon if needed.

Kea stuck close to me as Koi and Brennan snuck ahead, keeping low. She pulled me close to her side as we made our way across the steep sloping flowerbeds. A waterless moat between the Keep and the wall was all that separated us from the rest of the castle grounds. We all quickly shrunk under the cover of shadows behind the wall, just as a trio of red-clad guards appeared, flashlights in hand. The stamping of heavy boots in the distance told me that there were plenty of eyes, ready to spot us. Once they had passed, we climbed quickly and fluidly over the ancient wall and squatted again, listening for more guards. The diamond dagger poked into my shin whilst the Soul stone on my bracelet warmed me from the outside in. I rubbed it, and the smooth little piece of stone calmed my nerves whilst sending a bolt of heat racing up my arm, which caused my mark to suddenly light up.

"Who goes there? Wallingford, is that you? If you're playing funny buggers again, I'll be writing you up this time!"

I gasped and covered my face with my hands. Kea pulled me into her. With one gentle touch, she dulled my mark back to nothing. "We really need to work on that when we get outta here," she whispered.

"I'm sorry!" I whispered back. "God, I'm such a failure!"

"Oh, stop being a drama queen, we've all been there. Now, *shhh*!" she whispered again.

"Sir, I'm at my post. What are you on about?" called Wallingford through the walkie-talkie.

"I saw a light by the Keep," said the first voice. "I'm going to check it out, stand by," he ordered.

Fantastic, I blew it again!

A flashlight clicked on nearby. At the same moment that the torchlight hit our huddled group, someone lit up like a brief atomic bomb's blast. Koi flew over to the guard in an instant and dragged him back to us. He was stunned and rigid as Koi laid him carefully on the ground.

His large bearskin hat had fallen off. Koi whispered in the guards' ear whilst resting a glowing hand across his forehead. The guard seemed to suddenly emerge from his coma-like state. Koi stood him up. I held my breath as Koi put the walkie-talkie to the guard's mouth.

"Base, this is Stanford, over. Just a few squirrels, over."

The guard holstered the walkie-talkie, and then knelt down right in front of me. He fumbled around looking for something. I reached for his hat and silently passed it to him. He looked up at me; in fact, he seemed to look *through* me. He took the hat, stood up, put it on, and then marched away, toward the southwest exit.

"What did you do to him, Koi?" I asked.

"A little mind bending. Only sparingly do we use this tool to protect ourselves from discovery. He does not know what he saw. Now, let us move on."

We approached the beautiful chapel from a side entrance. The huge, ornately designed wooden door was barricaded with a metal gate. Koi made quick and quiet work of it, heating the steel to its molten point, which allowed the locks to drip away to the ground. As he pulled at the remnants of the frame, it squeaked loudly. We froze. The noise could've woken the dead. Luckily, the guards seemed to have moved to a different section, so we quickly squeezed through the narrow slit and pushed through a wooden door into the church.

"Remind me, Sophia, that the first thing I teach you when we get back is how to transfer! And properly, not randomly!" Koi uttered, slightly annoyed. He walked purposefully across an aisle. He stopped, turned, and retraced his steps. "It's a damned labyrinth!"

"Yeah, it kinda looked more straight-forward on the floor plan," quipped Brennan. The place was impressively ornate. Pillars and banners, statues and plaques punctuated the dim surrounds. The overly busy decorations made it hard to connect the right way forward with the floor plan at hand.

"Pass me that wretched device, Brennan, will you?" I couldn't help but giggle as Koi had to defer to a human gadget to find his way.

After turning the phone every which way and arguing like a married couple, they indicated forward, and then to the right.

We followed solemnly through a candlelit corridor. There was a prominent plaque marking the resting place of the current Queen's mother. We then made the turn into a smaller, inner chapel.

"I believe she lies somewhere in here," Koi assumed, as he picked up a thick altar candle to light the way. I grabbed one, too. The floor was crammed with memorial engravings. I happened to look down, just as *King Henry VIII* was illuminated by the glow of my own candle. I was both surprised and elated. This little tour was like Hollywood boulevard for me. The Tudor period of British history was my favourite. I couldn't help myself—I knelt down and grazed the lettering with delighted wonder.

"Princess, look! Over here!" Brennan whisper-shouted.

"Come on, Soph. Let's get this done," Kea said, pulling me up.

By the far wall, surrounded by marbled engravings, was a simple granite inlay in the floor that revealed the names: *Edward IV* and *Elizabeth Woodville*.

My heart skipped a beat.

"This feels so wrong," I said.

"Worry not. You are expected in this place," answered Koi.

"Take out your dagger, Sophia," he instructed.

I pulled it from my pocket.

"Without question, it will be only you who can touch this sacred place. Do as your heart tells you." Koi motioned for the others to step back and give me space.

I grasped the dagger in my hand firmly, knowing all too well what was coming. I knelt over the grave, resting my palm on the cool stone. The gilded letters warmed under my touch. Everything that was connected to me seemed to react when I touched it, by either warmth or vibration. It was a welcome consistency where all else seemed quite random, aka stubborn wings! I sighed, then took the dagger and pricked the tip of my thumb again without the same hesitation as before. Red oozed down the blade, coating it. I didn't wonder what I had to do next—I just did it. My body worked as though it innately knew what was required. Another unexpected piece of random but at least it was doing something helpful this time.

I jabbed to point of the reddened blade into the fine mortar space between the gravestone and the surrounding tiles. Energy flowed down my arms and into the dagger, which glowed white and hummed. I dragged the sharp point around the entire perimeter of the stone. The floor chimed as the blade scraped musically along its course. Once I had completed the perimeter, I stood up and waited. Everyone waited.

The stone memorial sank fluidly into the floor and slid off to the side, out of sight. Inside the tomb, the candlelight shone upon two coffins, each featuring the effigy of the person within. I hesitated noticeably.

"Go on, you are not disturbing anything," Koi reassured me.

Easing myself down into the cramped hole was no easy feat. It was dark and menacing, making it hard to breathe. I got my bearings with one foot balancing on the lid of each coffin. Creepy was the only way to describe the situation. I leaned down to run my hands over the marble faces and hands in riposte. It was then that I saw a faint engraving along the side of her face—a mark, identical to mine. I touched it tentatively. The cool stone was a poor substitute for a motherly touch, but it seemed as though it was as close as I was ever going to get, so I savoured it.

I stilled my quivering lip as a hot tear irritatingly escaped. It rolled slowly down my right cheek, moistening my now fiery mark and dropped silently onto the marble face. There was a sizzle and small spark as it made contact. This brought me out of my emotional haze. The lid rumbled. I moved quickly, edging back as far as the tight space would allow. I looked up at the faces peering down at me.

"*What's happening?*" I whispered.

"You've unsealed the tomb, princess. Just stand back and watch," said Brennan with an uncharacteristically reverent tone.

I looked back down as I felt my feet lose traction. The lid over Elizabeth shimmered. It undulated, and became hazy. I moved quickly to the edge of Edward's coffin just as the other lid became liquefied and vanished in the same way as the door in the shed.

There, below me, lay a thing of awe and beauty. The diamond skeleton of my grandmother in silent repose, glistening with perfection.

Clasped in her hands was a scroll.

Chapter
Forty-Six

"Oh my God! I gasped.

"Unbelievable!" exclaimed Brennan.

"Blessed be her eternal soul," Kea uttered solemnly.

"I have never seen such a thing! It's amazing," said Thomas.

"Sophia, quickly, take the scroll. We cannot linger," urged Koi.

I was frozen with wonder as I looked at her. I tilted my head to the side as my vision clouded. I felt woozy and thought I was going to faint. I knelt down to steady myself, and accidently grazed part of her. Electric sparks shot through me like I'd been injected with a speedball. My heart galloped wildly as my vision slowly cleared.

As I blinked the last of the cloudiness away, I was overcome by the sight of a flesh and blood woman lying where the skeleton had been. White hair was neatly curled up beneath a delicate golden crown. She was dressed ornately in a lace-embroidered white gown. Jewels dripped from her ears. She opened her fluid, blue eyes and smiled. She spoke in my mind.

"Beautiful child of mine son. I have awaited you an eternity. Feel thy love I have for thee."

My heart raced even faster as a wave of warmth, of pure love ran through me. I smiled. She smiled.

"Take from me this scroll to illuminate your journey. It is but an arrow to guide thee. I await success and repatriation with thee, my beloved granddaughter, amongst the plains of A'vean. Beware thy love of loves, sweet child. Beware thy heart. Thy heart is full and vulnerable. The Unseen shadow thee and shall use thy purity to bring thy fall. The way forward is incomplete, may caution be your tutor."

She smiled at me once more before she vanished. Nothing but the sparkling skeleton remained. I pinched at my eyes. "Please come back?" I whispered to myself.

"Hurry, Soph! The guards are on their rounds. Grab the scroll!" Kea called in the distance of my mind. I shook my head to clear it. I grabbed the cylinder from the bony fingers that were now open, unclasping the scroll for me to take easily. Sitting underneath it, caught between the tiny hand bones was a small necklace. I picked it up, too. The thin, golden chain carried a delicate, teardrop blue opal. I quickly clasped it around my neck, just as I felt hands yank me up and out of the tomb.

"Sorry I took so long. I needed a moment."

"What do you mean? You were in there for thirty seconds, max!" Brennan said.

"You're kidding! I—but I saw—"

Koi pulled me aside as the granite floor restored itself, resealing my grandparents in their mortal resting place.

"She communicated with you?" he asked, somewhat surprised.

"Yes," I answered simply, as we moved carefully out of the small, inner chapel.

"Your power grows infinitely stronger by the day. Convening with the ascended is a gift of the highest order."

We retraced our steps carefully back through the Keep and tunnel into the pub. Kristen was waiting for us there, sitting on a bench seat and laughing animatedly with the Steve.

"I can't believe I saw her. It was as real as anything could be. It seemed she was expecting me, too. It was just amazing."

"Was she beautiful?" asked Kristen who, within seconds, had extracted every detail of our encounter from Thomas.

"Like an angel." I embedded her face into my mind. It was the closest thing that I had to my own mother.

"Indeed she was, and *is*," Koi added.

The screeching of car tires in front of the pub stopped the conversation.

Through the window, I saw Jude race out of the car and head towards the front door. Showing no respect for the lock, he just rammed right through, leaving it hanging from one hinge.

"Get in the car, now! Rogues are rolling out all over the country. Let's make like last night's news and get outta here!"

We followed him without question and crammed into a different car.

"Keep the energy low. They're within miles of us. Something or someone has tipped them off. They shouldn't know we're here!" Jude fumed, as he floored the accelerator.

"Ged reckons there's been a double agent among us for a while. I'el better protect him if I find out who he is!" growled Brennan, as he rammed one fist into the other. I held on for dear life as the car took the corners at alarming speed.

"Who would do that? One of us? How could they?" I asked, confused, now grabbing the seat in front of me to keep steady. "It doesn't make sense. To help the Unseen is to guarantee that they don't get back home!"

Brennan yelled over the screeching and revving of the car. "True, but perhaps they've been offered something that's more tempting? We've been here so long that the memories of home have faded. Too many temptations and fascinations here. It's not hard to imagine the promise of something tangible that they can have now over only the possibility of getting home. There are some who don't want to leave, even if—"

The car screamed around a corner and accelerated faster, cutting off Brennan. Then it rocked, as something crashed into it. Kristen screamed. Jude swerved, and I slammed into the door. My face lit up with the spike of adrenaline and fear.

"Keep the face in blackout mode, Soph. That was a Rogue we just hit!" yelled Brennan.

I breathed deeply to quell the glow, well I tried to. The current situation was too frantic. I ended up just holding my breath and hoped for the best. Just as my face calmed, my damned wings started to emerge in reflex to the danger. The car must have looked like a lighthouse on the rocks as we sped down the motorway, with me trying to dull the glaring light.

"Soph, stop it, you're going to let the entire universe pinpoint us!" Kea screeched, as we swerved another zombie thing that flung itself at us from an overhanging tree branch above.

"Crap! I can't control it! Koi! Help me! I thought these cars were Chromious lined!"

"Not this beast! Had to lift this one. Argh, the bastards are coming from every damned direction!" yelled Jude as he swerved again. The four wheel drive then bounced twice over lumps on the road. I didn't even have to wonder what they were.

"Sorry, sorry!" I panicked as I kept trying to shove the wings back in. A decomposing face slammed into my window. The skin and bone shattered with the impact, making me scream in revulsion. *How could they match the car's speed?*

Jude swerved again, and the car rolled. Kristen screamed, then went silent. The car rolled four or five times down an embankment before crashing into a tree. It felt like slow motion, a dream. It was a dream, until we were stopped and the pain began. Thomas was yelling as he tried to pull his leg free from under his crushed seat. I was hanging over a front seat, wings still showing. Koi, Kea, Jude and Brennan were gone. I could only hear the panic of Thomas, and my rapid breaths.

"It's okay, Thomas, calm down. We'll be okay." I could just reach him. "Here, grab my hand."

He did. We could just wrap the tips of our fingers together. I concentrated on soothing the fear and pain emanating through him. His aura was faltering. I drew it in and sent him some warmth and strength. This took my mind off myself and allowed my wings to—*finally*—retract, leaving the car in pitch darkness and silence.

Then I felt a little shuffling.

"Thomas? Are you okay?"

"Yes, Sophia. I'm fine. Thank you. I am still stuck, but you have eased my pain." His voice was markedly weak.

The car rocked unexpectedly. I *smelled* it before I heard it. I scrambled down from the upturned seat with a few twists and wriggles. I was fairly sure I had a dislocated ankle, yet that pain evaporated as a flesh-less hand smashed through the window nearest me.

I lit up again, but just enough to find Thomas in the dark, and I let myself fall across him. I turned in the tight space and shot out a bolt of energy at the foul creature. It sizzled into nothing in an instant.

"*Stay quiet and still,*" I whispered to Thomas as I covered him like a shield. He did as he was told, though I think he had actually passed out.

Another lurch, and the car rolled upright. I was ready for another Rogue as I righted myself quickly, staying near Thomas.

Nothing came.

"Come, Sophia," was the last thing I remembered as I felt a hand on the back of my head.

The next thing I recalled was waking up. I was tucked under a knitted rug in my little room in the sanctuary, and Elizabeth's scroll was tight in my grip.

Chapter
Forty-Seven

Nik'ael had searched for Belial for hours. His thoughts of returning to the Daimon realm were quickly tempered by his sharp survival instinct. *Something was not right.* He knew he was vulnerable if he returned to that cesspit now. Someone or something was triggering the Rogues. It should have been him, but it wasn't. If he didn't know who or what it was, then there was most certainly something very wrong with the plan. He had never been out of the loop, until now.

He kept his distance in the trees lining the drive of the Tudor manor. He saw the battered car pull up. He also saw them carry out the two humans, but Sophia was nowhere to be seen. His heart did a flip in panic. *Was it about his or her safety?* He didn't know. He tossed the small vial in his hand. He knew they'd been to Windsor—the Afflicted spy was more than willing to tail them for two sniffs of his precious container. He didn't, however, know what they'd found there. The defilement of the air with the aroma of Rogues told him that it must have been something worth chasing them down for. It must have been the next piece of the annoying, bloody puzzle.

He ignored the distant yells, calling for him. They could wait. He would finish this himself. He would prove that he was equal to the task, equal to them. He was in control now. He didn't want to leave, but he had to. He relaxed his mind, unfurled his wings, and rose into the air. He reached a lofty height, above the snowing clouds. He made his way towards Windsor, to try to find what he was missing. He was just one step behind now. His heart raced as he glided away. It was not from the effort of physical exertion, but from the inner turmoil and effort it took to quell the unruly, disobedient emotions inside. As he disappeared through a bank of thickening clouds, he let out a desperate, primal scream that sent birds flying in all directions.

He didn't notice the figure following his same flight path.

Chapter
Forty-Eight

Lorcan was hovering by my bedside when I woke. Not literally, but pacing nearby. The scroll that remained in my hand brought memories of the past evening crashing back.

"Time to get up. Eat your breakfast and quickly. Enl'iel will escort you from the dining hall, meet her there. Then we are to meet Gedz'iel in the library to read that scroll." No, *how are you? Glad you're alive.* He was blunt and to the point.

It was the first time he'd spoken to me since he'd left for the Cavern of Souls. He left quickly before I could ask him if he'd found my mother. I felt immediately gutted that it meant he probably hadn't found her. I dressed quickly, wondering how I'd gotten into my nightwear. I hoped that had been Enl'iel's doing. I downed a bowl of fruit salad and a lifesaving black coffee on the move. I found a backpack by the door, shoved both scrolls in it, located the dagger in my pocket and left, following the trail of Lorcan's sea breeze scent.

I met Enl'iel in the dining hall which was practically deserted. Long, empty tables were the only evidence of a once thriving and bustling underground community.

"Good morning, Sophia." Enl'iel kissed me in a human way with a peck to my cheek. "How is your ankle?"

I'd forgotten about that. It felt normal, totally pain free. "Was that you?"

She answered with a smile. "You were rather battered. I am so pleased you are safe and feeling better," she blinked away a tear as she smoothed away a stray hair from my face.

"How did I get back? Last thing I remember, I was upside down in that car!"

"The others chased down most of the Rogues who attacked you. Koi got back to you just as you vaporised one. He righted the car and transferred you here. He had to sedate you in order to dull your energy for a safe trip. Your power is very strong now, and is growing rapidly as your birthday approaches. How you develop so fast is beyond our understanding. The enemy is getting closer for every day that you grow, Sophia. You are a beacon for danger."

"You mean the Daimons?" I grabbed another coffee as my skin crawled at the thought.

"Yes. They are sending so many of their bloodhounds out now. They somehow know that you are in this region." She looked troubled as she poured herself some tea.

"There's a traitor. How can we get ahead when one of our own is a double agent?" I asked, as I stirred an extra sugar in, taking a seat at the closest table. While I quietly crossed off those whom I thought couldn't possibly be guilty, Kristen appeared opposite me. Her head was bandaged. There was evidence of healed bruises around it, already faded to green and yellow.

"'Ow are you?" she asked "Nervous? You look tense, like you 'ave been caught wearing last year's fashion!" She smiled, and so did I. Her candour was refreshing.

"Yes. I'm nervous. This isn't how I thought I'd be spending Christmas. I'm not nervous about my ability so much as what the next scroll is going to say!" I answered.

"I expect zis 'as been confronting. You 'ave been thrown in at zee deep end as they say. You suddenly are living in a fantasy. Don't you worry though, no matter what is to come, we all 'ave your back. Thomas and I know zees vile creatures well. We 'ave many reinforcements. We 'umans are very 'andy. Zee Daimon cannot sense us. You see 'ow 'zey did not notice you slip out to Windsor? We kept zem busy for hours yesterday. You trust me, okay?"

I nodded. "Thanks for seeing me as a person and not just a means to an end."

"Oh no! Is zat 'ow you feel?" Her sweet face was an impressive masquerade for the huntress that lurked beneath.

"A little. Would I be as valued if I was not the Earth-born?"

"*Oh, la verite!* Sophia, you are loved for who you are, not just what you can do. Yes, you 'ave a special purpose, but if 'zat disappeared tomorrow, I would still lay my life down for you. You are kind and loyal and respect life above all else. Zat by itself makes you truly special."

She pepped me right up with that, though I felt like a selfish kid, needing an ego massage every five minutes to keep me going. I vowed to myself then and there to stop sulking and just get on with it. No more overthinking. Just ride the wave I was on, with as much confidence as I could muster.

"Your brother doesn't have the same accent as you," I commented.

"Zat is because 'e was raised on 'zee move with my Papa. Papa was an instructor for zee human militia. Thomas travelled and learned with 'im."

"Where were you then?"

"Oh I was in 'zee countryside. Anjou actually. My Mama trained me and many others. We were part of a group who hunted zee Demon Countess, Anjou'elle. She 'as not been seen for so long 'zat we were disbanded a few years ago to prepare for your awakening." *The Demon Countess? That title made her seem exponentially worse.*

At that moment, we were interrupted by Theus, of all people. I'd never seen any of the Eloi move out of the library—*aside from my little temper tantrum in the training room.*

"With respect, Soph'ael, it is time for you to open the next scroll for us." He offered me his charcoal hand, I took it as he rested his comfortably in mine.

"I will meet you there Sophia, I shall just check in on Jasmine." Enl'iel blinked out with a brief flash. The three of us then made a quiet journey down stairs, each in our own contemplation of the next move in this game.

Back in the library, I was seated in the same chair, with the same faces peering down expectantly at me. Except for Eilir. Her lack of presence was glaring. She seemed part of the fabric of this world, and without her bustling around, it just seemed—colder.

I opened the tube and let the brittle paper slide out. It wasn't sealed like the first which provided for a lot less drama. As I unravelled it, I was surprised to find it adorned beautifully with intricate decorative illumination. It was a far cry from Enoch's simple scroll. It resembled a medieval biblical manuscript. The script was ornate, the opening letter of the document was an exaggerated gothic *C* entwined with red and white roses. Down the margin were faded crowns, drawn by a skilled hand. The necklace I'd retrieved from Elizabeth's palm burned against my neck as the scroll came into contact with my skin. I read aloud, and with a renewed confidence this time.

> *"Child of mine son, feel the love of thy heart, through time and distance.*
> *Evil is near and known, but unknown.*
> *Beware the devil beside you.*

Heed the humans who adore you.
Thy father, mine own son, his love does not unravel for you in his absence.
We are all of but one origin, alas no longer of one spirit.
Evil has sliced through the core of our heritage.
The key to salvation is in your soul, protected deep within you.
Your blood runs pure, misunderstood by thy enemy.
Seek that which your blood shall resurrect.
I share the divine words of Enoch with thee:
"The Kaladai is the key to be bathed in your purity.
Thrice created, twice destroyed and hence scattered in pieces by the disciple of learning.
His words shall guide thee in the end from deep within his earthen retreat
Find the circle most misunderstood.
That which was once the Northern portal to A'vean.
The Giant's Dance entreats you
Tainted by the human ancients of thy land.
Stand upon its heart
Light the way as dawn arises
The East beckons the sun's humblest of days, when the moon lingers long.
Illuminate from within, stones shall crumble.
Impervious to the Unseen, bathed in cold,
The treasure of salvation awaits where naught a breath is drawn.
The light of the spirits shall guide thee."

I came out of the haze of the reading, having heard every word I'd said clearly this time.

"How would Elizabeth know what Enoch had written?" I asked as they all moved about with contemplative agitation.

Gedz'iel answered, as the Eloi continued to pace the room, digesting the words.

"I suspect it a combination of sources. Uriel, who walked the Earth with Enoch for a time, shared some universal knowledge with me as he may have done with others. It may also be visions from I'el. As you yourself have experienced Sophia, I'el can communicate across time and space. Throughout our extensive history, He has made revelations to those deemed worthy, either directly or through an Archangel such as Uriel. Only the smallest of snippets, however. Just enough to push us along, but not enough for a Daimon to gain an advantage if one were to come across such information. Not enough to redeem ourselves. I received such a vision, eons ago. This is how I knew of the Prime scroll and chamber, and how it was to be opened. A few revelations have made their way to the ears of the Unseen, though. Traitors lurk among us as you now know—the attacks on you in Windsor are evidence of this." This strong, imposing Watcher oozed exhaustion. His fight had been long, it was easy enough to see that in his drawn expression. The endless suffering of isolation they had endured made me cross. *Why would I'el enforce such an extended punishment?* I didn't much like I'el right then. I gently placed my hand on top of Gedz'iel's in sympathy. The buzz that exchanged between us was incredibly strong; reassuring. He placed his other hand across mine and smiled, we shared this silent moment before he nodded for me to continue. "Thank you, Sophia."

Just as before, I ran my fingers across the words, teasing their meaning out of the parchment. They leaped out and off the page, moving and spinning and dancing in front of me. Teasing me. Three dimensional images popped in and out, wanting me to decipher their meaning. I'el's words through my grandmother, they were meant for me. I believed immediately that I would understand them, that I could and should understand them.

"Clearly I'el wants you to return, he wouldn't do what he's doing otherwise. It can't be that hard then, can it?" I asked no one in particular. One sentence kept looming out at me, begging to be understood.

"*The circle most misunderstood.* This is where we need to go, but where and what is it?" I pondered thoughtfully.

Amais spoke. "It most assuredly refers to an ancient portal. In the beginning, there were many, however over time they were reduced to just four. The Southern portal is that of your homeland, Soph'ael. The others were the North, here in England, the Middle East, and South America. They were disabled one by one, long forgotten by all. Now, somewhere, there is just one."

"*The Giants dance and the disciple of experience!* Does that mean anything to you, Amais?"

"That I am not so clear about. The disciple of experience would appear to be a person, the Giants dance is more perplexing.

"Why not just say it as it is?" I was annoyed.

"Here, here!" Brennan piped in. I looked his way, only then noticing what he was doing.

"Brennan, you're brilliant!" A blue light glowed in his hands.

"Well that's just stating the obvious."

"Oh, pull your head in! Have you ever heard of the word modesty? Can I borrow that a second?" I asked, exasperated with his perpetual facetiousness.

He moved to pass it to me.

"What is that thing?" asked Pineme, just as I was about to take the phone. He leaned in for a closer look. His eyes narrowed in suspicion as he eyed the device.

"You are so last millennia, Pineme! It's a smartphone, man!" Brennan teased.

Pineme huffed and gave him a look that could have cut most to the bone. Brennan tapped at the screen giving it a small zap of current, not noticing his glare at all.

"Brennan, Sophia, how can this be of help to us?" Gedz'iel asked, he stepped forward with interest also.

Just as Brennan was about to slap the phone in my hand, the door banged open.

"Where is she?" a familiar voice demanded in a barely withheld scream.

"Jaz!" I exclaimed, jumping to my feet, nearly dropping the scroll. I shoved the phone back at Brennan. "Hang on," I said to him.

"Soph, you gotta get me outta here! Ben, where is he? Do you know? Can you find him?"

Her eyes were dilated, glassy and desperate. She pulled away from the Alchemae who ran after her into the room. She was dressed in ill-fitting, standard issue white clothes, which hung from her too thin frame. I hadn't noticed her weight loss before. She was gaunt.

"Get me out of this frigging place, Soph!" She was stopped by two sentries at the door as she strained to run in my direction. At this, she broke down and cried like a small child, falling to her knees. Jaz rarely cried.

"Let me go, for God's sake, please let me go!" she gushed in a way that was alien to the Jaz I knew.

I put the scroll gently down and rushed to her. They tried to stop me.

"Get out of my way!" I demanded.

They did.

She completely broke down in my arms. A thousand tears of every emotion poured from her. Her grief made me stronger and even more determined to make right what was wrong in the world for so long.

Enl'iel entered the room at a run with a tray of medicinal supplies and got just a little too close to Jaz. She may have been hazed by the tisanes they'd clearly been giving her, but she was sharp enough to turn and slap the tray right out of Enl'iel's hands. Glass and fluid sprayed everywhere.

"No more of your bloody hocus pocus! I just want to find my brother and go home!" she sobbed desperately.

"It's okay, Jaz, no one will force you to take any more medicines." I glared at Enl'iel and the other Alchemae who were calmly picking up the mess. Jaz's hair was threaded with bits of herbs and she smelled like a hundred beautiful fragrances. Her voice though, sounded defeated and was thick with the remnants of drug-induced sleep. I knew they were just trying to protect her, but this was not going to fly with her for much longer. I decided I was going to be *her* wingman—*so to speak*— from this point on.

"You can stick with me Jaz, okay?" Someone tried to object, but I put up a hand to hush whoever it was and continued, "*But,* you have to do what you're told. No more flying off the handle, okay? I'm having enough trouble controlling myself. They promised to help me find Ben. We *will* find him—*I* will find him, and then I promise I'll get you home."

She considered me for a moment through her lush, tear-moistened lashes as she sat on the floor, exhausted. I cuddled her. Enl'iel passed her a cup, but Jaz went to swipe it away.

"It is just water, Jasmine," she said sympathetically.

I took it first and had a sip.

"Water, *au naturel*! Have some." She took it from me and gulped it down. After a few moments, she seemed calmer.

"Don't bullshit me, Soph. These *people,* or whatever they are, have no interest in my brother or me, for that matter. Why would they bother looking for him? They want you and your magical mojo, that's all."

"Perhaps they don't have interest in him, but *I* do. I love you both, you're my best friends, and I'll do everything I can to protect you and to find him." I had a sudden flashback to the cavern, where I swear I thought Ben was going to kiss me. I lost track of my thoughts for a second.

"Soph?"

"Sorry, I was just thinking about how important you both are to me." It was the truth mixed with a longing that I couldn't reveal, even to myself. I snapped out of the reverie, stood and pulled her up. "Can someone get her into some decent clothes, please? She'll need some protective gear too. She's coming with me."

"Jude, remove the girl," ordered Gedz'iel.

After Jaz was hurried just outside the doors by an incredibly annoyed Jude, Gedz'iel immediately questioned me.

"Sophia, this is not wise. She is a human, and a liability for you. For us all."

"You take other humans into battle. I'll make sure she's out of the way," I countered.

"Indeed we do, but they are well trained in our ways. But with her fragility, this is a heavy weakness that may weigh dangerously over you and us all. She is strong willed, but I see the pain that courses through her. She is impulsive and explosive. Her temper makes her vulnerable, which in turn makes all around her so. She is safe here. She is not a trained warrior. No one can guarantee her life out there." He pointed to the roof.

"Gedz'iel speaks the truth, Sophia. We know you mean well. But she can be impulsive, as you have just seen. How are you going to control her? She has been sedated for her own safety," Enl'iel added.

"Her outbursts will put others in danger. She could cause more trouble than I care to consider. This is no time to pander to childish tantrums, Sophia. She is not our responsibility, and if we face battle, I fear she will become a casualty. Enough children of the Earth have bled for us." Gedz'iel was grave, but I was indignant.

"Jaz has been bullied and harassed for half of her life! She's the product of a crappy childhood. If you just give her a morsel of trust, put that trust in *me*, you'll see that she can shine like a diamond when she doesn't feel like a caged, wild animal. Please?" I looked to him, hoping he could see in her what I did.

"And who is going to watch her? You cannot," Theus spoke up. "Your responsibilities are too great. You cannot afford to be distracted by a human."

"Give the human a chance. She may well be helpful as an undetectable scout," Pathos joined in the debate.

"Pathos, with respect, you do not know this human. She is volatile," Enl'iel cautioned.

"Her name is Jaz, not Human," I was compelled to add.

"Indeed, no slight is intended. What may be of benefit though, is that she is invisible to the Daimon. She is of no interest to them at all. If we place a scout nearby her to read her thoughts and emotions, her eyes and ears in the right place could well be of value. If you wish to keep her, Soph'ael, she must earn her place. Left here though, I believe she would be more of a liability. Her escapee habit could compromise the safety of the Sanctuary," Pathos concluded.

Before I could say another word, Brennan spoke up.

"I'll sort it. Just leave her to me. Poor kid's been dragged into this mess. I'll make sure she's taken care of. You're in, aren't you Jude? A little paying it forward old friend?

Jude glowered at him from the doorway where he'd quietly reappeared. He clearly didn't want to air whatever dirty laundry there was between him and Brennan. He sighed in a resigned yet clearly non-gratuitous way.

"Brennan, this is foolhardy. Your responsibilities to Sophia and your kindred come before this girl." Gedz'iel warned.

"Don't worry Ged, have I failed you yet?" He gave the now bristling Gedz'iel a confident smile that bordered on irreverence. Gedz'iel's dark expression said as much.

"One mistake by that girl, one foot out of place and you alone will answer to me Brennan," Gedz'iel conceded.

"She will be invisible, I swear," Brennan added as he looked Jude's way.

I beamed at them both. That was the best I was going to get. "Just keep her safe, okay?"

"You know I will," Jude responded surprisingly. He leaned heavily by the doorframe, arms crossed looking as dirty as he could. "Go tell her to keep her mouth shut and her head screwed on straight then," Jude nodded his head towards the door.

"I'll be back in a minute," I headed for the door feeling Jude's none too pleased stare as I ducked past him.

With Jaz now safe under Brennan and Jude's watch, I stepped out of the room to find her being consoled by that same red haired girl that kept her company days before.

"Thanks. What's your name?"

"Rosalyn." She did a quick bow.

"Oh for God's sake, don't do that!" I put my hand out to her and smiled. "I'm Soph, thanks for keeping Jaz company." She shook my hand shyly.

"You're most welcome," she smiled sweetly. "I can take her to refresh and change if that is your wish?"

"That would be great, thanks." I turned to Jaz as Rosalyn stepped away. "Jude will make sure you're okay. This is the only way you can stay and be safe."

"He doesn't look too thrilled," she glanced back at the doorway that was ajar, with Jude's back blocking us from a heated discussion between the Eloi inside about me having too much opinion.

"Well, can you blame him? You just need to be civil, not friends, just civil, otherwise they will sedate you again. I don't know how much I can push them, I think this was a pretty good deal, Jaz. You owe Brennan big time."

"You promise me you'll find Ben and I'll do whatever I'm told," she answered.

"Jude, did you get anything out of those Afflicted about Ben's whereabouts?" I called out, realising I'd heard nothing about them.

"One expired quickly, the other responds to nothing. I have had no success unfortunately. They suffer so much already that any means of persuasion are rarely successful." The inference of torture was disturbing.

"Well, one way or another I'll find him, I promise." I secretly hoped that was not an empty promise. Jaz wiped her tear-reddened nose and pinched her cheeks, instantly looking a little brighter.

"Fine, let's do this then. At least my prison warden over there is eye candy," she whispered as she crossed her arms and gave Jude a sweet-as-pie fake smile.

"Stop it will you, this is serious!"

"I know, can I put it down to being slightly off my face? Don't drink the tea, I'm serious!" She had a point, she looked awful. I could forgive her practically anything at that moment.

"Get some rest and eat something, you're skin and bone. I'll be with you soon. You absolutely *must* do what you're told, or I'm going to get my butt kicked, okay?"

"Got it." We embraced briefly before she disappeared down the corridor with Rosalyn, Jude begrudgingly in tow.

"Hurry up human, I haven't got all day!" he growled impatiently.

"Hands off, freak!"

Less than ten seconds and the truce was already broken. This could go so very wrong, and that was without any Daimon. Those two might just kill each other.

"Enough now, return to the scroll, Sophia," called an impatient Gedz'iel from within the library. I re-entered just as Brennan started complaining.

"Where's my damn phone? I put it on the desk!"

"What? I was going to check out something on the web. Find it Brennan, it could be important!" I exclaimed.

"I put it right there Soph!" He pointed to the edge of the desk.

"Forget about such trivialities, Bren'ael. They are but magic tricks," scoffed an unimpressed Pineme. "Perhaps you would not have misplaced it had you not been so caught up in babysitting humans."

"Argh," Brennan was clearly annoyed as he hunted for it for a few more minutes, until Gedz'iel ordered him to stop and focus on the scroll.

"We will decipher it ourselves Brennan. Stop now and help us."

We worried over the ancient words for a while. I examined each illustration, every word and full stop. All in the room held the scroll. Each of us tried to extrapolate meaning from the same line, *The Giants Dance*. For some reason that one line drew us all in. If only Brennan had his phone on hand.

"Hmm, perhaps we should recall Eilir?" Gedz'iel mused. They all laughed lightly at that.

"Master Gedz'iel, perhaps some training to clear our minds?" suggested Matias.

"Indeed. Combat is an excellent refreshment."

The next few hours were punishing.

Combat with Lorcan and Brennan was more than brutal. The soft approach was long gone as I was flipped, rolled, kicked, and zapped. Brennan received a few good strikes from me though, underestimating the improvement in my agility.

"When did you get so damn good?" he breathed heavily as he came out of a commando roll, rubbing the kick I'd managed to plant on his thigh as I dodged a bolt from him.

I just raised my eyebrows in mock confusion. I was still too scared to use my elemental power in full during practice, despite them encouraging me to have a go at it.

"You really need to use more elementals though Soph, you have to get that fire power down to a precise art," Brennan said.

"I want to see how strong and accurate you are. C'mon now, give me a quick blast to the hand," he got ready and looked on expectantly.

"But you said I could kill you if I did that, Lorcan!"

"Did you say that, bro?"

Lorcan's cheeks bloomed crimson. Then he fessed up.

"Didn't want her getting a big head too quickly. Besides, she needs the stealth and physical combat practice more."

"You tricked me!" I immediately let a zap fly out that cracked so hard onto Lorcan's armour that he was flung to the ground.

I stood over him. "You're an idiot!"

Brennan was nearly crying with laughter. "Man, you have a way with women!"

That was when I saw Jaz enter the arena with Jude. Expecting a firestorm to erupt, I watched from a distance.

No yelling or shouting ensued, however. She simply followed him to the mats and proceeded with his warm-up. They began with some basic self-defence. She was swift and focused. I moved in just close enough that I could feel her energy. She was centred. Calm. Each time she fell under Jude's moves, she got straight back up. There was fire in her aura, but not towards him. She inspired me.

I moved onto the orbs, feeling motivated by Jaz' impressive effort. For the first time, I ran an entire lap without a single sting. Koi congratulated me as I took out all but one orb.

"That burn from within is working with you today, Sophia. This is progress."

The success of finding Elizabeth had boosted my confidence all round. I had opened and read two scrolls. I knew I was capable of more. After a quick break to eat, Lorcan tapped me on the shoulder.

"Our turn. Let's go." He turned his back on me and walked away. *Ouch!* I must have really stung his ego. *For the second time.* I wasn't looking forward to this.

"Give him hell, princess!" I gave Brennan a thumbs up.

Back in the ruins, Lorcan disappeared immediately into the shadows. I stopped and listened. He was going to get me good and proper if he could, as payback for humiliating him again.

At first there was just silence. Only the distant sounds of weapons practice in the other room.

Then there was something—a thrumming, pulsing, rhythmic vibration. I could feel it tickle the tiny hairs on the back of my arms. I shrunk within the shadows of a crumbling colonnade for cover. The burn within me rose, but I swallowed it back down. Waterfalls flowed through my thoughts as the feeling dissipated. I would call for it when I wanted it. It would behave itself until then. I hoped.

I jumped as I felt a shift in the air nearby. *The breeze of wings rustling the stale air.* I held my breath for some reason and grabbed a hold of Elizabeth's necklace. It was hot. As my hand closed fully around it, I sensed something pull in my gut, like plucking a guitar string. My grandmother spoke across distant realms to me, her voice echoing in my mind.

"*From within you, I dwell. My strength is your strength. Where you see yourself, so you shall be.*"

Darkness and silence reigned again. I snuck out of my hiding place and received a nasty sting to the back of my knee.

"Got to do better than that, or you'll be toast within the week. Try harder, Sophia!" With that rebuke, he was gone again in a flash, lurking somewhere else, ready for the next strike.

I was mad now. He was being a jerk. I breathed through the burn and snuck through the rubble, listening for him again. The faintest hint of ocean mixed with cedar was in the air. He was sweating. My senses were becoming so precisely honed that I could sense someone's proximity just by the lingering of their scent. It reminded of Ben—ashes and spice. I missed that.

I ducked away and back towards the colonnade until the scent dissipated. I wanted to blitz him this time. I needed to prove myself to him, and also to myself. I grabbed the necklace again and thought of Elizabeth's words. I imagined myself standing behind Lorcan. I squeezed my eyes shut and willed it to happen, with every atom of myself.

Everything became dull. Something yanked hard behind my bellybutton from within. The ground disappeared. Blackness became blacker, until it was peppered with pinpricks of light. Silence—then a *thud*. I suddenly had a mouth full of dirt. I looked up, spitting it all out, just as a very surprised Lorcan turned around to see me.

"How the hell—"

Before he could say another word, I jumped up and zapped the hell out of his smart mouth. He flew backwards onto the ground before recovering quickly, just as I was letting my wings unfurl.

"Come on, let's play for real!" I teased as I forced his sorry arse down again.

"You transferred! How did you do that?"

"Granny taught me!"

Chapter
Forty-Nine

With a thorough examination of my necklace by the others after Lorcan rather humbly reported what I'd done, no one was the wiser as to how this connection occurred.

"It is not a Soul stone, but it is also not a stone I have seen before," observed Koi.

"Whatever it is, its vibrations are beyond ancient," Gedz'iel added. "It could well be a relic of the old world. Keep it close, Sophia. Its purpose is clearly for your benefit."

I could barely keep my hand from it for the rest of the day, constantly twirling it through my fingers.

We finished with a cool-down run with the human battalion, which was actually fun. They were so competitive. They tried to outrun us, even though they knew it was impossible. The bond that we shared was incredible. Generations of families served and protected the Watchers and Eudaimonia in secret, for no reason other than a deep love and kinship that spanned the history of time.

I met Jaz for the evening meal, and she looked exhausted. Jude was nearby, his eye constantly on her. Watching for any wrong move, I imagined. *Brennan owed him!*

"Well, my faculties have finally been cleared of that god-awful stuff, at least. That dimwit over there is not so bad, either." She pointed her fork at

Jude. "He promised me he would find Ben."

"Well that's a change from the other day. Friends now?"

"I wouldn't go that far. He's tolerable, nice to look at, but just tolerable."

She was feeling low. I could tell this by the fact that she was eating a vegetarian meal without complaint.

"Promise me, for your own safety, you'll listen to Jude, or whoever you're with? I don't want anything to hurt you."

"I'm a one-woman trip to destruction for anything that touches me right now, so those things better stay the hell away."

I giggled. "I've never wanted to cross your path! I remember year seven all too well!"

"So you damned well should! You know who's boss!" she smiled. "You okay, Soph? For real?"

"I'm going with the flow."

"Seems like that's all you can do with these people."

Two more days of training followed, but brought no progress with the scroll. We were convinced *The Giants Dance* was the key to understanding where we had to go, but with Brennan still hunting for his phone, we were blind to outside help. Apparently it was too dangerous to head outside until we were armed with knowledge as well as weapons.

I walked through what I'd seen and done in Elizabeth's tomb over and over again, trying to remember something I might have missed. Nothing jumped out.

I took a walk with Jaz for a break. Today was the day before the winter solstice. I knew this because I heard some sentries discussing the different shift change times for the shorter day. It was just days until Christmas, which was about the right time for the shortest day of the year. That was hinted at in the verse too. *When the moon lingers long.* I felt the pressure, we all did. What would happen if the solstice came and went before we figured it out? Would the prophecy still work?

Jaz and I found ourselves at the entry level, sitting amongst the lush but flowerless foliage. It was the most outdoorsy place I could find since above ground was off limits. The warmth from the huge light orb, when my eyes were closed, felt almost like the sun. *It would have to do for now.* The sound of the waterfall behind us added to the effect, and for just a few moments, I felt relaxed—nearly happy, even. Jaz sat quietly beside me.

I was running those verses through my head again when I heard the delightful squeal of a child nearby. Surprised, thinking they'd all been moved to safety, I looked up.

"Who's the munchkin?" asked Jaz as she sat up, hair askew.

"Oh, that's little Av'ael. I met her when I first got here. She's a sweetie."

"Yeah, I suppose, if snot and dribble is your thing."

"Oh, don't be so cold. You were small and cute once, too."

"Never! What's she doing over there anyway?" she asked, pointing to the little building Av'ael was constructing out of dirt and stones. "Looks pretty damn good for an ankle-biter! Damn fine effort for a blind kid!"

I started explaining that she could see a little bit when I caught sight of her construction as well.

"Actually—what *is* that?" Av'ael's back was to us, so we walked over to where she was playing by the far end of the waterfall. She was plucking stones out of the small pond and using them to build a circular structure. She only noticed me when I peered right over her shoulder.

"Pretty Sophia, pretty Sophia!" she hugged my leg.

"What are you making there, Av'ael? It looks very impressive."

She beamed, clasped her hands under her chin, and swayed in coy shyness.

"Oh, I don't know! I had a dream last night and a nice man showed me how to build it. Mama is taking *soooooo* long, so I'm making it for the man now," she said as she picked up a finger-sized stone and placed it down to complete a circle.

"It's pretty cool, kid," said Jaz.

"Thank you. What's your name? You look sad."

"Uh, I'm Jaz, pipsqueak. I'm fine, don't you worry." She ruffled Av'ael's hair in a way that didn't impress the little girl as she tried to push her soft white locks back into place. She took her Soul stone from her pocket and cuddled it to her face.

"This is for you, Sophia." She pointed to the structure of concentric grey stone circles.

"For me?"

"Yes, the man told me to make it for you,"

"Who was the man in your dream?" I asked, just as her mother called from down the nearest corridor.

"I don't know. He had pretty, rainbow eyes, though," she answered.

"Come, Av'ael. Oh my goodness, forgive us, Soph'ael. Blessings to you," she said as she recognised me.

"Oh no, please, it's no trouble. We were just admiring Av'ael's artwork."

"See, Mama, she's the nicest lady-Watcher ever!"

"I hope she was not interrupting you," the mother said.

"Not at all. In fact," I knelt down onto my knees and looked intently at the tiny sculpture, "Jaz, what does this remind you of?"

Jaz squatted next to me. Av'ael took a step forward and ruffled Jaz's hair. "Hey kid, what're you doing?"

"You're pretty, too. You're pretty in there," she pointed at Jaz' heart.

It was a moment of pure innocence, and it left Jaz speechless.

"Come, darling, Papa is awaiting us. Leave these ladies alone now. May the blessing of I'el be forever upon you," her mark glowed warmly as she picked up the little girl and disappeared down the corridor. We were alone once more.

In the vast silence, we both circled the rubble masterpiece.

"Why is it so interesting?" I asked, more to myself than to Jaz.

"Beats me. Kind of cute kid, though."

I looked up in surprise.

"Don't say a word. Repeat that to anyone, and I'll *have* to kill you!"

"Understood." I smiled as I looked back at the intriguing circles.

I looked intently at the stones. My heart skipped a beat as I quickly pulled the scroll from my backpack that was almost a permanent attachment now. I dared not let the scrolls out of my sight.

Could it be? Could I'el have connected with a child? I wondered with a growing excitement.

I inspected the page again. Not the words, but the colourful artistry.

"What is it Soph?"

"I don't know, well, actually, I think I might know. I'm just looking for-"I sucked in a breath.

"What?'

"Look!" I ran my hand down the margin, along the line of coronation-style crowns, until my finger rested on the one third from the bottom of the page.

"It's a crown. Yeah, okay. There's a whole bunch of them," Jaz commented.

"No, look at this one!"

She looked closer.

"Oh! It's not a crown. It kinda looks like…" I cut her off.

"Jaz, I think it's Stonehenge! The clue is in the scroll artwork and Av'ael has somehow shown us too! Can you see it?" I pointed to the scroll first and then Av'ael's creation. "Look, an outer and inner circle, with the alter-stone in the middle. She's even tried to put the lintel stones on the top. She's a miniature genius!" *The circle most misunderstood.* No one had ever really deciphered what this ancient structure was, that much I knew to be true.

I dragged Jaz at a run until I finally found Brennan, with Koi. They were visiting Cael in the Stasis room. Cael looked much better now. He was asleep still, but the wounds were healed to silvery scars. His leaflets had been obliterated. I didn't know if he would be able to fly again. Despite my own excitement, my heart lurched in grief for him. I kissed his cheek gently. He stirred, so I stepped back through the white veil, beckoning Brennan out.

"Brennan, have you found your phone?" I whispered.

"Ironically yes. Would you believe it was stuffed behind a loose stone in the library hearth! Some git is messing with me! Anyway, what did you want it for? You wanna make a call? Who is he? I'll need to shake him down first, with this and this!" He held up each fist, one at a time.

"Stop messing around. I think I know where Elizabeth's scroll is sending us!"

He pulled the phone from the leg pocket of his pants in a nanosecond, and fiddled with it to power it up.

"God, do they *ever* wear shirts around here?" Jaz commented, trying not to look like she was gawking at the roomful of sleek muscles.

"Feisty, aren't you!" Brennan said as I saw him stretch his chest out, showing off. If Enl'iel were here, she'd cuff him over the ear, at the least.

"Okay, what am I searching for?" he asked as he held his typing finger ready.

"Oh, just give that thing here!" I snapped as I snatched the phone from his grasp.

The screen was dull. "A little more power, please. Quickly!" I snapped.

"You're feisty, too! Okay, okay, keep your knickers on straight," he said as he pointed at the phone. A small spark arced out of his finger, hitting it in the middle of the screen, giving me a strong signal to the outside world.

"Brennan, do not *ever* mention my knickers again! " I ordered as I typed a search into the device.

I waited a moment. It took a little longer for reception this deep down in the Earth.

"Yes! That's it! The Giant's Dance is an old term for Stonehenge!" I jumped up and down with excitement. I typed in tomorrow's date as well and waited. "Tomorrow is December 21, the winter solstice—*the night when the moon lingers.* It's the shortest day of the year. Just as the scroll said. We have to get to Stonehenge by sunrise tomorrow!"

I raced out the door in search of Gedz'iel, with the others on my tail.

Chapter Fifty

Brennan and I hunted everywhere for Gedz'iel. He'd left a few days ago to monitor Daimon movement. He hadn't returned yet from the perimeter of the Empyrean realm—the Daimon realm.

"Can't you just call him back?"

"Not that easy, princess. It's one of those funky places, like the Bermuda Triangle. Nothing works like it should. The energy is thin in the atmosphere, because the Daimon suck it all up into their hellhole. This makes it hard to use our power, or get messages in and out. We might just have to use the muscle and brainpower we have here if old Ged doesn't return ASAP," Brennan explained.

"It could work in our favour if he actually stayed there, he's an expert at monitoring whatever is slithering in and out of that place. He would know by their movement if something of significance was occurring, and news of that would bring him straight back," said Lorcan, who'd appeared in the doorway of the deserted library, peeling an apple with a small dagger.

"Everyone who helped the other day is still on standby. We have all the backup we need, but we should probably still try to get through to Ged."

"Don't let him hear you call him that again, Bren. He'll deck you, like this!"

He threw the apple so hard that it was obliterated when it hit the side of Brennan's head. They tussled a little, like teenage brothers, before I stepped in.

"That's enough! Both of you, we've no time to mess around. I want everyone available called back and in order, ready to go first thing in the morning. I *have* to be there before dawn. Now cut it out, and get yourselves together!"

They both stopped and glared at me. Then clapped. That annoyed me immensely.

"Just do it. I'm going to find Enl'iel."

They mocked me further with a salute, but disappeared with a touch to their faces, off to do what needed to be done. I looked around the ancient room. It was so quiet yet spoke loudly to me of an incredible world hidden in plain sight. I wanted to spend hours here, going through all the books to learn of the heritage I'd only just discovered. The dagger banged against my leg, reminding me of what I needed to do though, and that began with finding Enl'iel.

This time I tried something different. I wanted to prove something to myself. No one else was here. I'd dropped Jaz back at her room on the way down, so I couldn't make a fool of myself in public. I closed my eyes and concentrated really hard on Enl'iel, wishing myself to be with her. I stopped for a moment and opened my eyes, looked around the room to gather some reassurance that I was not under anyone's glare, then shut them tight again and concentrated. I placed my right palm over my mark and let energy flow from it onto my skin. Snaps of electricity zapped across between my face and palm. I pictured her long white hair, her warm smile and sparkling eyes. My body began to warm. Then my stomach churned. I sharpened the image of her face as clearly as if it were right in front of me, and willed myself to be with her. My mark scorched.

Suddenly, I was jerked into blackness—quiet, cool, tepid, then warm. Just as suddenly, I was met with the brightest of light again. I came to an ungraceful thud. I opened my eyes as someone grabbed my arm to pull me up. It was Enl'iel.

"Sophia! You have transferred! Did you mean to?"

"Yes! I did it! Oh my God, I can't believe I did it!" We were standing in the corridor, leading to the training rooms. She was in her fighting gear. Loose white pants, thick black boots and armour plating across her chest. Word must have travelled quickly. She hugged me as we continued to move at a brisk pace.

"Brennan told me that you discovered the meaning of the words, and then gave orders for action. I am so proud of you."

"I only hope I can keep it all under control!" I quipped.

"You have more control than you know." She responded as we approached the large entrance to the training arena.

We were met at there by Koi, Kea, Brennan, and Jaz.

"Where did you get to?" Kea asked me. "Found this one wandering on her own."

"Yeah, you forgot me back in my room Soph! Lucky she found me! God!" Jaz rolled her eyes at me. "I kinda rock this outfit though!" She was dressed in protective gear already. She looked like a warrior-goddess in all the white and metal. I hoped she didn't need any of the gear. I really hoped that she wouldn't see fighting at all.

"Sorry everyone, I took a different route."

"She transferred to me!" boasted Enl'iel.

"No way! Well done, princess!" There were glowing marks of approval all around as we walked through the milling troops of Eudaimonians and humans. A large contingent of Watchers stood up on the stone platform at the head of the room. They observed solemnly the mustering of troops. There was still no sign of Gedz'iel or the Eloi. I was hoping that wasn't an ominous sign.

Jude approached just as we were about walk up the steps.

"I will take you from here," he said to Jaz.

I faltered. Panic set in over the decision to let her stay near me. *Near danger*. I knew she wouldn't tolerate any other choice, though.

"You *will* listen to Jude. Don't be a hero or a hothead. If you get yourself killed, *I'll* kill you myself!"

We hugged goodbye. "Yes, ma'am," she saluted, then looked serious for a moment. "Just find Ben, please?"

"I will, I promise." And then she was gone, lost in the mass of people and the promise that she would be safe.

I saw Dash follow Jude, and it was the first time I'd seen him dressed like the Watcher that he was.

"Will Dash be okay? He hasn't fought for a long time, right?"

"He was a Seraph warrior in his time. He will mirror Jude with the humans. Don't worry, he will be fine," Lorcan said as he joined us.

Up on the platform, I could clearly see the magnitude of bodies. Thomas and Kristen were loud enough that I could hear them shouting orders to the human troops under the direction of Jude. He, who I could just make out, had a firm grip on Jaz's arm. She was not going to be able to move a centimetre without him by her side. I was relieved and somewhat amused by that thought.

A line of Alchemae healers entered behind us with trolleys laden with food, water, herbs, and lotions.

"We are in for the night. We eat and sleep here tonight," said Brennan as he watched them enter, too. Weapons clanged and banged as they were sharpened and adjusted. A few groups were in the ruins, practicing stealth tactics. I could hear and feel the popping of elemental explosions.

Kea suddenly pulled me aside. "We've had word from Gedz'iel. At least one of the Unseen has left the Empyrean realm. This is not good news. We want you to rest for a few hours. Tomorrow most likely will be hideously more challenging and dangerous than we had anticipated. A dozen humans have been lost to Rogues overnight already. They are buffeting their front line on the outskirts of the county. They know we are on to something. They are trying to distract us with small, frequent melees."

"Couldn't Gedz'iel have stopped them from leaving that place?" I asked.

"Gedz'iel is powerful, Soph, but they are originally our kindred—ancient souls who are equally as strong."

That knowledge was humbling. Then I burst out, "I can't rest while everyone else is preparing!"

"Yes, you can, and you will." She pulled me into a small room carved out of a sheer wall of rock at the back of the platform. The room was hidden behind a simple white curtain. I didn't think I was tired until I saw the bed.

"It's only three hours until we must leave, anyway. It isn't long, but enough to rest your body, if not your mind."

I complied. It was just easier. I'd gotten things started, which was a feat in itself. I didn't want exhaustion to defeat me just when I was needed tomorrow.

As she turned to leave, I asked, "Do we really have a traitor among us? It's the only way they could know we are about to make a move, right? Who would do such a thing?"

"Someone with a grudge. That's how it all started so long ago with Yeqon and Lilith."

I sat on the cot. "I've heard that name. Who exactly is she?"

"She's a girlfriend you really don't want. History says Eve plucked the forbidden fruit. Well, history forgets Lilith. Anyway, rest up. I'll make sure Jaz plays nice with Jude. If not, I'll keep her under my wing—literally!" She smiled to me as she left.

My head was in a tailspin. *Roaming Daimon and spies among us.* I lay down and played every face through my mind, but could not find fault or suspicion with anyone. Sleep crept up on me without warning, and I drifted off.

Horns and pitchforks poked at me. I ran through stinking wastelands. Hands grabbed at my legs as they reached up through cracks in the dry, packed ground. It was dark. Smoke made the air hazy and unclear. There is a flash of white hair,

then black hair. Blue eyes, then black. Someone is following me. I trip as a hand catches my ankle, and I fall hard. I am yanked back, with an iron grip. I try to summon some elemental power, but nothing, not even a molecule of energy, would come. I am empty, powerless. I am being pulled down into the earth by this strong, huge hand. I release a silent scream. My skin scrapes and rips open as I'm being dragged roughly across shards of rock. I claw desperately, with no effect. Finally, I tip backwards as the ground gives way. The hand releases me and I fall backwards into a long, dark abyss. I pray for forgiveness for failing, for letting everyone down by dying in a stinking hellhole. I close my eyes, awaiting the inevitable thud. It doesn't come.

Instead, I am cocooned in strong arms. Heartbeat pounding, nervous, anxious.

Whoever is holding me is doing so with great fear.

"Don't speak."

A deep, throaty, familiar voice.

I panic. I struggle to escape, at all costs.

The arms tighten. I am trapped.

"You are safe."

Too familiar. Everything brightens slightly when a light is struck. A flame burns on a dirt wall in a sconce made of—God— was it a leg bone? Red and orange licked away the darkness.

I struggle a little more in the muscular arms.

"Do not struggle if you wish to live. Quiet yourself, and you will be safe."

I crane my neck back to see who this voice belongs to. Who my captor is. My eyes adjust quickly. I blink a few times. A curved horn. Another horn, broken in half. My heart thunders in panic now. I force myself to look at the face that gazes down upon me. He is beautiful. Perfection.

It is Belial.

I awoke from this nightmare thrashing at someone, drenched with sweat.

"Get away! Get off of me!" I yelled at whoever was grabbing my hands.

The pressure was immediately released. I sat up, clearing my eyes.

"It's three in the morning, Soph. Time to get up." Lorcan stood over me. He couldn't wear any more weapons if he tried.

"What are you doing here?"

"Why so surprised? I'm hardly the bogeyman. I was sent to wake you. Get up, we leave in thirty."

Lorcan glared at me a little too long before he turned to leave. I looked down to see that at some point, I had wriggled out of my clothes and was just in my underwear. I could hear him swallow and sense his pulse quicken. The scent of salt was on his skin, sweat glistening in the orb light as he lingered by the curtain.

"I need to get dressed. Would you please leave?" *Awkward.*

"Of course." He pushed a chair out of the shadows as he left. It had fresh clothes on it.

After dressing, I ran out of the room quickly and bumped into Kea. The place was bright and alive with orderly squads awaiting the orders to move out.

"Great, Dash came to wake you."

"No, Lorcan woke me," I answered, confused.

"Oh, I asked Dash to—never mind. It doesn't matter. Here," she handed me two Eccles cakes that were hot and smelled delicious. "Eilir insisted that they were sent and warmed up for you. All the way from her safe house in Wales. You are the charmed one."

I ate quickly as everyone started to mill around the entrance. I was strapped back into all manner of protective gear, the breastplate being my least favourite. But Kea combing lavender oil and herbs through my hair was by far the highlight. I felt heavy and awkward in the outfit but smelled amazing. The thick wrist bands seemed over the top, but apparently they came in handy for weapon deflection and punching down Rogues in an emergency. It was all a bit Wonder Woman to be honest.

There was some shouting off to my right. Of course it was Jaz, escaping Jude's clutches. She dashed through the crowds, making a beeline for me.

I saw Enl'iel chasing her, but she got to me first.

"Just wanted to see you before—you know—whatever it is you're doing!" she huffed, out of breath. Then she dragged me into a tight hug. Her body was shaking. "Don't get hurt, Soph."

"I'll be fine, you just watch yourself. You've already run off from Jude, and we haven't even left yet!"

"I know, I just needed to say—" Enl'iel finally caught up with her. "I just wanted to say—*uh*—Soph, you rock that sexy goddess look too!"

"Come, Jasmine. Back you go, or it's another special drink of tea for you."

Jaz mumbled something rude as she went back down to the arena. She looked back at me, and there was real fear in her eyes.

Brennan, Koi, and Lorcan appeared from three sudden flashes of light.

"Ready, Sophia?" asked Koi, who gleamed in gold and silver armour, as did we all.

"Let's just get out of here before my nerves fry."

Chapter
Fifty-One

The cool night air nipped at my skin, and I pulled my camouflaging jacket more snuggly around my body. Despite my elevated body temperature, I could appreciate how cold it was and I worried for our human soldiers. Close to seven in the morning, the motorway behind us was quiet. Maybe one or two cars had sped past since we emerged to hide between the monolithic stones. It had been another long, evasive trip. Replaying that dream of Belial in my mind and worrying about Jaz had me on edge. I felt sure then that I'd made the wrong decision in keeping Jaz near me, but facing off a great white shark would be easier than leaving her behind. I was so scared that she'd run off to look for Ben at the first chance she got.

Oh Ben, where are you?

Brennan scouted the outer circle of stones, while I concentrated on tracking the energy within them. The soft pulse underfoot had drawn me in from miles away. It was getting stronger by the minute, as though beckoning. The air was alive here with an unearthly buzz. The E'lan was the most powerful I'd ever felt. The closer we got to Salisbury, the more irritable I'd felt. I'd been on edge to get out of the car. I'd tried to the point of exhaustion, to keep my power dulled to the minimum for the entire trip. I didn't want any more stuff ups. This wasn't easy with the unpredictable grasp I had on controlling myself. I imagined waterfalls, waterfalls, waterfalls! I think I held my breath more often than not, lest I light up like a one-woman firework display.

Elizabeth's scroll crackled in my pocket as though it were alive. Its words burned with encouragement, as though it knew I was close to something of great significance. Kea and Koi were down by the Avon River. They were patrolling the area whilst Enl'iel kept a distant watch on the other side of the motorway. Jude should have been there already to run an advanced reconnaissance, but he was nowhere to be seen. Not a footprint was in the snow to show that anyone had passed through, and this worried me.

My heart was racing with apprehension as I allowed a faint light to emanate only from my face. I kept my hands clasped tightly together, lest they betray me. I could feel each vein glowing warmly, providing an extra and welcomed barrier against the winter breeze. I wasn't one hundred percent sure what I was looking for, but I knew I would find it. I simply had to.

Brennan whispered inside my head, "*Heads up, princess. A mist is rolling in. The Rogues are coming.*" *How do you do that?* I asked in my own mind, knowing this was an ability I was yet to understand or conquer. Of course there was no reply.

I looked up to see the grey blanket slithering over the landscape towards us. I had learned from experience now that they liked to emerge from sudden influxes of thick fog, masking where and how they arrived. It was as though they literally appeared out of thin air, clawing their way up from the ground, like the walking dead that they were. This time, though, despite the billowing fog coming our way, I knew they were not too near, as the stench of decomposition had yet to accent the air.

I recalled the instructions of the scroll.

Light the way as dawn arises… The East beckons…

The light would lead the way. I was yet to know what this light was, but I did know it meant waiting until sunrise to find out. I was hoping it would be as simple as the first sunrays highlighting the place amongst the stones where the next clue was concealed, but it felt like we didn't have much time to wait. It would be another half hour or so before the first hints of winter sun hit the ground, and the pressure of attack and the lives already lost weighed heavily upon me. If I could circumvent the prophecy just a little to cut out some time, I was going to try.

I called back in a muffled whisper to Brennan, "*Anything? I'm feeling a vibration, but it seems to be all around us. The whole ground is humming,*" I said as I bent down, placing a palm to the ground. It warmed me and pulsed up my arm.

"*Yeah, there's definitely something here, princess. We're in the right place, it's just where to look without drawing those bastards out. Damn it, it would be a slam dunk if we could light this place up!*" The mind-talking made me slightly dizzy.

"I know," I sighed with the frustration of it. "Let's just keep poking around. I want to find this thing before the others get here. I don't need them in any more danger."

"Okay!" He whisper-shouted back to me. "Sorry about the head invasion!" He must have sensed that it unsettled me.

I inspected every inch of the stone circle. Nothing seemed to jump out or look even remotely like a secret something could be hidden somewhere. There was not an ancient swirl or scrawl to be found. It was the polar opposite from the symbol riddled scroll chamber.

The ground was sticky with the mud of recent rain. My feet crunched though a thin layer of icy snow, leaving me ankle deep in a cold, black sludge. Logically, I knew that if we were supposed to wait for dawn and I knew which direction East was, I could try to work out a general search area for the location of the next artefact. Based on the scroll, we believed that sunrise would cast a ray of light across the henge from the eastern horizon, hopefully landing somewhere near the location we needed. The general hum of the ground was confusing, though. It didn't seem to be drawing me anywhere specific.

"Which way is East?" I whispered again as I came up behind Brennan.

"If you're standing by the Heel stone, facing the henge, it should be at a slight diagonal to the right," he whispered back.

"What if I just head in that direction? I might come across whatever it is by luck." I asked as I pointed northeast.

"You really want to walk out into that fog in the dark, with no clue if you're going to find it? Be patient, princess. The prophecies were given to us for a reason. Let's follow them through, sometimes we need to have a little faith," he answered, all too sensibly.

This winter solstice sunrise was the key to finding the next part of this puzzle. I could feel the desperation inside me to end this nightmarish adventure. This was not the way I'd ever envisaged seeing the world—running and hiding under constant attack, wracking every neuron trying to figure out ancient riddles. I needed to be strong and patient. Thankfully, I had ancient teammates to guide me, beings who had a patience and depth of character I could only dream of.

A rumble, ever so slight, shook the ground. Brennan appeared suddenly, pulling me back protectively behind him.

"We're not going to be alone for long," he announced ominously.

"We have to get to this thing! I'll dig through the ground with my bare hands if I have to, just where is it?"

"We're going to have to ride it out 'til dawn. If the prophecy said sunrise, then there's a reason for that. If we were meant to take shortcuts, I'm sure we would have worked this out a thousand years ago, Soph. Let's dull down and just wait at the Heel stone. The second that sun is up, you get yourself onto that altar stone so you can see where the sun points to. You're the key to this so make sure you meet and greet that light. Okay?" I nodded.

We huddled closely in front of the large, bluish Heel stone. It was impressive, both in its size and mystery. Another rumble came, followed by the faint whiff of something rotten. It swept in on a newly emerging breeze. I was fairly sure the temperature dropped suddenly, as scant snowflakes began to fall. My hair whipped up in the breeze. Brennan was swiping his from his eyes as well, trying to keep a good line of sight. Pent up, nervous energy buzzed between us. Crackling electrons sparkled sporadically in the air around us.

"There aren't enough of us here! You and I can't fight a horde of Rogues ourselves!" I felt panicked. The two of us arriving here alone was not ideal, but travelling in numbers was a risk as well. We were more detectable when in large groups, but a group sounded much safer right about now.

"Speak for yourself! I'm quite impressive as a solo performer!" He smiled and pulled me into his side in a brotherly hug. "Don't worry, princess. The others aren't far off—five, ten minutes max. And remember Koi, Kea and Enl'iel are nearby, we're not so alone. The Rogues will pinpoint us instantly if they transfer here, you know that by experience. We all have to stay on foot, unfortunately, and be patient if we want to remain invisible to the enemy."

The sky was starting to lighten now, the pale hue of the horizon seemed clearer than the air above us. As dawn approached, there was another earthy rumble, quickly followed by a blinding flash of lightning in the distance and a loud crack of thunder.

"What was that?" I craned my head apprehensively around the stone, looking for the source.

"The reinforcements have arrived!" Brennan exclaimed. He fist-pumped the air, and then gave the sign of thanks to I'el, touching his hand to his face and then raising it to the sky.

I noticed an immediate change in the atmosphere then. The air cleared as the fog rolled away to the South, towards the light. The cool breeze dulled, and was once more sweet and dewy.

I heard a new, faint whisper in the back of my mind. "*Got your back, kid. Don't make me regret putting my faith in you.*" It was Jude's all too familiar, vexed tone.

It was growing painstakingly close to sunrise now, and the Eastern horizon glowed orange with the waking sun. Silhouetted flocks of screeching birds flew haphazardly overhead. They emerged from the South, as though frantically fleeing something.

"That'll be the troops." Brennan said, indicating up towards the frightened flock. Jude had definitely drawn the evil out towards himself and the human battalion. I worried momentarily for his safety, but then I reminded myself that he'd survived longer than written history. I'd heard Jude had even fought with the troops of human wars just for fun. He was strong and cunning. I felt less sure for the poor humans, though. I hoped Jaz was tucked away somewhere safe.

I stood up and bounced up and down on my toes to let the blood run back into them after crouching for so long. *Who knew when I might need to run?* My eyes never left the darkness in the distance, lest I miss something. I felt strong, physically. My training had given me a strength I'd never imagined I could have. My muscles felt tense and ready to spring into action, and the heat in my veins burned, yearning to explode.

Deep breath in, deep breath out, repeat.

Footsteps in the distance caught my attention. I peered into the faint blue light behind us.

"Someone's here," I whispered to Brennan, as we both crouched down again behind the stone. I strained my eyes against the murky backdrop, looking though the shadows cast by the giant stones. I knew someone was behind one of the monoliths on the outer circle, as I saw a darkened figure dart behind it.

"I'll go check it out, it's probably just a homeless guy. Plenty hang around here, trying to make money from the tourists. They're probably just getting in early. I'll give him a nap for a while—that'll keep him out of trouble," he said.

"No, I'll go! I've got to start doing things on my own."

"If it's not what you're expecting, best if I'm there too, princess," he made to stand up but I grabbed his arm and pulled him back down.

"No, it's only a few feet away. I'll call if there's a problem, okay?"

"Then take this," he passed me a curved chromious dagger. "I know we haven't touched on weapons yet but just in case, even a small nick with that thing will slow anything down, giving you enough time to get away. Ram it wherever you can if need be, I'm right here anyway. I've got your back as always." He smiled as he passed up the shiny blade with a nod of encouragement.

I took the weapon which was heavy for its size and shoved it down the band of my pants.

"I'm sure it will be nothing, just like you said, a wayward tourist hunter. I don't want some poor human hurt, let alone killed by whatever is surfing in on that mist. Hang on, how do I put someone to sleep?"

"Easy as. It's a skill the young ones learn with the second right of sevens. You'll kill it. Look here," he cupped his hand behind his own head. "You just have to get within a foot of someone. You feel for the brainwaves that surge and fluctuate within this space around their skull. You can slow them right down by sending a small, gentle pulse of energy out. Just like when you heal. It works in an instant with humans, a little longer for our own kind. Don't try it on a Daimon or a Rogue!"

I gave Brennan a reassuring squeeze on his arm. "Okay, hold the fort, big guy. I've got this." I didn't really think I had it, but I needed to rely on myself more. I hated the dependence I had on everyone else. Just like nursing school, I was going to learn on the run with practical experience. I hoped.

"Yes, ma'am!" He saluted me with a dimple rich smile again. I kind of adored him, in a completely big brother way of course. "Make sure you're on that stone before the sun is up, though." He gestured to the horizon. "We've got one chance at this. We need to get in first, before the Daimon just nuke everything while they look for what *we're* looking for."

"Promise. See you in a minute," I said as I snuck off.

With feather-light steps, I cased the perimeter, passing one stone at a time, pausing, and then moving on. As I passed the altar stone, I could hear and feel the beat of a heart. It was rapid, panicked, and disturbingly familiar. My stomach lurched, as a wave of nausea rolled through me, making me stop for a moment to squat down and still the feeling. The ever-increasing ground vibrations from the encroaching battle heightened my sense of urgency. I listened hard and heard panicked breaths, which suddenly stopped for a moment, as though this person was listening, too. After a sharp intake of that breath, the breathing continued. The familiar emotion of fear blanketed me. It chilled me, and my mind was screaming to turn around and go back to Brennan.

Instead, I felt for the dagger and crept forward, willing my energy to remain down so as not to give away my position. I was fairly certain that whoever was hiding was not a homeless person—he or she was emitting a different feeling altogether. My head ached like a hacksaw was working through it. I hadn't felt this way since I'd arrived in the UK. Something was very, very, wrong. I was only two stones away when I decided to double back and approach from within the circle.

Koi's voice was suddenly in the back reaches of my mind. *"Know your enemy's position at all times. Attack first and fast—the element of surprise is most powerful."*

I was sure I was going to throw up any second, I rubbed my stomach in an attempt to settle it. The feeling was overwhelming, but I pushed forward. Whatever was ahead had to be fairly questionable because of the effect its negative energy was having on me. I came up silently behind the twin stones connected by a massive lintel, I couldn't tell whether the pulse pounding in my head was from whoever was hiding, or my own. I could feel Brennan trying to whisper to me from afar, but I couldn't listen to him with all of the noise already banging about in there.

A sharp intake of breath and sudden movement had me sprinting into action with an animal-like instinct. I was around the monolith in less than a second, unfortunately losing the dagger as I grabbed for the large silhouette trying to flee. My arms managed to get a good tight grip around its neck. We wrestled to the ground, grunting, panting and struggling. The cold snow melted under the heat of my rising anger, as I couldn't help the release of my energy. I glowed, hot and furious, above this mysterious being who was surprisingly strong. He definitely couldn't be human. He grunted and groaned while trying to fling me from his back, but I had his large, muscular torso flat on the ground, pinned underneath me. My legs were wrapped around his, with one arm tight around his throat while the other twisted his left arm up behind his back.

"Who are you?" I asked, close to his ear through gritted teeth, and with an aggression that surprised me. As the words escaped me, I caught the scent of ashes and spice. I gasped, shocked, and jumped immediately back, letting him escape from my grasp.

He scrambled quickly from under me and turned around. He sat, panting heavily as he wiped mud and slush from across his face with the back of his hand. His bare chest heaved from the effort of our struggle. He looked up at me with his emerald green eyes that were glistening in the very first rays of the sun.

"Ben!"

Chapter
Fifty-Two

With the initial shock at seeing him, I nearly forgot my purpose at Stonehenge in the first place. The sun was rising, and I needed to be on that altar stone. I grabbed Ben by the arm, and dragged him wordlessly with me. He didn't resist as my mind raced with confusion.

I pulled him at a full run to the central altar stone—the heart of the henge. I jumped up on it with the lightness of a cat. I pushed him down at the base of the stone. I looked down at him, both furious and scared all at once.

"Stay there! I don't know what the hell you're doing here, but just stay there!" I glared at him, daring him to move. A loud buzz cranked up to blaring in my head, making me wince. The ground rumbled, and the stone beneath me hummed as the sunlight hit my back. I looked up to the sky as snowflakes fell overhead. They descended from a single cloud formation, surrounded by pink and orange hues. Humming and rumbling and voices all invaded my mind. I shouted out loud, my hands pressed firmly over my ears.

"What do I do?"

"Light it up, princess! Light it up!" Brennan appeared, running around from behind a leaning stone.

Inside my head, I could hear a million voices screaming at me, on repeat. *"Light up, light up!"*

I glanced down at Ben. I hadn't seen him for what felt like an eternity. He glared back at me. His expression was unreadable, but his eyes never left me as he stayed crouched, motionless on the ground.

I closed my eyes then and relaxed my body. I let the warmth in my veins unfurl, allowing it to escape the flesh and blood that contained it under duress. The heat spread quickly throughout me, up my legs and down my arms, as my face pulsed with the light. My spine screamed to break free as the burn coursed down it. I breathed in and out slowly, vaguely aware of Ben at my feet, feeling his heartbeat match my own.

My wings burst from my back and fanned around me. Surprised at how quickly I was able to do this, I dared to open my eyes. My breaths were hard and heavy as I scanned around me to see what was happening. Ben was now standing, looking at me oddly with his head tilted to one side. I could have sworn his expression was love and hate intertwined. Brennan was just behind him, regarding him with confusion before drawing nearer to me.

"Something's happening, Soph, hang in there! Look!"

His eyes followed something though the henge and across the landscape to the Northeast. I followed his line of vision. That's when I noticed that the light of sunrise refracted from my wings to the stones and back again in a complicated pattern of light, converging into one piercingly bright light that reflected off the altar stone and carved a path through the still dark horizon. It hit something far off in the distance. There was an increase in the Earth's magnetic field, a hum like the rev of a jet engine, whirring before take-off. A white light shot up vertically into the night sky, followed by a brief but ear-piercing explosion. This strange light lingered in the air like a beacon.

Enl'iel, Koi, Kea, and a few others emerged through the stones at that moment.

"Sophia, you did it!" Enl'iel reached up to help me down with the broadest of smiles.

"Come now, let's follow the path of light. We must hurry—Jude is outnumbered, and we will be inundated all too soon." Panic was evident in her voice, which made me panic, too. She suddenly caught sight of Ben, and swung her focus in his direction. "Ben! How did you get here?" She pulled him close, looking him up and down for sign of injury. He remained silent, but compliant. Her face reflected the same confusion I felt. She took off her coat and put it around him.

"That's a very good question," I said, still bitter for the worry he'd put me through, and the nagging feeling that there was so much more to this than I cared to know.

With no more time for words, as the clang of metal and screams of mortal wounds edged closer, we ran.

And we ran *fast*. We veered with an inhuman speed towards the pulsing vertical white light. I had my hand vice-tight around Ben's as he silently kept up with surprising ease.

"What do you think is over there?" I puffed to Enl'iel as we ran.

"Looks like the old henge they call the Durrington Walls," she answered.

The mist was rolling in again as we ran. Thankfully, it wasn't too thick yet. The dawn light began to dull to a stormy grey as we crossed the couple of kilometres between the two ancient sites. Over another motorway that bisected this area, we arrived to find the dissipating beacon of light being replaced by the emergence of a swarm of little glowing orbs. *Keepers.*

The fog was thickening rapidly now and full of stench.

"Hurry, Sophia! Follow the Keepers, they will guide you," she urged as she pushed me forward and hung back, taking over my grip on Ben.

"Watch him. Don't let him out of your sight!" I looked at him quickly, urging him to explain himself. He was so distracted by the screams and flashes of light in the distance that he hadn't even registered our exchange. He looked frightened.

"This young man will not leave my side. Now go!" she yelled over the noise.

With one last lingering look back at Ben, I ran toward the bustle of orbs to find the rubble of an exploded rock, scattered along the chalky ground. The Keepers buzzed around me in an instant, as though they were excited to see me. A kindred feeling emanated from them, but also one of urgency. The thicker the fog became, the faster they swirled around me, shielding me. A couple zipped away and then back again, as if urging me to follow.

"Get the hell going, Soph!" called Brennan from the distance.

"They're coming, and it's a bloody swarm!" I glanced back as I saw him running towards the fog. He threw off large white orbs that exploded into a thousand shards of white-hot arrows of light that sprayed down towards the oncoming enemy. "I'll cover you, now run!" he turned and fired continuously as I ran after the little lights, whilst he disappeared into the malevolent fog. The others must have joined in as the sky behind me was lit up less by the sun than the by Angelic war munitions. The clash of weaponry was all too close as I heard the encroaching battle.

I stopped looking back and followed the Keepers at a furious pace. They buzzed ecstatically. They drew me toward the Avon River as the wind whipped up suddenly and ferociously.

My breath was catching in the frigid air but I didn't falter. The clouds above began swirling and darkening from grey to black. Lightning crackled across the sky. The smell of rotten eggs and decay was an assault to my senses and a frightening warning. One last glance behind me had my legs working even harder. The stinking fog was now at my heels. Tendrils were reaching out to grab at my feet. *Or were they fingers?*

I skidded to a halt at the river's edge, heaving for breath. Guttural screams that were way too close sprung hot tears down my cheeks. The snow was thick and icy along the banks, the edges slippery as I followed where the little spirits were guiding me. The rushing water melded with the howling wind, drowning out the distant screams. My Keepers darted out over the water and hovered under the naked, white-capped branches of a willow tree that hung long and low. It brushed sorrowfully over the water. The storm that brewed was loud and wild, rustling through the dormant branches. In the back of my, mind I could hear warnings to hurry, that we were under attack.

The Keepers dove in and out of the water, inviting me to do the same.

Without hesitation or question, I kicked off my boots and singed coat and dove into the freezing water.

Despite the murkiness, I could see clearly. My vision was crisp. The little lights swam in front of me as I swam. Suddenly I realised that I felt no need to breathe. It startled me, and I thrashed for a moment until I was drawn along in the current, encouraged by the little white guides. They hovered over a spot on the bottom, and I felt around through the slimy silt. A fish rushed past, scaring me half to death. I dug in harder as the Keepers became frenzied while they lit up the slimy hiding place.

When I was elbow-deep in the sludge, I hit on something hard. My excitement built and my heart pumped furiously. I dug fast, and within moments had pulled a metal box from within its watery grave. I could tell by the feel of it, by the engravings under my fingertips, that it was the same as the Prime scroll box. I clutched it to my chest and floated quickly to the surface.

I emerged about fifty metres or so from where I dove in. The climb out with heavy, waterlogged clothes and armour up the icy bank was hard going whilst holding the chest under my arm. The Keepers surrounded me and worked together to levitate me up and out safely onto the bank.

"Thank you," I puffed, reaching out to them as they danced across my palm. With that, they dulled down rapidly and disappeared, leaving a fearful energy swirling around me. Biting rain was falling now, and I could again hear and see the sounds of fighting that was all too close. I screamed out to Enl'iel, Brennan—to anyone that I thought could hear me.

Like static on a radio, I could only make out in my mind, "Run! Run, princess! Run!"

I got up, shoeless and dripping, and I ran in the opposite direction of the fray. I wrapped my wings around myself, encasing my body, protecting it from the cold and the danger. My instinct was to go back and help, yet I now knew better than to ignore such a warning.

Lightning struck the ground in front of me. I dodged to the side and ran harder, not knowing where I should end up. I flung my free hand out and shot a hot blast haphazardly in the direction it came from. There was no point hiding now. I had to defend myself. I tried to transfer away. I thought of the sanctuary, of Cael, of little Av'ael, but my panicked mind couldn't get a firm grip on any one thing. I felt my body fade in and out a couple of times, but the effort was pointless. The pull in my gut just wasn't there. So, I ran as hard as I could to anywhere but where the screams were coming from, and it felt cowardly.

The sun was now completely dulled by the wild weather, the sky as black as night. I felt sick again, and my stomach lolled and ached, slowing me down. The feeling in the air was nothing short of dread. I stopped a moment as I arrived back in the middle of the henge. The stones were charred, and the white snow spoiled by foul piles of ash and crimson. A body lay under a sarsen stone, bloody and lifeless. I knelt to see who it was. *A human male whom I didn't know.* His skin, a few shades darker than mine, was ripped apart. I closed his eyes as I placed my hand over his heart. I silently prayed to whoever might be listening. I looked back at the lightshow that was ablaze back near the river. My keen ears could hear the guttural sounds of the Rogues and the screams of my kindred. I shivered as I stood up. Shock was setting in.

I turned to continue running and smacked straight into someone, falling heavily backward to the ground. I hit my head on the side of the altar stone, leaving a hot trickle of blood running down my face.

"How ironic, the blood of the Earth-born upon an altar of sacrifice." A cool and calm voice spoke.

I looked up, still clutching the box, only to see something truly frightening.

A huge, horned figure, dressed waist down in black and holding a glowing red trident stood over me. He glowered at me as his bare chest heaved with cruel laughter.

Behind him, I saw four others just like him. Dark hair with white streaks and beautiful beyond words, yet they emitted a feeling of utter ugliness. A swirling storm encased us. We seemed separated from the rest of the world.

"Get away from me, whoever the hell you are!" I tried to sound as defiant as I could in the face of this frightening sight. I inched back a little, not sure of where to run.

"Dear, dear, if you don't know who I am, you are very much the poorer. A disservice has been done to you that you remain so naïve. Yet, it serves us all too well." His voice was cruel and methodical.

"Stop with the Oscar performance and just tell me who you are!" I screamed.

He was in my face in an instant, teeth bared and smelling like the remnants of a long dead fire.

"I am your worst nightmare, Sophia, Soph'ael, Earth-born, stupid child!"

Thwack. My head flung sideways as his fist met my face. The sting was blinding. I clutched the box tighter as I tried to clear my vision, blinking rapidly, not wanting to let him out of my sight.

"Oh, Yeqon, just get on with it. Your theatrics bore me," said the one to his left.

"Know your place, Ged'erel. I've waited an eternity for this, and I shall have my fun." His black ringed irises glowed red as they seared into mine.

"I'll have that box, and I'll have you, too." He spat the words at me as though I was nothing.

He grabbed at me with an immense strength, instantly wrenching the chest from me.

"*Argh*, the damn thing burns!" he threw it somewhere behind him, and the smell of his burnt flesh gave me a gruesome satisfaction. I smiled.

Thwack. Another slap across my face.

"Cover it up and bring it with us," he commanded. "Damn them!"

I could feel my energy building up, and I let it grow. It had saved me before, just when I needed it. My eyes burned, my chest heaved, and my wings fanned wide, ready to attack these beasts. I counted five of them. Then my heart sunk as I realised who they were.

"Ah, it has just dawned upon you? You're disappointingly slow for the Chosen One. I would put that little power show away that you're brewing, too—it could get a bit messy," he growled, hot breath and spittle blowing across my face. "Pineme, bring me the girl!"

I heard her before I saw her.

"Jaz!" I screamed in horror as she was brought out of the shadows. Her body was bloodied, her armour gone, she was bound hand and foot, screaming.

"Kill them, Soph! Fucking kill these animals!"

Then she was smacked into silence.

"What an awful creature she is, so unbecoming," he said, as she was thrown to the ground at his feet. He raised his glowing weapon above her. "You will do as you're told and come with me, or I will gladly use her head as a drinking vessel."

"No! No. No, okay, just don't hurt her, please? I'll do whatever you want!" Tears brewed as my weakness shone through. I would never be able to watch another suffer if I could stop it. Especially not someone I loved. I let my body dull and slacken, no longer ready to pounce.

He leaned in and smacked me hard across the face a third time for good measure. The sting was excruciating. I bit back new tears, my chin trembling like a traitor with the effort. He hauled me up by my arms, kicking Jaz out of the way, back into the shadows as he did so.

"By I'el, that felt good." He laughed in my face and then spat at the ground with disgust.

He looked up to the sky. "Did you hear that, old man?"

As I dangled there in his grasp, I heard a new voice and a familiar heartbeat getting closer and louder. Suddenly, I was flung from Yeqon's grip to the ground.

I looked up, dazed.

A figure slithered around Yeqon, wrapping itself around him, cooing in his ear. *A woman.* She was tall and thin, with an alabaster complexion. As my vision cleared yet again, I took in long legs wrapped in tight black pants and thigh-high red stilettos. Spindly arms rubbed lustfully across Yeqon's chest as she dug her talon-like nails in, drawing drops of blood. He growled at her, but gathered her in closer, planting an aggressive, deep kiss on her all too willing mouth. She giggled like a child as she regarded me through long lashes and eyes smudged black. She was as beautiful as she was scary, like a killer porcelain doll.

"You have him?" Yeqon asked the sultry woman as she continued to peck and kiss at his neck. She licked the length of it, from collarbone to ear. He half-smiled, as his eyes never left mine. He didn't return the obvious affection.

"My love, my life, I have hunted him down." She disappeared for a few moments, then reappeared with a hunched, shadowed figure. She flung it to the ground in the darkness near where Jaz lay. I could smell blood. *A lot of it.*

"You may partake, my Queen. Well done." Yeqon beckoned her back to him and bent his head to the side, offering her his neck.

Not sure where to look, my eyes remained riveted as she bit into Yeqon's neck. Like a car wreck, it was impossible to look away. The storm thundered overhead. He groaned with pleasure as she drank from him. Her head moved rhythmically back and forth as she drew circles on his chest with her fingers. It turned my stomach. I couldn't help myself—I threw up. Wiping my mouth with the back of my mud-caked hand, I looked back to see that she had finished, and they both laughed at me. She teasingly, seductively licked her lips clean of the iridescent red dribbles, mocking me openly. Large, clear, and dangerous eyes burned like a sunset as she glared at me. She then turned and sauntered away casually without another word.

"You are lucky I don't rip you to shreds, boy!" Yeqon suddenly growled at the figure groaning in the dark. His hunched over back was to me, and the light too dull to see who exactly it was that rewarded that woman with a meal of blood. A light began to glow from his hands which were running up and down Jaz's body. I recognized it as the light of healing. I was confused by this.

Who was this?

"Don't touch her!" I yelled at the silhouette.

"Quiet!" thundered Yeqon

The figure healed her to the point that she stirred, but he laid a hand across her head and quieted her into a sleep.

Through gritted teach and barely repressed tears, he addressed Yeqon.

"You don't need the human girl. We have what we need. Let me deal with the Chosen One as I promised."

The voice cut me to the bone.

"Boy, you test me! Do you wish this trident through your chest?"

"Have I not brought her to you? Have I not done all that you have asked? Thousands of years of your bidding. Murdering and interfering. Never once have I wavered. Just leave this one, please? She is an innocent." His glowing hand was pointed at Jaz.

The one named Ged'erel spoke. "You have become weakened living amongst the humans, Nik'ael, and you show mercy where none is warranted. It is sickening to see."

The womanly figure appeared again from behind Yeqon. She towered over the disgraced accomplice and pushed viscously at his back with her stiletto heel. He fell, but caught himself before he crashed onto Jaz by unfurling huge wings of murky light that flapped hypnotically. Sparks of orange, red and green flicked from the edges of his immense wings. I'd seen those before. *No!*

"Indeed, Nik'ael, you have done our bidding to a point. But you kept the Earth-born to yourself for too long. You have disobeyed your master for your own selfish desires. You wish to keep her for yourself, but she is not yours!" The woman screamed so loud that even the thunder seemed to meow like a kitten. "Do not deny it! I can see into your weak, half-breed heart." She inspected her hands for a moment. "I broke a nail hunting you down, you worthless dog!" she spat the words in a high-pitched trill. I remained speechless. Surely, I must be dreaming.

"I was trying to gather as much information as I could, Lilith. You know all too well that we are forsaken if we act too soon!" he answered as he cowered from her threatening stature in the dark.

"You don't fool us. You have fallen for her, as we all fell at some point." Yeqon laughed heartily and looked around. "Is that not why we are all here in the first place? For a woman!" They all laughed as the slithering Lilith wrapped herself around him again. "Admit your weakness, and you shall suffer little. Lie to me and Tartarus shall seem a luxury compared to the pits of the lowest realm!"

"Lilith, partake of the girl. Perhaps that will persuade the truth from his lips?" Yeqon peeled the sultry vampire from his chest.

"*Ooh,* yummy!" She made her way to Jaz. I froze in horror.

"No! No, stop! Yes, all that you say is true. I've fallen, but I have never indulged in it, in *her*. I have struggled through this and I have not failed you yet. Please, allow me to send the innocent away and I will do as you wish, without hesitation." He was on his knees, begging. Shadowed hands raked wildly through his hair. I squinted hard, but still could not make out his features. My heart didn't really want to.

"There, was that so hard? You are as weak in your heart as she is." He inclined his head to me. "By the soul of I'el, I do not understand you, boy. You are lucky I have the smallest morsel of pity for you. I will pay for this with incessant moaning for weeks, Nik'ael. Lilith, let her go. I've got no more time for this. You've had your fill on me." The awful, bloodsucking woman dropped Jaz heavily to the ground, whinging with disappointment.

"Get on with it then, Nik'ael. You have by the rise of the Empyrean evening to bring Soph'ael to kneel before my feet. This is your last chance. Do not disappoint me."

Yeqon turned his back and walked away. They all followed him casually, slowly disappearing into the thick fog.

The shadowed figure immediately tuned back to Jaz. I was still frozen, like a coward. His wings glowed brighter now, a more pure white and immensely beautiful. It seemed impossible that they could belong to someone who was working with the devil. He kissed her head, and then waved his hands quickly over the length of her body. In a sudden flash of light, she was gone. I screamed.

"What have you done?" I came out of my state of fear as anger surged. I rose from the ground and unfurled my wings, but he was up and on me in a flash, my arms were pinned to my side in an iron grip. The devils were gone, so this was his show now. I struggled violently, clawing to get my hands free enough to blast him.

"Let me go!" Our wings thrashed and clashed together. The strange familiarity weakened me each time his wings grazed mine. I awaited the pain of death, which didn't come. His strength eclipsed mine. I realised quickly that while I was fighting against him, he was merely holding onto me. Not hurting me—just holding me close to his bare, burning chest.

Ashes and spice.

No!

The ingestion of the smell took my remaining strength. Our heartbeats matched, thrumming in sync, as they had countless times before. Only now, it was the last thing I wanted to feel. I couldn't look at him. The winds howled though the stones that looked on like voyeuristic spectres. I could no longer hear fighting. My heart screamed behind my ribcage as he drew me impossibly close, wordlessly. His breath on my ear was calm and measured as it both intoxicated and frightened me. He was both my safety and my danger all at once.

Nothing separated us now. He was shaking.

Ashes and spice! How could this be?

The soft touch of his hand drew my face towards his. *Don't look!*

"Please, no," I cried, my voice weak.

He bent his head down as his wings enveloped us both, forming a warm barrier from all that was real and unreal. I felt suffocated. He hesitated ever so slightly, his breath faltering as his heart hammered next to mine.

"Just once," he said softly, breaking my heart in an instant.

The storm was like a distant memory. I felt like my heart would seize any moment, my mind paralysed with denial. He gently caressed his face against mine, a K'ufili shared. A small yelp of grief escaped me as he cupped my face with both hands. The screaming in my head was shoved far away as his tear-moistened lips met mine. Soft and tentatively at first, as if testing the waters of a deep pool. Then the kiss deepened, firm and panicked, as if there was no time left for us. The urgency emanating from him drew me further in as I matched his passion. My own will was a crumbled wall. The fire between us burned as we stood in the stone circle, surrounded by the storm. I was elated and hungry for this feeling. A feeling I had pushed down and away countless times, convincing myself it wasn't real, that I didn't need it. As I retuned his desire with vigour, I was disgusted with myself, yet I pulled at his neck and drew him as close as we could possibly get. He groaned with pleasure. *How could something so dreadfully wrong feel so perfectly right?* There was a certain kind of desperation in this forbidden act between an angel and a devil.

He pulled slightly back as I felt my breastplate burn into his chest. It seemed to alert me to my senses, as I remembered that evil could not touch Chromious metal. I pulled sharply away and slapped him with every ounce of strength I had left, leaving a hand-shaped mark across the white scar on his face. I knew now that it had never been a scar at all, as his mark burned white through the inflammation. I looked into his sorrowful emerald eyes. I was breathless, destroyed.

"I'm so sorry, Sophia." With these words, his emerald eyes flickered cerulean blue and then turned black as night.

"Oh, Ben. Why?"

That was the last thing I said before I was dragged into oblivion.

Surrender
Book 2 Coming Soon

Acknowledgments

To keep things short and sweet, I want to thank my amazing family for supporting me as I ventured into the world of writing. I have the best fan club under my own roof.

Thank you to my beautiful children for putting up with the many, many times I've pulled the car over and said, "Quick, I've just got to right an idea down!" Each one of you has made mum feel so special because you share your pride and excitement in what I am doing.

Thank you to my husband, who is not a book worm, yet has lovingly read through my many versions of this book and ensured me that I was going to succeed.

Finally, to my sister who has from the beginning been my unofficial editor and book critic. Your honesty and encouragement have single-handedly propelled me to the finish line.

You have all given me confidence in myself to follow a long held dream.

Thank you and I love you so very much.

Follow me on twitter @grthomas2014
& my website www.grthomasbooks.com